A SIME~GEN NOVEL

A CHANGE OF TACTICS

CLEAR SPRINGS CHRONICLES #1

THE SIME~GEN SERIES

OTHER BOOKS BY JACQUELINE LICHTENBERG

OTHER BOOKS BY JEAN LORRAH

BOOKS BY JEAN LORRAH & LOIS WICKSTROM

A SIME~GEN NOVEL

A CHANGE OF TACTICS

CLEAR SPRINGS CHRONICLES #1

MARY LOU MENDUM, JACQUELINE LICHTENBERG, AND JEAN LORRAH

WILDSIDE PRESS

CONTENTS

DEDICATIONS

MARY LOU MENDUM

To Jacqueline Lichtenberg, for letting me travel through her universe for so many decades, and to the crew at Borderlands for sharing the journey with me.

JEAN LORRAH

As always, my work in the Sime~Gen Universe is dedicated first to Jacqueline Lichtenberg, for welcoming me into her universe.

My work on this particular book is also dedicated to Mary Lou Mendum, whose approach in *A Change of Tactics* is the mirror image of mine in *To Kiss or to Kill*. Both books concern ordinary citizens facing huge changes to the world they live in and the beliefs they have grown up with, brought about by leaders whose stories become the text of history books. The main characters in both our books are not the Famous Names, but the ordinary people who actually have to do what their leaders have agreed to in their treaties.

A Change of Tactics shows how people cope in Gen Territory, while *To Kiss or to Kill* shows the same sort of everyday people in Sime Territory, struggling to understand the promise of an amazing new world while wondering if they can survive to live in it.

JACQUELINE LICHTENBERG

To all the fans who have written Sime~Gen fanfic for the half-dozen or so magazines, on paper and on line, and especially those who have encouraged Mary Lou Mendum to present her fanfic stories of Den and Rital's adventures opening an Out-Territory Sime Center during the first explosive growth of technology in the Sime~Gen world. Mary Lou's stories of convincing out-Territory Gens to donate selyn lay the foundation for the space program that will blossom, and for the eventual space wars with the various Aliens that Earth will encounter.

CHAPTER 1

TOURISTS

It was all the fault of Den's cousin Rital, of course. It usually was. Who else knew Den spoke English, the language of the out-Territory Gens? And who else could have talked Den into agreeing to help with the Gens touring the Old Sime Center?

"Oh, come on, Den. I'm only asking you to fill in for a week, so Ersov can help me make arrangements for the new Sime Center in Clear Springs. The Mayor and her delegation will be here to sign the final agreement in three days. You'd think I was asking you to move out-Territory and join the Church of the Purity. Please?" Hajene Rital Madz's warm brown eyes sent a pleading look across the cafeteria table from under a mop of unruly brown curls very like Den's own.

Den had never found it easy to resist his cousin's signature kicked-puppy look, even when they were children. "Pick on somebody else," he suggested weakly. "I don't like tourists."

"There *is* nobody else." The channel's fists clenched and four handling tentacles emerged from the orifices just above each wrist, lashing restlessly. The smaller lateral tentacles remained sheathed, so it was just a display of frustration, not an attempt to sneak a closer read of Den's emotional state.

Seeing that a show of temper was unlikely to win him the Donor's cooperation, Rital sheathed his tentacles and took a hasty sip of soup. "It's almost Faith Day, Den. Everybody who can speak even broken English is already handling out-Territory visitors."

Den nodded stiffly. The holiday was still three weeks off, but the seasonal increase in tourism plus the opening of a new Sime Center had strained the English-language capacity of the Valzor District employees. Each year at this time, mobs of general-class selyn donors descended upon Sime Centers located either out-Territory, or conveniently close to the ter-ritorial borders. It put a huge extra workload on the channels and highly trained, technical-class Donors like Den.

Den much preferred spending his days serving channels' personal Need, helping them heal their patients, or even performing as the channels' own physician. Unfortunately, not only was he fluent in English but, unlike District Controller Monruss, Rital knew it. It was his cousin, after all, who had decided when they were eight that English would make a fine "secret language" for the two of them.

"It's only for a week," Rital wheedled. "Just while the delegation from Clear Springs is here."

"I don't understand your obsession with Clear Springs," Den complained. "You're a First Order channel. You're as good as most specialists at healing. You've been Sub-Controller under Monruss for almost a year. Isn't that enough of a challenge?"

"There's never before been a Sime Center so far away from the border," Rital enthused. "It's an historic moment and I want to be a part of it."

"Don't they have diplomats for that?"

"Most of them have been sent to the Southern Continent to handle that mess between Cordona and the local Gen Territories. I like playing host to our out-Territory guests. Now, about the tours: there's a script for most of it, although you'll want to be prepared for questions, too…"

In the end, of course, Den gave in.

About a dozen and a half "guests," as he was supposed to think of them, waited in the small auditorium. They were a mixture of children and adult Gens like Den, talking to each other or curbing the excesses of their offspring. They stole surreptitious glances at his bare forearms as he entered, relaxing slightly when they found no tentacles. Most of this group, Den understood, had come all the way from Clear Springs, eight hours away by train. They were spouses and children of the Gen Territory delegation negotiating the last details for their new Sime Center. Why otherwise sane people would voluntarily spend eight hours on a noisy, cramped train if they didn't have to was beyond his understanding, but now Den was responsible for keeping them occupied. He adjusted his crisply ironed Tecton uniform like the armor it was and began his hastily memorized script.

"Good morning. Welcome to Sime Territory and the city of Valzor's Old Sime Center. I am Sosu Den Milnan. The 'Sosu' means I'm a technical-class selyn Donor and I work with the channels across the street at the New Sime Center. Before I show you around, I'd like to take a moment to explain how the Sime Centers got started."

None of the audience seemed inclined to lob souvenirs at him in protest so Den continued, concentrating on maintaining a cheerful, friendly attitude. With his perpetually disorganized mop of hair he couldn't manage dignified, but friendly should work well enough for this audience.

"Long ago, the Ancients built a civilization that has never been equaled in modern times. They built huge cities run by machines that could think. They built other machines that could fly, even as far as the moon…"

Some of the tourists looked skeptical and Den couldn't blame them. There was abundant evidence that the Ancients had used flying machines as a common means of transportation. But all the way to the moon? There was no air up there for them to fly on! Den and his friends built models of those Ancient designs, some of which could be persuaded to fly for short distances when powered by tightly wound elastic belts. He knew wings, or even air-screws, had to have air to support them.

Still, he supposed the experts who had written the script had some good reason for entertaining visitors with the more outlandish speculations of Householding Frihill's historians.

"The Ancients all looked like Gens, with no tentacles on their arms, although nobody knows whether they produced the selyn—life energy— that Simes must have every month to live. What we do know is that when the first Simes appeared, there were Gens available. Unfortunately, when a Sime took selyn from one of them, the Gen usually didn't survive. Simes had to view Gens as food animals to live with their sanity intact, so it's hardly surprising Gens viewed Simes as inhuman, murdering monsters.

"To make matters worse, both Gens and Simes soon learned that segregating themselves from each other was no solution. You all know it: at adolescence, one third of the children of two Simes establish selyn production and become Gen adults, while one third of the children of two Gens go through changeover and become Simes."

Den saw frowns on some of the faces in his audience and even a few heads shaking in denial of this most tragic and inescapable fact of human life pre-Unity. It fell within the anticipated range of reactions, so he continued, "Ancient civilization collapsed, starting a thousand years of war between Territories claimed by groups of Simes or Gens."

A carrot-headed, eight- or nine-year-old boy in the first row bounced in his seat at the idea of armed conflict, but the adults were all sober. In many parts of Gen Territory, Clear Springs included, their own newly Sime children still posed a frequent, mortal threat to the adults around them.

The modern Sime Territories had found a better way.

"About five hundred years ago, some Simes, the channels, discovered how to take selyn from Gens without harming them and give it to other Simes, who could then live without Killing Gens. The channels formed Householdings: communities of Simes and Gens who lived together without the Kill. However, most Simes were not Householders. They were junct—addicted to Killing Gens—and every citizen had a right to claim a farm-raised Gen from the government Pens each month."

The orange-haired boy's eyes shone with morbid delight and he grinned broadly, bringing his freckles into high relief. The adults shifted nervously in their seats as the script deliberately touched on deeply ingrained fears.

This tour had been specifically designed by psychologists specializing in public relations to help them overcome those fears.

Den wished the experts luck with that.

"One hundred and twenty-five years ago, a severe drought turned the western reaches of our continent into dust. Crops failed and the Pen system in Norwest Sime Territory collapsed. Simes who had depended on it swarmed out across New Washington Gen Territory on their way to plunder Nivet Sime Territory's Pens, Killing as they went. Faced with the impending destruction of both Territories, the Gen soldiers of New Washington and the Sime army here in Nivet formed an alliance of desperation."

Den gratefully signaled for the projectionist to start the movie. Safely obscured by the darkness, he closed his eyes and cursed his cousin once more.

The movie told the story of Faith Day, the only holiday observed officially on both sides of the border. After a hard-fought campaign drove the marauders from Norwest back into the mountains, winter storms had prevented supplies from reaching the combined armies, stranding them without food … or Pen Gens. To survive, the Householders had brokered an astonishing exchange between the starving Gen Army of New Washington and the Kill-addicted Sime soldiers of Nivet: the Nivet Army would turn over its remaining rations to feed its Gen allies and in return, the Gens would donate the selyn their Sime allies must have through the channels.

Only on the battlefield, where Simes and Gens fought shoulder to shoulder against a common enemy, could such a thing have happened: Simes and Gens had come to regard one another as people, as colleagues, and sometimes even as friends. By the time they defeated the invaders and won the war, neither Sime nor Gen veterans could imagine going back to fighting one another and the modern world was born.

The legend had been retold many times on both sides of the border, with wildly varying degrees of historical accuracy. The acting in this version was dismal compared to the famous, out-Territory-produced epic starring Faffard Ebert as the heroic Gen commander, General Dermott. On the plus side, the actors playing Simes in this film actually *were* Sime, eliminating the unintentional comedy of fake rubber tentacles. The Gen audience gasped as the "Norwest invaders" attacked the combined armies with the augmented strength and speed only Simes could muster.

The final portion of this account, however, had a very different emphasis than the out-Territory visitors expected. The Gen film they knew cut directly from General Dermott's famous speech urging his troops to stand by their allies to a dramatic final battle and ended with the leaders of both sides agreeing to turn their temporary alliance into a permanent peace. The Gen production had won a well-deserved award for the artistry of that final scene, which featured the principals silhouetted against a beautiful sunrise in a rustic mountain pass while orchestral music swelled.

Trust Gen Territory producers to omit what had actually made Unity possible. Or perhaps those producers had realized that Gen actors wearing prop tentacles would have made a farce out of what was arguably the most important event since the discovery of channeling.

The Gen audience watching this in-Territory version squirmed restlessly as the actor playing General Dermott outlined the famous Faith Day exchange for his troops. When he finally finished, they leaned forward in anticipation of the battle scene.

Instead, they were shown what really happened after that famous speech, the thing for which Dermott was still honored in Sime Territory, but which most out-Territory Gens would rather forget: not how the General had destroyed his enemies, but what he had done to preserve his allies.

The Gen actor playing General Dermott might not have Faffard Ebert's famous rugged features, but he gave a convincing performance of a man pushing down fear to do what the moment required as he rolled up his sleeves to expose his forearms. The Sime actor playing channel Klyd Farris reached gently for the general's hands.

This, the visitors had not expected. Eyes widened in shock all over the auditorium, spines stiffened, and the morbidly inclined boy cheered in unfettered glee. Out-Territory culture preferred to think of selyn donation as something distasteful occurring far away and to somebody else. Since the entire Old Sime Center tour was designed to convince visiting Gens to celebrate Faith Day in a less abstract fashion, the film concluded by showing them what their heroic ancestors had actually done.

A collective gasp greeted the emergence of the Sime's handling tentacles, which embraced the Gen's bared forearms. The tentacles that were so fearsome to out-Territory Gens were photographed here as something beautiful, the act of selyn donation as life-enhancing. Den looked from the screen to the faces of the audience, knowing that most people out-Territory still chose to live in fear of being Killed by their own Sime children. Something inside him wanted to scream, *You fools! The Tecton exists to prevent your child from turning into a helpless Killer, or you into your child's murderer! Why do you still reject what your honored ancestors won for you, more than a century after Unity?*

Den returned his attention to the screen, hoping against hope that this audience would appreciate what was being shown to them—for it was an actual donation that had been filmed, the only acting the Gen's pretense of fear. When the Sime's grip was secure, the vulnerable nerve-rich laterals extended to touch the Gen's arms. The two actors leaned toward each other and touched lips to complete the circuit. Two adolescent schoolgirls hid their faces with little shrieks, although Den saw the pretty, dark-haired one in the red skirt peeking avidly through her fingers.

Instead of supplying adolescents with cheap thrills, Den fumed to himself, *I could be spending my free mornings flying models of Ancient airplanes with Jannun and Eddina.* Their latest effort, the largest yet, was suffering because Den wasn't there to work on it—and for what? Another failed attempt to reach a group of ignorant Gen tourists determined to reject a better life. *Rital, you owe me.*

Den stood as the lights came back on and braced himself for the question-and-answer session.

The audience was still in shock from witnessing the act they wanted to pretend had nothing to do with them. They looked anywhere except at Den, clearly wanting to flee their discomfort.

Den allowed the awkward silence to drag on long enough for them to realize it was a lesson, then let them off the hook by suggesting the most-asked question from out-Territory tourists who had not just been traumatized. "Doesn't anyone want to know whether Sime tentacles really *are* slimy?"

Relieved laughter stuttered around the room and a man in an eye-searing, lime-green sweater said, a little too heartily, "Yeah! Are they?"

"Not at all. The four handling tentacles, the ones sheathed on the tops and bottoms of Sime forearms, are dry and smooth, like extra fingers. Only the laterals, the smaller tentacles along the sides, are moist with selyn-conducting fluids." He looked around. "Next question?"

It came from the disturbed eight-year-old. He obviously hoped to restore the "ick" factor and upset his sisters, but his question was the one the final scene of the movie was intended to evoke but almost never did: "What does it feel like when a Sime sucks your selyn out?"

"Raymond Ildun!" his mother admonished, flushing with embarrassment.

"It's all right," Den reassured her. The few times young Raymond's question was asked, his notes had warned, it almost always came from a precocious child. The scripted answer was what the Tecton most wanted the adults to remember. "Channels take selyn from general-class donors very slowly and only from the shallower storage levels. So, there's no sensation of selyn movement at all and no injury, even if the donor is frightened and resists."

At Raymond's expression of disappointment, Den abandoned the script and added, "Channels do take selyn more rapidly to satisfy their own Need with a technical-class Donor like myself. We don't resist, though, so we don't get hurt. It feels…" Den searched for an English adjective that could adequately describe that transcendent bliss and finally had to settle for, "…very good, indeed."

Den nodded automatically when another hand went up.

"Do you worship the Devil?" That was the pretty, red-skirted peeker.

Den's briefing materials had warned that this annoying question would be asked frequently, strange though it was. "Why would anyone do that?" he replied impatiently. "By all accounts, the Devil is notoriously unreliable and destroys his own followers more often than his enemies. You won't find many citizens of Sime Territory willing to waste their time worshipping such a being…if he exists at all."

Den answered the remaining questions with as much patience as he could muster. When he could stand no more, he urged everyone to follow him to the Old Sime Center and his next memorized speech.

"For almost two hundred years, this building housed the Pen for the town of Valzor. After Unity, a lot of the old Pen buildings were repurposed as Sime Centers. Valzor outgrew this building about twenty years ago. When operations were moved to the new complex across the street, it was decided to keep the old building as an historic monument."

Some of the tourists looked nervous at the idea of entering a former Pen, but none actually refused to go inside. The carrot-headed Raymond, predictably, was delighted. In the empty changeover ward, Den explained how a channel could not only help a child survive the dangerous transition into an adult Sime, but could then prevent that new Sime from Killing the nearest Gen in the madness of First Need.

"I won't turn into a Sime, but that gossip, Myra, might," Raymond announced, pointing to the red-skirted girl's friend. In all fairness, his victim was a little smaller and thinner than average, as many Simes were as children.

"Mrs. Ildun, you STOP him!" the girl whined to Raymond's embarrassed mother.

"Dear, he's too young to understand," the mother replied.

"No I'm not!" said Raymond. "Only bad children turn Sime. Everybody knows that!"

To Den's surprise, several adults nodded in agreement. Was this something they used to keep their children in line? Such an idea was very dangerous. Those children who went into changeover would add guilt to the volatile mix of pain and anxiety that attended even the easiest of changeovers. Orders to stay on script or not, Den had to challenge this fallacy.

"Raymond," he said, "you're old enough to know that isn't true. No one knows until it happens whether they're going to be Sime or Gen. Nothing you can do or think, nothing you can eat or take as medicine, absolutely *nothing* can make you turn one larity over the other. It was built into you when you were born, just like the color of your eyes. One day you will simply become a Gen or Sime adult, just as you are now a Gen or Sime child."

"Hey!" objected a tall man in a checkered shirt, "We didn't come here for you to tell lies to our children!"

Den forcefully curbed his temper. "We do not lie about larity in Sime Territory, Mr…?"

"Jess Rebens, Clear Springs City Clerk."

"Mr. Rebens. We cannot lie because Simes and Gens live here together. All our children get changeover training, no matter which larity their parents are. That way, those who go through changeover recognize what is happening early and get help from the nearest Sime Center. There, a channel helps them through changeover and gives them First Transfer, while their friends and family plan a changeover party to celebrate their becoming adult."

"You're insane!" Rebens gasped. "Only heretics would celebrate their child turning into a monster!"

"What are you doing in this delegation if you think Simes are monsters?" Den asked.

"Somebody has to represent common sense!"

Den took a deep breath and then another before he thought of a neutral response. "Arithmetic is common sense, is it not?"

Grudgingly, the man nodded agreement.

"I'm sure that as City Clerk, you keep records in Clear Springs of the births of babies and also of your adult population. All the adults living in Clear Springs are Gen, correct?"

Rebens nodded suspiciously. "Yeah. We don't let the ones that sprout tentacles live. One day, we'll drive the demon taint out and all our children will be human."

Den winced at the thought of so many unnecessary murders, but kept his voice level as he continued. "Your town records, if they are accurate, *will show* that one-third of your children in each generation change over. Furthermore, your records will document that one-third of your best and brightest children go through changeover, while two-thirds of your indifferent, lazy, or cruel children establish as Gens. Nature plays no favorites. It has nothing to do with climate, custom, philosophy, good behavior, or whether or not a community believes in it. For centuries after the channels discovered how Simes and Gens could safely live together, people of both larities rejected that solution as immoral. You just saw the history of Faith Day. If the exchange of food for selyn—the essential social contract of Unity—had not taken place, human beings of both larities would quite likely have been wiped out across the whole continent."

Den stopped, looking at faces showing varying degrees of anger, hope, and skepticism. If he let this continue, it could interfere with Rital's dream of seeing a Sime Center open in his guests' hometown—all because he could not stand the ideas they held.

He took another deep breath and said, "My apologies, Mr. Rebens. You are our guest, here to discover what a Sime Center could mean for your community. Perhaps you will find selyn-based technology of more interest." Returning to the script, he offered, "Let me show you how your own selyn can be used to enrich your world."

While the tall man appeared willing to continue arguing changeover statistics, the rest of Den's tour group were happy enough to change the subject. Everybody liked fancy modern machines.

The power plant in the basement was still operational. The towering banks of selyn batteries, connected to humming transformers with a spider-web of orgonics tubing, drew exclamations of wonder. Like most Donors, Den shared the channels' aversion to batteries and the "dead" selyn they stored, essential as the resulting energy was to powering modern technology.

However, out-Territory Gens were just as partial to having a clean, cheap, reliable source of power as their in-Territory neighbors. Even those who might otherwise be unalterably opposed to letting channels operate in their communities might be open to accepting a Sime Center to gain discounts on industrial selyn. Den reminded himself that if out-Territory Gen towns did the right thing for the wrong reason, at least the right thing got done.

When his group had gaped their fill, Den herded them toward the last stop on the tour. "The industrial selyn that fills those batteries and provides cheap power to the citizens of Valzor is produced by Gens just like you," he told them, stopping by an insulated window that provided a view of a small room. "The quantity of selyn available depends on the willingness of general-class donors to provide it. That happens here in the Collectorium. It is still staffed when the Old Sime Center is open, which gives you an opportunity to see this vital function of all Sime Centers for yourselves."

Den was forbidden to mention the other reason that the Collectorium in the Old Sime Center was open during tour hours: the remote possibility that some of the visitors might follow the example of their great-grandparents and donate selyn. It was Tecton policy to accommodate such impulses promptly, before prospective donors could change their minds. After his exchange with Rebens, he could appreciate why the psychologists didn't want the tour guides to lead a more open discussion: one forceful rejection of donating by a vocal opponent might discourage several potential donors.

With the exception of the boy, Raymond, the out-Territory tourists did not appear overjoyed at the opportunity to see a Tecton channel at work. The filmed donation they had seen earlier, while more explicit than many preferred, had been non-threatening: a filmed performance recreating heroic events in the distant past. This would be a live donation happening only a few feet away to an average person just like them. However, they did peer through the window.

The donations that the tour groups were allowed to watch were all taken from steady, experienced donors, of course. There was never any shortage of Gen volunteers, especially during the holidays, since in exchange for the loss of privacy, the donors were able to make firm appointments in advance, avoiding the holiday crowds and inevitable delays.

Hajene Tellansar was just showing a client into the collecting room. Den recognized Kirri Hoplard, who worked in the New Sime Center's library. She walked calmly over to the peculiarly shaped couch and lay down, settling into the comfortable contours.

"Isn't she afraid?" one of the women asked in a classic example of projection.

"Not at all," Den answered, keeping his voice calm and reassuring. "Kirri has donated every month since she established selyn production. She knows she isn't in any danger and that Hajene Tellansar will issue her a nice, fat voucher when she's done." Gens were, of course, paid for their selyn. It was the only reason many out-Territory donors bothered.

The dark-haired girl in the red skirt had ended up close to Den. She chewed her lip nervously and tugged at the name tag pinned to her blouse. When Tellansar sat next to Kirri on the channel's seat, designed to allow him to reach both of his client's arms easily, she prepared to hide her face again.

On impulse, Den suggested, "Why don't you watch..." he mentally sounded out the odd English letters on her badge and took a guess at the proper pronunciation, "...Bethany?"

Her eyes widened. "Oh, I couldn't!"

"It's not nearly as bad you think." Den nodded toward the window and the girl looked through it reflexively.

Hajene Tellanser was hamming it up, as usual. He took Kirri's hands in his own, striking a pose. There was a collective flinch from the adult observers as his handling tentacles emerged, but even Bethany kept watching. Young Raymond pressed his nose against the glass as the graceful, muscular appendages extended in excruciatingly slow motion to wrap comfortably around Kirri's forearms, giving the watching tourists an opportunity to examine each separate tentacle.

Kirri was having a hard time keeping a straight face, but she remained still as the slender, moist lateral tentacles emerged from each side of Tellansar's wrists and slid into contact with her skin.

"Those lateral tentacles are very fragile," Den explained. "If they are dislodged during selyn flow, the channel could suffer a painful or even fatal shock." In-Territory Gens all knew how much more durable Gens were than Simes, but out-Territory Gens never seemed to understand that simple truth. "Channels have two separate selyn systems," Den continued. "Hajene Tellansar stores the selyn from donations in his secondary system, which he can control very precisely. Look at Kirri."

The special glass in the window blocked selyn fields quite well, but not sound. On cue, Kirri looked over to the viewing window and winked. Then she looked up at the channel and nodded. Tellansar leaned down to touch lips with her and a moment later, it was over.

Innocuous as the scene was, Bethany nonetheless stiffened, as if she were watching a bloody murder, not a routine procedure. She did not, however, try to hide her eyes again.

As Tellansar dismantled his grip, Den completed his speech. "Kirri didn't feel a thing, as you can see, because Hajene Tellansar controlled the rate of flow to below her level of perception. She would not have been injured even if she had resisted—but she didn't, which enabled Hajene Tellansar to tap her maximum capacity. That gives her a bigger paycheck, as well as providing more power to run the lights."

Most of the adults' expressions ranged from fear to disgust as the obviously unharmed Kirri got up from the transfer lounge. Den didn't hold out hope that this tour group would add to Valzor's selyn balance today, or that of their own city in the near future. It would, after all, be some years before young Raymond was physically able to donate, if he established at all.

Sighing, the Donor led the group through the double doors at the end of the hall and bade them farewell. The group dispersed toward the bathrooms, gift shop, and exit. None turned back through the yellow door to the Collectorium. Den sighed morosely and followed the group heading toward the facilities.

When he emerged, it was to the sight of Raymond pursuing his sisters with an anatomically correct Sime doll from the gift shop. "I'm a channel and I'm gonna suck your selyn!" he threatened as the girls screamed. The rest of the tour group had vanished, their involvement with the Tecton finished.

Glumly, Den trudged back across the courtyard to the auditorium to repeat the futile process with his next group.

CHAPTER 2

A SELYN ECONOMY

Although Den's job playing host to tourists at the Old Sime Center seemed to go on forever, eventually the week ended and with it, his mornings in purgatory. He whistled cheerfully as he headed to the New Sime Center to cover his shift at the infirmary.

There, Den spent the afternoon helping Hajene Nalod, the First Order channel handling the more difficult cases that shift, care for a thirteen-year-old girl who had conducted an unsuccessful flight test of a homemade flying harness. Through a combination of favorable weather, better than usual engineering, luck, and a providentially placed rose hedge, young Mandle had escaped serious injury during her flight off the roof of her house.

Once the intrepid test pilot's broken thumb had been set, her relieved father, a tall Gen with a bushy mustache, began conducting a stern post-flight analysis as Den and Nalod cleaned and healed the cuts and scratches adorning her face, arms, and legs.

"…And if people were meant to fly, we'd have wings," the scold concluded. "Leave flying for the birds. They're built for it."

"The Ancients built flying machines," Mandle protested, "and they looked like us. Like Gens and children, anyway. If they could do it, I can, too."

Den moved a little to the right, blocking the father's reaction from Nalod's perception. The man had donated selyn within the past week, so his emotions did not project to nearby Simes as strongly as they would later in the month. Still, even low field, intensity mattered.

"Only birds and bats can fly, young lady…" the distressed father continued, disrupting Nalod's focus again.

A diversion was obviously required. "Actually, your daughter's right," Den observed in a slightly apologetic manner. "The Ancients built both gliders and powered flying machines."

Mandle straightened and opened her mouth to claim victory.

"However," Den cut her off, "they built their gliders out of very strong, lightweight materials that we don't have today, and there were still very few places where there was the right combination of height and wind to fly them."

"It almost worked," the unrepentant test pilot insisted. "I just ran into that stupid rose bush."

"It didn't work at all, because you didn't know what you were doing," Den corrected her. "If you want to fly, you have to study the experts."

"Fine," Mandle said, tossing her head. A rose twig detached from her hair and fluttered to the floor. "You find me an Ancient and I'll ask her."

"You don't require an Ancient," Den corrected. "If you want to fly, look at birds." His voice warmed as he talked about his pet obsession. Only the ironclad discipline ingrained in him during his training kept part of his attention fixed on supporting Nalod. The channel tolerated his distraction because the impromptu aeronautics lecture was preventing his patient and her father from arguing.

"Birds fly more efficiently than any Ancient machine," Den continued. "But the ones that are really good at it share certain traits. The best fliers don't flap their wings much. They glide on the air, so they don't have to work very hard. Take vultures, for example. If you stretched one out, its wingspan would be about as wide as your father is tall. But do you know how much one weighs?"

Mandle admitted her ignorance of this avian statistic.

"About as much as ten oranges. You could lift it easily. Birds have very light, hollow bones to reduce their weight. So you see, if you want to glide, you have to have wings large enough to lift your weight—and *you* don't have hollow bones like a bird. The wings must lift their own weight, too. Now, the Ancients also had heavier flying machines, with powerful, lightweight engines to pull them through the air. We can't reproduce them because we can't recreate their engines."

Seeing Mandle's disappointment, which matched his own so closely, he winked and added, "Yet."

The girl's father frowned, no doubt anticipating further unscheduled trips to the Sime Center. Den cut him off again.

"Mandle, if you want to help redevelop the Ancient flying machines, you've got to go about it right. Learn how air lifts a wing, about weather and navigation, and the properties of various materials, so you can select ones that are both strong and lightweight. Develop an engine that can provide enough power without being too heavy to lift. And when you've put all those things together, *that's* when it's time to build something and try to fly."

Mandle frowned. "But all that will take *years!*" she complained.

"Yes, it will," the Donor agreed. "But at the end of it, you just might have a working flying machine. Isn't that better than a broken thumb, a lot of scratches, and a smashed rose bush?"

* * * *

When Den's shift ended, he retired to his office with a mug of trin tea to catch up on his mail. However, he kept thinking back to Mandle and her homemade glider.

After reading the same memo three times—yet another update about the Tecton delegation to the Southern Continent—he went to the over-stuffed bookshelf for a slim volume with a cracked spine and dog-eared pages.

This book had come by its dilapidation honestly by inspiring his child-hood. Ornate, gold-tinted letters spelled out "A History of Ancient Aviation by Vanrell ambrov Frihill" and underneath, in metallic grey, was a picture of an Ancient flying machine with the sleek proportions of a hawk. It was pulled through the air by a single propeller attached to the nose. In short, it was a design that might be simple enough for modern technology to du-plicate.

With due care for the crumbling spine, Den untied the string that held it together and carefully opened the book to the section describing the craft. The Ancient histories, Vanrell explained, alleged that the 'Spirit of St. Lou-is' had crossed the entire Eastern Ocean. If it had really done that, such an aircraft could reach anywhere on the Northern Continent. He stared at the book, lost in dreams of flying, until his tea was cold.

The next day, Den was scheduled for an evening shift in the change-over ward. That left him with the afternoon free, so he walked to the di-lapidated warehouse that housed the workshop of the Valzor Flyer's Club.

As Den had hoped, his friend, Jannun, was there, carefully hand-sand-ing the rounded topside of a wooden plank. He looked up as the Donor entered and called a greeting.

"You got the wing planed into shape!" Den exclaimed in delight, grab-bing a second piece of sandpaper and setting to work. "How is Eddina coming with the propeller?"

"She hasn't found anything better than the bicycle wheel to wind the rubber belt up with, but that's good enough for a test flight, anyway."

The scale model of the 'Spirit of St. Louis' was the largest flier the club had attempted to date, with a four-foot wingspan. Built of lightweight but strong birch, it would be as sleek and beautiful as the original—if it could fly.

"I'm still worried that it will be too underpowered to get off the ground," Den muttered, voicing a frequent complaint among flying enthusiasts. "We ought to have a motor, not a glorified rubber band."

"Tell that to the Economic Development Board," Jannun grumbled. "They might listen to a First Order Donor like you. There must be dozens of applications for smaller, more powerful motors."

Den sighed. Jannun's specialty in their club was woodworking. He left propulsion to Eddina and design issues largely to Den. "It's not just a matter of small motors," the Donor explained, "it's the selyn batteries that *power* the motors. They're bulky and heavy, which is fine when they sit in the basement and power a building. But in a train, half the batteries are there to move the mass of the power plant so the other batteries can move the train—and that's just to pull it along a level track. I don't think anyone has yet made a selyn battery efficient enough to lift its own weight."

"Someone must be working on it," said Jannun. "It would be worth a fortune. The Economic Development Board should develop the motor and a lightweight battery to run it as a package deal. Surely they can see the value in that."

"While we wait for them to zlin sense, let's see if we can make a glider that will actually glide," said Den. "We're working on lift," he gestured at the graceful curve of the wing they were sanding, "and lightweight material." He recalled his conversation with Mandle. "Have you ever held a bird?"

"Chickens," Jannun replied. "My folks raised them for eggs."

"Chickens are kind of heavy," said Den, "which is why they don't fly like songbirds. Ever have a tame jay sit on your finger? You hardly know it's there until it pecks you for a peanut. Gens and birds both use muscle and bone to move, but we're built for strength and durability, while birds are built for flight. They also eat high-energy foods and their lungs supply more oxygen to their muscles, so they have more power applied to less mass."

"Then selyn power ought to be the ideal solution," Jannun argued. "Simes get a lot more power from selyn than Gens can from food."

"Well, yes, theoretically," the Donor agreed. "But to get rid of the weight of the battery, our flyer would have to be powered by augmenting Simes, pedaling madly the whole trip!"

They laughed at the absurd notion, but then Den sobered. "The Economic Development Board gets a lot more proposals than it can fund. They pick the ones that can deliver a usable product in a reasonable time. We'll have to design our airplane propulsion system from scratch. The Ancients didn't use orgonics technology, so it's not just a matter of asking Householding Frihill how they did it. The Ancient engines were powered by combustion and made out of metal alloys we don't have."

Jannun sighed. "I know. But still..." He smiled wistfully. "I want to fly."

They were giving the wing its first coat of varnish when Eddina arrived, grinning broadly and waving a piece of paper in two tentacles. "They're having a challenge at this year's East Nivet Model Flyer's Convention!"

"What is it?" Jannun asked. He started to reach for the paper with a sticky hand, but Eddina snatched it away from ruin.

"Tell us," Den urged, continuing to wield his own brush with steady efficiency.

"We're not the only ones who want to fly ourselves instead of just making pretty toys," she began, bouncing with excitement. "Nobody will fund research for a flying machine to carry people while there are so many problems to solve. So, the convention's issuing a challenge to design a functional wing for powered flight."

"What are the rules?" Den asked, mentally flipping pages in *A History of Ancient Aviation* in search of potential designs.

Eddina consulted her flier. "First, entries must have a wingspan of at least twenty feet and no more than forty feet."

Jannun's eyes widened. "That's big enough to carry a person."

"I expect that's the point," Den said.

"The wings must attach to a packing crate weighing 300 pounds," Eddina continued. "They'll be launched from the top of a hill using a catapult, and the winner will be the wing that flies the farthest."

The three considered the problem for a moment.

"A double wing?" Eddina hazarded. "Box kites are most stable."

"Chances are, the catapult launcher would interfere with that," Den pointed out.

"I could build a larger version of this wing," Jannun offered.

"We require something designed to glide," Den pointed out. "There won't be any more power after the initial launch."

They discussed alternatives as the men cleaned up the workspace and Eddina made trin tea on the battered old hot plate.

"What should we call our entry?" she asked, handing out steaming mugs.

"I have the perfect name," Den said. Holding up his mug in a toast, he continued, "I give you...the 'Spirit of Valzor'!"

Den met Rital at the latter's office later that day, still bubbling with excitement. However, the channel seemed even less interested in his cousin's dreams of flight than usual. After Rital changed the subject for the third time, Den protested, "Someday airplanes will be as important as trains, just as they were for the Ancients. I want to be in on that."

Rital shook his head slowly. "Den, I'd like to recreate some of the legendary Ancient technology as much as you. However, technology takes a reliable source of power. The Ancients' civilization would probably have collapsed even if they hadn't mutated into Simes and Gens, because they powered their technology with irreplaceable fossilized hydrocarbons."

"We've got selyn-based technology," Den argued. "As long as there are Gens, we'll have power."

"Theoretically," the channel agreed. "But there's always the gap between theory and practice." He settled back in his desk chair, wrapping hands and tentacles around his tea mug. "Working with Monruss in the District offices has given me a different perspective. The in-Territory Sime population is growing. Our reliance on selyn-powered technology is growing even faster as the sliderail trains expand out-Territory … but out-Territory Gens seldom donate. The current population of donors is barely large enough to support what we've got. That's why the Economic Development Board funds so few proposals. New gadgets benefit nobody if you can't run them."

"Then they should fund research into improving selyn technology," Den insisted, "so in the future, the available selyn will power a lot more machines than it does now."

"It's more than that, Den," Rital told him. "Monruss is deeply concerned about the long-term trends in the numbers of Simes and Gens. Simes have been living longer ever since Unity—and having more children, two-thirds of whom are also Simes."

"I know that," said Den, recalling his encounter with the math-challenged Gen tourist. "Any population in which Simes and Gens have comparable lifespans and fertility will, over five or six generations, tend toward half Simes and half Gens. But that's theoretical. For one thing, Sime women tend to bear fewer children, on average, than Gen women."

"Nevertheless," Rital stated, "the Sime population is growing faster than the subpopulation of Gens who donate selyn. Out-Territory Gens in border communities are more likely to deliver a child in changeover to their local Sime Center than their own parents were, but almost none of those parents will defy local custom by donating selyn to support their Sime offspring. If those trends continue for another decade or two, Simes will outnumber the Gens who support them and we won't have enough surplus selyn to maintain even our current tech base."

Den enforced strict control on his field to keep Rital from being affected by his surge of anger. "Those bloody lorshes!"

Confused, Rital asked, "Who? What lorshes?"

"Non-donors who expect to profit from our technology without contributing one dynopter of selyn for its maintenance!"

"That makes them misers, but not exactly lorshes," Rital said mildly.

"No, they're *worse* than lorshes," Den explained. "You should give the shenned tour to out-Territory Gens sometime and hear them talk. You sure won't want to zlin them. They don't abandon their children in change-over—they *murder* them! And they're proud—*proud*—of doing it. They have some sort of sick ethical system that requires them to murder their Sime children, even now, when they know all they have to do is take them to a Sime Center."

Rital inexplicably seemed to find something positive in Den's words. "*That's* why I've fought so long and hard to open a Sime Center in Clear Springs," he said, his passion unmistakable even to Gen eyes. "Out-Territory culture doesn't care about supporting renSimes and honestly, we don't expect *our* Gens to travel to another city to donate every month. But out-Territory Gens want to redevelop Ancient technology as much as we do. Put a Sime Center where they can reach it easily, show them that some of the renSimes who Need their selyn are their own kids, not just strangers from a foreign Territory, and they'll start to donate regularly. We'll end up with enough selyn to support our renSimes and build your flyers, too."

The Donor shook his head. "You're delusional. I hope Ersov got your paperwork in order, Rital, because for sure, nothing else got accomplished in my week at the Old Sime Center. I must have talked to hundreds of out-Territory Gens, but I doubt even one of them dropped by the Collectorium. I've never met people so determined not to listen or learn."

The channel frowned. "They still deserve access to channels, just like anybody else."

"Rital, if the Gens I showed around the Old Sime Center are typical, they don't *want* access to channels." He got up from his chair to pour himself more tea.

"Actually," Rital said, leaning back in his desk chair and swiveling it back and forth in a calming motion, "the Clear Springs City Council and the leadership of the university there came to *us* to suggest a Sime Center. They want to expand and they've reached the practical limits of their current, electrical-based grid."

"How were they planning to support a selyn-based power grid?" Den asked sarcastically. "Import batteries from Valzor?"

The channel refused to share his cousin's pessimism. "Perhaps at first, but I think when they don't have to travel to the border to donate, some Gens there will discover advantages to dropping by the Collectorium. If nothing else, it's a university town and students are always short of cash."

"It sounds like a sentence of death by entran to me," Den insisted, exaggerating only slightly. While the painful secondary system cramps a channel experienced when unable to work could be managed by a competent Donor, complications from chronic entran could be severe.

"I sincerely hope you are wrong," his cousin said. He looked thoughtfully into his tea for a moment, then set the mug down and looked at Den. "You see, I've asked District Controller Monruss to let me be the Clear Springs Sime Center's first Controller. The assignment came through today."

Den's just-filled tea mug hit the floor, sending pottery shards and hot liquid flying. "Rital, no!" he protested. "You can't live out in the middle of nowhere, an eight-hour train ride away from civilization. Who will look after you when the out-Territory Gens get you all tied up in knots?"

Rital grinned weakly at his cousin and reached into the top drawer of his desk. "I was hoping *you* would look after me," he admitted, holding out a neat, pocket-sized reassignment packet. "I asked Monruss to assign you to my staff and he agreed. We leave for Clear Springs in twelve days, to be there for a Faith Day opening ceremony."

CHAPTER 3

MIDNIGHT TRAIN

The next few days passed in a blur for Den. In addition to his normal work shifts, his belongings had to be sorted and those he wanted to keep packed for shipping or storage. He had been stationed in Valzor for three years, rotating through different departments rather than moving between Sime Centers, so he had accumulated more detritus than a young, bachelor Donor ought to allow. Possessions were a bad habit only a Donor whose seniority or family obligations rated a permanent assignment could afford. While Den had submitted a request for such an assignment six months before, he had known that it was unlikely to generate any response other than amusement from District Controller Monruss.

There were planning meetings with Monruss and his staff to make sure that the new Clear Springs Sime Center had all that was required for it to function smoothly from the beginning. There were also briefings on out-Territory culture given by junior diplomats and *their* staff, all designed to ensure that nobody offended the good citizens of Clear Springs, broke their laws, or violated the more obscure provisions of the First Contract. This was supposed to ensure that large numbers of said citizens would welcome their new channel with bared arms.

Den didn't believe, even for an instant, that *that* would happen.

His primary consolation as he contemplated his forthcoming banishment from civilization was that as the only Donor in Clear Springs, he would be working exclusively with Rital and would give the channel his personal transfer most months. They were well matched and had always been close. Having family around might make the hostile surroundings more bearable.

As the endless meetings dragged on, Den got to know some of the other staff Rital had picked for the Clear Springs Sime Center. Most were Gens although Alyce Tobeas, the head groundskeeper, and Gati Forsin, one of the receptionists, were renSime. The other receptionist, Seena ambrov Carre, was a Householder. However, unlike many Householders who were traditional enough to use their House name instead of a last name, Seena seemed willing to work under non-Householders. Den decided to withhold judgment and see if she proved able to take orders from him. It wasn't easy to find people ready to move so far into Gen Territory, after all. The Donor felt much more confident about the chef, Ref Maxin, a large, cheerful man whose rounded belly hinted that his cooking was at least good enough to win his own approval. All spoke the Gen language fluently enough to refer to it by the Genlan term, English.

Any moment that Den could steal from his other duties he spent working on his wing design. While a wing was a surprisingly simple sort of machine, at least theoretically, designing an efficient one required making dozens of choices to optimize function under specific conditions. The best length, width, angle of attachment, and degree of top-surface curvature had to be calculated for several possible wood types and then recalculated for several possible weather conditions that might occur on the day of the test.

Not all his aviation research was devoted to the wing project, however. In a fit of well-deserved guilt, or perhaps in an attempt to make a sojourn among the Wild Gens seem more palatable to his cousin, Rital presented Den with an early Faith Day present: a paperback novel written in English that had sat unclaimed for over a week in the lost and found at the Old Sime Center. It purported to be a translation of an Ancient biography, although Den was skeptical. Why would anybody lucky enough to have a working airplane risk it in aerial jousting, shooting bullets at other pilots? The sky was big enough to accommodate dozens of pilots and their craft, after all, so there was no reason for conflict. And why would any sane man taking up such an odd sport make himself a better target by painting his aircraft bright red? Not to mention that Rick Toeffen was an odd name, even for an Ancient.

Improbable as the plot was, however, the flying sequences were vivid enough to give the reader a taste of what powered flight might be like.

The staff left for Clear Springs five days before Faith Day to make sure everything was ready. Den and Rital would take the train out four days later, giving them a night's rest and time for Den to give Rital his personal transfer before the official opening ceremony started at noon sharp on Faith Day itself. It was a tight schedule, but it would give Rital the chance to carry a normal workload as long as possible.

Den was still worried that, Faith Day or not, too few Clear Springs Gens would volunteer to donate to prevent his cousin from suffering entran. The Donor had taken the precaution of slipping a text on entran management into his luggage, but he was by no means an expert on treating the condition.

By two days before Faith Day, there was nothing more Den could do to prepare. His luggage was packed, color-coded with yellow stickers for the boxes going into storage and purple for those he wanted sent to Clear

Springs. The diplomats and administrative types had given all the advice they had to offer and he had worked his last shift at the Valzor Sime Center.

For the first time in over a week, he had time to spend as he wished. Donning an old, grease-stained coverall that was still unpacked because it was too disreputable to be worth keeping, he slipped away to the warehouse. Jannun and Eddina greeted him enthusiastically and they spent an hour poring over the specifications of the flying wing contest. The required payload was to be a standard packing crate. Two opposite sides would be reinforced and three holes drilled to allow wing assemblies to be attached. The interior would be filled with stones to bring the weight up to the specified 300 pounds.

Eddina had drawn scale pictures of a standard packing crate and had several ideas of how wings might be attached to it. They discussed each in detail, trying to strike the proper balance between being able to attach the wings in a reasonable period of time and ensuring that they did not become unattached prematurely. None of the available options satisfied Eddina.

"There's going to be a lot of stress on the attachment sites," she complained, poking two tentacles at opposite sides of a small cardboard box that held used bits of sandpaper. It was close enough to the proportions of a packing crate to act as a three-dimensional model and facilitate discussion. "The stress won't necessarily be in a constant direction, either. I'm worried that the wings will snap off if a gust hits them the wrong way. Three hundred pounds is a lot to carry."

Den's education in practical engineering had been limited by the demands of Donor training. Over the years, he had taught himself quite a bit about wing shapes and what they were supposed to do, but he had only a vague idea of how they might be constructed, much less attached.

His Donor training, however, had instilled in him the habit of working *around* a problem when working through it wasn't possible. While Jannun and Eddina argued hotly about the shear strength of bolts, the structural integrity of the reinforced packing crate, and just how well the 300 pounds of weight would be secured inside it, Den's eyes wandered randomly around the shop and eventually came to rest on the neglected wing for the 'Spirit of St. Louis' replica, still waiting for its final coat of varnish before it could be attached to the main body of the model. The excitement over the contest had caused the project to languish unfinished.

He checked the contest rules once more, then nodded. "Here's what we'll do," he announced, with the confidence of a Donor who was used to making critical decisions with insufficient evidence, in situations where not acting could be fatal. "The rules say our wings have to carry the crate and its contents. They *don't* require that the crate be a structural element or that we use their attachment points."

Eddina looked confused. "How else can the wings lift the crate?"

"As cargo." Den appropriated the box of sandpaper from Eddina, set it on the bench, then picked up the incompletely varnished model wing and placed it on top. "If we make the wings one piece, running over the top of the crate, we can maintain structural integrity. The crate can be strapped on underneath. It still has to hold, but the attachment points won't have to take the jolt if a gust of wind hits in the wrong direction. The wing will."

"But that means a whole section of the wing, the part attached to the crate, won't be contributing any lift at all," Jannun objected. "The crate is heavy enough by itself. Can we afford to add more dead weight?"

"You're looking at the problem backwards," Den said, his excitement growing. "We're not trying to design a wing that can lift a packing crate. We're trying to design a wing that can be used on an airplane. A real one, which could carry people up to the clouds if we had a propulsion system that was powerful and lightweight enough to push it there."

His friends' eyes widened in sudden understanding, then they grabbed paper and pencils and began sketching, throwing ideas back and forth in a frenzy of creativity. Den left them to it—they both knew a great deal more about building things than he did—and went to make tea.

He had just poured the hot water onto the tea leaves and set the cracked old teapot aside to steep when the door to the warehouse burst open. Rital charged through, carrying a large satchel. Drawn by Den's peaking nager, the channel's eyes settled immediately on his cousin. "Den! I've been looking all over for you." He frowned. "Whatever possessed you to go wandering so far from the Sime Center?"

It didn't take the ability to zlin to see that the channel was almost frantic with worry. However, there was a principle to uphold. Even channels tended to get short-tempered when in Need, but that was no excuse for bad manners.

"This is where I usually go, when I have time off," Den pointed out in mild indignation. "You know that." He waited for Rital to nod, conceding the point, before he asked, "Is something wrong?"

"Yes. Or actually, no." The channel waved his ambiguous answer away with two tentacles and explained, "There was a phone call from Clear Springs an hour ago. They have a child in changeover at the Sime Center, confirmed by Gati Forsin. And there isn't a channel or Donor in hundreds of miles who can give her First Transfer!"

"Shen!" Den swore. "How long does the kid have?" Briefly, he fantasized about being able to fly an airplane directly to Clear Springs in just an hour or two, then set the dream aside to deal with the possible.

"Monruss has been on the telephone with the Transport Authority," Rital said. "There's a freight train heading that direction this afternoon. It will make an unscheduled stop at Clear Springs to drop us off."

"Good," the Donor agreed. He waved an apologetic farewell to Jannun and Eddina, who broke off their discussion long enough to wave back and wish him luck, then followed Rital out of the warehouse.

"I can change out of these coveralls and pack a bag in ten minutes." He turned right, only to be brought up short by two tentacles wrapping around his upper arm.

"There's no TIME, Den," the channel said. He started briskly in the opposite direction, half-dragging the Gen after him. "They're holding the train for us. I packed you a dinner, but your things will have to come later. Don't worry, I left a message about your color-coding."

The portion of the Valzor train station dedicated to passengers was a showpiece of modern architectural design: spacious, clean and inviting. The portion dedicated to freight was merely utilitarian and no cleaner than it had to be. Den and Rital paused just inside the fence that kept unauthorized visitors away, surveying the bewildering maze of tracks, switches, warehouses, detached boxcars in various stages of loading or unloading, and freight handlers shouting over the hissing of the locomotives.

"Which one is ours?" Den asked.

"I've no idea," the channel admitted, zlinning the ambient for any nager that carried the confident signature of authority.

Their own nageric signature, of course, marked them as interlopers. The patterns formed by a channel's secondary system and the discipline required to use it were quite distinctive, as was Den's own field, which at the moment was brimming with far more selyn than a general-class donor would carry.

A harried renSime carrying a clipboard trotted up to them and asked, "Hajene Madz?" At the channel's nod, he gestured for them to follow. "I'm Stationmaster Plovitt. If you and your Donor will come this way, your train is ready to leave. Then I can get to work unsnarling my schedule."

"We do appreciate the cooperation of the Transport Authority in this emergency," Den told the man before Rital could snap at him. The presence of a Donor helped soothe a channel's Need anxiety, but Donors still automatically ran interference when their channels were particularly edgy.

Plovitt stopped by a locomotive attached to a long string of boxcars, flatcars and tanker cars. A pair of Gen women in Transport Authority uniforms leaned casually against its side.

"Here they are, Getta," he announced. "Get them settled quickly. I'll have you cleared to go in five minutes."

"Sure thing," the taller woman agreed amiably to Plovitt's back as the stationmaster charged off down the track, shouting for the switch handlers. She shook her head sadly and remarked, "Now, there's a man who's headed for an early grave, if he doesn't learn to relax." Turning to her passengers, she smiled. "We've cleared space in the third boxcar for you. Come on and I'll show you."

The accommodations could have been worse, under the circumstances. They had almost half the boxcar, crates on which to sit, and fire blankets for padding.

"All the comforts a hobo could want," Den observed, looking around.

"Better get your retainers on now, Hajene," Getta advised before she left them to help her colleague prepare for departure. "We cross the border five minutes out and I'm told it's easier to put the things on when the train isn't moving."

"Would you get them for me, Den?" Rital asked as he arranged some of the crates for more comfortable seating. "They're in the satchel."

Despite the intensive schedule of briefings, Den had forgotten that his cousin would have to make the eight-hour journey to Clear Springs with his tentacles confined in retainers. The devices had been invented centuries ago by the Gen military to confine a captured Sime's tentacles and render the Sime incapable of Killing Gens. That they did so in a particularly painful way also made them effective instruments of torture.

When the First Contract was being negotiated, the Gen Territory representatives had insisted that out-Territory citizens retain the legal right to murder Simes on sight, a necessary defense against their Sime children. As a compromise, they reluctantly agreed to criminalize the murder of any Sime whose tentacles were confined in retainers.

The practical result of the retainer laws was to prevent Simes from traveling in Gen Territory for any but the most unavoidable reasons. Even then, because the manacles were so crippling, Simes could not linger to see the sights or enjoy the amenities. Den sometimes wondered if that was the real reason the New Washington government insisted that Sime visitors wear them.

Den opened the satchel and pulled out the metal gauntlets. Modern retainers were custom-fitted, but they still forced the handling tentacles to stay retracted, made the laterals extend unnaturally, and interfered sickeningly with a Sime's ability to make sense of the ambient nager. A Sime had to be very careful when wearing them so as not to pinch a lateral.

"Do you want help getting them on?" he asked his cousin sympathetically, holding the left-arm one out.

Rital stared at the gleaming device and all four of his vulnerable lateral tentacles retracted far up their sheaths in dread anticipation. He swallowed apprehensively, then reached for the retainer.

By the time they had gotten the things properly seated, the train was winding its way through the switches toward the open track and Rital was looking distinctly pale.

"Are you all right?" Den asked in concern.

"I will be, I think," the channel said. "The combination of the retainers and the movement of the selyn fields out there is making me nauseated."

The train picked up speed as it left the station. Rital huddled closer to his cousin to take advantage of the Donor's selyn field, which was at least stationary with respect to his own.

About five minutes after the train left the outskirts of Valzor, the noise altered subtly. "We're on the bridge over the river," Rital explained. "The other side is Gen Territory."

The train accelerated again as they left the bridge, passing isolated farms and small towns occupied only by Gens. Each time they did, Rital got a fraction paler.

It's going to be a long night, Den thought grimly as he focused his full attention on Rital to control the motion sickness. To distract his cousin from the discomfort, he asked, "If opening the Clear Spring Sime Center means so much to you—and it obviously does—why didn't you ask Monruss for a real expert instead of me? Say, a Donor with diplomatic experience who's used to managing that sort of tricky situation?"

"I did," Rital admitted. "Monruss asked the regional office for a troubleshooter, but they said they couldn't send one until summer at the earliest. All their diplomatic staff is working overtime on that Cordona business."

The small, independent Sime Territory of Cordona, far away on the southern continent, had pretty much given up the junct lifestyle in the last generation, but its fiercely independent channels had refused to join the Tecton officially or make peace with the two neighboring Gen Territories. Under intense pressure from the Tecton and its affiliated Gen Territories, a three-way peace conference had been arranged for the following month. Sosu Quess ambrov Shaeldor, the Donor who was the official leader of the delegation, had been quoted as having hopes of gaining a permanent peace—and not incidentally, three new signatories to the First Contract.

"They can't have sent every competent troubleshooter off to the southern continent," Den pointed out.

Rital shrugged, slowly and carefully so as not to pinch a lateral. "Perhaps not, but the regional office wasn't about to offer me any of the ones they held back in reserve. That left me with the resources I had in my tentacles. Most of the people in Valzor who have the necessary language skills and experience are either Sime, married to people who can't afford to leave their jobs, or are raising children."

"Clear Springs is not going to be a child-friendly post, particularly at first," Den agreed.

"Exactly." The channel was looking a little less pale as the conversation distracted him from the movement of the train. "If I couldn't have a diplomatic expert, I at least wanted someone I know I can work with and who I can trust not to misread the situation and offend the out-Territory authorities."

Den gave a politely skeptical snort. "I'm no diplomat."

Rital looked at him earnestly. "Really, Den, you did an excellent job handling the tourists over at the Old Sime Center. I kept track and the groups you hosted averaged nearly twice the usual number of donations."

The Donor felt his jaw drop. "They did? I was watching for that, too, and during the whole week, I only saw two Gens from my groups head into the Collectorium."

Rital grinned. "Didn't you pay attention during the briefings? A lot of out-Territory Gens think of donating as vaguely shameful, something done by other people who are desperate enough to prostitute themselves to a channel for money. Those who want to try it prefer not to let their friends or neighbors know. So, they linger in the bathroom or gift shop until the rest of their group has left and only *then* sneak into the Collectorium. The ones who aren't even considering a donation usually just leave."

Den made a quick estimate of the number of tourists from his groups who had headed for the bathroom or gift shop. It completely contradicted the impression of their attitudes he had gotten from their responses to the tour. "Are you sure it's not just the holiday?" he asked. "Out-Territory Gens are always more inclined to donate around Faith Day."

"That's true enough," Rital agreed. "However, it often takes a certain amount of discreet persuasion to turn that inclination into action. You have a gift for convincing out-Territory Gens that they don't have to be afraid of channels. It would be a shame to waste a talent like that."

"But I don't *want* to work out-Territory," Den protested. "I want to stay in Valzor, where people aren't ashamed to use the Sime Center's services and there are plenty of channels and other Donors to share the workload. I like knowing that when I have time off, I can spend it building flyers without worrying that some easily solvable problem will become a disaster because there wasn't another Donor around to look after my channel. With just the two of us, we'll never have a moment when we aren't on duty."

"We'll be able to bring in another channel or two in a few months, when we have a good, solid base of regular general-class donors," Rital said confidently. "Then you'll have free time again."

Den was less optimistic.

Rital reached out to rest a hand on the Donor's, started to give a reassuring squeeze, then stopped with a hiss as the retainer threatened to pinch. "I know this wasn't what you wanted, cousin, and I'm sorry. There simply wasn't any other Donor available who speaks English and is a good match for me. I'm overdue for a really good transfer and I won't be able to manage this assignment without one."

It was completely unfair, Den thought, for Rital to advance the one argument that no technical-class Donor could or would dispute. When he had Qualified as a First Order Donor, able to serve the most sensitive, demanding channels in transfer, he had sworn an oath that he would never abandon a channel who needed him. That the channel in question was family—the only real family either of them had—just made it more unthinkable to continue fighting the assignment.

Rital zlinned the moment Den's resistance crumbled, of course. To his credit, he was a gracious victor. "I promise you, I'll do my best to see that you can rotate back to Valzor in time for your flyer meeting and contest. If it's any consolation, Monruss was seriously considering granting you that permanent assignment to Valzor that you requested, even though you're not raising a family. The only reason he sent you with me instead is that the higher-ups decided to make the Clear Springs Sime Center part of Valzor District for administrative purposes. So officially, we're both still based in Valzor."

Around sunset, the train paused briefly at Cottonwood Crossing to drop off six cars of lumber and other building materials and take on eight cars of corn bound for a distillery beyond Clear Springs. Den and Rital took the opportunity to stretch their legs and use the station facilities.

Unfortunately, this station was too small to maintain separate areas for freight and passengers. There were a dozen people in the big main room, waiting for the regular passenger express. The channel and Donor tried to be unobtrusive, but a small child caught sight of Rital's retainers and shrilled loudly, "Mommy, why does that man have shiny things on his arms?"

"Hush!" the embarrassed mother warned, pulling the child back against her, but the damage was done. The Gens in the room pulled back as if the channel and Donor carried some deadly infection, staring at them in open hostility. They whispered to each other. Den couldn't make out much of the thick local accent, but the word "Sime" was repeated frequently.

Then a tall, middle-aged man with ill-kempt hair and a permanent frown stepped forward and spat contemptuously on the floor.

"We don't like murdering Simes staying in Cottonwood Crossing," he announced, looking around at the other Gens for support.

"And we at the Transport Authority don't like trouble-causing fools on our trains." Getta stepped around Den and Rital and glared down her nose at the would-be ringleader. It was quite a feat since tall as she was, she was a full six inches shorter than the troublemaker. "The channel here is passing through. He's no threat to anyone in Cottonwood Crossing, as you well know, and he'll be on his way shortly. If you insist on making trouble, though, I'll leave orders with the stationmaster to cancel that ticket of yours. For cause, which means no refund."

"You're bluffing."

Getta smiled, not pleasantly. "I never bluff," she promised.

The man looked around for support. When he didn't find it, he grumbled, "Aw, it's not worth it," and turned away.

"No, it's not worth it," Getta agreed. "Come on, Hajene, Sosu. The new cars are secured and we've got to clear the track so the express can take on its passengers."

Outside, she said softly, "I think it would be better for you to use the employee facilities. They're around the side there. Don't linger; we really do have to clear the track."

When the train was safely on its way again, Den asked a question that had been bothering him for some time. "Rital, the tourists I guided around the Old Sime Center actually chose to visit Sime Territory. They were self-selected for being willing to have contact with Simes, at least in principle. If those people in Cottonwood Crossing have a more typical attitude toward Simes, even channels wearing retainers who couldn't possibly harm them, why did Clear Springs ask for a Sime Center in the first place?"

The channel settled back on his crate. "Clear Springs is an odd place, not at all like the farming community back there. It's bigger, for one thing, and it's a regional hub for the towns around it. Mostly, though, it has a top university that specializes in engineering, architecture, and materials applications in addition to the more usual agriculture, law, and economics."

"So why does that make it a good place for the Tecton to put a Sime Center?"

"They like their gadgets in Clear Springs," Rital answered. "Four years ago, they decided to open a brand new flagship institute, the Center for Technology. The idea was to put the engineers, builders, and materials professors in state-of-the-art labs right next to each other and see what technological marvels they could develop."

Den, who had started the conversation mainly as a way to distract Rital from the continuing discomfort of the retainers, leaned forward with real interest. "I wonder if there's anyone there trying to build a working flyer?"

The channel shrugged. "I don't know, off hand, but it wouldn't surprise me. In any case, the new department and the extra students and staff it will bring are forcing both university and town to expand their infrastructure. Right now, they have a power grid that runs on electricity, like the Ancients used."

"Electricity?" Den asked. "To power a whole city? The expense of all the copper you'd use to run wires to every building would be prohibitive in itself."

"It is," Rital agreed. "Not to mention that those expensive wires have to be run through buried conduits so nobody will steal them, which makes what should be routine maintenance anything but routine. They generate much of the electricity from windmills, but they have steam generators for backup, which makes fuel another big expense. Since they had that nice Center for Technology in the planning stages, they asked the professors who would be joining it to find them a better and cheaper solution for their new complex."

"They recommended using selyn instead of electricity?"

"Yes. Orgonics tubing is so cheap it isn't worth stealing and useless for anything but conducting selyn, which means you can string it from poles where it can be repaired easily. However, Professor Willum Ildun, one of the social economists attached to the Center for Technology, pointed out that the Tecton charges a great deal for imported selyn batteries, but much less for selyn collected at a local Sime Center. The university decided to save the extra money."

"How'd they get the rest of the town to go along with them?" Den asked.

"They didn't have to," Rital said. "The university directly or indirectly employs about three quarters of the people living in Clear Springs. There's an idiom for it in English: *company town*. Essentially, the Board of Regents told the City Council that they were going with selyn power for their new construction and wanted a Sime Center to service the batteries, and that was that."

"What do the rest of the people living there think of all this?"

The channel shrugged. "There's some hard feeling in the community because there was no popular vote or referendum. However, there isn't a whole lot they can do about it, outside of complain. Once the City Council made the initial request to the Tecton, the issue was largely out of local control. Some people tried to stall construction of the Sime Center by contesting the zoning and by intimidating local merchants into refusing to do business with the Tecton, but that was a minor inconvenience. With the support of both the university and the City Council, there was no question that the Sime Center would open on schedule. Things might be a little awkward for a while, but the rest of the town will come around when they have a chance to get used to us. And when their power bills drop. You'll see."

Try as he might, Den couldn't share his cousin's optimism. His cousin had forgotten that converting to selyn power also meant buying all-new equipment that could run on it. How many people would be willing to do that?

CHAPTER 4

CHANGEOVER

The freight train dropped them off at the Clear Springs station shortly after midnight. The platform was deserted and the waiting room was locked. There wasn't even a stationmaster on duty, since the channel and Donor were the only cargo being delivered at Clear Springs.

While Den was glad not to face another hostile crowd, he had hoped that they would be met after their long journey. He squinted, trying to see into the shadows, of which there were many. "Do you know where the Sime Center is from here?" he asked his cousin.

"It should be roughly a mile that way," Rital said, nodding toward the exit at the right end of the platform.

The Donor sighed. After the long train ride, he wasn't looking forward to a mile-long hike through potentially hostile territory while lugging Rital's satchel to spare the channel's retainer-abused tentacles. "I suppose we'd better start walking, then," he said glumly. "I don't see a taxi and our patient—and our staff—are at risk until we can take over her care."

"Yes," Rital agreed. He led the way to the exit and out into the night air.

Den had assumed that the emptiness of the station was due to a lack of passenger trains scheduled during the next few hours. Outside, however, the street was deserted and the businesses and office buildings were shuttered tight, only an occasional spark of light showing where some night watchman or janitor was making the rounds.

"Where is everyone?" the Donor muttered uneasily. It reminded him too much of the climactic scene in a horror film that had given him nightmares as a child. It was set in a pre-Unity Sime town in which winter storms had blocked the roads, leaving the inhabitants to Kill each other when they ran out of Gens.

Rital didn't answer. He walked slowly, looking around in a dazed fashion. "Den, it's beautiful," he whispered. "Even through the retainers, I can zlin it. A whole city full of Gens and I'm the only Sime. There's enough selyn here to supply half of East Nivet. What an untapped treasure!"

Rolling his eyes in exasperation, Den stepped closer to his cousin, using his nager to block the surrounding selyn fields. The channel shook his head as his attention returned to business and his pace picked up.

They had reached the corner and paused to consider how best to navigate through a town with roads that didn't form a true grid when a car pulled up beside them. "It's Seena," Rital identified the driver, with some relief.

"Sorry I wasn't there to meet your train," the Gen apologized as they climbed in. "It got in earlier than the Transport Authority estimated."

"They gave us a good crew," Den explained. The car accelerated smoothly, weaving through the maze of streets, and the color drained from Rital's face. Den was sure it didn't help that a Gen was driving a selyn powered vehicle even if she was the receptionist Rital had picked.

Den placed a soothing hand on the channel's arm, just above the retainer. "It's only a mile," he murmured. "Then you can take the retainers off."

Rital gave a jerky nod, then asked, "How's our patient?"

"Not good," Seena summarized succinctly. "Nozella Duncan has no training at all, of course. She had never met a Sime before yesterday and is terrified that she's going to Kill somebody."

"She's been burning too much selyn?" Den guessed.

The receptionist nodded, her distress apparent even to Gen eyes. "She's too afraid, of us and of herself, to cooperate with her care. Gati and Ref—he's the highest-field of our Gens at the moment—have been on the phone with Hajene Anfrit in Valzor all night, trying to figure out how to keep her selyn consumption low enough for her to survive until breakout."

"Anfrit's good," Rital observed, nodding in approval. "You were able to manage, then?"

Seena tilted a hand back and forth to indicate uncertainty. "Yes and no. She's still alive and we think she's got enough reserves to survive until breakout. That is, *if* she can be kept from squandering what little selyn she has left. She entered Stage Four about two hours ago."

In Stage Four, the new Sime would be unconscious as her tentacles developed rapidly and her metabolism shifted over from burning calories to consuming selyn. It was not a simple or easy transition, but with the watchful support of an expert channel/Donor pair, most complications could be avoided.

Nozella, of course, had not enjoyed the benefit of such expert support until now.

Another turn and a large, well-lit new building could be seen ahead: an imposing structure with three rows of windows, a neatly trimmed lawn, plantings in front, and a sturdy fence enclosing the rear.

"That's the Sime Center," Seena told them.

Den squinted, trying to match the finished building with the blueprints Rital had displayed on his office wall all winter. The basic shape was an "H," with four wings leading from each corner of a central lobby. At the street level, one of the front wings would house the Collectorium, where it would be easily accessible to visiting selyn donors. An in-Territory Sime Center would also have had a Dispensary, where renSimes in Need of selyn would come for transfer from the channels, with an entrance at the opposite end of the building to minimize contact between the high field, non-donor Gens and the renSimes in Need. In between would be an admitting area for those who required medical assistance and the upper floors would house the wards, examination rooms, and offices.

The Clear Springs Sime Center didn't require a dedicated Dispensary, however, because the only renSimes living in the city would be the Sime Center's two renSime employees. Instead, the infirmary and changeover ward had been placed in the back wing farthest from the Collectorium to minimize the chances of an untrained out-Territory visitor entering them by mistake. The other back wing had a library and conference room, the Donor recalled, and the upper floors had a cafeteria, offices, and living quarters. Eventually, it was anticipated, a separate residence building would be necessary, but that was in the future.

Far in the future, Den thought, remembering the hostility of the waiting room crowd at Cottonwood Crossing. Some Gens in Clear Springs might be impoverished or idealistic enough to donate selyn, but seeking medical help from a channel would require a much more fundamental alteration in their accustomed worldview.

Seena drove around the building on an access road and parked the car beside an ambulance with the Tecton logo painted prominently on the doors.

"We're here at last," Rital said, opening the door carefully so as not to pinch a lateral. Den couldn't tell whether his cousin was elated or terrified at the prospect of staying in this strange place. Perhaps it was both.

"Let's get you inside where there's better light so I can help you off with those retainers," he offered, handing the satchel to Seena to carry.

Rital nodded stiffly and led the way.

Den followed his cousin up the loading dock stairs. The doors at the back opened onto a large storeroom filled with crates and boxes of supplies, equipment, and furniture. It was obvious that the staff was still unpacking the essentials that had been forwarded from Valzor.

Rital made a beeline for the pool of light under the closest selyn-powered utility lamp, then turned and offered his retainer-encased right arm to his cousin in a pleading fashion.

Den hurried over and carefully released the catches. Rital hissed as the retainers cracked open and moved very slowly as he worked his tentacles out of the interior pockets.

The Donor set the retainer on a convenient crate and surveyed the damage to his cousin's arm with dismay. After eight hours of continual abuse, the handling tentacle sheaths were red and swollen. Even worse, there was an incipient bruise over one lateral sheath. He rested a gentle hand on it and asked, "How bad is this?"

Rital inspected the area, then his eyes went blank as he zlinned. "Not as bad as it looks, fortunately," he assured Den. "The damage to the sheath is superficial and doesn't extend to the lateral itself. There's no impairment to function and the bruise will heal quickly after we have transfer."

"Good, we don't want the good citizens of Clear Springs to wonder if their new channel has some odd and possibly contagious disease of the tentacles."

He reached for his cousin's left arm and helped the channel work it free of the metal gauntlet. Another inspection reassured him that the damage on that arm was limited to swelling and redness on the handling tentacles. "You managed not to pinch your other lateral sheaths," he announced. "As your Donor, I advise you not to take any more eight-hour train rides out-Territory until you've learned how to wear the shenned things properly."

"I guess I'll have to postpone that vacation in New Washington, then," Rital agreed with feigned disappointment. He glanced at the discarded retainers gleaming malevolently on the crate, shuddered, and turned to Seena. "Where is our patient?"

"Just down the hall," Seena said, setting the satchel down and leading them out of the storeroom. The hall outside stretched off into the gloom on the right but was blocked with double doors on the left. Seena pushed them open, revealing the spacious lobby. The architect had tried hard to make it a pleasant space in a dignified, institutional sort of way. There were abstract murals on the walls, potted plants here and there, a desk for a receptionist, a waiting area with comfortable couches and chairs, and a grand staircase leading to the upper floors. The effect probably worked well enough when sunlight entering through the large windows would minimize the shadows and people were around. At night, it simply looked lonely.

They crossed the lobby and entered the other back hallway through another set of double doors that were prominently posted "No Admittance" in English. Just inside was the infirmary, which meant that beyond it should be…

"Here we are," Seena said, stopping in front of a door labeled "Changeover Ward" in both Simelan and English. She grinned. "Gati and Ref will be very glad to see you. I don't think they realized they could be drafted as emergency changeover attendants when they agreed to come out here. I'll take your things up to your rooms and have someone bring you tea." With a wave, she hurried briskly back the way they'd come.

Den looked at Rital. "Well, cousin, shall we go meet the patient we've come so far to help?" he asked.

Rital's back straightened and his face assumed a calm, dignified expression as he made the mental transition from Den's cousin Rital, who had just finished an exhausting eight-hour journey, to Hajene Madz, the Clear Springs Controller. It was a surprisingly effective illusion in spite of the rumpled uniform and unbrushed hair.

Den had no uniform to help him establish professional dignity, but he pushed his hair back out of his face, squared his shoulders, and ran a quick mental exercise to calm his nager and focus his thoughts on the task at hand.

Rital nodded his appreciation of the effect, then the two turned and entered the room, the channel slightly ahead to control the effect of their strong selyn fields on the ambient nager.

The changeover ward was a nicely appointed suite. The first room had a reception area with a desk and several couches for the comfort of anxious family members. It was currently deserted.

The door to the first treatment room opened a crack and Gati peered out, keeping the door mostly shut. When she saw Den and Rital, an exhausted but genuine smile lit her face.

"They're here, Ref!" she called over her shoulder, then she opened the door more fully. "We are so glad to see you, Hajene, Sosu," she greeted them with heartfelt relief. "We were afraid that you wouldn't make it in time and we'd have to help the poor girl die."

Until that moment, Den hadn't realized—hadn't let himself realize—that if he and Rital had suffered any substantial delays in their journey, the Sime Center's staff would have been forced to murder Nozella or risk having her Kill one of them in the ravenous hunger of First Need. The Simelan term for a person who would abandon a child to die in changeover, lorsh, was the vilest insult the language contained, for good reasons.

"What is the patient's status?" Rital asked crisply.

Den shot his cousin an admonitory look. It was not Gati's fault that she wasn't a channel. The receptionist had obviously decided that it was more humane to murder the girl than to let her die in the agony of Attrition. That spoke well of her sense of personal responsibility, however horrifying the prospect might be. It spoke even more to the barbarity of life here, where it took eight hours to get back to civilization.

"Nozella is still in Stage Four," Gati reported. "Her tentacles are developing nicely as far as I can tell." She spread her hands in apology. "I don't have a channel's sensitivity."

"You've done very well," Den assured her, since it looked like Rital wasn't going to do so. Making a mental note to remind Rital that he was the one who had sent Gati and Ref to Clear Springs without a channel, he followed the channel into the room, letting Rital meld their nagers together into a harmonious whole that wouldn't disturb their patient.

The adolescent girl lying unconscious on the bed was slender, with sweat-matted hair of an undistinguished brown. Den guessed her age at about fourteen natal years. Her left arm was under the covers, but the exposed right one had quite visible tentacle sheaths developing in long streaks from elbow to wrist.

An exhausted Ref was sitting by the girl's bedside, trying to keep his attention firmly focused on her. Done properly, the exercise allowed a Gen to control a Sime's emotions and selyn consumption. Unfortunately for Nozella, Ref had neither the training nor the aptitude for such work.

"We'll take it from here, Ref," Rital assured the chef. His voice already had the deep, relaxed tone of a channel working to manipulate the selyn fields around him. He moved closer to the bed and reached for Nozella's hand as the chef stood and retreated to stand with Gati in the doorway.

"She'll transition to Stage Five before long," the channel announced. He extended his laterals to zlin the developing tentacles more closely, reciting a highly technical series of observations for his Donor's benefit.

The last number on the list made Den frown. "That's not much of a selyn reserve, when she's only at the end of Stage Four."

"The girl's been fighting us all night," Ref explained, his frustration obvious even to Gen eyes. "First, she wouldn't let Gati zlin her. Next, she wouldn't believe that Gati could tell she was in changeover and then, when she couldn't deny that she was becoming Sime any more, she still wasn't interested in anything we had to tell her about how keep her selyn consumption under control so she could survive until you got here. She kept saying that you'd never come to the Sime Center."

Gati nodded. "It got so bad, Hajene Anfrit had us dose her with arceinine. That finally calmed her down, although she still wasn't very cooperative."

"Arceinine? For a changeover?" The drug was a powerful sedative, but it was slow to wear off and had side effects. Most notably, it interfered with a Sime's ability to distinguish her own emotions from those of the people around her, a difficult task for a new Sime under any circumstances.

Den looked down at their patient. "Won't that make her…?"

"Twice as vulnerable to outside nageric influences as she ought to be?" Rital finished the thought. "Yes, it will. I expect that was the point. Wasn't it, Ref? To make her vulnerable to your nageric projection?"

The chef nodded. "I'm no Donor. Without the drug, I didn't have the field strength or control to force her to calm down and cooperate with us."

"It worked," Rital assured him. "She's alive and has enough selyn to see her through breakout and First Transfer. Barely."

"She'll be even more disoriented than most new Simes over the next week or so, as she tries to figure out how to make sense of what she's zlinning," Den added. "On the other hand, she will live long enough to figure it out, which wouldn't have happened without you and Gati. You've done an amazing job to keep her alive and with enough selyn for a reasonable chance to stay that way."

Rital, finally realizing that he had been less than polite, seconded Den's praise, then sent Gati and Ref off to get some well-earned rest. When he and Den were alone with the unconscious girl, the channel zlinned her again. "Another ten or fifteen minutes until the transition to Stage Five, I think."

"Then we wait," Den agreed, sitting in the chair that Ref had abandoned.

"Yes," his cousin agreed. "Changeover and childbirth happen at their own pace." The channel walked over to a cart in one corner that held cups and a teapot. He lifted the lid off the teapot, inspected its contents, shrugged, and filled two cups with over-steeped, lukewarm trin tea. He handed one cup to Den, pulled up another chair, and settled down to wait and watch.

Something was niggling at the corner of Den's mind, now that he had time to think instead of just react. "Am I remembering correctly that the changeover ward only has three beds?" he asked.

Rital, who had followed the design and construction of the Clear Springs Sime Center more closely than his cousin, nodded absently. "That's right."

"That doesn't make sense," the Donor objected. "Not when this Sime Center was purpose-built instead of adapting an existing building. How in the world can we expect to take care of all the changeovers in a city this size with only three beds?" The changeover ward in Valzor had fifteen, although there were usually a few beds unoccupied.

"The people who live here are all Gens, Den," Rital reminded him. "There are a lot fewer changeovers than in an in-Territory city of the same size. Also..." he hesitated, reluctant to face an unpleasant reality. "Realistically, we'll only see a small portion of the changeovers that do occur. At least, that's what the experts decided. If they're wrong, which I sincerely hope, we can put any overflow in the infirmary. Since the people here have their own medical system, it's also going to be underused."

"The Collectorium has a full wing, though," Den observed.

The channel shrugged. "That's because the whole purpose of putting a Sime Center out here is to tap all that unused selyn. Our primary mandate is to recruit selyn donors. Enough to provide the industrial selyn to run the trains and factories and maybe, just maybe, enough to let us take on more long-term, power-hungry projects like powered flight."

"So saving this girl's life is just an afterthought?" Den asked, nodding at their unconscious patient. He didn't try to conceal his displeasure with such open disregard for the value of a child's life. "If that's true, why did we go to so much trouble to get here in time instead of just letting her die?"

"Of course we're not going to let her die, or Kill, for that matter," Rital said, obviously annoyed at Den's question. "However, we're here on the sufferance of the local people. The psych experts agree that giving out-Territory adults a place to donate if they want is less threatening than, say, offering to teach their children that everything their parents, teachers, and religious authorities have told them about Simes is wrong. Yes, we'll offer changeover training and assistance, medical care, and other services, but our primary focus, at least at first, has to be on building up a reliable cadre of general-class donors."

"I suppose that makes sense, in a cold-blooded sort of way," the Donor admitted. Privately, he promised the children of Clear Springs that he would do what he could to make sure that those of them who went through changeover didn't end up sacrificed on the altar of political expediency.

Ten minutes later, as Den was finishing the dregs of his now-cold tea, Nozella stirred. The Donor came to full alert.

Rital zlinned her closely, then nodded. "Stage Five transition," he announced.

The girl tossed her head restlessly, as if resisting or rejecting something, then her eyes opened. She stared from Den to Rital and back to Den. "Who are you?" she asked apprehensively. A new Sime was particularly vulnerable in Stage Five and nature compensated with hostility, withdrawal, or even paranoia, all designed to make the child in changeover seek a safe place to hide.

"I'm Hajene Madz," Rital said in an encouraging tone. "This is my Donor, Sosu Milnan, and you, I'm told, are Nozella Duncan." Den felt his own nager modulate as his cousin borrowed strength to reinforce his verbal reassurance with a projection of warm welcome and safety.

"You're the channel?" For some reason, Nozella seemed to find this confusing. "But Reverend said you'd never get here because..." She paused, obviously rethinking her words. "I was told you'd never make it as far as the Sime Center," she continued more cautiously, "and that you weren't supposed to be here for another day, anyway."

"We came out from Valzor early to take care of you," Den told her.

"So that's one more thing gone wrong," the girl said. She closed her eyes with a dry, hiccoughing sob.

"Oh, it's not so bad," Rital assured her, sending out another wave of reassurance and calm.

Instead of leaning into the offered comfort as an in-Territory child would have done, their patient resisted the channel's projection. Her selyn consumption spiked with the cognitive dissonance created by the conflict between Rital's projection and her own distrust of Simes. Thanks to the arceinine, both emotions must seem to her as if they were her own deeply held feelings.

Rital backed off his projection and signaled for Den to take over.

"Our luggage will catch up with us," the Donor agreed, smoothly capturing Nozella's attention with his words and trying his own projection of cheerful acceptance. "Helping out the very first person in Clear Springs to survive changeover without Killing is well worth rearranging our travel plans."

Nozella was more accepting of the Donor's coaxing, perhaps because she didn't view Gens as a threat. That would change as she met more Gens and discovered the power a knowledgeable Gen had over any Sime, but for now her ignorance was useful. Encouraged, Den continued talking.

"You were very lucky, you know," he told her. "Your family saved your life by bringing you here early so you could get help."

"It wasn't *my* family," Nozella insisted. "*My* family is respectable. It was Professor Ildun's fault, curse him for an interfering busybody."

"Ildun?" Den asked. The name sounded vaguely familiar, but he couldn't remember where he'd heard it before.

"My next door neighbor," the girl explained. "I was babysitting his kids yesterday when I got sick. When he got home, the oldest brat told him I was turning Sime. Since my own parents were at a church meeting, Professor Ildun brought me here. Said he couldn't turn me loose in case the kid was right, he didn't see any reason to do my parents' dirty work for them and in any case, that's what the Sime Center was for."

"He sounds like a very sensible man," Rital said.

"He had no right to just haul me off and drop me here like dirty laundry!" Nozella's fists clenched in anger.

Den concentrated on calmness. The girl's outrage melted away like snow on a hot stove, leaving her confused. The Donor lightened his projection, allowing her the freedom to feel her own emotions, but preventing them from overwhelming her.

"It worked out for the best, since you actually *were* in changeover," he pointed out. "If you had stayed home you might have died in changeover, or Killed someone if you survived."

Nozella was not quite ready to concede the point. "But Professor Ildun didn't *know* I was turning Sime," she said with an adolescent's keen sense of injustice. "For all *he* knew, I was throwing up because of something I ate."

"If you had just eaten spoiled food, Gati would have found you some-thing to settle your stomach and sent you on your way," Rital said firmly. "As it is, you have a very nice set of tentacles growing and in another few hours, you'll be a full-grown Sime."

For the first time since she regained consciousness, Nozella's eyes fo-cused on her arms. Her face twisted in disgust. "They're hideous," she an-nounced. "Lumpy, nasty things. I look like I got my arms caught in a meat grinder."

Rital chuckled. "Your tentacles are still developing. Give yourself a few days and they'll look like completely normal skin."

Their patient compared her forearms to the channel's skeptically. "Yours don't look like normal skin. They look sunburned."

"That's because he had to wear retainers for the train ride out from Val-zor," Den explained. "That redness will disappear in a day or two. It's just like the rash you get when your clothes rub."

Nozella looked back at her own arms, tracing the lumps of the tentacle sheaths. Her focused attention caused the newly developed nerve control-ling one handling tentacle to fire and it twitched, raising a lump at her wrist as it tried to extend. This was not yet possible: the skin over the wrist open-ings would not thin enough to rupture for hours.

"It moved!" The girl's eyes widened in incipient panic.

"Of course it did," Rital said. "You'll find that your handling tentacles are very useful, sort of like having extra fingers. For now, though, you should let them be. If you wiggle them like that, you could trigger breakout contractions before you're ready."

"Why don't you nap for a while?" Den proposed, reinforcing the sug-gestion with a projection of security and sleepiness. The latter emotion came almost too easily. He had worked a full shift that morning before the train ride, during which he had kept his attention focused tightly on Rital to control the channel's retainer-induced motion sickness. Sime stamina might leave Rital functional after such a marathon, but Den was exhausted. "You're only in Stage Five," he told Nozella with a yawn. "It'll be hours yet before anything interesting happens."

Nozella did fall asleep as the sky began to lighten. When it appeared she would stay that way, Rital zlinned her closely again. "Her development is normal except for the confusion from the arceinine," he reported. "Her selyn reserves are low, but I think she can last until breakout if she stays calm. The arceinine will actually help us, there."

"It's like she's never been taught to keep her emotions steady," Den complained.

"I expect she hasn't," Rital said absently. "With no Simes around, emo-tional control as we know it isn't necessary out here." He zlinned again, then nodded in satisfaction. "She'll sleep for a while. Why don't you let me keep her comfortable while you grab a nap in the next room? Stage Six is going to be critical and from the zlin of things, she'll respond better to you than to me."

Den yawned his agreement with this sensible suggestion. However, when he tried to relinquish control of the ambient to Rital, Nozella resisted. She moaned in her sleep, reaching an arm toward the Donor as if to hold him back. Den immediately resumed control of the projection and the girl calmed, settling back into restful sleep.

The cousins exchanged a worried look. "Try again," Rital suggested. "Very carefully."

"Give me a moment."

Den ran through a centering exercise designed to focus his concentration along a single path. Tired as he was, walking that path felt more like slogging through a marsh. When he thought he could manage his half of the effort, he nodded to his cousin and began to surrender control of the ambient again.

This time, they were a little more successful. Rital meshed his field with Den's and assumed control of their combined projection. However, when Den began to fade toward the door, the Donor's focus wavered. Nozella again reacted with anxiety until Den returned to her bedside.

Rital sighed. "I think you'd better nap in the chair."

The Donor nodded. Settling back into the chair, he closed his eyes and let himself doze. He napped in fits and starts for most of the day. Every hour, when Rital checked their patient's progress, he would wake as the channel leaned more heavily on his support to keep Nozella calm and tractable.

Seena brought them reheated leftovers on an irregular schedule because Ref was still sleeping. The rest of the staff, she informed them, were busy with last-minute preparations for the following day's official Faith Day grand opening.

As the sun began to set, Den was jolted out of his latest catnap when Nozella yelped loudly.

"My arms hurt!" she complained, holding them protectively close to her chest.

"You've entered Stage Six," Rital told her. "Those new nerves you've been growing are starting to carry selyn and they're not very good at it yet, which is why your tentacles are cramping. Don't worry, they'll get better with practice. You've got to let your arms relax, though. You can't afford to waste any selyn."

"It *hurts*," Nozella repeated, with the full weight of adolescent indignation.

After the long train ride in retainers and almost a full day of supporting Nozella, Rital was getting perilously close to the end of even Sime stamina. Being a mere eight hours away from his own scheduled transfer with Den wasn't helping the channel's ability to deal with the situation.

From somewhere, the Donor found the strength to intervene before his cousin snapped. Signaling Rital to back off, the Donor talked their patient through some relaxation exercises, using his own brimming nager to enforce her cooperation.

Rital took a short break and returned with a freshly scrubbed face, damp hair, and hot tea. For the next few hours the cousins tag-teamed, swapping primary control of the ambient nager whenever concentration lagged. Thanks to the arceinine, Nozella remained controllable even as her tentacle sheaths filled with fluids and she began to consciously zlin selyn fields.

Then Nozella's hands clenched into fists as the random cramps turned into rippling contractions. "It's time, Nozella," Rital told her, moving in to take the girl's hands. "Squeeze hard, then fling your hands open as hard as you can like we showed you. That's right. And again!"

Den doubted the girl could hear Rital's instructions. Her eyes had the vacant, unfocused look of a hyperconscious Sime: focused so tightly on zlinning the selyn fields that she lost all awareness of her other senses. It didn't matter, though. Caught up in primal Sime instinct, she strained to extend her tentacles. On the third contraction, the thinning membranes at her wrists yielded and her tentacles burst free in a shower of blood and fluids.

She fell back on the bed for a moment, panting in triumph, then First Need hit. Still running on instinct, she attacked the nearest source of selyn: Rital. The channel entwined his tentacles with hers, leaning forward to complete the contact.

Den watched the transfer with profound relief, glad that the long vigil had come to a successful conclusion. When Nozella's post-transfer reaction had run its course, there would be time for him to get at least a little proper sleep before giving Rital his transfer.

Nozella dissolved into sobs as Rital released her and relief, grief, anger, and other emotions washed over her. That, Den had expected; it was the natural consequence of the tight emotional control he and Rital had imposed to prevent her from using up her selyn reserves before her tentacles were mature enough to take selyn.

However, when half an hour passed and she showed no sign of stopping, the Donor began to worry. He glanced at Rital, who looked equally concerned.

"I think it's the arceinine," the channel explained softly in Simelan. "There's a reason why it's almost never used during changeover. She can't control her own emotions or separate them from what she's zlinning. If we can't teach her control, the internal conflict will drive her to violence or suicide."

Den nodded in reluctant agreement as the opportunity to sleep was postponed once again. He turned to their patient and began. "Nozella, listen to me…"

CHAPTER 5
OPEN FOR BUSINESS

By the time Nozella was stable enough that she wasn't an immediate risk to either herself or the Sime Center staff, Rital was three hours overdue for his own transfer and far closer to his breaking point than a channel had any business getting, particularly when out-Territory among the Wild Gens. When the channel failed to respond to subtle hints, Den exercised a Donor's prerogative.

"Nozella, Hajene Rital will help you more with those concentration exercises this evening but right now, we've both got to get ready for the opening ceremonies. I'll ask Gati to come sit with you for a while."

Rital opened his mouth to protest, then shut it as his cousin glared at him and gave the hand signal for a Donor's Call. A Donor had both the legal and moral obligation to overrule a channel whose actions, in the Donor's best professional judgment, posed a danger to himself or others. It wasn't an authority any Donor took lightly since it was not only rude, but made the Donor legally responsible for any consequences.

Obeying his Donor's order, the channel swallowed his objections and followed Den out into the hall.

The objections did not stay swallowed any longer than it took to close the door, of course. "Den, it's a full hour and a half until the official part of the program starts. There's time to work a little more with Nozella."

"No, there isn't," the Donor said, setting off down the hall. "You're in hard Need and that changeover took a lot out of you. Your control is compromised and you're in no condition to go party with several hundred Wild Gens."

While Den didn't remember where the architects of this Sime Center had put the deferment suite, the heavily insulated room where channels normally had their transfers, he knew where the Collectorium was and that it would not be open until after the opening ceremonies. While smaller, the collecting rooms would also be well-insulated against interfering nagers.

"It's just intil," Rital objected, following the Donor's replete selyn field as if he were attached to it by a strong leash. "I'll survive."

Den, whose own exhaustion had reached the point at which tact was impossible, uttered a choice expletive expressing his disbelief. "You, Rital

Madz, are suffering from Need-induced delusions of invincibility. It's not just intil. We were supposed to have transfer three hours ago."

"Which would have been a little early for me," his cousin pointed out. "I survived worse, the last time I went in for Proficiency Testing."

"The whole point of Proficiency Testing is to know your limits so you can stay far away from them and…"

Den's line of argument lost what little coherence it had when Gati flagged them down.

"Hajene, Sosu, Seena's been looking all over for you. Nozella's grandfather, Joziah Duncan, is here. He brought her things and he wants to see her and…"

Rital somehow set his Need aside and pulled himself together. "Where is he?" he asked crisply, every inch the Tecton channel again.

The Gen waiting for them in the main lobby had probably been taller than Den in his prime, before age had diminished him. He walked with the aid of a cane, a stylish accessory of polished cherry wood with a carved bone handle, and a thick mass of snowy white hair drifted down over his forehead. There were laugh lines on his face, although he wasn't smiling at the moment. His gaze moved from Rital's rumpled Tecton uniform to Den's shabby coveralls, both of which had been splattered with blood and fluids during Nozella's breakout. To his credit, he withheld judgment.

"Mr. Duncan?" Rital asked as they approached to conversational distance. "I'm Hajene Madz and this is my Donor, Sosu Milnan." He smiled politely but in an unusual display of common sense, refrained from offering to shake hands in the out-Territory greeting.

"Good to meet you," the old man said. "Word is, you were coming out on this morning's train and didn't show."

"We came early to look after Nozella," Den explained. He looked down at his coveralls and sighed. "Our luggage will catch up with us, some day."

For some reason, this news evoked a delighted cackle from their visitor. "And won't *that* set the kitten loose in the dovecote," he observed cryptically. Putting a hand on the large trunk that stood on a wheeled dolly beside him, he continued, "I brought my granddaughter's things for her. Figured she could use them more than the church."

"I'm sure she'll be very glad to have them," Rital agreed.

"So if you'll take me to her?" Mr. Duncan prompted.

"I'm afraid I can't allow you to give Nozella the trunk in person," Rital told the old man apologetically. "She is very new to being Sime and can't yet separate her own emotions from those of the people around her, particularly when those emotions are carried on a strong nager. The Gens who work here all know how to keep their selyn fields from overwhelming a Sime, but that skill takes time to learn."

"Rital's right," Den confirmed. "Nozella's been through a lot. You don't want an unguarded reaction to hurt her."

"I think I understand," Mr. Duncan said. "But isn't there a way to weaken my field so that I won't disturb her?"

"Well, yes, there is," the channel admitted. "If you're not carrying so much selyn, your ability to accidentally project your emotions to a Sime will be reduced. It will be safe for you and Nozella to talk to each other. Is that what you want to do?"

The old man nodded slowly. "I believe so. Nozella deserves a chance to say goodbye to at least one person from her past, before she has to face her future."

"So she does," Den agreed.

The elderly Gen looked at Rital. "I was wondering if it would come to that." He patted the pocket of his worn flannel shirt. "I've got an old letter here from my grandfather that I brought to share with Nozella. He was a soldier under General Dermott and wrote it to my grandmother about six weeks after the Battle of Shen. He said having a channel strip him of selyn that first time was the worst he'd ever been scared by nothing at all, but he took no harm from it." One bushy white eyebrow elevated. "How do you channels manage that trick, anyway? It's not just wanting to, or a lot of kids wouldn't Kill the people they love."

"No, it's not just wanting to," Rital admitted. "When a Sime berserk with First Need stalks a Gen for selyn, the Gen almost always panics. Gen fear enhances Sime Need. If there is no channel to step in, the Sime attacks. The Gen instinctively resists, the Sime draws against that resistance, the Gen's nervous system shorts out, and the Gen dies."

Den was not sure that offering a potential new donor a glib description of the mechanics of the Kill was a good idea, but Mr. Duncan seemed to take it well. "So what's different about channels?" the old man asked.

"Most important is that we can take selyn from Gens and transfer it to Simes. The Gens are not harmed because the channel mutation allows us to control the speed at which we take selyn," Rital explained. "If we match our draw to the speed at which a donor can release selyn safely, nobody gets hurt."

"It sounds simple enough in theory," Mr. Duncan observed, "although I expect it's a lot more complicated in practice. Most things are, where people are involved."

"Well, yes," Rital admitted. "But I don't have time to summarize centuries of research. What matters is, I can draw enough selyn from you to keep your field from bothering your granddaughter without harming you, even if you resist."

Yellowed teeth were bared in a grin of challenge. "Are you so sure I will resist?"

"Chances are, you will," Rital warned him. "When you've lived most of your life in danger of being attacked by a Sime just through changeover, your reflex is to view any Sime as a threat, even when you know better. If you want to do this, I can and will control *what* you feel, by keeping the selyn flow too slow for you to perceive. However, there's not much I can do to control how you feel about it. It takes experience to overcome that sort of ingrained emotional response."

"So it does," Mr. Duncan agreed. "I remember it took three months after Nozella's father was born before I could hold him. He was my first child and I was afraid I'd drop him, you see." He winked. "Of course, my wife insisted to the day she died that I was making it all up to avoid diaper duty."

Den and Rital both chuckled, then the Donor said, "Nozella would be glad of a visitor. There's still time for Rital to take your donation before he has to look pretty for the cameras at the opening ceremonies." Den wasn't sure it was the smartest thing for Rital to attempt, under the circumstances, but he had no real grounds to forbid it. Besides, it was clearly the right thing to do, for both Nozella and her grandfather.

"There's enough time," Rital agreed. "Although…" his eyes lost focus briefly as he zlinned the Gen with Need-sharpened senses. "Do you have any medical issues that could complicate matters? Heart problems, asthma, angina, or that sort of thing?"

"Why, no," Mr. Duncan said, his eyes betraying second thoughts. "Why would that be a problem? I thought you said donating doesn't cause injuries?"

"It doesn't," Den reassured him. "However, we can both see you're a little nervous. Fear and stress can trigger problems all by themselves, in people who have underlying medical conditions. It's still possible for such people to donate, but that would take more time than Rital has, just now."

"Oh, I see." The old man digested the information for a moment, then nodded as he reached a decision. "I don't know of any reason why it would be a problem for me, so let's do this."

"Very well," the channel agreed, turning to lead the way. "The Collectorium is just down the hall here. You'll be our first customer, so you'll have to tell me if our staff did a good job with the decorations."

When they showed him into a collecting room, the old man looked around at the polished desk and chair and the cheery yellow slipcover on the transfer lounge. "It's a bit pleasanter than the drafty tent my grandfather describes," he allowed.

Rital chuckled. "Indeed." He gestured toward the lounge. "Now, we're a bit pressed for time, so if you'd lie down over there, we can get started. You can fill out the paperwork with Seena afterward."

After his experiences with the Old Sime Center tourists, Den was a little concerned about how the out-Territory Gen would respond to being rushed. However, Mr. Duncan seemed steady enough as he stretched out comfortably on the lounge and when Rital sat beside him, he placed his hands in the channel's with only a little hesitation, signaling his consent.

Just in case, Den moved closer and put one hand on his cousin's shoulder so his field could offer support if the other Gen's courage faltered. He couldn't block it entirely, of course, but his emotional stability would help Rital set his Need aside and focus on the task at hand.

Rital gave his client an encouraging smile, then shifted his hands to the Gen's forearms, handling tentacles reinforcing the grip with his usual neat economy.

Mr. Duncan flinched.

"You're fine," the channel said, pausing for a moment to let the Gen regain his composure. "I'm going to make lateral contact now. They're a little moist with selyn conductors and if you move while they're touching you, you could hurt me. Can you hold still?"

Den was not sure if his cousin's approach was the best one. Mr. Duncan was apprehensive enough about letting Rital touch him without adding the fear that he might hurt a channel. Besides, a Sime's handling tentacles were more than strong enough to immobilize any Gen's arms, no matter how much he resisted.

However, the elderly Gen nodded and held still as Rital's laterals slid into position, seeking out the selyn-rich forearm nerves. "That is the most peculiar sensation," he complained, his voice trembling.

"It won't hurt you," Rital murmured. "Now, I'm just going to glean the selyn in the shallowest, GN-3 storage level. That will still reduce your field enough that you can't overwhelm Nozella. It will take less than a minute and you won't feel anything happening. Ready?"

Reminded of his reason for donating, the old man promised, "I'll behave." He braced himself as Rital leaned forward to make lip contact, then gradually relaxed as no further sensation occurred to disturb him.

Den, who had been poised to distract their client verbally if he seemed likely to panic, held his peace. The Donor still wasn't convinced that his cousin's decision to rush this donation was the right one, but couldn't deny that a visit from her grandfather had distinct advantages for Nozella. Whether it turned out to be best for the Sime Center would depend on how her grandfather chose to view this encounter in the weeks to come.

A moment later, Rital straightened, breaking the lip contact. "All right, you're low field now," the channel said as he started to retract his vulnerable laterals. "You can't overwhelm Nozella as easily—no, keep still until I let you go—although she'll still be able to zlin what you're feeling. Seena will show you to her room as soon as the two of you have finished filling out the paperwork." He released the elderly Gen and stood. "Right now, I've got to go get ready before they decide to open the place without me."

Den frowned at his cousin and followed him to the door. Seena was hovering outside in the hall, but Rital simply walked past her, turning back toward the door that led to the lobby. There were channels who made a point of ignoring the administrative workers, but Rital wasn't usually one of them.

"Go through the standard donation paperwork with Mr. Duncan and then take him over to see Nozella," the Donor ordered Seena quietly. "We'll get him a voucher later." Then he hurried after his cousin.

"Just where are you going?" he demanded quietly when he caught up.

"I want a shower and a clean uniform."

"Haven't you forgotten something?"

Rital frowned. "Forgotten something? I don't think so."

Behind them, the door to the collecting room opened. Voices echoed as Seena escorted Mr. Duncan down the hall in the other direction, toward the Collectorium's waiting room and its stacks of medical history and donation consent forms.

Too tired to argue coherently, Den decided that a demonstration was in order. He stopped focusing his attention on his cousin, withdrawing the nageric support he had been offering since they boarded the train.

The channel staggered as the reassuring conviction that Den's selyn was *his* disappeared. His laterals extended in involuntary protest, seeking the life he had to have or die.

"You can't go out there and hobnob with a mob of nervous Gens in that condition," Den stated the obvious. He resumed his support and the channel steadied.

"There isn't any choice," Rital said, also stating the obvious. "I'm Controller here, so I've got to attend the ceremony."

"Strangely enough, I agree you have to attend the ceremony," Den admitted. "But *not* when you're in hard Need. If there was a fresh Donor available it might work, but I'm too tired to control your intil in a hostile crowd."

"There isn't time for you to have a nap." Impatient with Need, Rital was inclined to charge forward at all costs.

"I agree with that, too," Den said, walking briskly down the corridor. Rital followed, drawn by his nager. "But there *is* time to give you transfer.

Barely." He lured Rital back into the insulated collecting room, thumbed the "in-use" signal to warn the staff not to enter, and firmly closed the door.

"It's been so long since we were assigned together," Rital complained feebly. "I didn't want to rush this transfer." He did not, however, try to leave.

Den, too, had wanted to make the most of the rare opportunity to give his cousin transfer but being Gen, he was still clear-headed enough to consider the necessities of the situation. "We're both stuck out here for the foreseeable future. We'll have other opportunities," he promised, urging his cousin over to the transfer lounge.

Between Mr. Duncan's nervousness and Den's temporary withdrawal of support, Rital was primed to attack any available source of selyn, shaking with the effort to maintain some shred of self-control.

Under most circumstances, a Donor's job was to support and reinforce a channel's control. The exception was when a channel took personal transfer. To reach full satisfaction, the channel had to draw selyn at full speed and capacity—and a channel's speed and capacity were far greater than those of a renSime. It was sometimes necessary for a channel to hold back, when the available Donor could not fully match the channel's demand, but too many such transfers could have serious effects on the channel's health.

"We're well matched," Den reminded his cousin, sitting beside him and reaching for his hands. He let himself savor his own eagerness for the transfer, knowing that it would help free Rital's intil. "I'm not in any danger even if you lose control completely."

The reassurance finally allowed the channel to shift mental perspectives from channel to Sime. Den grinned as Rital's much-abused tentacles gripped his arms tightly and his cousin leaned forward for the fifth contact.

There had been no time for either of them to prepare properly for the transfer. The channel had made himself function for hours past his scheduled transfer time by telling his Need that it would have to wait. Now that it finally had a Donor in hand, Rital's Need was inclined to strip Den quickly before the channel could change his mind and deny it once more.

Fortunately for both of them, Den was in full agreement with this plan. Rital's draw had a harsh edge of desperation. Den flattened his barriers and released selyn as fast as Rital could take it, maintaining only enough conscious control to prevent Rital from stopping before they both were satisfied.

Afterward, he held his cousin as they both cried in sheer relief.

Fifteen minutes later, Rital stiffened. "Shen!" he swore, hastily grabbing a tissue from the box on the little desk and mopping the tears off his face. "I've got to go. They're waiting to open the Sime Center."

"Are you ready to go out there yet?" Den asked. "That's a big crowd, they're not used to Simes, and I'm not high field enough to block any unpleasantness."

The channel spread his handling tentacles in a gesture of helplessness. "I'll be fine. Ref is high field; I'll ask him to stick as close as he can. Make sure Mr. Duncan and Nozella are getting along, then grab some food and take a nap. I'll require you alert and functioning when the show is over and the Collectorium officially opens."

Den opened his mouth to protest but found himself yawning hugely. Faced with that unwelcome evidence that he was, in fact, asleep on his feet, he conceded the argument with a gesture. Rital was the Controller here in Clear Springs and therefore had the authority to take him off duty. Besides, his cousin was right.

Gati woke Den two hours later. He was still far from rested, but the nap had restored him enough that he could function again. She had laid out clean clothes for him: a plaid shirt and soft, stretchy knit pants that were so oversized that she could only have borrowed them from Ref.

"I thought my luggage was supposed to come on today's train?" Den asked, eyeing the overlarge offerings skeptically.

"It was," she confirmed. "There's been some sort of major disturbance at the train station—the stationmaster was too frantic to give me any details—and he hasn't had a chance to deal with the cargo from today's train yet. He suggests checking back tomorrow."

Once Den had rolled up the cuffs of both garments, tucked in the shirttails, and belted the pants, they were at least no longer threatening to fall off. Checking the mirror, he decided that decorum could be maintained, although dignity was a lost cause.

Gati's eyes widened as she saw him in the absurd outfit, but she managed not to snicker. Much. "I'll see that your coveralls are cleaned for tomorrow, just in case," she promised by way of an apology. "Our initial supplies didn't include the usual assortment of spare uniforms."

Of course they didn't. Den had known that and had carefully packed accordingly. "Are they nearly done with the speeches outside?"

She shrugged. "It's hard to tell. If they follow the program, when Regent Serra Fillmore is finished with her speech, Senator Jas Bowman will cut the ribbon and he and Mayor Ann Kroag will come in to be our first official donors. The Collectorium will be staffed for another few hours, then we close until tomorrow morning."

Den decided that he could stay awake long enough for an abbreviated Collectorium shift and a meal, then leave Rital to manage any further problems with Nozella while he caught up on his sleep more fully. It wasn't as if he could unpack his things, after all.

He took the stairs down to the first floor, pausing on the last landing to readjust the overlarge pants and tighten the belt one more hole. When he entered the lobby, his opinion of the architect improved considerably. Golden sunlight streamed through the large windows, reflecting off warmly colored murals to make a cheerful and welcoming space. The upholstery on the couches in the waiting area glowed in jewel tones and the plants brought the space alive.

He had paused in the middle of the open space, turning in a slow circle to admire the effect, when he heard a brief scuffle of footsteps and caught a glimpse of furtive movement out of the corner of his eye, near the door that let out onto the Sime Center's fenced grounds.

Den frowned, worried that Nozella had decided to ignore their orders to stay in her insulated room. She might think it was perfectly safe for her to take a walk, but the uncontrolled fields of visiting out-Territory Gens would make that hazardous for all concerned.

When he followed the noise to a particularly oversized potted plant, however, the face peering out at him from between the plate-sized leaves was that of an eight-year-old boy. The carrot-colored hair and freckled cheeks looked vaguely familiar.

"Hey, you're the tour guide!" the boy said, boldly emerging from his hiding place.

"And you're trespassing," Den responded. "We're not open for visitors yet." He remembered the boy chasing his younger siblings with the channel doll and scanned the area for other places that might provide refuge for a small child. "Did you bring your sisters..." What had his name been? Roton, Rayman, something like that? "Rimon, was it?"

The boy shook his head, not at all disconcerted at having been caught. "It's Raymond and my sisters are with my mom, outside."

"Won't she be wondering where you are?" the Donor asked.

"Nah, she thinks I'm with my dad." An impish grin threatened to split the boy's face in two. "I came to see my babysitter, Nozella. Did her tentacles burst out yet? Did they splatter yucky stuff everywhere? Can I see?"

Den found new sympathy for Nozella's conviction that she had been ill used by her charges. "Yes, Nozella is now a grown-up Sime, complete with tentacles," he told the boy. "And no, you can't see her." Catching sight of one of the maintenance workers, he waved the woman over and entrusted her with the task of returning young Raymond to his family.

Rital was waiting in the Collectorium's records room. This was a small, windowless alcove that was accessed from behind the receptionist's desk.

Mr. Duncan's brand-new file looked lonely against the expanse of empty shelving.

Although he no longer showed the urgent, predatory nervousness of Need, to the Donor's experienced eye his cousin looked slightly over-whelmed. "How did it go?" he asked.

The channel shrugged. "There were a lot of speeches. The crowd was small: about a hundred people. I'd estimate two thirds of them were college students looking for free food. They put me up on the speaker's platform, so I wasn't in with the crowd. That suited everyone, I think. Nobody was really hostile, but most were nervous about me and Ref is no Donor."

Den put a hand on his cousin's arm and Rital steadied enough to actually look at him. The channel's eyes widened. "What are you wearing?"

"No luggage," the Donor explained. "Gati borrowed these from Ref."

"They lost it?"

"There was some problem at the train station. Gati will try again tomorrow." Den frowned at his cousin, whose uniform was clean and only a little wrinkled. "I see you packed yourself a change of clothes before leaving civilization. Couldn't you have grabbed one for me while you were at it?"

"There wasn't time," Rital explained apologetically. "What I'm wearing is the spare I keep in my office." His attention strayed to the waiting room. "Ah, here's Seena with the paperwork for our first two customers. We're in business at last!"

The two files Seena handed Rital were thinner than Den was used to, since the two Gens had obviously not donated at Clear Springs before. Reading over Rital's shoulder, the Donor discovered that Senator Jas Bow-man donated regularly at the Sime Center in New Washington. Apart from some joint stiffness and an age-appropriate tendency toward high blood pressure, there was nothing to suggest that he would present any difficulty. Ann Kroag, in contrast, was younger and healthier, but had never donated before.

"Is Mayor Kroag going to be a problem?" he asked.

Rital shrugged. "She's emotionally invested in making this Sime Center succeed and we got to know each other a bit when she came to Valzor to sign the final agreement. That will help." He turned toward the door and held his hands out, laterals extending to zlin the waiting room. "She's nervous, but it's under control, at least for now."

Den sighed. "I suppose we'll be seeing a lot of that at first." He checked to make sure his belt was holding, aware that his appearance was hardly professional, then nodded to his cousin. "Let's go."

The two Gens stood as they entered the waiting room. Bowman seemed calm, but Kroag's hands were twitching as if she was fighting the impulse to wring them. Rital smiled and said, "Senator Bowman, Mayor Kroag, welcome to the Clear Springs Sime Center. This is my Donor, Sosu Den Milnan. We're told his luggage will get here tomorrow."

Ann Kroag's eyes widened as she took in Den's outfit. She gave him a sympathetic smile…and her twitching hands relaxed as the news of such a common dilemma made Den, and by extension Rital, more human and accessible.

Den still felt ridiculous and unprofessional, but gave Rital full credit for turning that liability into an asset.

Senator Bowman cleared his throat. "If it's all the same with you, Hajene, I'll go first. I've got a train to catch."

"Certainly," Rital agreed. "If it's all right with Mayor Kroag?"

"Yes, of course," Kroag agreed, a little too quickly.

Senator Bowman followed them back to the collecting room with the confidence expected of an experienced donor. He stretched out on the transfer lounge and when Rital sat beside him, placed steady hands in the channel's without prompting.

"Would you like me to work a bit on those stiff knees, while you're here?" Rital offered.

"Please do, Hajene," the Gen said with real gratitude. "Otherwise, they'll be throbbing by the time I reach New Washington."

The Senator's donation was routine, as expected. Rital had gleaned barely half of the selyn he had provided Nozella at her changeover from the nervous and inexperienced Mr. Duncan. From the relaxed, experienced Senator Bowman, Rital drew selyn not only from the shallowest, GN-3 level but also from the deeper GN-2 and GN-1 levels. In the process, the channel recovered the rest of the selyn he had provided to Nozella and a bit more, placing the Sime Center's accounts in the black. With luck, that would continue even after the selyn-powered Center for Technology opened.

Even to Gen eyes, Senator Bowman was walking more freely as he left the collecting room. Rital left Bowman's file for Seena to put away and took the other back into the waiting room.

"Mayor Kroag, we're ready for you now," the channel said quietly.

"Yes, of course," she said, standing.

She followed them back to the collecting room, looking around curiously. "They did a nice job with the decorations. I like the pattern on the sofa and that painting…is it one of Grisilda Imman's?"

"I'm afraid I don't know," the channel admitted. "We only just got here."

Ann Kroag remained calm until Rital sat down beside her on the lounge, at which point she swallowed convulsively.

The channel gave her a reassuring smile that somehow acknowledged her apprehension and accepted it—and her—without condemning either. "It's all right to be afraid," he told her.

Kroag turned scarlet with embarrassment. "After the weeks of studying, you'd think I'd know better. I even saw a donation when we visited the Old Sime Center in Valzor. It's silly of me to be so nervous. I know there's nothing to it."

"Watching isn't the same as doing," the channel pointed out kindly. "Even Gens who grow up in-Territory can be a little apprehensive when they start donating." His eyes twinkled with infectious good humor. "Most of them get over it pretty quickly, once they get a little experience."

Kroag smiled and offered her hands. "Then by all means, I'd better get some experience!"

"As you wish," Rital said gallantly, taking her hands. Without making an issue of it, he shifted his grip expertly to her wrists and completed the full transfer contact. Den watched carefully, ready to provide the channel support if Kroag lost her nerve, but after an initial startle reaction, she steadied and held still until Rital broke lip contact.

"That was harder than I expected," she admitted, her voice shaking a little.

"You did very well," Rital told her as he retracted his laterals. "It's a deep-seated reflex, to pull away, but you overcame it." He released her and smiled. "And as I said, it gets much easier with practice."

"That went better than with Mr. Duncan," Rital commented, when the mayor had collected her voucher and left.

"Yes," Den teased. "For some odd reason, you're a better channel when you're not three hours overdue for transfer and in a rush to finish because you have to be elsewhere."

The channel looked around at the empty waiting room. "There's no rush here," he observed. His disappointment was clear even to Gen eyes.

The Collectorium stayed open for business another three hours. No additional Gens volunteered to donate. By the time Rital gave up and told Seena to close half an hour early, the channel's post-transfer euphoria had turned to bitter disillusionment. "A hundred people turned out for the opening ceremony," he complained. "If they can sit through the speeches—and believe me, they were as dull as you'd expect—why can't a single one come inside and see what we're all about? Is all that work getting a Sime Center out here going to be wasted?"

"Rital, you're expecting them to behave like in-Territory Gens," Den told him. "Remember my tour groups? You told me that the tourists who decide to donate after their Old Sime Center tours try not to be seen entering the Collectorium. Isn't it logical that the Gens here in Clear Springs will also choose a time when they are unlikely to be observed? You'll see. They'll start coming, especially the students."

Whether or not Den's prediction proved accurate, the channel seemed comforted as they headed up the stairs to a well-earned supper.

CHAPTER 6

RESEARCH

Only two donors visited the Collectorium on the next day, despite front-page coverage of the Sime Center opening ceremonies in the *Clear Springs Clarion*. One of the donors worked as an aide to Mayor Kroag and the other was Ref. Rital was both disappointed and worried: if the workload did not improve, he would be facing entran before much longer.

"I guess the planners were overly optimistic, dedicating an entire wing to the Collectorium," Den admitted. "It's going to take a while before we require seven collecting rooms."

His own disappointment at the poor showing was mitigated by the news that his luggage had finally been shipped over from the train station and was waiting in his rooms. He bounded up the stairs to the third floor and entered the three-room suite Seena had selected for him, whistling all the way...then stopped short when he saw the yellow stickers on the crates.

He walked around the pile of crates, checking each one carefully, then dropped into a chair and hid his face in his hands, fighting the urge to scream. Somehow, somewhere, the key to his color coding system had been garbled. As a result, the crates of books, winter clothing, model aircraft, and other detritus that he had packed for long-term storage in Valzor had been meticulously sorted out and shipped to Clear Springs. Given the Valzor staff's usual diligence, the purple-stickered crates that contained seasonally appropriate uniforms and civilian clothing had probably already been sent to long-term storage, where they might take a week or more to retrieve.

Of course the Valzor staff was not accustomed to shipping belongings with departing staff. Channels and Donors usually traveled with hand luggage and picked up a standard kit on arrival. Clear Springs had still not been supplied with spare kits.

He hadn't realized how much it bothered him to be seen in public in Ref's oversized garments or his own stained and tattered coveralls until he was faced with working another week or so without a proper Tecton uniform. He had worked his way to the top of an elite, highly paid profession and was used to receiving respect from those around him. He was *not* used to having everybody he met snicker when they saw him.

Because the walls of his quarters were well insulated against nageric surges and he was alone, Den indulged himself, wallowing in frustration and anger at the pointless and unnecessary complication for a cathartic minute or two. Then he set it aside. It wasn't his uniform that made him a First Order Donor, after all. If mixing up his luggage was the biggest setback that happened during this assignment, he was doing just fine.

Turning his back on the yellow-tagged crates, he went to the window and looked out. Den recalled Rital complaining about how difficult it had been to find land on which to build the Sime Center, because the local Gen businesses objected to having Simes move in next door, scaring their customers away. In the end, Clear Springs University had stepped in and sold the Tecton a property it had inherited as part of a bequest. Since the land was some distance from the campus, the university was glad enough to get rid of it while facilitating their new Center for Technology.

As a result, the Sime Center building stood at the edge of several acres of overgrown lawn, woodland, and garden, all surrounded by a sturdy fence. Alyce, the groundskeeper, had not been idle. The grass near the back entrance was trimmed and some of the hedges pruned into submission. Now, Den saw her in a sunny area near the fence, breaking ground for a kitchen garden.

The prospect of eating fresh tomatoes and corn in a few months finished restoring Den's perspective. He explored the crates and, nestled among his winter clothes, he found a fashionable shirt and dress pants that he had bought for dancing. They weren't a uniform, but they fit properly. The silk shirt's brilliant turquoise and blue paisley pattern even matched the decorations in the main lobby.

It also attracted salacious whistles from both Alyce and Gati.

That evening, he placed a cross-border telephone call to the New Sime Center in Valzor. When he finally managed to track down the night shift facilities manager, she apologized profusely for the packing crate mix-up and promised that Den's essential, purple-labeled crates would be shipped to Clear Springs as promptly as could be managed.

With that necessity accomplished, Den was free to take advantage of the already-established chain of operators to place a call to Jannun. After describing his current sartorial dilemma and getting a snicker in lieu of sympathy, he asked what progress Jannun and Eddina had made toward constructing their full-scale wing for the contest.

"Not much," Jannun admitted reluctantly. "Your idea of building one large double-wing and strapping the crate on worked well in the small-scale model. But when we looked at making a full-sized version, it was pretty clear that a double wing would be too heavy to manage. We might be able to make it in sections, but that would put back the same structural weakness we were trying to avoid in the first place."

Den frowned. "We know it can be done, because the Ancients built airplanes with that design."

"Well, see if you can figure out how they did it," Jannun suggested. "Since you have your books with you, after all. In the meantime, Eddina is going back to looking at bolts and fasteners."

On the Sime Center's third day of business, it had four visitors: a quartet of college students out for an adventure. One of them was from a border town and had donated twice before moving to Clear Springs. As there was no crowd of impatient Gens filling the waiting room, Rital took his time with each donor, making sure they were as relaxed as possible before gleaning the scant trickle of selyn a new donor could provide. To Den, that made the process interminable, but the students didn't seem to mind.

On the fourth day, no Gens came to donate. However, Mr. Duncan returned to visit his granddaughter before she was sent to Sime Territory to start her new life. While showing the man up to Nozella's room, Den learned the nature of the Faith Day disturbance at the train station that had caused the delay in sorting cargo.

"It was Reverend Sinth, the pastor at the Conservative Congregation," the old man told him. "He's a new fellow, so of course he wants to make an impression. For some reason I've never understood, he decided to make a cause out of fighting the Sime Center. When you folks were set to open on schedule, he decided the only way to stop that was to get a bunch of his followers together and prevent Hajene Madz from getting off the train. Of course, Sinth didn't know that you'd come out early."

A broad grin split the wrinkled face. "He looked like a proper idiot, blundering around the train station with a dozen followers demanding to know where the Sime was."

"I take it you don't like this Reverend Sinth?" the Donor asked, pausing on a landing to let Mr. Duncan catch his breath.

"He's a blustering bully," came the reply. "Reverend Holder, who had the job before him, was a nice enough fellow. Spent his time telling people to be good to each other and collecting postcards. Sinth, though, is purely mean. Wants everybody to follow his rules and likes to cause trouble just because he can."

"You're a member of this…Conservative Congregation, then?"

"Well, not anymore." Mr. Duncan shrugged. "When he found out I'd brought Nozella's things to her here instead of giving them to his church, he decided to shame me in front of the congregation. I learned about it from my daughter, Carla, and decided to save him the trouble of kicking me out by going to services over at the Rational Deists, instead."

"It was good of your daughter to warn you."

The old man shook his head. "She wasn't warning me, she was getting in her scold first. In some ways, she and my son are more traditional than Sinth in their views of Simes. It'll take 'em a while to resign themselves to having you folks around."

That first week in Clear Springs was both frustrating and boring. There was very little actual work for a channel or Donor to do, but because there was no other channel or Donor available, they were never truly off duty, either. They couldn't leave the premises, even when the Collectorium was closed, in case a child in changeover or other medical emergency should materialize.

With so few Gens volunteering to donate, Den and Rital spent most of their Collectorium shifts sorting through the cabinets and drawers, making sure they knew where everything was. It wasn't long before all seven collecting rooms were ready for instant use, in the remote possibility that six more channels and enough donors to keep them busy should magically appear.

When they ran out of supplies to organize, they left Seena or Gati to watch the Collectorium while they tackled the now-empty changeover ward and the infirmary. The latter got its first customer when Alyce succeeded in trapping the feral cat that lived in the toolshed. It was a measure of how bored Rital was that the channel spent almost an hour on the project, first helping Alyce shave the mats out of the creature's fur and then healing the incidental scratches it inflicted on its would-be benefactors.

After catching his cousin massaging his arms twice in the same day, Den checked the Sime Center's library for advice on managing entran. He didn't know whether to be pleased or alarmed when he discovered no less than three texts covering the condition. However, after he applied what he learned, Rital seemed more comfortable.

Mindful of Jannun's plea, Den also thumbed through his aviation books, seeking how to build a functional wing out of something that was both strong enough to fly and significantly lighter than wood.

The solution came from a surprising source. Den had spent a frustrating evening over his books. The only possible solutions he found were descriptions of wings built from the lightweight metal, aluminum, which would have been prohibitively expensive to use for a full-sized wing even if anyone in their small group knew how to work it.

Den finally gave up and turned to the biography of Rick Toeffin, Ancient aviator and participant in the sport of aerial jousting. Improbable fiction or not, the author did include thrilling descriptions of what it might be like to fly. The best such passage described a joust between Toeffin's red aircraft and an opponent from a team that used a camel as its totem. The author (or perhaps translator, if the bit about the book being a translation of an Ancient biography was not a literary device) did not bother to explain whether the Ancient term "Sopwith" referred to the one- or two-humped beasts used as desert pack animals in the distant lands across the ocean, or alternatively, to the non-humped beasts used for the same purpose in the mountains of the Southern Continent. He was rereading the sequence for the third time when his eyes paused on a paragraph describing how Rick's bullets "shredded the enemy airplane's wing fabric, leaving it in tatters," thereby forcing his opponent to make a crash landing.

"You are a proper idiot, Den Milan!" the Donor exclaimed, as his mind considered the possibilities that suggested. "After lecturing young Mandle that she should look at how birds fly, you'd think it would occur to you to follow your own advice…"

He reached for a notepad and began to sketch. Both bird and bat wings used a scaffold of bone over which skin and/or feathers were stretched. This resulted in a sturdy but very lightweight wing that allowed muscle-powered flight. It should also be possible to lighten an aircraft wing by using a structural frame covered by fabric, much like a kite. As an additional advantage, fabric was less expensive and more flexible than lumber, although it was also less strong. Den played with a few designs, but didn't find one that satisfied him.

"Cloth is flexible," he explained to Rital as they sorted through a box of informational pamphlets. "It has to be supported on all sides or it flutters and tears."

"You mean, like a sail on ship?" he cousin asked. "Or a kite?"

"Exactly!" Den agreed. "I don't know anything about building ships or kites, though."

"I expect the university library has some books that would explain it," Rital suggested. "They are opening a Center for Technology, after all, so building is a big part of what they do."

It wasn't until the following week that Den got a chance to visit the university library. That was when the Sime Center received a one-day record number of visitors: eleven general-class donors and a Second Order Donor, Sosu Risetta, who had been sent out from Valzor to Escort Nozella to Sime Territory.

She arrived in the evening and, because of the train schedule, could not leave until the next afternoon. While a Second Order Donor couldn't manage the more technical feats of a First like Den, Sosu Risetta was quite capable of assisting Rital with routine donations. Or so Den's cousin assured him, and the Donor was eager enough to leave the frustration of the too-empty Sime Center that he allowed himself to be persuaded.

The rest of Den's belongings did not, to his disappointment, arrive with Risetta, though she'd been told they were on the train. Instead, they got a shipment of standard kits for channels, but nothing for Donors. Since he wanted to save the paisley dancing outfit for his Sime Center work shifts, he dressed in the stained coveralls. Then he tucked a notebook under his arm and set out through the downtown business district toward the university's campus.

Making the most of his holiday, Den strolled in a leisurely fashion, looking through the shop windows. The mix of businesses was similar to parts of Valzor, apart from an excess of cafes that served full menus. That made sense, once he thought about it: with a clientele consisting only of Gens, proprietors would provide more than a place to sit and have a glass of trin tea.

There were, of course, more striking cultural differences. A group of children in the park hadn't just swapped the blades on their ice skates for wheels when the local pond thawed. Instead, they had attached the wheels to planks from old shipping pallets. Balanced precariously, they attempted to steer through a maze of improvised ramps and obstacles. Because shoe and board were only held together by friction, any time one of the children lost balance, the board would go shooting off on its own, endangering fellow enthusiasts and innocent bystanders in equal measure.

The university campus was an expanse of very large buildings, trees, and lawns adorned with groups of students enjoying the sun. He asked a passing student for directions.

"The library? It's right there." She pointed toward a relatively new building built in the hulking, fortress-like style of modern Gen architecture.

The library's cavernous entrance hall rose a full three stories, with a wide staircase leading up to the second and third floors. Directly inside the door was a series of glass-covered display cases with documents that depicted the history of the university. Curious, Den examined the first exhibit.

The narration explained that the university had been chartered by the New Washington Territory government 257 years before in response to a wave of Sime raiding. Its primary purpose was to develop technological superiority sufficient to maintain the borders. Den realized that the era in question was the time which in-Territory history texts called the Golden Age of the Gettisky Administration. During those years, several new vaccines against common Pen diseases and a critical new mine yielding phosphorous fertilizer allowed the Sime population to expand.

On this side of the border, both university and town had prospered and expanded. The last display case showed an architect's rendering of the new Center for Technology but, much to the Donor's amusement, the accompanying text said nothing about the switch to selyn power for the new building or about the equally innovative Sime Center that would provide that selyn to make it possible.

Once past the display cases with their odd history, the rest of the building was simply a library. Den located the card catalog, scanned the labels on the drawers, and only then realized that he didn't know the English words for "flyer" or "glider."

Looking around for a collections manager, he discovered a middle-aged woman watching him from behind a desk that guarded shelves of particularly well-worn books. The sign hanging above the desk said "REF-ERENCE," which was ambiguous. It seemed to be derived from the English word "refer," which could mean either to pass an issue on to a greater authority or to quote an expert opinion, neither of which was directly applicable to his situation. However, the woman's age made it likely that she worked here and would know enough about the library's organization to help him.

The woman looked up as he approached the desk. Her eyes took in his age—slightly older than the general population of students—and his stained coveralls. To her credit, she didn't immediately summon library security to throw him out.

"May I help you?" she asked in a carefully neutral voice.

"I am looking for books on Ancient flying machines," Den told her.

"Stories about flying machines, or more technical works?"

"The latter, please," the Donor said.

With a brisk nod, she got to her feet and gestured for Den to follow her over to the card catalog. In less than five minutes, she had explained the basics of the cataloging system to him, located several potentially helpful books in the card catalog, jotted their location numbers down on a piece of scrap paper, and annotated a library map with specific directions in how to find that section.

"…And be sure to check the other books in the area," she advised him. "We catalog by subject, so you might find them interesting, too."

"Thank you," he said, a little awed by her efficiency. "You've been most helpful."

Soon he was browsing through two whole shelves of books on Ancient aviation. To the Donor's delight, a full dozen of the offerings were completely new to him. He spent half an hour drooling over two English translations of Ancient works, one on pilot training and the other on navigation using instruments. However tempting, though, these didn't address the immediate issue of how to construct a lightweight but durable wing.

In the end, it was a book on an adjoining shelf that gave him the information he required. The title was *Eyes in the Sky*, and it detailed a program that the Gen military had developed to aid reconnaissance. During the endless border wars with Sime Territory, the New Washington Army had sometimes used giant balloons inflated with heated air to support aerial observation platforms. It had been a surprisingly effective way for Gen generals to keep track of the battlefields they couldn't zlin.

What Den hadn't known was that shortly before Unity, the Gen Army had started to develop reconnaissance gliders in the western regions, where the geography provided favorable launch sites and reliable updrafts. Although these aircraft were not powered and could only fly in daylight with good weather and favorable breezes, their wings still had to lift both their own weight and that of the observer.

While Den's command of English was good enough to handle general conversation, it was not quite sufficient to understand a detailed discussion of glider construction. However, there was a very informative series of illustrations that detailed several wing designs. One variation used a wooden framework with fabric stretched over it like a kite.

Contentedly, Den opened his notebook and began sketching.

He returned to the Sime Center at lunchtime, humming under his breath as he mentally compared possible wing designs. How best to combine the strength of spruce with the lightness of silk for optimum lift? If silk could not be found, would cotton or linen be the best substitute? Perhaps Eddina's aunt, who was a tailor, should be consulted on how best to attach the fabric onto the frame to optimize strength and reduce the risk of tearing under stress. He was still mulling over the options as he approached the Sime Center, pleasantly tired from the walk.

As he turned the last corner, noise penetrated his creative fog and he stopped to stare. About thirty people were milling around on the sidewalk in front of the Sime Center. Most were adults, with a few children and adolescents mixed in.

Under the direction of a tall, gaunt Gen man in a long black cassock, several men unfurled a banner that read, "SIMES OUT OF CLEAR SPRINGS!!!" Others held up professionally printed signs with the slogans "Save Our Kids" and "Keep Our Children Innocent." Not content with that, one turmeric-haired fellow on the edges of the crowd carried a handprinted placard with "The Onlee Good Sime is a Ded Sime!" As the Donor stared in disbelief, the man in the cassock called the crowd to order in the deep, booming tones of a professional orator, directed them to spread out, and turned to face the Sime Center.

"No longer will you corrupt our fair city and its children!" he shouted. "We command you in the name of God to depart for the vile and debased land that spawned you!"

"Simes go home! Simes go home!" chanted the clergyman's followers.

How was Den supposed to get through the angry mob to the Sime Center? He was considering going around the block and climbing the fence when an earnest, middle-aged woman broke out of the picket line to accost him.

"You don't want to go in there, sir! It's dangerous!"

"Dangerous?" he asked mildly.

"Oh, yes! They don't tell you half the terrible things that go on in there. You don't want that to happen to you."

The woman was Gen and thus couldn't zlin his Donor's nager. In his old and stained coveralls, Den must look like a general-class donor coming to the Collectorium. Thinking back, the Donor realized that none of the press coverage of the Sime Center's opening ceremonies had included a picture of him, although there had been several of Rital with Ref.

The anti-Sime demonstrators were generating quite a respectable volume as they marched back and forth on the sidewalk. The chant shifted to, "Keep your tentacles off my city!"

The woman smiled up at Den. "Look, I know a nice little coffee house right around the corner. Why don't I buy you a snack and we can talk about it where it's quieter?" She must assume he had come to the Sime Center simply to donate selyn for money, and wanted to talk him out of it if she could. Such an opportunity to observe the unsuspecting enemy in action was unlikely to come again.

Den wavered for a moment. However, neither Rital's goal of making the Clear Springs Sime Center a success nor his own of developing powered flight would be possible unless they could recruit more donors among the Clear Springs Gens. Any plan to do so would have to survive contact with this well-organized opposition. Den's stomach rumbled, reminding him that it had been a good five hours since food had last passed his lips, and that decided him. With a mental apology to Sosu Risetta for leaving her to handle Rital under such trying circumstances, he smiled back at the woman and said, "Sure."

"My name is Carla Lifton," the woman said, patting her greying hair back into its neat bun as she led the way down the street. "I belong to the Conservative Congregation over on Second Street."

The Conservative Congregation, Den recalled, was the religious group that Mr. Duncan had left. That implied that the tall leader in the cassock was their new pastor, Reverend Sinth. If Mr. Duncan was correct that the man had made driving the Tecton out of Clear Springs the focus of his ministry, the good Reverend was unlikely to give up harassing the Sime Center any time soon.

Recalling his manners, the Donor said, "Pleased to meet you, Miz Lifton. I'm Den Milnan." The omission of his title "Sosu," reserved in-Territory for technical-class Donors, might be misleading but was not technically a lie.

"I'm pleased to meet you, Den. I don't think I've seen you around."

"I haven't gotten out much since I arrived in Clear Springs last week."

Carla seemed to like this answer. "So, you're new in town." She looked at the notebook he carried. "A student, perhaps?"

Continuing his strategy of remaining as close to the truth as possible, Den admitted, "No, I came to Clear Springs to work."

"Well, I'm sure you'll love our community…"

She made small talk, describing the municipal virtues of Clear Springs, as they sat at one of the outside tables of the Eight Mice Cafe and Grill. It was clear that Carla knew her city and its residents well and that she cared deeply about what happened to them. At her urging, Den ordered a cheese sandwich while Carla asked for lemonade.

Once the waiter delivered their order and left them, Carla's whole manner changed. The friendliness and concern were still there, but now that Den had committed to staying long enough to eat his sandwich, it was clear that she was ready to get down to business.

"Den, I'm so glad I caught you before you went into that place," she began. "You're too nice a person to fall victim to a murdering demon."

"A murdering demon?" Den had heard his cousin Rital described many ways, but this was a bit excessive even for a channel who had taken the last pastry at breakfast, leaving his starving Donor to make do with toast.

"You can never trust a Sime," Carla assured him. "They all live on selyn and Gens like us are the only place they can get it." She pulled out a pamphlet. "Here, this tells all about it."

DON'T BE A VICTIM! was splashed across the page in blood-red letters an inch high. Underneath was a drawing of what Den assumed was supposed to be a Sime. The poor thing looked like an octopus convention, with a least a dozen tentacles on each arm, dripping blood as they reached toward the viewer. An untentacled corpse lay at its feet, an agonized grimace on its features, the outstretched arms dripping from bloody, helical cuts.

In the purple prose inside, Den was amazed to discover that there was a secret Pen in the Sime Center basement, in which unwary general-class donors were imprisoned for the resident Simes to Kill at their leisure. There was also witchcraft used to lure children into the Sime Center, causing them to go into changeover, and midnight orgies where unspeakable debauchery held sway. That last sounded interesting, if exhausting.

"My goodness, I had no idea," he said, taking a bite out of his sandwich. The cheese was rich and creamy and the lightly toasted bread crunched: delicious. "Are you sure that this pamphlet is correct? This bit about stealing children seems a bit fanciful, don't you think?"

Grief washed over Carla Lifton's features. "That part I know is true. My own niece, Nozella, was abducted and corrupted. She's now a tentacled monster, lost to the service of the Lord. Not satisfied with that, the Simes also corrupted my father and turned him away from the True Church. I can't bear to have that happen to my own children."

That explains why she looks familiar, Den thought. There was a definite family resemblance to Mr. Duncan around the mouth.

"You aren't the first to fall victim to the Tecton's propaganda," Carla assured him, beginning what was obviously a well-rehearsed speech. "Oh, they talk a good line, all those tales about how none of them Kill anymore, and peace and goodwill between the Territories, but Killing is the Sime nature. They live on Gen lives and they never forget it, even though they try hard to make us forget. 'We just want to help,' they say. 'We'll keep your children with the Devilseed from Killing.' And when the unsuspecting government agrees, they move in and take over. Once we give them a hold on us, we'll be locked behind bars in their Pens before you know it, just waiting for them to get around to Killing us."

She believes it, Den thought in amazement. *She believes every word she's saying.* "I thought Tecton channels only took donations from Gens who volunteer," he objected mildly.

It was, in fact, a bedrock principle of the Tecton, even in Sime Territory. Whatever legal, social, or moral circumstances brought a Gen to the Collectorium, no channel would lay a tentacle on an unconsenting donor.

"I hear they pay well for donations, too," he added, finishing his sandwich and reaching for the check.

"My treat," she said, picking it up. "If you're bad enough off that you'd consider earning money *that* way, it's the least I can do."

"No, really…" Den began. He was beginning to feel guilty about leading her on in the face of her obvious sincerity.

"I insist," Carla said, breaking into another, obviously rehearsed speech. "My church has created a special fund to help people who are in danger of falling for Sime lies. There are a lot of people who are down on their luck, or have families to feed, and they might think the Tecton offers an easy way out. But by believing the snakes' propaganda, they lose their faith in God and the purity of the Gen species. We offer a less spiritually dangerous alternative." She gave him a measuring glance. "You, for instance. From your accent, you're a long way from home. You're new in town and you don't know anyone. You're just the kind of victim they like to get their slimy tentacles on. But we can help tide you over until you can get back on your feet, maybe even help you get a job. Do you have any particular job skills?"

"Why, yes, I do," Den admitted with an admirably straight face. "For the last eight years or so I've worked for the Tecton as a Technical-class Donor. I came to Clear Springs to look after Hajene Madz." As he spoke, he ran his thumb over the distinctive Tecton crest ring that had adorned his right hand since his Qualification, with its diamond declaring him First Order.

Carla's eyes went to the ring and then back to Den's face. Her jaw dropped, but no sound came out.

"Your niece, Nozella's, changeover was diagnosed before we left Valzor," Den continued. "That kind of makes it impossible for Hajene Madz to have caused it. We did arrive in Clear Springs in time to prevent her from Killing, however. If you would like to visit her before she leaves for Valzor this afternoon, I would be happy to facilitate that. You have only to ask."

The Donor smiled into her still-stunned face. "Speaking of Hajene Madz," he continued, standing and pushing in his chair, "I really ought to report in before he starts worrying. It's been a most interesting chat. Thank you for the lunch and by the way," he added, tossing the pamphlet back onto the table as she continued to gape at him, "Simes only have six tentacles to an arm."

CHAPTER 7

FAMILY FEUDING

As Den had feared, Rital had not taken well the appearance of thirty chanting anti-Sime Center demonstrators on his doorstep. The Donor found his cousin in his second floor office, uncharacteristically idle, handling tentacles wrapped around a cold cup of trin tea as Sosu Risetta hovered in concern. She looked up as Den paused outside to announce his presence and smiled in open relief, beckoning him inside.

Rital lurched to his feet as Den entered, arms outstretched to zlin his cousin for damage. "Den! Are you all right? Are those people still out there? How did you get through them?"

"I'm fine, Rital," Den assured his cousin. "Reverend Sinth and his followers are still outside, but they didn't do anything but wave their signs at me. Annoying, but not dangerous."

"They're a mob," Rital insisted. "And mobs of frightened people are dangerous by definition."

"They didn't look very frightened to me." Den picked up the teapot steeping on Rital's desk, warmed the channel's cup, and filled a second for himself. "Mostly, they looked annoyed. Which is understandable, because when we opened they lost their argument with the city, the university, and the Tecton."

"What if they scare all the donors away?" The channel massaged his arms reflexively, as if fighting off another bout of entran.

"Don't worry," Den assured him. "Standing around waving signs is boring and accomplishes nothing. They'll decide they've made their point and leave us in peace, soon enough."

Seena drove Nozella and Sosu Risetta to the train station in the ambulance, to spare them having to confront Reverend Sinth and his followers. She returned with the back end stuffed with packing crates. The balance of Den's luggage had finally arrived from Valzor along with the shipment of standard kits for traveling Donors.

Den's joy at once more being able to wear a proper Tecton uniform was marred by concern about the situation on the sidewalk. Some of the demonstrators left, but fresh replacements soon joined the group and chanted enthusiastically until the Sime Center officially closed for the day. A somewhat smaller group of demonstrators showed up the following morning and stayed until suppertime. That set the pattern for the next two weeks. During the hours when the Collectorium was open, there were never fewer than ten people chanting or singing on the sidewalk outside the Sime Center, accosting any Gen who showed interest in going inside.

Despite their efforts, a steady trickle of Gens came in to donate. Most were students seeking extra spending money for their upcoming spring break, although a few were long-time residents of Clear Springs. The workload was barely enough for Rital to avoid entran.

It was not, however, enough work to keep him particularly healthy. As Rital descended into Need again, the channel began to worry that none of the new donors who had come in over the past month would return to try again, if they had to do so under the public condemnation of the demonstrators.

"How will we generate a selyn surplus for Valzor District like this?" he complained fretfully to Den one evening. "Only three donors came in today. At this rate, we'll barely be able to fulfill our contract with the Center for Technology."

This was not a trivial concern, as the professors would move their offices, students, and labs into the new, selyn-powered building over the summer. However, before the building could be turned over to the university, the contractor had to run a full test of all its selyn-powered systems. The in-Territory subcontractor who had installed the selyn battery bank had worked with empty batteries because they were much safer to transport and handle than live ones. Before the shakedown tests could be run, those batteries had to be filled by Rital with the selyn he had so painstakingly gleaned from local Gen donors.

Early one morning, two days before their second transfer was scheduled, Den met Rital in the Sime Center's lobby. Together, they worked Rital's tentacles into the gleaming retainers.

"They feel even worse than I remembered," the channel complained, poking fretfully at the catches on the left-arm manacle.

"At least you won't have to wear them for eight hours this time," Den pointed out. He opened the catches, relieving the pressure that was ironing a pleat into a fold of skin on one tentacle sheath, then closed them again. "Better?" he asked.

"Yes," Rital said, then muttered, "For very small values of 'better,'" as they stepped out into the cool morning air. Den automatically started around the building toward the loading dock where the Sime Center's staff car and ambulance were parked, then stopped short as the channel headed down the path that led to the street instead. "We *are* driving, aren't we?" he asked his cousin.

"Of course not!" Rital answered. "It's only a mile, no university campus ever has decent parking, and besides, it's too nice a day to waste the opportunity for a walk."

"Look," said Den, as persuasively as he knew how. "Fresh air is marvelous stuff and I like it as much as you do, but there are an awful lot of non-donors out there and you're not in very good shape right now."

"Nonsense," the channel said firmly. "This early, the streets will be practically empty. I haven't left the Sime Center since we got here and you only got out once. Come on, the exercise will do us both good."

Realizing that it was useless to argue, Den gave in. "At least there aren't any sign-waving fanatics today," he said as they reached the sidewalk.

"They may be fanatics, but they're pragmatic fanatics," Rital explained. "They know the Collectorium is closed now. I expect they'll be waiting for us when we return."

"Humpf."

They walked briskly through deserted streets. The closed and shuttered shops seemed unnatural to Den. "Don't the shop owners lose a lot of business, staying closed so much?" he asked Rital.

"What good would it do them to stay open when all of their customers are sound asleep?"

"I keep forgetting," Den admitted sheepishly. Gens tended to sleep eight hours or more each night; Simes, only an hour or two. "It must be very strange, living in a town without Simes."

"Not to them."

Now the closed storefronts no longer seemed so sinister. There were a few people about. A delivery van passed them, as did a woman walking a dog. When they reached the park, Mr. Duncan waved a greeting from a bench. "I'll see you tomorrow!" he called, reaching into a paper bag for a handful of seeds that he scattered for the birds. "Even if my children don't approve!"

That earned a real smile from Rital, who waved back and told his cousin, "He's an independent old fellow. I like him."

The Center for Technology was located on the far side of the university's campus. As the spring break had started the day before, there were very few people about.

Den stopped to scan a bulletin board covered with a patchwork of colored paper. The Drama Department, he learned, was performing some obscure play by an equally obscure playwright. A visiting scientist had given a lecture on maize genetics the week before. A roommate was sought for a two-bedroom apartment starting in the fall. The chemistry club was having a picnic and warned its members to "be there or we'll mutate your cat." Then a red flyer with bold black lettering caught his eye.

"**WARNING!**" splashed across the top in letters two inches high. **"The university and the city government have conspired to sell Clear Springs to the Tecton,"** it continued in smaller print beneath. "The following people have actively aided this treason by donating selyn—support which the Sime Center *must have* to remain open!" There followed a list of names, with occupations or business affiliations beside some of them. "Remember," the flyer warned, "if you give these Sime-lovers your business or your friendship, you are showing your approval of their actions!" At the bottom, in small print, was, "A public service message from Students for a Sime-Free City."

Den pulled the flyer down and shredded it. "No wonder so few Gens here are willing to donate," he said, tossing the scraps into a nearby trash barrel.

"Yes, no wonder."

The almost-completed Center for Technology was even larger and more fortress-like than the library. It was surrounded by an orange construction fence and a sea of churned-up mud bridged by temporary walkways. A steam engine provided power for an assortment of saws and other machines. More noisy, steam-powered machines graded the steep sides of a gaping pit that exposed the foundation and basement level of the building.

Unlike the rest of the campus, the construction site swarmed with people. Some carried supplies and equipment into the building. Another crew worked at laying forms for a sidewalk. Inspecting the angles between the new building's doors and the surrounding buildings, the Donor predicted that the sidewalks would not successfully prevent students from shortcutting across the lawns. To Den's relief, the work crews seemed quite willing to avoid the lone Sime and his Escort.

"Do you know where we're going?" he asked his cousin quietly.

The channel was scanning the area. "We were supposed to be met by… Ah, that must be him now."

A stout man carrying a clipboard was hurrying in their direction, scowling. "There you are! You're five minutes late. Don't you know we have a schedule to keep?"

In an unsubtle rebuke to such rudeness, Rital said, "Den, this is Mr. Nid Fulson, the manager of Fulson Construction. Mr. Fulson, this is my Donor, Sosu Milnan, and I'm Hajene Madz. We're here to fill your selyn batteries."

Fulson beckoned for them to follow him. "Yes, yes, hurry up. I don't have all day."

He led them to a solid, fire-resistant door in the side of the building. Large letters stenciled across it proclaimed "No Admittance" and in smaller letters beneath, "Sime Territory." That made the space beyond officially part of Sime Territory, a legal fiction necessary to allow Rital to take off the retainers and work with the selyn batteries.

Fulson pulled a fist-sized tangle of keys from the pocket of his heavy denim pants and began sorting through them. The third try produced the right key and he pulled open the heavy door, revealing bare concrete stairs leading down to the basement. "Go on, then." He gestured angrily for Den and Rital to enter. "I don't know what the world is coming to, when site managers have to waste their time showing Simes around," he muttered under his breath as he slammed the door shut behind them, leaving them in darkness.

"What a charming person," Den said sarcastically as Rital threw a switch. Temporary safety lights came to life, throwing just enough light that a Gen could avoid a fatal stumble.

"I believe Fulson Construction pushed hard for a more…traditional power source for the building," Rital explained, putting a steadying hand on the Donor's elbow as they started down the stairs. "One with a higher profit margin for his company and which didn't require him to hire an in-Territory subcontractor. You can hardly expect him to be enthusiastic about me, when the switch to selyn caught his family right in the pocketbook."

"If he objects so strongly to letting you in, why didn't he just send somebody else over with the key?" Den asked.

"He can't. His contract with the university only allows him to provide keys to shift managers and subcontractor shift bosses. You can see why: the combination of heavy equipment and prank-prone youngsters can be… explosive."

The Donor nodded. "So can't he make you a subcontractor shift boss for the summer? They've got to have a way to do that."

"Unfortunately for Fulson, his contract with the construction workers' union does not allow non-union members as company employees or subcontractors. I understand there were some heated objections before the union allowed the in-Territory subcontractor in to lay the orgonics—on the condition that they were all Gens."

"Typical."

The stairs ended in a gloomy, musty-smelling cavern. It appeared that the in-Territory construction crew had appropriated the space for a break room over the winter. Muddy footprints crisscrossed the floor and the threadbare carpet that adorned the middle. An ancient, olive-green couch sagged against the wall, stuffing showing through the rents in its cushions.

A battered table stood in front of the couch, listing slightly because one leg was shorter than the rest.

"They must have furnished the place using stuff even students rejected as hopeless," Rital observed.

Looking totally out of place among the dinginess, a shiny new safety grating blocked off the back third of the room. Large signs warned the untrained of danger in Simelan and English both and as a further safety precaution, the door in the grating was secured by a Gen-proof, and thus theoretically child-proof, lock.

"Why didn't they put the batteries in with the rest of the utilities?" Den asked as he carefully helped Rital remove the cumbersome retainers.

"They did, almost." The second retainer came off. "Oh, that's so much more comfortable." The channel stretched, working the stiffness out of his handling tentacles, and pointed to where orgonics tubing disappeared through a conduit in the back wall. "The steam plant, water heater, and ventilation fans are just on the other side of the wall. That way, they won't have to evacuate their physical plant to keep the staff from disrupting the ambient nager while I'm trying to work."

"That makes sense." Den set the retainers on the table, propping them open to dry, and followed the channel over to the grating. Rital pulled the door open as easily as if it were unlocked, using Sime strength and his handling tentacles to manipulate the catches, and Den had his first unobstructed view of the selyn battery bank.

"That's *all*?" he asked incredulously. "Three batteries for a whole department's worth of labs and research equipment? They aren't even the largest size!"

"It turns out that a lot of the professors have expensive equipment that runs on electricity, since that's what the university has used to date," Rital explained. "It would cost a lot to convert so many machines to selyn power and neither the professors nor the university are interested in paying for it. Some star professors were even making noises about staying in their old labs rather than joining the Center for Technology. So, the university compromised and told Fulson to run wires for electricity down the orgonics conduits to power that equipment. The Center for Technology's first group project will be converting an electrical generator to run on selyn power, but it won't be working until midsummer."

Den shook his head. "Wouldn't forgoing the cost of running wires for their duplicate electrical system pay for converting a lot of the machinery? And doesn't wasting selyn to generate electricity defeat the whole purpose of converting to a selyn-powered energy grid in the first place?"

"The selyn-powered generator will just supplement the electricity they generate with wind power. Windmills power the rest of the campus. Also, they use a lot less powered equipment than a comparable in-Territory university would, because electrical systems are so expensive to build and maintain."

"Using cheap, efficient selyn to generate expensive, wasteful electricity in a building designed as a showcase of modern efficiency," Den summed up, still trying to wrap his mind around the concept. "It's the sort of irony that only happens when a decision is made by committee."

The channel shrugged. "It was never going to be a clean conversion. Given the lack of enthusiasm for donating among local Gens, it's just as well that we'll only have to provide enough selyn for basic utilities, at least for now. Maybe by the time the labs manage to convert that generator, we'll have grown the donor base enough that we won't have to import selyn batteries from Valzor." He contemplated the batteries for a moment, then made a face. "I suppose I'd better get started."

Kneeling beside the first battery, he unhooked the leads to the orgonics cables and placed them carefully to one side. Gripping the handholds, he reluctantly extended his laterals to contact the terminals. Den took a half step to his right, feeling for the location that would give him optimum control, and held the ambient nager steady. After a moment's pause to brace himself, the channel leaned forward, pressed his lips against the red fifth terminal, and began to void selyn.

By the time the third battery was filled, Rital was looking distinctly nauseated. Pulling the channel to his feet, Den walked him out of the restricted area, kicking the safety door closed with a clang as they passed through the grating. Urging Rital to sit on the ancient couch, the Donor sat beside him, holding the channel as he shuddered in revulsion.

"Shen, I hate batteries," Rital muttered against Den's shoulder. "The rest of the work here is fine, what there is of it, but the batteries are awful."

Den ran a soothing hand along his cousin's tentacles, letting his 'live' nager dispel the 'dead' feel of the batteries. "At an in-Territory Sime Center, you wouldn't have to work with batteries very often," he pointed out.

"No!" Rital stiffened.

"I know you like the challenge here," Den argued, "but there just isn't enough work for a First Order channel in this town."

"Den, I want to stay here." Rital straightened, reaching for his retainers. "At an in-Territory Sime Center, I would be in charge of one, maybe two departments, doing mostly routine functionals. I'd probably get drafted as Controller, now and then. Oh, it's valuable work and someone's got to do it, but here?" The channel's eyes lit with enthusiasm. "Here, if I do my job correctly, the children of this town won't have to fear being murdered if they go into changeover and their parents won't have to spend years wondering if their own children will Kill them. Have you any idea what a difference that will make in their lives?"

"They don't seem particularly interested in living their lives differently," the Donor pointed out, steadying the retainer so his cousin could work his tentacles into the pockets. "In the month we've been here, seventeen children have gone into changeover." Den had taken to reading the *Clear Springs Clarion* every morning. The obituaries were particularly depressing. "That's thirteen murders and two Kills when the murders didn't happen soon enough. One poor kid died before breakout, trying to escape from the mob out to murder him. Only Nozella was brought to us, and that was likely just because her parents weren't around to murder her and the neighbor didn't want to do their dirty work for them."

Rital gave a flinch that had nothing to do with pinched laterals. "What about the selyn?" he asked, in a blatant attempt to dodge Den's too-accurate line of argument. "We can't recreate the wonders of Ancient technology without tapping the resources of out-Territory cities like Clear Springs. Having the technology will force people to donate, donating will force them to see that Simes are human, and that will lead them to accept their own Sime children. Isn't it worth the inconveniences," he snapped the catches on the second retainer closed, "to be a part of making that happen?"

Den sighed. "I can't argue against that," he agreed, getting to his feet. He followed Rital to the stairs. "Just remember, you can't do anybody any good if you collapse."

The stores had opened while they were working and the streets were now crowded with shoppers. The bustle stopped as the channel was sighted and people stared with alarm, revulsion, or (occasionally) curiosity. Nobody tried to stop them, but the walk back through the crowded streets was nerve-wracking. Den was uncomfortably aware of how little it would take to turn the shoppers into a mob. He was so glad to see the Sime Center that he didn't even mind the thirteen sign-waving demonstrators on the sidewalk in front of it. Their chanting ground to a ragged halt as channel and Donor approached, but they stepped aside to let the pair pass, faces twisted with hatred.

"Family-destroying devil-worshipper!" Carla Lifton hissed at Den.

The Donor gave her his most impudent wink as he went by.

Over steaming mugs of trin tea in Rital's office, Den asked his cousin, "Why didn't they just string orgonics cable to the battery bank here in the basement of the Sime Center, instead of forcing a channel to travel all the way across town?"

"The City Council voted not to. The official reason was economic. The extra cable would have laid a portion of the cost for a university project on the city, since the city is responsible for utility maintenance outside the boundaries of the campus. The unofficial reason was political, of course. The university wanted to be able to show visitors the selyn batteries to prove that its new building is a modern wonder."

Den shook his head in bewilderment. "It's not as if the building would be powered any differently if the batteries were stored elsewhere. In-Territory towns always put the battery bank in or near the Sime Center. If they want to show people where the power for the Center for Technology comes from, they could easily just bring them over here."

In a flat voice, Rital intoned, "Ah, but the university refused to ask its valued patrons and guests to set foot in a Sime Center. Too many of us ferocious demons about. They hope to leave that to the less-well-off students, who are too young to know any better and struggling to pay their expenses." He raised his eyebrow over the rim of his mug and continued in his normal voice. "Judging by the tenacity of the demonstrators, I suspect the City Council had another motive: not providing a mile of orgonic tubing to guard constantly, lest somebody cut it. It might actually work out for the best. If I'm out and about every time the batteries want charging, it gives the townsfolk who won't come to the Sime Center a chance to get used to me."

"*Used* to you!" Den sprang to his feet in indignation. "They won't set foot in the same building with you, they act as if you have shaking plague when you walk down the street, there's a horde of them demonstrating outside the Sime Center every day, and you think they're getting *used* to you?"

"That's right. This is the first time you've been posted out-Territory, isn't it?"

"And the last, if I have anything to say about it! I've never seen a ruder, more ungrateful and *ignorant* bunch of people in my life." Den sat down again and frowned morosely into his tea. "We're wasting our time here, trying to help people who think you're a murdering demon and I'm a devil-worshipper, so that their precious university can prosper while they teach their kids to hate us even more. Maybe the Distect rebels had the right idea: let those Gens who won't accept Simes die of their own phobias, so they won't go breeding another generation of lorshes."

"Oh, Den, you know Simephobia isn't a genetic trait." Rital set his tea mug aside and leaned back in his desk chair, lacing his handling tentacles together. This close to Need, the channel was reluctant to face the possibility that the Gens of Clear Springs might choose to withhold their selyn from him. "Also, the fear of Simes isn't as widespread as you seem to think it is, at least when it comes to channels. Two weeks ago, there were half again as many demonstrators on our sidewalk. Sure, it's a slow process. The local Gens are apprehensive or even afraid of me, but that's normal enough, considering. Until we came here, very few of them had ever seen a channel. However, they all know someone who was Killed by a berserk Sime in changeover. It takes time to overcome such fears, but we've been getting a steady trickle of general-class donors."

"Trickle is right," Den retorted. He was also just two days from transfer but being a Donor, that condition manifested as resentment toward any Gen who made things unnecessarily difficult for his channel. "You could triple our donor rolls and still suffer occasional entran. Do you think that mob outside on our sidewalk is about to learn anything you might teach? They'd rather believe their own lies."

"Don't underestimate them, just because you don't agree with them," Rital warned. "The worst anti-Sime fanatic is capable of learning and once they have changed their minds, their hearts will follow."

"They won't change either if we can't find some tactic that gets past the hate and fear."

That afternoon, Den offered to fill in for Seena as Collectorium receptionist so she could help Ref and Gati finish their inventory of the storeroom. After assuring her that he wouldn't mess up her filing system, he surveyed the empty waiting room, pulled out a translation of an Ancient text on the "Spirit of St. Louis" and its purported flight across the great Eastern Ocean, and settled down behind the desk to read.

Only two Gens braved the demonstrators to donate during the shift. One was the student from a border city who had donated on the Sime Center's third day of operation and the other was his equally impoverished roommate, who was donating for the first time.

If that's the 'progress' that Rital is making with donor recruitment, Den told himself cynically, *I'd hate to see his idea of stagnation.*

The following morning showed every sign of being a beautiful spring day. The sun shone warmly without being too hot and a gentle breeze caressed trees just starting to show the yellow-green of new leaves. Sparrows, bees, and a virtuoso mockingbird combined their songs into a springtime symphony.

All of which, Den reflected as he stepped outside the Collectorium entrance with a steaming cup of trin tea, *shows that Nature has no particular respect for the trials and tribulations of one frustrated Donor.* Sourly, he watched the day's corps of demonstrators deploying their signs under Carla Lifton's direction.

Reverend Sinth was not present, the Donor observed. The clergyman had attended the demonstrations every day for the first week, then cut back to once or twice a week, leaving Carla to run the project as his able lieutenant. Idly, Den wondered if the daily demonstrations would have continued without her personal grudge against the Sime Center.

Exactly five minutes before the Collectorium opened, the group broke into song, sending the sparrows and the mockingbird flying in alarm. The selection was one of their favorites, a traditional hymn that praised parents who raised their children well. Veterans of a lifetime of choir practice and church services, the group managed the four-part harmony with authority.

After weeks of hearing the thing several times a day, Den knew the words by heart. They had reached the next to last verse, which admonished parents to turn to religion to ensure that they found the courage to bid their children farewell if that test should come, when the dapper figure of Joziah Duncan turned the corner, white hair neatly combed and cherry wood cane gleaming in the sun. Carla Lifton, who was conducting, broke off to watch her father approach. The singing ground to a ragged halt as members of the choir realized what was happening.

In the unaccustomed quiet, Den could hear Carla plead, "You don't have to do this, Father. Come back to the Path, to the Church. Reverend Sinth will forgive you, if you are penitent."

"Forgive me for what?" Mr. Duncan asked. "Being happy to see my grandchild live? Giving her my best wishes for a successful future?" He shook his head. "I've done nothing for which I need forgiveness." He looked beyond his daughter to stare down the others defiantly. "I do not believe that a merciful God would ask loving parents to murder their children when a responsible alternative exists."

"Nozella has no future," Carla insisted. "She is a shadow of herself, possessed by a murderous demon. How many Gens will die before it is sent back to Hell where it belongs?"

"Not a single Gen will die because Nozella lives, Carla," her father said earnestly. "*That* is what the Tecton offers us. Your children won't have to die the way your sister did, even if they become Sime."

Carla flinched, then lashed out in defiance. "That survival comes at a price. What of the Gen who must provide the selyn that keeps the demon inhabiting Nozella from Killing? Can you make the choice to condemn another Gen to suffer that, month after month for their entire life?"

Mr. Duncan shook his head. "I've never been a freeloader and I'm not going to start now. If Nozella must have a Gen donate selyn every month to support her, I'll do it myself."

"Father!" came the anguished protest. "What would Mother have said?"

"She'd have said I was a stubborn old coot and she'd be right." Mr. Duncan smiled fondly at the memory of his late wife, then met his daughter's eyes calmly. "My mind's made up, Carla," he told her, not unkindly. "You can stand out here and rail uselessly against progress if you want. You won't change the city's mind about having a Sime Center in Clear Springs and you won't quiet your own doubts about whether the folks at the Sime Center might, just might, be exactly who and what they say they are."

Turning away from her, he started down the path to the Collectorium entrance.

W hen the day of Den's transfer with Rital arrived at last, he took the precaution of getting to the deferment suite half an hour early to avoid being dragged into any last minute emergencies. He puttered around a bit, checking the cabinets, putting on water for tea, and unplugging the phone jack. The hushed solitude of the sound- and selyn-insulated room helped him find the state of relaxed anticipation necessary for a good transfer.

Rital arrived a scant ten minutes before their transfer was scheduled. "Sorry I cut it so fine," he said, flopping face down onto the lounge with a sigh. "It's been one of those days."

"Well, no one will bother us for the next hour, so relax and enjoy it."

Den sat down beside his cousin. He could barely feel the Need underlying the ironclad self-control Rital had been using to enable himself to function at almost his usual efficiency. When the Donor placed a cautious hand on one tentacled arm, he saw that the ronaplin glands were barely swollen, although the channel's laterals responded to his high field. If Rital attempted transfer in such a condition, as he had the previous month, there would be no real joy in it for either of them.

"Why don't you turn over and let me get to work?" he suggested.

When Rital complied, Den began to ruthlessly provoke the Sime, letting his high selyn field and his anticipation dissolve away the other's self-control. Soon he could feel his own body's response as Rital's Need soared, a bottomless hunger that he ached to feed.

"Careful" the channel warned, handling tentacles restraining the Donor's hands. "It's not quite time yet."

"Relax," Den said again. "This one's for fun."

This time, when he checked, the ronaplin glands were swollen to almost three times their normal size, pumping selyn-conducting fluids into the channel's lateral sheaths. The dripping laterals had emerged and were quivering with anticipation. They left pleasantly tingling streaks on Den's arms between the handling tentacles that now gripped him with the urgency peculiar to personal transfer.

When the proper moment arrived, Rital didn't wait for the Gen to bend over, but instead pulled his Donor down to make the lip contact. Den abandoned himself enthusiastically to the channel's deep, swift draw, an irresistible demand for selyn that reached the very core of his being, to be fulfilled in an ecstatic celebration of life.

This was the bond that held the Tecton's First Order together, that made all the hard work and loss of personal freedom worth enduring. Transfer was always pleasurable, even when the channel whose Need Den served was merely a colleague. To reaffirm that bond with Rital, the only family either of them had, was far more.

The demand for selyn slacked off as Rital reached satiation and Den felt a flash of pity for the out-Territory Gens of Clear Springs, so caught up in their fear of Simes that few could even find the courage to donate. They would never know this double satisfaction, never even believe, most of them, that a Sime's touch could bring anything but pain. *How can they bear such a crippled existence, cutting them off from everything that makes life worth living?*

There was no time to consider the matter. Rital had just completed his best transfer in months and Den had no intention of letting distractions interfere with finishing his job. As Rital's handling tentacles released him, Den reached with one hand to help the channel sit up and with the other, deftly snagged a tissue from the newly opened box he had placed beside the lounge.

Rital gave an anguished cry and collapsed forward into the Donor's arms, sobbing convulsively as he was overwhelmed by the accumulated emotional pain that he had been unable to experience fully while in Need. Den had known that his cousin was hurting, but this was far worse than he had anticipated. As Rital wailed, "Why do they have to hate me so much?" Den's earlier pity for the out-Territory Gens evaporated, to be replaced by anger. Frightened or not, no Gen had the right to mistreat a channel that way.

They're ignorant, but not stupid, Den thought as he savagely pulled yet another tissue from the rapidly emptying box and handed it to his cousin. *They know exactly what they're doing to Rital, with their signs and their chants and their hatred.*

And I'm not going to let them get away with it!

When Den and Rital finally emerged from the deferment suite and entered the cafeteria for lunch, they walked into an ambush. Gati cut between them as they entered and herded the channel off to one side with a neatness and efficiency that would have done a champion sheepdog proud. The receptionist had taken an excellent transfer from Rital two days before. In Simes, the sating of Need left room for other basic desires to emerge. Den watched long enough to determine that Rital did not object to her plans and then went to get a sandwich.

Before he could take the first bite, Alyce sauntered over to his table. She took her time looking him over and the gleam in her eyes suggested that she liked what she saw. "Do you mind if I join you?" she asked.

Den didn't mind at all. It wasn't only Simes, after all, who responded to a good transfer with heightened interest in other physical drives.

CHAPTER 8

RITAL AND THE NIGHT VISITOR

To Den's relief, about two-thirds of the Gens who had come in to donate selyn during the Sime Center's first month braved Reverend Sinth's demonstrators to try again during the second. Although not all were as punctual about it as Mr. Duncan, some of them brought friends. The result was an overall increase in the Sime Center's selyn balance.

The increased donations did not result in any shipments of industrial selyn back to Valzor, however. The Center for Technology building was officially turned over to the university in an opening ceremony that was memorialized in a three-page spread in the *Clear Springs Clarion*. Viewing the pictures, Den concluded that the Sime Center opening ceremonies had been paltry indeed, by local standards.

As the professors moved into their new accommodations, the demands on the selyn batteries increased. The first charge lasted a month but the second, only two weeks.

"And that will get worse if they figure out how to convert that electrical generator to work on selyn power," Rital observed glumly, as he rested on the old couch after filling the batteries for the third time. That morning, Den had helped his cousin through a rough turnover, the point at which a Sime had metabolized half the selyn taken during the last transfer and began the descent into Need. Like most Simes, Rital found it difficult to be optimistic during the Need half of his cycle.

"At least we're breaking even," Den pointed out. "We haven't had to ask Valzor to ship filled batteries out."

Rital shuddered. "That would be a disaster. The final agreement between the city government and the Tecton stipulates that all selyn sold to the university for the Center of Technology be billed at the rate for locally collected selyn. Everybody on the negotiation team assumed that in a city full of Gens, there had to be enough donors to cover one building."

"I guess it never occurred to them that we'd have an organized mob on our sidewalk every day, trying to discourage donations," the Donor observed.

"Foolish negotiators," Rital agreed.

* * * *

Den did not provide his cousin with his personal transfer that month. To prevent potentially crippling dependencies, the Tecton rotated transfer assignments so that no channel-Donor pair shared transfer more than twice in a row. This was easy to accomplish in-Territory, where even small Sime Centers were staffed by several channel-Donor pairs who could simply swap partners as necessary.

However, the Clear Springs Sime Center only had Rital. It made sense for a First Order channel to open a Sime Center so far from the border. Firsts had more control than Seconds or Thirds and could better handle inexperienced donors, who were often nervous or even frightened during their initial donations. Everyone had assumed additional channels and Donors would join the Sime Center's staff long before a rotation was required.

Unfortunately, the workload in Clear Springs was insufficient for two First Order channels. Instead, District Controller Monruss decided to send a Donor out to Clear Springs to give Rital transfer and pull Den back to Valzor for a few days to give transfer to Hajene Nalod. The Donor felt guilty about leaving Rital alone to face Reverend Sinth and his friends, but promised to present his cousin with an assortment of really good trin teas on his return.

The train ride back to Valzor was uneventful, since Den had taken the precaution of dressing in civilian clothing for the trip. With no easy way for passing out-Territory Gens to tell that he worked for the Tecton, he was able to travel in a regular passenger car without attracting the sort of hostility that he and Rital had experienced at the Cottonwood Crossing station.

It was strange to be back in civilization. He was no longer accustomed to seeing a normal mix of Simes and Gens when he walked down the street, or to receiving nods of respect for his profession from passing strangers. His transfer with Hajene Nalod would not be complicated by entran because the channel had had plenty of work in the previous month.

"It's as if Valzor, of all places, was some legendary paradise where hardship doesn't exist," he told Nalod as they shared a late dinner in the cafeteria. "Workaday, boring Valzor, where the only excitement is the annual flyer's conference. Who'd have thought?"

Nalod chuckled at his joke, then sobered. "Everyone knew that Clear Springs would be a hardship post at first, but this sounds far worse than anyone expected. Should you start pressuring District Controller Monruss to replace Hajene Rital with, say, three Third Order channels?"

Den considered, then shook his head. "No, I don't think so. There might not be much work, but what work there is, is best done by a First until the Sime Center can build a reliable base of donors. Besides, Rital wants to see it through."

After his transfer with Hajene Nalod the next morning, Den had a full six hours before he had to catch the train for the long ride back to Clear Springs. He purchased Rital's tea assortment and a few odds and ends for the other Clear Springs staff, then headed for the warehouse to check the progress his fellow aviation buffs had made on bringing his design for the 'Spirit of Valzor' to life.

Jannun wasn't there, but Eddina showed Den the pieces of strong, flexible spruce that he had selected for the outer edges of the wing. "There will be an interior framework of lightweight pine, too. It adds weight but without it, Jannun thinks we won't be able to hold the fabric taut enough to generate lift."

Den nodded thoughtful agreement. "It doesn't take much distortion to aim a wing down instead of up, especially if that catapult launcher generates a lot of push. Look at the pictures of Ancient aircraft. They had those little flaps for steering, so small in proportion to the wing that you'd think they'd do nothing at all." He traced the spiderweb of framing that had been sketched onto his design. "This is an excellent compromise."

Eddina nodded. "Jannun also wonders whether he should build the wing flat or design it with the ends lifted up at an angle, like some of the Ancient aircraft. That would be harder to build and possibly not as strong, but it might glide better."

"It's the launch I'm worried about. That's a lot of force being applied all at once." The Donor considered. "Can I get back to him on that? There are some books I found at the Clear Springs University library that might help me calculate the best compromise wing angle for lift at launch and stable gliding afterward. Jannun can decide how close he can get to that angle with the available materials. He knows the limits of wood better than I ever will."

"Does Clear Springs University have any books on how the Ancients built their lightweight engines for aircraft?" the renSime asked wistfully. "It would be worth making the train ride out, to learn that."

"Eddina, no!" the Donor protested. Just the thought of having his obsessive mechanic friend subjected to the abuse of Reverend Sinth's followers, who would see her as a mass murderer even though she'd never Killed, was enough to give him nightmares. "It's not just the train ride," he explained. "Things in Clear Springs are still much too unsettled for visitors."

Seeing her disappointment, he added, "I'll see if the university library has anything interesting on Ancient motors the next time I can get free."

Eddina nodded so reluctantly that Den changed the subject before she could protest again.

"Were you able to get the silk for the covering?"

Eddina shook her head. "The only bolts of silk we could find in Valzor were very narrow. It's expensive enough that it's mostly used for trim and accents, after all, and they don't require large swaths. There was also a huge variety of weights and surface textures because a lot of silk fabrics come with pre-embroidered patterns. I talked to my Aunt Lorna—she's a tailor—and she suggested a solution."

"What was that?" the Donor asked.

"Muslin," Eddina answered. "Plain, sturdy, tight-woven muslin, of the sort they use for making sheets. It comes in extra-wide lengths, which minimizes the number of seams, and we can get enough cloth in a single bolt. Aunt Lorna said that if we make the wing surface from new cloth and stretch it over the frame, we can wet it down and it will shrink for a really tight fit. Besides," the renSime grinned, "my helpful aunt happened to have a bolt of new muslin in the back of her shop that one of her sewers spilled tea on. After some sweet-talking by yours truly, she donated it to the cause." The renSime pointed proudly at a dust-covered bolt of off-white fabric standing in a corner. An irregular darker patch showed on one end.

Den sighed. "I can't fault your Aunt Lorna's logic. And I'm sure she knows fabric much better than I ever will. But muslin…it's just dull. Ordinary. It would have been beautiful, to see silk wings shimmering like a peacock in the sun."

"Falcons are duller than peacocks," Edinna pointed out, "but they fly a lot better."

Den's short visit to civilization made life in Clear Springs even more oppressive. Nothing had changed during his absence. The Collectorium yield continued to barely keep pace with the demands of the new Center for Technology. Between fifteen and thirty demonstrators chanted and sang on the front sidewalk every day, so as the weather warmed the Sime Center's staff was forced to choose between leaving windows open to relieve the stuffiness or closing them to gain something approaching peace and quiet.

There was, of course, no chance to return to the university library. Den pored over his personal library for clues and finally settled on a compromise. He wrote Jannun with a suggestion that the interior bracing be built first, on the slim hope that Den could get free before the main, structural pieces had to be cut.

An opportunity finally came at the end of the month, when the Sime Center admitted its second child in changeover. Unlike Nozella, Samit voluntarily sought Rital's help when he developed the symptoms of changeover. It turned out that he had lived the past five years in an orphanage run by the Conservative Congregation, since his father had been attacked and

Killed by a neighbor's berserker child. Samit wasn't willing to Kill, but neither was he willing to let the staff of the orphanage turn him over to Reverend Sinth. The clergyman openly boasted that he saw no reason to "coddle" evil Simes with a quick and relatively painless death. The Sime Center offered Samit a more palatable option.

The university's spring semester had ended the week before. Without student pranks and misdemeanors, the *Clear Springs Clarion* was experiencing a slow news week. An enterprising reporter noticed that the obituary submitted by the orphanage lacked the customary funeral details. When further investigation revealed that Samit had survived changeover, she wrote a story on it.

Hank Fredricks, the paper's owner and editor, used the story as filler on the page he normally reserved for university doings. Fredricks also used the incident as fodder for his weekly editorial, pointing out Reverend Sinth's inconsistency in expecting children in changeover to turn themselves over to him when he refused to reward them with the traditional quick shot to the head.

Reverend Sinth was predictably furious, both at the public criticism and at being deprived of what he viewed as his lawful prey. For a full week, he attended the demonstrations in front of the Sime Center, leading his followers in chanting, "Shoot the gut or shoot the eye, Scripture says all Simes must die!" He also persuaded a member of his congregation, Len Dusam, to run against Mayor Anne Kroag in the upcoming election on a platform of closing the Sime Center.

Legally, the land on which the Sime Center stood belonged to Nivet Territory until and unless both the New Washington Territory Senate and the Tecton decided otherwise. The city's mayor no longer had any say in the matter. However, if Dusam won and made an official request that the Sime Center be closed, it would permanently tarnish Rital's professional reputation and probably Den's, as well.

The Third Order Donor who was sent out to Escort Samit back to Valzor arrived the evening before Den was to give Rital transfer. As before, Rital insisted that Den take some time off while there was another Donor available. Thus, after Rital's post-transfer reaction had passed and the channel left to work on the Center's monthly report, Den gave into temptation. He changed into civilian clothes, wheedled a picnic lunch from Ref, grabbed his notebook, and set off.

He spent a satisfying few hours immersed in the aviation section of the university library. The array of forms that the Ancients had used for their aircraft wings was bewildering. The purpose of particular designs was often difficult to deduce from the reconstructed wreckage and surviving bits of writing. Because the Ancients had built the important parts of their engines out of steel, very little information could be gleaned from the remaining rust regarding the exact design of the propulsion systems that had been used with the various configurations.

Finally, Den decided to try a different approach. If the specific applications of Ancient aircraft designs were unknown, there were other flyers with shapes and sizes of known design, function, and propulsion strength. Following his own advice to the young test pilot, Mandle, he asked the librarian at the "REFERENCE" desk where books on bird flight might be found.

He was quickly able to eliminate the elliptical wing shapes found in songbirds like sparrows, thrushes, corvids, and finches. Such wings were highly maneuverable, but required bursts of energy to maintain flight. Without a lightweight, powerful engine to provide propulsion, maneuverability was irrelevant. The same argument eliminated the thin, medium-length, high-speed wings used by terns, falcons, and swifts. Long, narrow wings used by gulls for active soaring were closer to what he was after, but again required the ability to adjust quickly to small changes in wind and moisture.

The 'Spirit of Valzor' would be an un-powered glider with no steering capability. Its wings had to soar and glide, maintaining stability for as long as possible. The bird with the most comparable behavior was the turkey vulture, which seldom flapped its wings as it soared on thermals. Those wings were long and almost square, but the tips ended in feathers with visible slots between them. The wingtip of a glider could be tapered to provide a similar distribution of lift. The ornithology books also yielded the information that vultures soared while holding their wings angled upward.

Den left the library and settled under a maple tree to finalize his sketch and eat lunch. He ate his sandwich slowly, enjoying the warm day and remembering his own student days at Rialite.

He fed the last scraps of bread to a passing duck, tore a page out of his sketchbook, and began idly folding it into a dart-shaped flyer. His research that morning had explained how some of his favorite boyhood toys actually worked. He adjusted the wings of the dart carefully to the proper angle and launched it.

His concentration was interrupted by giggles. Startled, he looked up and saw that he had attracted an audience: two adolescent girls, twelve or thirteen years old. Neither had the solid muscle that most Gens acquired shortly after Establishment, but one had the small size and light bone structure that often characterized Simes as children.

Not that small size necessarily means that a child will be Sime, Den reminded himself. *Some just turn out to be skinny Gens.* Still, he couldn't help worrying that the girl would go through changeover out here, where even channels were considered less than human. His concern made him smile at her more warmly than he had intended.

Emboldened, she came a little closer.

"Hello," Den said. "Lovely day, isn't it, umm… What's your name?"

"Annie," she said shyly, twisting one light brown braid around a finger. "This is my friend, Rachel."

"Den," he introduced himself. "I'm pleased to meet you both."

"I've never seen a grown-up making flying darts before," Annie observed.

"I'm conducting research on wing design. The basic dart design is easy to fold, but it's pretty limited." He tore another page out of the sketchbook and began folding. "For instance, if you alter the design a little to put some of the weight back toward the center, you can get more stable flight because the nose isn't pulling it down."

He launched the modified dart and it flew a little farther then the first one. "See?"

Both girls nodded thoughtfully.

He pulled out another page and the girls sat down on either side of him to watch him fold it. "If you really want to go for distance, though, you have to use a wing that's proportionally longer and weighted toward the leading edge." This design flew half again as far as the others.

The girls cheered in honor of its performance.

"Aren't you a little young to be college students?" Den asked, as he got up to collect his flying darts.

"We go to the middle school," Rachel confirmed, shaking her dark curls. "We came with Annie's brother, Rob. He's meeting with some friends over at Wilson Hall," she pointed at one of the ivy-covered buildings that surrounded the lawn. "Then we're going to a movie."

"Quite intelligent of you," Den approved. "No one with any sense would stay outside in the afternoon heat."

"You're outside," Rachel pointed out.

"I never claimed to have any sense." The Donor grinned. "It's a requirement for anyone in my profession."

The pleasant conversation was interrupted by an outraged shout. "Annie, Rachel, get away from that man this instant! Can't you stay out of trouble for fifteen minutes?"

"But Rob, we were just watching him make flying darts," Annie whined in the universal matter of a younger sibling. "You never said we couldn't."

Rob, a solidly built young Gen with a strong resemblance to his sister, jerked the two girls to their feet and glared at Den. "Don't you try your Sime tricks on my sister," he snarled.

Den took an instant dislike to Rob.

"Haven't you got any sense at all, Annie?" Her brother shook her, not gently. "That's the man who always goes with the Sime to the power plant. The one who tricked Mom into buying him lunch out of the church fund. And now I find you talking to him! Do you want to turn into a Sime?"

Annie, who it seemed was Carla Lifton's daughter, covered her mouth in terror: terror of Den, not her brother. In an effort to calm her, Den said, "Come now. If associating with in-Territory citizens made children become Sime, I would never have Established."

Rob ignored the Donor. "Mother's going to be furious." He dragged the two girls away, continuing to scold them. Rachel never looked back, but Annie did, once. The look of horrified revulsion she gave Den showed quite clearly that she was prepared to believe anything her brother cared to say about him.

His holiday mood spoiled, Den threw the flying darts into the trash and returned to the Sime Center.

That evening, Rital announced that he was going to bake cinnamon rolls and recruited Den to help. By the time they had made a mess of Ref's kitchen, Den's spirits had lightened considerably. The kitchen was uncomfortably hot with the oven on, so they stepped outside while the rolls were baking. The full moon cast a silvery glow over the garden but a brisk breeze brought the smell of rain. Lightning flashed on the horizon and there was a distant grumble of thunder.

Suddenly, Rital stiffened, holding his arms out, laterals extended to zlin the garden. "There are four…no, five Gens out there. Non-donors. What the bloody shen do they think they're doing?"

He trotted off down a twisting dirt path. Den stumbled in his wake, unable to see the ground clearly because of the bushes on either side. The path ended on the strip of lawn bordering the vegetable garden. He could just make out the intruders on the far side, blithely trampling the knee-high corn.

"Hey!" he yelled in English. "Get out of the garden!"

"Damn!" one of them swore.

"It's the Sime," another yelled in panic as he caught sight of Rital. "Let's get out of here!"

They stampeded for the fence. Den clenched his fist in anger as one tripped over the peas, bringing down half a row. The culprit scrambled to his feet with a curse and sprinted after his friends, who were already swarming over the fence.

An Augmenting Sime could run faster than any Gen but Rital, running around the garden instead of through it, had a much greater distance to travel. He was still a good forty feet away as the last intruder reached the fence. Pounding along behind the channel, Den saw the Gen make a desperate leap, scramble halfway up the fence, miss his footing, and fall. There was a clearly audible *thunk* and he lay still, one arm held stiffly off the ground in the unmistakable sign of a head injury.

Rital staggered, grunting at the nageric shock, then recovered and knelt by the unconscious Gen's side, zlinning for injuries. The Gen's four comrades disappeared into the darkness.

"How…how badly is he hurt?" Den panted, sliding into position across from the channel.

"Not fatally," Rital answered, slipping a diagnostic hand under the limp head.

Den obligingly shifted a knee underneath to support it, allowing Rital's laterals to seek the injury.

"Hmm," the channel muttered abstractedly, "Skull's not broken, but he's bleeding underneath it. Got to get it stopped or he'll never wake up."

With a nod, Den slipped into working mode, blocking out extraneous nageric influences and their patient's pain, freeing the channel to concentrate on healing. Applying a nageric backfield to control bleeding was a routine functional that posed little challenge to a First Order channel of Rital's ability. However, the selyn field associated with a living brain was much more complex than that of, say, a muscle, and a wrong move could lead to nasty complications for both patient and channel. The procedure was also made more difficult by the insulation provided by their patient's skull. Judging by the behavior of its owner, Den suspected that this skull was thicker than average.

Den monitored Rital carefully, ready to stop his cousin at the first sign of distress. The Donor had no intention of letting the only channel in hundreds of miles take unnecessary chances to save the life of this out-Territory trespasser.

When Rital straightened a few minutes later, Den blinked in relief as he came out of his semi-trance.

"That should do it," Rital said with a sigh. "He'll come to in a few minutes."

"Good thing; the rain won't hold off much longer."

The wind was gusting stronger and thick clouds were blowing across the face of the moon.

"What brought them here on a night like this?" Den wondered aloud.

"If I had to venture a wild guess, I'd say vandalism," the channel said, nodding toward the bundles the intruders had dropped in their haste to escape. "At least, I can't think of any other reason for them to be carrying spray-paint and stencils, can you?"

"Terrific." Disgusted, Den looked down at their patient. Mentally, Den erased the dirt and bruises and then recognition came. "He's Rob Lifton, Carla Lifton's son and Mr. Duncan's grandson. I met him and his sister this afternoon." Briefly, Den described their confrontation. "So it may be my fault that Rob and his friends paid us this visit."

Rital shrugged. "Maybe. On the other hand, maybe not. Anti-Sime slogans have appeared all around Clear Springs, mostly on businesses owned by donors and other Sime Center sympathizers. They may just have decided that it was our turn tonight."

There was a soft moan as Rob's head shifted on Den's knee. Rital put one hand, tentacles carefully retracted, on the boy's chest to keep him from moving. "Lie still for a moment, Rob," he advised softly in English.

Rob's eyes fluttered and opened cautiously, unable to focus properly. There was a louder grumble of thunder and the Gen flinched, lifting one hand to his injured head. "What happened?" he mumbled. "My head is killing me."

"I know it hurts," Rital said with brisk sympathy. "You gave yourself a nasty concussion. Next time you try to climb a fence, watch where you put your feet."

"Fence…" Rob repeated vaguely. There was a pause while the idea percolated through his scrambled brain, then his eyes opened wide with alarm. The moon chose that moment to come out from behind the clouds, throwing enough light on the scene that the Gen was able to see them clearly. "No!" he cried, trying to sit up. "Let me go!"

"Take it easy, Rob," Den advised, helping Rital restrain their patient before he undid all of the channel's hard work. *What does he think we're going to do to him, anyway?*

"Let me go," Rob kept insisting. "You can't keep me here. I want to go home."

"You are in no condition to go anywhere," Rital said firmly, cutting through the incipient hysteria. "Den will drive you home in a little bit, when you've rested, but right now, we'd better get you inside before we all get soaked. No, don't try to stand up," he warned as the boy tried to get his feet untangled. "We'll carry you."

Rob stopped struggling and let them lift him. Den let Rital lead the way, trusting the Sime to steer him around any obstacles. They barely made it inside before the rain hit, a solid sheet of water beating into the ground.

They installed their patient in a well-insulated treatment room on the empty changeover ward, where his uncontrolled high field wouldn't bother the staff renSimes. Rob looked around at the strange equipment, trying to force his eyes to focus. Den handed the young Gen a glass of medicine and he sipped automatically, choked, spluttered, and spat it out. "What is this stuff?" he demanded suspiciously.

"Fosebine," Rital told him. "It tastes awful, I know, but it will help your headache."

"I don't want any of your Sime drugs," Rob insisted, putting the glass down on the bedside table. "You're not going to poison me."

Den had had enough. "If we wanted to harm you, we could easily have just left you out there," he pointed out acidly. "If Rital hadn't stopped the bleeding before it put more pressure on your brain, you'd likely have slipped into a coma, stopped breathing, and died. Now drink that down before your headache drives him nuts!"

Rob glared back, but the Donor was projecting enough honest outrage to overcome simple bravado. Resentfully, the boy raised the glass and drained it. "There," he said, flinging it spitefully at Den.

Rital intercepted the glass effortlessly with two handling tentacles and set it on a counter. "Good. Rest for a bit and then Den will drive you home."

"I want to go now."

"You're pretty demanding, aren't you?" Den remarked sourly. "Particularly for someone who sneaks around at night, trampling other peoples' corn and peas. If you had to take a shortcut through the garden, couldn't you have gone for the zucchini instead? I'm not driving you anywhere until the rain lets up."

An extra-loud crack of thunder made Rob flinch.

"That was close," Rital said. He went to the window and pulled back the curtains. "Look, the lights are out all over town. It must have hit one of the transformer stations."

"But…" Rob looked up at the steady light of the ceiling bulb. "How come the lights here…? What kind of magic are you using here, anyway?"

"The magic of modern science," Den said dryly. "That's a selyn-powered lamp running off selyn batteries. This *is* a Sime Center, after all. What did you think we'd use, electricity?"

A particularly strong gust of wind hit the window and it rattled loudly. Rital sighed. "It started out as such a quiet evening."

Channel and Donor stiffened simultaneously, staring at each other as they remembered. "The cinnamon rolls!" Rital groaned, forgetting to use English as he made an Augmented dash for the door.

"What's wrong?" Rob asked.

"That was about my breakfast, which because of your little prank, is probably charcoal by now," Den answered, making no attempt to hide his anger. "We were baking cinnamon rolls when Rital spotted you and your friends."

Rob stared at the Donor in confusion. "But cooking is something only women do," he said.

"I expect more men can put a meal on the table than you think, or there would be a lot more of us starving to death."

As the fosebine took effect, Rob grew more alert. Soon he was complaining again, insisting that he be taken home immediately, despite the loud pattering of raindrops against the windowpane. After the fourth request in ten minutes, Den ordered the boy to stay put and stepped out to the changeover ward's nursing station.

Rummaging through the desk drawers, he located the small collection of books kept handy for patients. These were mostly English translations of popular in-Territory works, which entertained while introducing new Simes to in-Territory society. Scanning the half-dozen titles, Den selected a novel he had enjoyed at Rob's age. It detailed the improbable adventures of Slem, a cabin boy on the *Far Horizon*, one of Householding Shaeldor's early clipper ships. Perhaps storms, shipwrecks, and hairsbreadth escapes from unfriendly natives would silence Rob's whining.

I t was a much-subdued Rob Lifton who sat next to Den in the passenger seat of the Sime Center's staff car an hour later. He mumbled directions, casting sideways glances at the Donor as he clutched the book, which he had asked to borrow. Finally, he blurted, "Here, in the first chapter... Is that what that Sime did to me?"

Den tried to remember the convoluted plot. The first chapter... "Do you mean the part where Slem knocks the spice jar off the top shelf and it shatters on the stove?"

"Yes. What the ship's channel is doing to the cook's injuries in this picture...is that what that Sime did to me?"

Den glanced at the engraving, considering the question for a moment. "Well, I haven't read that translation, but if it's close to the original then, yes, that's pretty much what Rital did."

"Why?"

Den was surprised to be asked such a question. "Because you would probably have died if he hadn't," he repeated as patiently as he could.

"Oh." This was obviously not the answer Rob had expected. After thinking it through for a moment, he asked, "How can you stand living with that Sime? It must be terrible."

There was so much wrong with Rob's assumptions that Den didn't know where to start, but in the forlorn hope of getting through his patient's misconceptions, he said, "First of all, Rital isn't 'that Sime,' he's my cousin. We grew up together and I'm very fond of him."

"You grew up with a Sime?"

"Well, he wasn't a Sime, back then," Den pointed out. "He was a child, just like me. Our parents died when we were young, so we were raised by our grandmother. She lived long enough to see us grown, at least."

Family was apparently a more comfortable topic, because Rob asked, "She's dead, then?"

"Yes," Den said shortly, making a turn. "She couldn't work anymore and for channels, that's a death sentence."

"Your grandmother was a Sime, too?"

Den couldn't tell whether Rob was surprised or offended. *Perhaps some of both.* "Yes, she was a channel. For that matter, so were both of my parents and Rital's father, although his mother was a Donor like me."

That revelation was shocking enough to win him almost a minute of peace and quiet, and when Rob resumed his interrogation it was on a different subject.

"How can you do it?"

"Do what?"

"Let that Sime take selyn from you. I know there's a law that says you have to in Sime Territory, but here they can't make you do it, if you object."

Den, who was still feeling the rush of post-transfer vitality, censored his first two replies and eased the car through an intersection before answering.

"What on Earth gave you the idea that I object to giving him transfer?"

Rob stared at Den. "But Reverend Sinth says it's horrible."

"Rob, do you think Reverend Sinth has ever worked for the Tecton as a technical-class Donor?"

"Of course not!"

"Or even donated selyn?"

"Um…no."

"Then how could he possibly know that it's horrible? I've been a technical-class Donor for eight years now and I wouldn't want another profession. Especially not if it meant giving up transfer."

Rob shook his head in disbelief. "But everybody knows it's true. I mean, just thinking about letting those slimy tentacles…ugh!" He shuddered.

"Rob, who is 'everybody?' And how can they 'know' anything about what it's like to do something they've never done? My grandmother once told me that there are two ways to find out what something's like: try it yourself or ask someone who has. Have you ever asked any of the people in town who *have* donated how they felt about it? Your grandfather, perhaps?"

Rob shook his head.

"Maybe you should."

CHAPTER 9
THE VOICE OF EXPERIENCE

Carla Lifton was not at home to receive her injured son. Rob and his friends had selected that evening to vandalize the Sime Center because their parents were attending Reverend Sinth's weekly organizational meeting, settling on the week's roster of demonstrators to harass the Sime Center. To Den's relief, Rob was just as interested in keeping the evening's adventures from his mother as the Donor was. As he left, the young man was already swearing his sister to secrecy and concocting a story about falling down the stairs to explain his injury.

A week after Den's transfer with Rital, Annie Lifton's friend, Rachel, went through changeover. Too ashamed and terrified to ask the Sime Center for help and no more eager than Samit to face Reverend Sinth's idea of a proper execution, she hid in the basement of her home until her tentacles broke free. Driven by instinct to attack the closest source of selyn, the girl Killed a sister before her parents succeeded in beating her to death. In dueling opinion pieces in the *Clear Springs Clarion*, Len Dusam, the anti-Sime candidate for mayor, cited the incident as an example of the immutably evil Sime nature, while Mayor Ann Kroag, running for re-election, pointed out that both girls would still be alive if their parents had called the Sime Center for help. The letters to the editor the next day ran three to one in favor of Dusam's position.

Den was with Rital that afternoon, halfheartedly going over the monthly no-progress report, when the phone rang. Since Den was closest, he answered, mumbling a distracted greeting.

"Den? This is Seena, in the Collectorium. We've got a virgin down here. He's displaying an admirable amount of courage and a less admirable lack of control. Could you get Rital down here to take care of him before he paces a hole in the waiting room carpet? Gati really likes that floral design."

"That bad?"

"Worse."

"We'll be right down." He passed on the message to Rital, adding, "If he's that scared, I'm going with you to Attend."

The channel zlinned the stubborn determination in his Donor's nager and gave in gracefully.

Den was astonished to see that their visitor was Rob Lifton. The young Gen was pacing back and forth in the waiting room, shoulders hunched with tension. His face had the greenish-grey tint of someone who has been through a prolonged ordeal—or was anticipating one. It clashed horribly with his yellow T-shirt.

Rital cleared his throat and Rob started, whirling to stare at them, wide-eyed. Den could feel the channel brace himself against the other Gen's fear and moved between them to cut the nageric projection. *Does Rob think Rital is going to attack him?* the Donor wondered.

"Hello, Rob," Den greeted their visitor, trying to provide a distraction. "How's your head?"

Rob relaxed infinitesimally. "Much better; the headaches are all gone."

"I'm glad to hear that. How is your sister Annie?"

"Pretty upset about what happened to her friend, Rachel. She thinks God punished Rachel for talking to you and she's afraid that she'll be next. Mother is still furious at her for not staying away from you and at me for not looking after her better. She's forbidden us to talk to anyone who even enters the Sime Center. Including Grandfather."

"I'm surprised to see you here, if your mother feels so strongly about it."

"Well…" Rob gave a weak but genuine grin. "I didn't exactly tell her I was coming and I climbed the back fence to avoid the demonstrators." Correctly interpreting Rital's alarmed look, he added, "I was more careful about it this time, really. And I wore a disguise." He gestured toward one of the chairs that held a freshly purchased, wide-brimmed hat, price tag still attached, and a pair of sunglasses.

"Well, now that you're here, what can we do for you?" Rital asked.

"I was wondering," Rob began tentatively. At Rital's sound of encouragement, he nodded toward Den. "He told me that your mother was a Gen and that she died when you were young?"

"She did," Rital agreed patiently.

"How did she die? Did a Sime Kill her?"

It was obvious that the question had been disturbing the young Gen for some time. Rital was kind: he didn't laugh as he answered, "No, of course not. Kills are much more rare in Sime Territory than they are here. My parents died in a train accident."

"A train accident?" For some reason, Rob seemed to find this reassuring.

The young Gen's tension returned as he focused on Den with a kind of desperate courage. "I've been thinking about what you said," he began tentatively. "About all those folks out there," he waved a hand toward the distant chanting of the demonstrators outside, "not knowing what they're talking about, and…"

He swallowed convulsively. "Everyone I know except Grandfather thinks they're right, but I can't take their word for it any longer. I've got to find out for myself."

Shen. "So you've come to donate," Den completed the thought for him. Rob nodded.

Den groaned silently. It was patently obvious even to Gen eyes that the boy was frightened enough to turn what should be a routine procedure into something fully as horrible as he expected it to be. However, if they turned Rob away, he would assume that they had something to hide and he would never trust anyone connected with a Sime Center again. It was a classic no-win situation.

The final decision was Rital's, since it was the channel who would have to experience Rob's fear if they proceeded. One look at his cousin gave Den the answer. No First Order channel with such a light workload would turn down a donation. With a sigh, Den resigned himself to assisting. *The kid's going to panic—shen, he already is—but if he's handled properly and we're very lucky, he won't actively fight Rital.*

"All right, then," Den said in as reassuring a tone as he could manage. "Why don't you come with us?"

Rob squared his shoulders and followed them down the short hall to the collecting room that Rital preferred. The young Gen surveyed the room in quick, nervous glances, taking in the cheerful yellow carpeting, the desk and chairs, and the transfer lounge along the far wall.

Den faded smoothly into the background as Rital sat down behind the desk and, tentacles carefully sheathed, gestured for Rob to take the visitor's chair. Rob perched on the very edge of the chair and Den inched a little closer to the channel.

Rob watched closely as Rital fished in a drawer and pulled out the Tecton's substantial medical history form. Ignoring the scrutiny, Rital began collecting the endless list of information—demographic, biographic, and medical—required of all new general-class donors. By the time it had become excruciatingly clear that Rob was a normal, healthy young Gen, their client was sitting back comfortably in his chair and the wild look in his eyes had been partially replaced by the glazed boredom common to victims of the Tecton's lust for documentation.

In the same calm, matter-of-fact tone, Rital said, "Rob, donating selyn isn't very exciting or complicated. You give me your hands, I wrap my tentacles around your arms—no, they aren't slimy—we touch lips to complete the contact, I collect a trickle of selyn, and we're done. The whole thing takes less than a minute and you won't feel anything at all." The channel spread his hands, tentacles still carefully retracted, and gave an apologetic shrug. "I hope it doesn't disappoint your sense of adventure."

We should be so lucky, Den thought.

"Wh-what about afterward?" Rob asked. "Will people be able to tell I've been in here?"

"A Sime could tell, of course, because you won't be carrying as much selyn," Rital answered. "But as long as you're not seen leaving, I don't think your family, friends, or neighbors will know unless you tell them."

"So it won't change me at all?" Hope and fear warred in Rob's expression and Den wondered just what sort of contradictory information the young Gen had been provided by Reverend Sinth and his followers.

"Only in the way any new experience changes your perspective." The channel gave a reassuring smile. "Are you ready to give it a try?"

"I guess."

"All right, then, why don't you lie down on the lounge over there? Standing works just as well, of course, but we might as well be comfortable."

Rob moved to the transfer lounge and lay down as directed. He let Rital sit next to him, not quite drawing away, but not accepting, either.

"I know you're nervous," Rital said soothingly. "That's very common for Gens who didn't grow up among Simes; I'd be surprised if you weren't a little anxious. I promise I won't hurt you, no matter how frightened you are, but it's your decision." He held out his hands, tentacles still retracted, and waited.

Rob stared at them for a long moment. "I guess if I never try, I'll never find out what it's like, will I?" he remarked with the ghost of a smile. He hesitated a moment more, visibly gathering courage, and then timidly reached for the channel's hands.

Den had to admire both Rob's nerve and the skill Rital had developed at seducing out-Territory Gens, but he was pretty sure that neither would be sufficient. Laying a hand on Rital's neck, the Donor offered a steady support. He felt the channel's field mesh with his, accepting the help, and then Rital deftly completed the transfer contact, so quickly and smoothly that it was done before Rob could react.

The young Gen stiffened, the whites of his eyes showing clearly. For one long moment, Den thought the boy's nerve would hold, but then he began to struggle.

While consent was an absolute requirement before any ethical channel would dream of taking selyn from a Gen, cooperation was optional. Transfer lounges were designed to be comfortable to lie on, but they did not provide much leverage to a person trying to get up without using his arms.

Rital hardly had to Augment to keep the young Gen immobilized. Rob soon discovered that he was not going to escape, which fed his panic even more.

Because the Gen was locked tight against him, it took the channel half again as long as usual to finish the donation. When he had drained the shallowest, GN-3 level, Rital dismantled the contact, carefully sheathing his vulnerable laterals before he let his handling tentacles loosen their grip. Rob stopped struggling as he was released, sanity slowly returning to his eyes and with it, embarrassment.

"That's it," the channel told him. "You're all done. You're low field now."

"I'm…sorry," Rob said awkwardly. "I don't know why…"

Rital murmured something reassuring and stood. Their young client scrambled off the transfer lounge as soon as the way was clear. For a moment, Den thought Rob would bolt from the room, but he calmed as Rital did nothing more alarming than return to his seat behind the desk. The channel scribbled the relevant notations on the form with less than his usual briskness.

He's exhausted, Den deduced, *and no wonder!* The Donor neatly appropriated the file when his cousin finished and herded Rob toward the door, leaving the channel to enjoy some nageric quiet.

As they walked back to the waiting room, Rob admitted, "You were right, but so was my mother. I didn't feel anything happening, but…" He shuddered convulsively, revulsion twisting his face. "Still, I'm glad I came."

That makes one of us, Den thought, leaving Rob and the form in Seena's capable hands as he hurried back to Rital. The channel was slumped over the desk, massaging the back of his neck with all eight handling tentacles. Den pushed them aside and substituted his own hands, reaching out with his nager to undo the havoc Rob's terror had wrought.

Rital gave a small moan of relief. "Thanks," he said. "That was not fun." As his knotted neck muscles began to relax, he added, "I've never had a Gen panic on me like that. Not during a routine donation. I think he actually believed I was Killing him."

Like many technical-class Donors who had no reason to fear attack by any Sime, Den had little empathy for Gens who feared even a simple donation to a competent channel. "The kid had no business coming here, if he couldn't behave himself."

Rital, who could not take a donation without experiencing the emotions of the donor fully, was more sympathetic. "Now, Den, that's not fair," he chided. "First you say those frightened Gens should come in and find out what we're about and then as soon as one does, you want to kick him back out again. Besides, from what he said, you were the one who suggested he donate."

"I most certainly did not!" Den finished with his work and moved around to perch on a corner of the desk. "I just said that his mother and the other non-donors in her church weren't a reliable source of information about it. I thought he'd ask his grandfather, Mr. Duncan, or even go to the library and look it up. If I'd thought he was the type to go for experimentation, I'd have kept quiet."

"But you were right. How could Rob ever learn, without trying?"

"Learn?" Den scowled. "He hasn't learned a thing and he managed to give you both a very hard time while he was doing it. Maybe now that his curiosity is satisfied, he'll have the sense to stay away with the rest of the Simephobes." He gestured toward the front of the building.

Rital's eyes twinkled. "Your parents used to tell me, 'Never underestimate a Gen.' I think Rob has changed his mind about Simes…a little bit. That's really all we can ask for, at this point. Even our more vocal opponents can learn a little bit, but not unless we're willing to teach them."

"Oh, they're learning so much about Simes, standing out there waving signs with hate messages at you," Den said sarcastically. "There are more of them out there today than there were the first day they decided to occupy our sidewalk."

"I know. Most of today's demonstrators were bussed in from a sister Conservative Congregation church in Oak Ridge." Rital grinned mischievously. "They used to be able to harass us full time using locals only. Think about it."

The next few weeks passed quietly. There were no more changeovers in the town and five new Gens joined the Sime Center's too-short roster of donors. Fortunately, none was quite as panic-stricken as Rob had been.

With the design for the 'Spirit of Valzor' completed and construction in progress, Den turned his attention to a more long-term goal: securing a reliable source of enough industrial selyn to justify ongoing research on lightweight engines and batteries to power them. That meant making the Clear Springs Sime Center less of an isolated outpost and more a part of the community. As a first step, he sent a letter offering his services as a speaker on the services provided by the Sime Center to those of the university's service clubs that were not instantly identifiable as religious, but received no reply.

Rital was still suffering an occasional bout of entran and Den began to seriously consider recommending to the District Controller that his cousin be replaced. He knew Rital was as committed to the challenge of Clear

Springs as Den was to redeveloping powered flight, but the Donor had no intention of letting the channel ruin his health over it.

As election day approached, the protests outside the Sime Center grew noisier. After a particularly bad day, Den was in his office, skimming through the *Clarion's* listing of daily events in search of distraction when a notice caught his eye:

> 8:00, 155 Norvan Hall: Public Debate. Mayor Ann Kroag and challenger Len Dusam will discuss whether the Sime Center should remain in Clear Springs, followed by comments and questions from the audience. Come and let us hear your views! Sponsored by Students for a Sime-Free City, the Friends of Len Dusam, and the Conservative Congregation Committee for Political Action.

Den read and reread the sponsors' names, his anger growing with each repetition. He had no illusions about what would happen: before the evening was over, the town would be officially on record as strongly in favor of closing the Sime Center. *And won't Controller Monruss be happy about that!* The more the Donor thought about it, the more unfair it seemed. *They're not content anymore with just making Rital miserable while he's here. No, now they want to put a permanent blot on his record!*

The Tecton forbade its channels and Donors to meddle in out-Territory politics without specific permission, which was usually granted only to trained diplomats. But suddenly, staying out of trouble with the Tecton was unimportant to Den if it meant letting Carla Lifton and her friends speak unopposed.

I won't let them get away with it!

Den glanced at the clock hanging on the wall. It was 7:15. He threw a light sweater on over his uniform, told Seena he was going out for a while, and slipped out the back door. It wasn't until he reached campus that he realized he had no idea where Norvan Hall might be. After failing to find a name on the three closest buildings, he cornered a passing student and asked for directions.

"Norvan Hall?" she repeated. "Are you going to that debate thing?"

Den nodded.

"So am I. It's this way." She led the way down a brick path. "I'm Marcy Ingleston, by the way."

"Den Milnan. Do you belong to one of the sponsoring organizations?" the Donor asked as he followed her. He didn't recognize her, either as a donor or from the demonstrations in front of the Sime Center.

"Those fanatics?" she asked scornfully, tossing her long hair back over her shoulders. "No, I have better things to do. Besides, I don't particularly care if the Sime Center goes or stays."

"Then why are you going to tonight's debate?"

She shrugged. "I'm tired of studying and the poetry slam at Sudworks Brewery doesn't get going until 9:30. So why not?"

By the time they arrived at their goal, Den had learned that Marcy was an English major and aspiring poet, that she found her best inspiration going on hikes with her friends, and that she was dreading her physics midterm because vector mechanics was incomprehensible gibberish.

Norvan Hall, it turned out, housed the chemistry department and room 155 was a large lecture hall. Den lost track of Marcy as he looked around. Under the periodic table at the front, several frantic students were trying to hook up two microphones, one on the lectern for the speakers and one at the bottom of the center aisle, for audience members.

About three quarters of the seats were occupied with a mix of students and townspeople. At least a third were carrying anti-Sime posters or wearing "Tecton go home!" buttons. (Students for a Sime-Free City was selling them from a table at the entrance.) Almost all of the people who regularly demonstrated in front of the Sime Center were present, but Den was gratified to recognize a few regular donors as well.

Den wandered down the main aisle in search of a seat. Hearing a cheerful shout of, "Den! Over here!" he turned and discovered Marcy Ingleston waving from a group of informally dressed students who were not wearing buttons.

He was quickly introduced to a dozen or so students. They waved casually at him, either not recognizing his Tecton uniform or not caring.

When Den sat down, there was a crinkling of paper from underneath him. He investigated and discovered one of Students for a Sime-Free City's flyers, with a list of businesses owned by "Simelovers," and a familiar pamphlet. A glance around showed that all the seats were similarly decorated, ensuring that every person attending would have copies.

The Sime on the pamphlet still looked like an octopus convention.

The moderator, a formidable older woman, took the microphone to explain the rules. Each speaker was to make a fifteen-minute speech, followed by five-minute rebuttals. Members of the audience would then be allowed comments or questions, no more than three minutes, "...so long as they are relevant and politely phrased—this is a schoolroom, not a schoolyard."

The first candidate, challenger Len Dusam, took the microphone to a spatter of applause which was considered by Gens a polite greeting. Dusam was a balding, portly gentleman dressed in a suit far too heavy for the warm evening. He was obviously ill at ease as he adjusted the microphone.

Wiping beads of perspiration from his forehead with a wrinkled handkerchief, he began, "I'm not a big talker, but I'd like to tell you why you should vote for me, instead of putting Ann Kroag back in office and letting her do even more damage than she has already."

Dusam's critical review of Ann Kroag's last term added up to a blanket condemnation of her for allowing Simes into Clear Springs. He wasn't a terribly inspiring or even coherent speaker, but many of his statements generated murmurs of approval from the audience.

"On behalf of all of us here," he concluded, "I'm going ask my opponent just one question. Are you going to send those Simes back where they belong, or are we going to have to elect someone else who will … Sosu Kroag?"

A chorus of cheers, sneers, whistles, and hallelujahs applauded his sarcasm. Like Dusam, they seemed ignorant of the meaning of the Simelan honorific given to technical-class Donors, or of the respect that it implied.

Ann Kroag was not a large woman, but to Den's eye she had more poise and presence than Dusam and the moderator combined. She adjusted the microphone and suggested in a pleasant voice, "Perhaps it would be easier if you addressed me as 'Mayor Kroag.'"

Another chorus of applause erupted, especially from the women in the audience, this time sans hallelujahs. When Kroag held up her hand for quiet, everyone settled down to listen.

"Folks, Mr. Dusam has asked me to tell you why I support having a Sime Center in Clear Springs. I'll admit that when the university first approached me, I wasn't too happy about it. The other members of the City Council and I did a lot of research, and we concluded that the impact would be more positive than negative. The past four months have already justified our action."

There was a murmur of discussion, about evenly split between supporters and detractors.

"For one thing, everyone's electric bill has gone down because the power company is worried that selyn power might prove to be a cheap and reliable alternative. I don't know about you, but I'd rather not go back to last year's prices."

There was a swelling sense of agreement until a heckler yelled, "I'd rather have higher bills than be attacked by Simes!"

"And that brings me to my second point," Kroag continued smoothly. "There have been several dozen changeovers in Clear Springs since the Sime Center opened. The parents of most of those children did not call the Sime Center for help. Their children all died and three of them Killed friends, neighbors, or family members. However, neither of the two children in changeover who were turned over to the Sime Center Killed a Gen, and both are alive and well.

"Mr. Joziah Duncan, whom some of you know, tells me that it wasn't easy to see his granddaughter, Nozella, leave for a life among strangers, but he's very glad she's still alive—and didn't Kill anyone. He got a letter from her yesterday." She pulled an envelope from her pocket and showed it to the audience. "Nozella Duncan is happy, healthy, and it looks like she's going to be a sliderail engineer just like she always wanted. Can Rachel Grieve's parents say as much about their daughter? Either one of them?" Her voice firmed with utter conviction. "Having a Sime Center to take care of changeover victims has saved lives, not endangered them. And I, for one, think saving lives is a goal worth working for!"

Marcy and her friends applauded loudly and all but Dusam's most hard-core supporters joined in, in spite of Kroag's odd characterization of children who were going through the normal process of maturing into adult Simes as "victims." With an eye toward regaining his lost support, Dusam appealed to his listeners' fears in his rebuttal. He was describing the excruciating death of his wife at the tentacles of their own son when the moderator gave him the one-minute warning.

"I'm sure we all agree that the Sime Center has done good things for those children who turn Sime," he conceded. "However, I'm more worried about the Gens of this city! I don't care how they try to sanitize it, how innocent they make it sound, they are doing their level best to lure my friends and neighbors into their clutches. Friends, I don't know about you but somehow, a Sime's clutches doesn't strike me as a very safe place to be!"

It was nonsense, of course, but effective nonsense.

"A Sime's clutches is exactly where a changeover victim belongs!" Kroag retorted. Over the offended gasps she continued, "Dozens of children have died unnecessarily since the Sime Center opened, because people like you refused to take them to the Sime Center. Mr. Dusam, if the Sime Center had been here at the time, both your wife and your son would be alive today—but *only* if you had taken your son there. Lives are being wasted because of fear and prejudice. You're concerned about the people who choose to donate selyn? Look at the record: there are no reports of injuries during donations, in Clear Springs or elsewhere. None of the people who have visited the Sime Center since it opened have complained of mistreatment. Even if you don't want to donate selyn yourself, how can you forfeit to sheer ignorance the precious lives of your own family?" By the time she finished, even some of the people wearing 'Dusam for Mayor' buttons were nodding in agreement and Dusam was a very worried man.

But the first audience member to speak was Reverend Sinth, his soulfully handsome face invoking the otherworldly air of a mystic—or a fanatic. He was wearing his floor-length black robe and carrying a sign with "Sime-free Zone" stenciled on it.

"This should be entertaining," Marcy snickered in Den's ear.

"The good Reverend doesn't look happy at all," the Donor agreed, leaning forward in his chair.

"Very pretty speech, *Mayor* Kroag," Sinth drawled in a deep, resonant voice with the power to fill the lecture hall even without benefit of microphone. He lingered sarcastically over the title. "However," he continued, "just because no one's been physically hurt yet, that doesn't mean it won't happen. However, you have completely missed the point. For now the Simes may not harm your bodies, but what about your souls? I speak for most of the people in this town when I say that I don't want anyone in Clear Springs to lose themselves to the enemy! Those monsters are seducing you with what? Lower power bills?! They are ask you to pay for new toys with your very life force! Your souls! The souls of your children! Miz Kroag, your words defile the memory of all the sacred martyrs who have died at the tentacles of monster Simes."

The combination of voice and appearance gave Sinth enough charisma to rival the Sectuib of Householding Zeor, Den thought enviously. He wondered how he and Rital, neither of whom was a particularly compelling speaker, could hope to prevail against such a riveting performer.

The anti-Sime faction was out in force and many lined up to speak. They had even imported speakers from surrounding communities; these were easily identified because everyone who could, prefaced his or her speech by claiming to be "a Clear Springs resident and registered voter" did so without hearing objections. By 9:00, only two speakers had expressed support for the Sime Center: one businessman who liked his lower utility bill, so long as he "didn't have to deal with the snakes personally," and a student who depended on the income from donating to supplement her financial aid. The presentations ran two to one in favor of asking the Tecton to close the Sime Center.

To Den's utter surprise, many of the most virulently anti-Sime speakers—those carrying "Don't be a Victim!" pamphlets and identifying themselves as members of Reverend Sinth's Conservative Congregation—expressed concern about the welfare of the Sime Center's Gens. Apparently, it was an article of faith among them that Rital forcibly confined the Gen staff to the Sime Center's grounds to keep them from running away to join the Conservative Congregation. This spiritual deprivation was supposed to make the eventual confinement of in-Territory Gens into Pens easier.

After five speakers in a row had accused Rital of enslaving him for purposes of homicide, Den had had enough, Tecton policy or no Tecton policy. He took off his sweater and joined the considerably shortened line.

By the time he reached the microphone, seven anti-Sime speakers later, he was coldly furious.

"I am Sosu Den Milnan, Hajene Madz's Donor," he began, winning astonished stares from those members of the audience who hadn't recognized his uniform. "I am…deeply moved…by the expressions of concern for my well-being that I have been hearing from the members of the Conservative Congregation tonight. However, if they had come to me with their concerns, I could have saved them some sleepless nights. No one forced me to become a Donor. No one is forcing me to continue. I enjoy my job, or I'd find another.

"Many of you have also expressed concern about what exactly is happening inside the Sime Center, particularly to those people who come to donate selyn. My advice to anyone who wants to separate truth from fiction is to ask the people who know: the ones who have actually donated. For your convenience, Reverend Sinth's congregation and Students for a Sime-Free City have placed a list of such experts on your chair." Den held up the flyer and got a laugh.

"If you don't like second-hand information, come and see what's going on for yourself," Den continued. "We'll be happy to show you around and explain exactly what we're doing. But *don't* rely on the ignorant ravings of a fanatic who doesn't even know how many tentacles a Sime has!" Den waved the pamphlet with its octopoid Sime, ignoring the glares from Reverend Sinth's congregation.

Surrendering the microphone and suddenly remembering how much he hated public speaking, a weak-kneed Den sat down in the closest empty seat, surprised to hear applause. "Nice speech, son," a familiar voice praised from the seat behind him. It was Mr. Duncan, Carla Lifton's father. "It's about time you folks stood up for yourselves."

The remaining anti-Sime speakers moderated their language, accusing Rital of seduction, not enslavement, and they were not as well received as the earlier speakers.

CHAPTER 10

FORESEEABLE CONSEQUENCES

Rital was horrified when he learned of Den's adventure, of course.

"How could you do such a thing?" he demanded, bursting into his cousin's room before breakfast. "Are you *trying* to get the Clear Springs City Council to ask the Tecton to close down the Sime Center? Why did you break the treaty we spent so much time working out? You know that we aren't supposed to take sides in out-Territory politics."

"That's a little hard to do when our presence is the major political issue in this town," Den pointed out, calmly pulling on his trousers. "Until now, Reverend Sinth has been controlling the conversation. He can accuse us of auctioning off donors as Choice Kills if he wants—and he's come close—because nobody is willing to call a religious leader a liar."

"Did it never occur to you that there is a good reason I haven't called him on that in public?" the channel demanded. "Like it or not, Reverend Sinth is a citizen of Clear Springs. He and the other citizens of this town have a right to decide who their next mayor will be by themselves, without our help."

"I'm just as aware of the principle of non-interference as you are, Rital," Den retorted, letting some of his own anger show. He pulled on the less worn of his two clean uniform shirts. "I didn't say a thing about either candidate for mayor. All I did was point out that anyone who is interested in finding out what the Sime Center is doing, particularly to our donors, should get their information from primary sources."

"You said a little more than that," the channel said, shaking the morning's *Clarion* under his cousin's nose while resting an accusatory handling tentacle on the pertinent paragraph. "Something about the 'ignorant ravings of a fanatic who doesn't know how many tentacles a Sime has,' I believe?"

Den squirmed uncomfortably. The words sounded unprofessional this morning, although last night he had been proud of them. "Well, Sinth *doesn't* know how many tentacles a Sime has, judging by his favorite pamphlet. Of all the false things he's said or implied about us, that's the easiest to disprove. Once people start doubting him, his influence will wane."

"Unless his followers rally to defend him instead," Rital pointed out. "They won't appreciate your interference and with the situation so explosive, they just might retaliate."

Den knew that much of his cousin's paranoia was due to approaching Need, but he couldn't help being annoyed by it. "Rital, the folks who don't want us here can hardly dislike us more than they do already," he asserted, struggling with a stubborn button until it yielded.

"Yes, but the real question is, what are they going to do about their dislike?" The channel paced back and forth from window to door. "Neither of us has the training to deal with this sort of opposition. We really ought to have had a diplomat on staff from the start, to handle just this sort of situation. Unfortunately, Monruss claims the Diplomatic Corps is still tied up with that Cordona mess on the Southern Continent. Apparently, the negotiations have been trickier than anyone thought and they won't be able to send anyone out here for months." He offered a pleading look. "Will you at least *try* not to get us lynched by an angry mob or expelled from the city borders until then?"

"I'll be good," Den promised, gripping the channel's shoulder in reassurance. "I honestly don't think what I said last night is going to provoke retaliation beyond what they're already doing." He grinned. "Who knows? I might have reached some people who still haven't made up their minds about us. So stop being a spoilsport and come have some breakfast."

"I'm not hungry," Rital objected, but he followed the Donor to the cafeteria.

Over the next week, the demonstrations outside the Sime Center grew larger and noisier. "Mayor Kroag has gone rogue" was added to Save Our Kids' rotating roster of chants, and "Elect Len Dusam for Mayor" campaign buttons were much in evidence. In spite of this, over a dozen new Gens braved the barricade to donate, leaving the Sime Center with a small selyn surplus even after the Center for Technology's electrical generator was converted to run off the selyn batteries.

This was a mixed blessing, as far as Den was concerned. The extra work prevented Rital from having any more entran attacks but as their next transfer date approached, taking first donations from nervous Gens was taking a toll on the channel. Den left standing orders to be informed whenever a new general-class donor came in, so that he could bring the channel's intil factor, the psychological component of Need, down to an acceptable level afterward.

Still, the polls showed that Mayor Kroag had caught up to Len Dusam. A few people even nodded a surreptitious greeting when Den and Rital walked across town on their way to the university. Even Rital was less convinced of impending disaster, and that made Den happy.

Two days after Den's transfer with Rital, the Donor sought out a quiet corner in the garden in which to pour over Rick Toeffen's "biography" for clues to the performance of his craft's engine. He found the part in the first chapter where Toeffen first spotted his opponent on the horizon. He had remembered correctly: the passage clearly stated the lapsed time from that first sighting until the two flyers were close enough to make the first pass of their joust. He backtracked several paragraphs and found an estimate for the flyer's altitude: 15,000 feet. That put the flyer well into the clouds.

From such a height, it would be possible to see a great distance. More calculations gave him a range of distances from which Toeffen could spot his opponent. Dividing by the stated time to first pass gave him a speed four times faster than the fastest sliderail train on record.

Den rechecked the numbers several times, but they all pointed to an extremely powerful engine, one that in modern times would be far too large to fit on a flyer even without the boxcar full of selyn batteries it would take to power it. He struggled with the unwelcome conclusion that powered flight really couldn't be re-invented, not even on an experimental basis, without securing a reliable excess of industrial selyn. Nothing else would justify developing the technology for the Tecton, which had as its first duty to supply the world's renSimes with a reliable source of selyn.

So, I've got to make Clear Springs accept the Sime Center.

Just then Rital stormed up, waving an official-looking bundle of papers.

"This is your fault, you brainless escapee from a Pen! Everything was going along well and then you had to meddle!"

"What's the matter?" Den asked, unimpressed with his cousin's histrionics.

"This is the matter!" Rital thrust the papers into the Gen's hands. "Your prank the other day has backfired. If you hadn't gone on about the 'ignorant ravings' of a prominent and respected clergyman, the members of his congregation couldn't have convinced the City Council to vote against us!"

Den smoothed the wrinkled pages. Under the city letterhead was neatly typed:

Hajene Madz:

Due to the untrue and offensive religious slurs uttered by a member of your staff at a recent political debate, the city council has passed the attached ordinance by a vote of three to two. We request your immediate compliance.

Jess Rebens, City Clerk

Den read the text of the ordinance in disbelief. Apparently, Reverend Sinth and his followers had not appreciated being faced with incontrovertible evidence that Rital was not holding the Sime Center's Gen staff prisoner—so they had convinced the City Council to make the outrageous accusation true?! Effective immediately, no Sime Center employee was to leave the grounds except for an emergency or for the purpose of leaving the city, permanently.

"What are we going to do?" Rital paced back and forth, tentacles lashing in agitation.

"Hope Mayor Kroag and her supporters running for council seats win the election?" Den suggested lamely.

Rital's lip curled in disgust. "Oh, go back to your book. If the Clear Springs Sime Center closes, that means you can go back to Valzor and putter around building toy flyers and dreaming about the Ancients. Of course, our failure means there won't be any local selyn surplus, so nobody will be able to build a working flyer." The channel paused to zlin his point drive home. "Sometimes I wonder about you, Den. I know you don't think much of the local Gens, but you might show some consideration for those of us who have to deal with them! I swear, if you don't follow the rules to the letter from now on—"

"That's it!" Den interrupted.

"What's what?"

"'Follow the rules to the letter'… They'll repeal this nonsense in no time!" Den grinned at his cousin's confusion. "All we have to do is apologize and follow their orders, exactly as written." He pointed to the relevant clause. "See, they don't want us to leave the Sime Center except for an emergency, which this section defines as a life-threatening situation, like chasing down a child in changeover who might Kill somebody. They forgot to make an exception for nonessential services like," he drew it out, "say… refilling the batteries at their vaunted Center for Technology. Which has just finished converting its electrical generator to run off selyn."

"Go on strike?" Rital considered the implications. "There hasn't been a breath of wind all week. Unless it really starts blowing, the Center for Technology will be out of power by tomorrow night. But why punish the university, which has generally supported the Sime Center, for the mistake of three city councilors?"

"To me, the university's attitude toward the Sime Center looks more like benign neglect than actual support," Den retorted. "It's high time that the university with their shiny new Center for Technology learned exactly how integral the Sime Center is to their flagship department. Besides, if you were a councilman running for re-election, would you want the blame for a failure of basic utilities to the city's biggest employer? Particularly if the local newspaper doesn't let you get away with placing the blame elsewhere? I've read Hank Fredricks' editorials. He's as fed up with Reverend Sinth's fanaticism as we are." Den gave his cousin a wicked grin. "Let me do the talking and those poor idiots won't know what hit them."

It took some persuasion, but once convinced, Rital entered into the spirit of the thing. Early the following afternoon Hap Enstun, the Center for Technology's facilities manager, called to find out why Rital had not appeared to recharge the selyn batteries as planned and was most upset when Den apologetically read him the new ordinance. A staff reporter for the *Clarion* called shortly thereafter and Rital gleefully listened in on the extension as Den, dripping innocence, carefully explained that the City Council had passed an ordinance forbidding the channel to leave the Sime Center for such routine, non-emergency tasks which, as law-abiding visitors to the community, they were bound to obey.

The three council members who had voted for the ordinance called in the early evening. They threatened and cajoled, but Den stood firm. Rital would be happy to refill the selyn batteries, but not until the ordinance was repealed.

At eight, the power went out at the Center for Technology, bringing to an abrupt end a tour of the facility by six wealthy alumni expected to contribute substantial financial support to its endeavors. The university's chancellor was understandably furious at the humiliation. Twenty minutes later, a messenger arrived to inform Den and Rital that the ordinance had been repealed unanimously during an emergency session of the city council. Half an hour later, Rital had refilled the batteries and the Center for Technology was back in business.

The incident was covered by the *Clarion* in terms even more favorable than Den had dared to hope, including a scathing editorial accusing the three errant council members who had voted for the ordinance of "putting personal prejudice and political partisanship before the interests of the people of Clear Springs" and reminding readers that if the anti-Sime faction had its way, the Center for Technology and all its essential research projects would be at the mercy of the wind for however long it took to locate, purchase, and install a steam generator—at considerable cost to all concerned.

The next day's poll showed Mayor Ann Kroag pulling ahead of her opponent for the first time. The double setback provoked Reverend Sinth and his followers to a new level of savage determination as they turned their fury on any Gen who dared to defy their barricade.

For the first time since the Sime Center opened, Carla Lifton's father, Mr. Duncan, failed to appear on schedule for his donation. Also absent were the friends who usually came with him. Rital worried that the elderly Gens might be victims of the influenza outbreak reported in the *Clarion*. Den worried that the lack of work would give Rital more entran attacks.

That afternoon, Alyce, the groundskeeper, announced that the corn was ready to harvest. Den volunteered to take the afternoon shift as Collectorium receptionist to free Seena to help Alyce and Ref put up the agricultural bounty for the winter. For lack of anything better to do, the Donor spent the time perfecting a talk on the Sime Center's services. There was always the outside chance that one of the organizations he had contacted would change its mind and agree to hear it.

An hour into the shift, Den stepped outside for a breath of fresh air. A sudden spike in the volume of the protestors' chanting caught his attention in time to watch two young women in casual student dress try to cross the picket line. The response was both immediate and violent. The mob of demonstrators closed around the students and began to grab at the young women, sending them staggering from side to side.

"Stop that!" Den shouted, sprinting down the sidewalk toward the altercation. He was twenty feet away, still shouting, when the students saw him approaching. Encouraged, they struggled harder to push their way through. Den had time to recognize Marcy Ingleston and her friend Silva when disaster struck—literally.

The large man with turmeric-colored hair who customarily lurked on the outskirts of the demonstration looked around for what was encouraging the young women and spotted Den. An expression of uncontrolled fury crossed his face and his knuckles turned white around the handle of his sign reading, "This Sime Center is CLOSED!" As the students broke through, the man charged them, bringing his sign down on Marcy's shoulder with the full strength of his rage.

The cardboard crumpled on impact, but the handle was a sturdy piece of oak. The improvised club hit with a sickening thud and Marcy went down with a shrill scream.

At the sound, the mob drew back. Many of the demonstrators looked uncertain, even embarrassed. They did not object when Den moved in to examine the damage to Marcy's shoulder, or when he and Silva helped her slowly down the path into the Sime Center door.

"You've got a broken collar bone, Marcy," Rital announced, when he had completed his examination. "And both of you have an interesting collection of bumps and bruises, as well."

"They'll pay for this!" Marcy vowed, as Sylva nodded in agreement.

The next day's *Clarion* covered the incident in some detail, including a strongly worded editorial calling for police supervision of the demonstrations in front of the Sime Center to prevent further injuries. Well-expressed letters from students and faculty completed the editorial page.

It made no difference. Police Chief Tains, who spent his days off pounding the pavement in front of the Sime Center, flatly refused to act on Marcy's complaint, arrest her assailant, or assign an officer to prevent further injuries.

"The people who demonstrate outside of the Sime Center are law-abiding, upstanding citizens," claimed his official statement. "I will not interfere with the free expression of their beliefs. As for the alleged assault on a student seeking to sell selyn to the Simes, it is arguable whether the Clear Springs police even have jurisdiction because by Miz Ingleston's own account, at the time of the alleged incident she was in transition from the public sidewalk to the land claimed by the Sime Center, which is legally part of Sime Territory."

Needless to say, Tains made no effort to determine the exact location of the assault in the days that followed, despite the hours he spent outside the Sime Center among many of the witnesses.

One rainy night shortly before the election, the fourth day of a drizzle only a farmer could love, Den was passing by the back door on his way to the library when he heard a frantic knocking. He opened it to discover Rob Lifton: soaked, shivering, and sporting a spectacular black eye.

"It's Annie," Rob panted, grief thickening his voice. "You've got to help me find her before my mother does. Mom'll shoot her this time. Oh, come on, hurry!"

"Calm down. I can't do anything until I know what's going on. Now. What's this about your sister?"

"It's changeover," Rob announced. "Annie started running a fever this evening, throwing up. I thought at first that it was just her cold. She always gets a nervous stomach when she's got a fever."

Den nodded in understanding. In a society where changeover was a death sentence, any child of the proper age who caught a disease that mimicked any of the early symptoms of changeover would be likely to develop anxiety attacks.

"Mother didn't believe me," Rob continued. "She had Reverend Sinth come over and he said it was changeover. She wouldn't let me call you and said she would take care of Annie herself, like Reverend Sinth insisted was her moral responsibility. She took the carving knife and…" The young Gen shut his eyes, swallowing convulsively. "There was blood all over and Annie was screaming. I tried to hold Mother back and Annie ran out the door.

Reverend Sinth said I was a traitor to my family and when I yelled back that Annie didn't have to die, he took a swing at me. That's how I got the eye. Mother locked me in my room. She took the gun and went after Annie. I climbed out the window and came here. I think I know where Annie would go to hide. You've got to help me find my sister before Mother shoots her!"

Den nodded agreement as he rapidly led the way through the Center. He flagged Gati down as they passed through the main lobby and sent her to rouse Rital and the ambulance crew. Rital joined them and was quickly briefed.

"It's only been a few hours since she developed symptoms," the channel said. "There's plenty of time to get your sister here before she reaches breakout." He reached out, tentacles retracted, and gave Rob's shoulder a reassuring squeeze.

Den deftly took control of the fields as Rob shied away, then visibly forced himself to accept the Sime's touch. Apparently, Rob's one donation had not done much to mediate his emotional response to Simes, even if he was willing to ask Rital to rescue his sister. The channel released him and stepped back, giving him room.

"Where do you think your sister has gone?" the Donor asked, trying to curb his own impatience.

"There's a sort of cave under the bank of the stream that runs through the park," Rob explained. "We used to play there sometimes. I can show you where it is."

"You can tell us where it is," Rital corrected.

"I've got to go along," Rob protested. "Annie won't let you near her if I'm not there. She's terrified of Simes. You know she is," he appealed to Den. "Tell him."

"I know your sister's feelings about Simes," Den agreed. "*But,*" he continued, firmly overriding Rob's next words, "it's been a while since you donated selyn. You're high field again and you haven't the faintest idea how to behave properly around Simes." At Rob's indignant look, the Donor elaborated. "I know you don't mean to be rude, but your selyn field fluctuates in response to your feelings and induces a sympathetic response in nearby Simes that's proportional to the amount of selyn you're carrying, which right now is a lot." When this explanation also earned him a confused look, he simplified. "You could accidentally hurt your sister very badly by being in the same room with her. Understand now?"

"Yes." Rob's face firmed with determination and he began rolling up his sleeves. "If my being…high field," he stumbled over the unfamiliar term, "bothers you, that can be changed, but I'm going with you."

Rital looked at the Gen's offered hands, sighed, and signaled Den with one tentacle. Obediently, the Donor blocked the nageric chaos of the assembling ambulance crew, surrounding the channel with a bubble of nageric privacy.

Rob flinched and closed his eyes as Rital's tentacles secured his arms and pulled him forward to complete the transfer contact, but the young Gen didn't struggle. When the channel let him go he shuddered, then followed close on Den's heels to the ambulance.

It was a wild ride through the rainy darkness by the occasional dim glow of a bit of moon and the ambulance lights. The vehicle swayed alarmingly on the last curve, then coasted to a halt. Den helped Rital put on the loathsome retainers, grabbed a selyn-powered lantern, and climbed out after his cousin. He looked around, trying to orient himself. The park was large, with picnic areas, a playground, a playing field, and several acres of overgrown forest with hiking trails.

"There's a path over there, on the other side of the picnic area," Rob said, pointing across the playing field as he joined them. "It leads down to the stream."

Rital nodded and led the way, splashing through the puddles. Den and Rob fell in behind the channel, followed by two of the Sime Center's Gens carrying a light stretcher.

Rob stumbled over a grass clump and cursed. "It must be nice to be able to see in the dark," he remarked a little enviously, watching the channel's unhindered progress.

"Rital can't see in the dark any better than you or me," Den told him absently as the ambulance lights faded behind them and he held his lantern high. "Simes don't require light to zlin selyn fields any more than Gens require selyn fields to see light."

"Oh." Rob tried to wipe the water off of his face, then gave it up as a futile task.

They slogged onward in silence. Den shivered in the wet chill. He hoped they found Annie soon, before the cold and her injuries combined with fear and lack of training to bring her into Attrition before her new tentacles were ready for breakout.

When they reached the picnic area, Rob appropriated Den's lantern and led the way down a narrow, winding dirt path obviously created by the local children, not the Park Authority. Before long, it sloped sharply down toward the stream. A torrent of runoff gushed down the path with them, forcing them to wade ankle-deep in muddy water. Den skidded on the slick clay and was only saved from a fall by Rital's Augmented grab at his arm.

"Thanks," the Donor muttered as he got his feet on firmer footing. "Can you zlin her yet?"

"No. Either Rob's cave is deep enough to insulate her nager, she isn't here, or..."

"Yeah. Or she bled out and is already dead."

An anguished moan echoed down the trail. Den hastily slithered down the last of the path, landing knee-deep in the cold stream. Rob was inspecting a raw gash in the bank where a deep undercut, softened by the rain, had recently collapsed.

"Shen," Rital swore. "If she was under there when it went..."

"No!" Rob denied. "Look how high the water is. The floor of the cave must have been underwater before the cave-in. She'd have hidden somewhere else." Cupping his hands around his mouth, he yelled, "ANNIE!"

"Go away, Rob!" came a faint cry from above, barely audible over the stream's roar.

Rob scrambled up the bank of the stream and bolted up the steep hill like a goat. The remaining Gens sensibly let Rital lead the way. The channel wound through bushes and boulders, taking a less obstructed way to the top.

Den could hear Annie crying faintly when Rital stopped abruptly, uttering a string of soft obscenities in which the word "lorshes" featured prominently.

"What is it?" Den asked.

"She's no more in changeover than you are," the channel explained succinctly, working his way through the boulders that had prevented him from zlinning her earlier.

In the pool of light cast by the lantern, Den could see Annie huddled in her brother's arms. Her thin face was blotched with dirt, rain, tears, and blood from a knife slash across one cheek. She shrank back like a trapped animal when she saw Rital.

"No! I won't go! I won't be a Sime!" She doubled over in a convulsive coughing fit. When she brought her hands up to cover her mouth, Den could see that her arms had also been slashed by the knife. *Wielded by her own mother, just on the suspicion that she might be in changeover!* The Donor fought down his outrage; this was no time for it.

"You're right, Annie," Rital said in his gentlest tone. He knelt on the leaf mold beside her, but did not try to touch her. "You won't be a Sime, because you're already a Gen."

Rob and Annie stared at him with identical looks of dumfounded astonishment.

"But Reverend Sinth said..." Annie began.

"He was wrong," Rital said quietly. "You've Established, Annie. About a week ago, I'd judge. You're not in changeover."

She went limp with relief, took a deep breath, and began coughing again.

"However, that cough sounds like it's trying to turn into pneumonia and those knife slashes are filthy," the channel continued. "We have a stretcher here. Do you think you can get onto it?"

With encouragement from her brother, Annie let them put her on the stretcher and they started back down the trail to the ambulance.

At the Sime Center, Annie refused to let Rital treat her, asking for a Gen doctor instead.

"Leave her to me for a few minutes," Rob said, waving Den and Rital out of the treatment room. The room was insulated against both selyn fields and sound, so they couldn't hear what Rob was saying, but before long he poked his head around the door. "She'll cooperate now," he assured them.

"Robbie..." she wavered as she got her first good look at Rital's tentacles, now free of the retainers.

"It's all right," her brother promised, taking her hand. "I'll be right here."

Den wasn't keen on having an untrained Gen around when Rital was trying to do serious healing, but it was pretty obvious that otherwise, Annie wouldn't let the channel touch her. The Donor settled on a compromise, placing Rob behind him and to one side. That allowed Rob and Annie to see each other, but allowed Den's own nager to block Rob's from Rital's perception. *At least the kid's low field*, he thought grimly.

It took the channel nearly five minutes of coaxing before his patient would let him zlin her lungs. Even with Rob's continual stream of reassurance, she gasped in fear at the feel of tentacles on her back. Fortunately, the gasp triggered a thoroughly distracting coughing fit and by the time it was finished, so was Rital.

"You're in luck, Annie," he told her. "That zlins like a bacterial infection, not a virus. Are you allergic to any antibiotics?"

"No, I don't think so."

"Good." Rital unlocked the cabinet in which he and Den had stored a selection of the medications they had compounded during their first weeks in Clear Springs and rummaged through the vials. He selected one, double-checked the label, then extracted two pinkish pills and dropped them into Annie's hand. "These will start taking care of the infection."

Den handed Annie a glass of water and the young woman obediently swallowed the pills.

It was when they began to work on the knife cuts that the real trouble began. Annie gritted her teeth and endured as Den carefully washed dirt and bits of leaf from a particularly nasty slash that ran almost the length of her left forearm, but when Rital extended his laterals to heal it, she panicked.

Rital yelped in pain as he was shenned out of the contact and Den reached for his channel with both physical and nageric support. *I used to think Rital would have fewer problems if the locals would bring him their injuries!* Den remembered ironically as he worked on the damage. *I should be careful what I ask for!*

Annie watched Rital wide-eyed, knowing that something was wrong, but unable to understand what.

"A...Annie, I can't help you if you keep flaring fear at me that way," Rital told her when he could speak again. "I'm not going to hurt you, I'm just going to close those cuts so they don't get infected and leave scars. Relax, now, and let me work."

"I'll try," she promised meekly, but Den was skeptical that she would succeed.

He was right. The next attempt ended when Annie panicked again, this time before Rital could make a firm lateral contact. After a third unsuccessful try, Rital gave up and administered a sedative. When Annie's eyes began to glaze, the channel was finally able to gain the necessary control of her selyn field. Rob watched in utter fascination as the channel healed the deep cuts, using minute selyn currents to weave together the undamaged cells until all that was left was red lines. Afterward, Rital encouraged Annie's lungs to reabsorb the liquid accumulating in them, easing her breathing considerably.

"I didn't think it was possible to stop an infection that fast!" Rob exclaimed.

"It isn't," Rital told him as he coaxed another dose of the antibiotic down his sleepy patient.

Annie's lungs had to be cleared out twice more, but by dawn the antibiotic had the pneumonia under control, Annie had fallen into a restless sleep, and even Rital admitted to wanting a nap. Leaving Seena to watch their patient, channel and Donor headed upstairs for a few well-earned hours of rest before the daily contingent of demonstrators occupied the Sime Center's sidewalk and made sleep impossible.

CHAPTER 11

OLD SOKS

Den was tired enough to sleep in despite the chants and singing. Rital had left orders that his Donor not be disturbed for anything less than an emergency, so Den woke early the following afternoon. The rain had gone, leaving the sun to evaporate the puddles and raise the humidity to near saturation.

It was too late for breakfast, but lunch was still being served. Den had almost finished his soup, bread, and cheese when he was paged to the main lobby. He disposed of his dishes and headed briskly down the stairs.

The lobby was occupied by a most unlikely trio of Gens. Hank Fredricks, owner of the *Clarion*, carried the notepad and sharpened pencil that declared him to be present in his official capacity. Reverend Sinth, soberly dressed in an immaculate black robe, hovered over a haggard Carla Lifton. Her greying hair had escaped from its usual bun, there were dark circles under her tear-streaked eyes, and she appeared to have aged ten years overnight.

When she caught sight of Den, she gave an outraged shriek. "There he is!" she cried in mingled rage and grief. "He's the one who corrupted my daughter." Her voice broke. "Well, you succeeded with my Annie, Devil-worshipper, but you won't seduce another child in this town, not if I can prevent it!"

She started for the Donor as if to attack him, but was restrained by Reverend Sinth. "Patience, my child," he soothed her. "God's Might will prevail." When Carla was calmer, he let her go and announced to Den. "We have come to put an end to your campaign to turn our children to the worship of evil. You have deceived the people of this town long enough. I command you to stop in the name of the Almighty God!" The preacher ended with a dramatic, well-practiced gesture that seemed to impress both of the other out-Territory Gens.

Its significance completely escaped Den, who knew little and cared less about out-Territory religions.

"You can deceive mortal man, but God knows all," Reverend Sinth continued in his booming voice. "How long did you think you could hide your pact with the Devil, when his evil influence corrupts everything you touch?"

"I don't believe in your Devil any more than I believe in your God," Den said, able to partially understand that accusation, at least.

"Now, now, don't get excited," Fredricks interrupted, as Sinth drew another deep breath. "This isn't your church, Reverend, so there's no reason to give a sermon."

"You don't think the wholesale subversion of children is something to get excited about?" Carla asked.

Fredricks sighed. "Miz Lifton, Reverend Sinth, I'm here because you claimed to have uncovered a plot to harm the children of this town. So far, all you've done is make the same wild accusations you first made two years ago. I wouldn't print them then and I won't print them now. If you can't come up with solid evidence, I'm leaving." He turned for the door but before he had taken more than one step, Sinth reached under his long robe and produced a book, which he waved dramatically under the newsman's nose.

"Is this solid enough for you?" he demanded. "This…obscenity…has been circulating among the children of Clear Springs without the knowledge or consent of their parents. One of them has already suffered incalculable harm as a result." Sinth turned to Den. "Do you deny that this volume came from your Sime Center, or that it was given to Miz Lifton's daughter?"

Den took the book and inspected it. "Well, Miz Lifton's son, Rob, borrowed it, not her daughter, but it did come from here. It's a translation of a popular children's novel," he explained to Fredricks. "I understand it won several awards when it first came out. It's certainly not obscene."

"Not obscene!" Sinth snatched the book back, flipped feverishly through it until he found the page he wanted, and thrust it into Fredrick's hands. "Just look at that! Is that suitable fare for children?" He pointed to an illustration.

The book was opened to the chapter that described the hardships of the *Far Horizon*'s crew after storm damage stranded them in Gen Territory. The picture showed Slem, the cabin boy, and the ship's carpenter standing guard over a traveling peddler who had stumbled into their encampment. The peddler was watching the ship's channel take a donation from one of the Gen crew. Below the picture, the legend quoted Slem as saying, "Fortunately for you, channels aren't just a legend."

Fredricks inspected the picture for a long moment, then looked at several others. After reading the plot summary on the dust jacket, he closed the book and handed it to Den. "Reverend, I can see why you would want to prevent the youngsters in your congregation from reading a book like this," he told the clergyman judiciously. "However, I don't hold with censorship.

The fact that a book might encourage children to question the teachings of your church doesn't make it obscene or harmful."

"Not harmful!" Sinth said indignantly. "Mr. Carlon discovered his daughter, Jerri, reading this book two days ago. The girl admitted that she had gotten it from one of her friends, who in turn got it from another friend. At least five impressionable young girls have been exposed to this heresy. Five children, whose loss of faith may well cause them to become demon Simes…thanks to that evil and pernicious text!"

"You think reading a book can cause changeover?" Such ignorance had only been a theoretical possibility to Den. "That's the most ridiculous thing I've ever heard!"

"I have proof!" Sinth thundered. "We traced the volume back to Miz Lifton's daughter Annie, who, it now seems, got it from her brother. And last night…" He paused dramatically. "Last night, Annie Lifton went into changeover and her brother prevented his mother from giving her the death that would have freed her soul!"

"That book didn't make Annie Lifton go through changeover…" Den began.

"Liar!" Carla Lifton interrupted. "My Annie was a faithful and obedient daughter. God would have rewarded her faith by making her a Gen. Then your book got into her hands and turned her into a vicious, slimy…" her face twisted in disgust. "My girl was lost because of you, Sime-lover, and don't think you're going to get away with it!"

To hear her talk, you'd think I was the one who sliced Annie up, Den thought indignantly. "As I was about to say," he repeated, "neither I nor that book caused Miz Lifton's daughter to go through changeover. Annie Lifton is a Gen and Gens don't go through changeover."

"See how he attempts to deceive us, even now," Sinth told Fredricks. "I confirmed the changeover myself."

"You were wrong," Den repeated. "And because you irresponsibly made a medical diagnosis that you are in no way qualified to make, the young woman was almost murdered. By her own mother."

"You have seen Annie Lifton, then?" Fredricks asked.

"Yes," Den said. "Annie's brother believed Reverend Sinth's misdiagnosis. He came here last night and asked our help to prevent his sister from Killing. By the time we found her, she was half dead from blood loss and congested lungs, but she's as Gen as you or I."

Conflicting hope and disbelief warred on Carla's face and disbelief won. "Liar!"

"Come see for yourselves," Den suggested in exasperation.

The out-Territory Gens stayed close together as Den led the way to the infirmary. The "Do not disturb" light on Annie's treatment room was off, so Den thumbed the door signal.

"Come in," Rital called.

Den poked his head into the room. Annie was sitting up in bed, clutching a handful of cards and looking slightly better after a night's rest. Rob occupied a chair on the near side of the bed, scribbling on a scorepad, and Rital perched on the far side of the bed, frowning over his cards and, the Donor knew, encouraging Annie's selyn production to help her heal faster.

"Annie, Rob, your mother and Reverend Sinth are here," Den said. "Do you want to talk to them?"

What little color Annie's face had regained faded away. "Do I have to?" she asked.

"No, you don't have to," the Donor answered, "but I think you should."

Brother and sister looked at each other. After a long moment, Annie nodded and Rob said, "All right, we'll talk to them. But only if they'll leave when we tell them to."

Carla opened her mouth to protest, but Fredricks grabbed her elbow and shook his head. She hesitated, then nodded agreement to Den's raised eyebrow. Den entered first, to control the fields, but Carla followed close behind. She eyed Rital nervously, then met the accusing eyes of her children and forgot the channel.

"Mother," Rob greeted her coldly, not giving an inch as he let his bruised eye speak for itself. Annie, taking her brother's cue, crossed her obviously untentacled arms across her chest, displaying the red, swollen lines where Rital had closed the gashes in her arms.

Carla flinched as if she had been hit. "Annie isn't Sime," she whispered , turning chalk white. She buried her face in her hands. "And I tried to murder her," she mumbled, grief-stricken. "She wasn't in changeover, and I…"

"You had something to say to us, Mother?" Rob prompted.

Carla straightened. "Yes, I do," she said. "I was wrong and you were right. Thank you for stopping me from murdering your sister."

"Because I turned out to be a Gen after all?" Annie asked sweetly.

"No!" Carla said, a little too loudly. "Annie, I've always been taught, and believed, that it was better to help a child in changeover die than to condemn them to live as Simes. But…I spent last night hoping you'd made it here in spite of me."

Rob and Annie held their poses for a moment more and then Annie held out her hands to her mother. Hardly daring to believe it, Carla went to the bed and hugged her daughter, crying unashamedly into the girl's hair, then hugged her son as well.

As he watched the reconciliation, Den realized that his perception of Carla Lifton had changed. He could no longer view her as a fanatical lorsh who got sadistic pleasure from slaughtering helpless children. She obviously cared deeply about her children and wanted want was best for them—although he still found it hard to understand how any loving parent could honestly believe that her child was better off dead than Sime.

When she had dried her tears, Carla turned to Rital. Carefully keeping her eyes on his face to avoid the sight of his tentacles, she said, "Thank you for taking care of my children."

"You're welcome," the channel said politely.

Carla turned to her daughter. "We should get you home."

"Annie really ought to stay here for a few more days," Rital said, in a firm but non-threatening tone. "That pneumonia is only controlled, not defeated. I'd hate for her to end up with lung damage."

"You should have seen it, Mother!" Rob said enthusiastically. "Last night, Annie could scarcely breathe, she was coughing so hard. Hajene Rital fixed her in half an hour. I've never seen anything like it."

"Annie?" Carla asked.

"I'll be all right," Annie reassured her mother.

"Very well, then," Carla gave her permission.

"Are you blind, woman?" Sinth demanded. "Can't you see what the demon has done? You find your children with a Sime, playing who knows what evil card game, and you want to leave them in his care? He has already gained power over your father and your niece. Will you give him your children, too?"

Carla hesitated, casting a suspicious glance at the channel.

Bringing the full force of his charisma to bear, the clergyman proclaimed, "As your spiritual advisor, I counsel you to fight the Sime's evil influence and remove your children before they are irrevocably harmed."

This was one unfounded accusation too many, as far as Den was concerned. "Haven't you offered Miz Lifton enough counsel?" he demanded. "Her daughter almost died last night because she followed your advice."

"Silence!" Sinth turned back to Carla. "You must not listen to him. He is a Sime-lover, a Devil-worshipper..."

"And *you*," Den placed himself in front of the preacher and poked his chest with an accusing forefinger, "are an ignorant, superstitious, bigoted fool. How many of your followers' children have died because you never bothered to learn the difference between changeover and any number of common illnesses?"

Reverend Sinth stared disdainfully at the Donor. "It is far better to err on the side of caution in such cases."

"So it doesn't matter that you might be wrong? When Rital could settle the matter with one quick zlin?"

"You see?" Sinth addressed the frantically scribbling Fredricks. "They will go to any lengths to spread their influence." He turned back to Den. "My followers won't tolerate you threatening their children..."

"Shut up, you hypocrite!" Carla cried, pushing Den aside to glare at the preacher. "He's right, Sime-lover or not. The one who's endangering the children is *you*! *You* told me Annie was in changeover! *You* insisted that it was my duty to kill her!"

Den had a most improbable mental picture of a berserk Carla attacking Annie while wearing a set of those fake tentacles some in-Territory costume stores sold. Then he remembered that in English, the word 'kill' had a broader meaning than in Simelan.

"Now, Sister Carla, you know you don't mean that," Sinth said in a patronizing tone. "You're just upset."

"You're absolutely right, I'm upset!" Carla agreed. "I'm upset that I was foolish enough to believe that a man like you could speak for God." She glared up at him. "I don't believe it anymore, so take your 'advice' and offer it to the people who want it. And may God help their children!"

Sinth flushed at the insult, but before he could answer, Den grasped his elbow. "I think you have outstayed your welcome for today, Reverend," he said and propelled the indignant clergyman firmly through the door.

Several of the staff had congregated in the hall outside. Den beckoned to two of the onlookers, both high field Gens who were capable of shielding the renSimes from a non-donor's relatively weak nager. "Ref, Vonce, would you please escort Reverend Sinth to the front door?"

"I hope you will excuse me if I join them," Hank Fredricks apologized, still scribbling madly as he joined the three Gens. "I have a new front page to design, though it won't be the one Reverend Sinth wanted when he asked me to come here today!"

"That Sime isn't at all what I expected," Carla admitted to her son later, as Den escorted them back through the Sime Center.

"I know he isn't," Rob said, with more than a touch of sarcasm. "Not a horn or cloven hoof to be seen."

"I'm serious. He's polite, he's got a better bedside manner than Dr. Gilman... I have to keep reminding myself that he's the one who does those horrible things to the Gens who get tricked into donating selyn."

"Oh, it's not *that* bad," Rob said without thinking.

Carla stopped short, grabbed her son's arm, and jerked the boy around to face her. "Robert Sammel Lifton, have you been sneaking in to donate selyn? After I told you that you were not to set foot on the Sime Center grounds?"

Rob scuffed his shoe on the floor. "Yes," he admitted.

"Why?" Anger and betrayal colored her voice. "How could you?"

Rob straightened, looking his mother in the eye. "Because I had to know what it was like," he said passionately. "I had to *know* whether Reverend Sinth is right about the Sime Center endangering the community, or whether our whole family has spent nearly two years fighting a menace that doesn't exist. I found out, too. Reverend Sinth is wrong about donating, Mother. Just as wrong as he was about Annie."

Carla stared at Rob, taken aback. "Well," she said finally, "if you really want to donate, I won't forbid it. Not that that would make any difference, it seems."

"It wouldn't," Rob admitted.

"Just don't ask me to come with you," his mother conceded.

On election day, Den dressed in civilian clothing, climbed the back fence to avoid the protesters, and headed into town to reconnoiter. An hour of wandering through the downtown and university campus, listening to the conversations around him, failed to provide any real consensus regarding the outcome of the election, although interest was uniformly high.

In his preoccupation, Den forgot to return to the Sime Center via the back door.

"Sir!" a young man called urgently, hurrying up to him. It was one of the roving "counselors" who accosted anyone intending to enter the Sime Center. "Sir, please don't go in there! Those murdering demons might Kill you!"

The young man's face was unfamiliar, as were those of the other demonstrators. It appeared that Reverend Sinth had arranged for sympathizers from other towns to take over the blockade that day, to free his own congregation for last-minute campaigning in favor of Len Dusam. The protester confronting Den obviously didn't recognize him as a Tecton employee.

Den automatically accepted the pamphlet he was handed. To his surprise, it was a new one. "DO YOU KNOW WHAT YOU'RE GETTING INTO?" the heading asked. Den glanced inside. Instead of wild accusations about secret Pens, the text concentrated on gruesome descriptions of slimy tentacles. The illustration bore a suspicious resemblance to the engraving that Reverend Sinth had found so offensive and as a consequence, there were only six tentacles to an arm.

Den guffawed, put the pamphlet into his pocket, and started down the path to the Sime Center.

"But sir," the counselor called after him, "Where are you going?"

Den grinned at the young man over his shoulder. "I'm going inside," he said cheerfully. "I've got to tell a certain murdering demon he was right!"

Den snagged a copy of the next morning's *Clarion* as soon as it was delivered. **MAYOR KROAG RE-ELECTED!** the headline screamed. "In an election widely viewed as a referendum on the presence of a Sime Center in Clear Springs…" the story began. Almost shaking with relief, Den took the paper to the dining hall to read over breakfast with his cousin.

Rital was as relieved as his cousin at the outcome of the election. "You see?" he said, sipping his tea. "Progress toward Unity is possible, even in a place like Clear Springs. It moves at its own pace, not ours, but it's inevitable. Carla Lifton permitted her child to remain under my care. Carla might never find the courage to donate, but her son did. Her grandchildren will grow up fearing changeover less and accepting donating as a natural part of being a Gen. In twenty years, or a hundred, the out-Territory Gens will demand that their Sime children be allowed to live with them and the borders will dissolve."

Den's greater experience with the non-donors of Clear Springs made him more skeptical. "Before they can have a change of heart, their minds have to accept that most of what their culture 'knows' about Simes is wrong. That's the hard part. Anatomically accurate illustration or not, Sinth's new pamphlet contains the same wild conspiracy theories as the previous one." He considered the problem more deeply and conceded, "The change in illustration does suggest that even Sinth will stop using a particular lie once a sufficiently large portion of his target audience know it's false."

"While he doesn't care whether what scares people away from the Sime Center is true, he does object to public ridicule when he's caught in a bald-faced lie," the channel summarized.

"Yes, exactly," the Donor agreed. The insight suggested a possible new avenue of attack, but the complete indifference that had met his offer to speak to city- and university-sponsored public service groups suggested that a new tactic might be required.

The channel patted the newspaper. "At least their candidate's loss will force Sinth and his followers to pause and think. Who knows, they might even reconsider this blockade of theirs."

Rital's fond hope evaporated with the morning quiet as an earsplitting cacophony broke out on the front sidewalk. Channel and Donor turned to stare in disbelief through the large cafeteria window, which provided an excellent view of the uproar.

Almost sixty anti-Sime demonstrators crowded onto the sidewalk in front of the Sime Center, shouting at each other as they got organized for the day. Most were middle-aged, although there were a few younger couples with children. Den couldn't see Carla Lifton—the day's blockade was led by the mother of Annie's deceased friend, Rachel—but otherwise most of the usual suspects were present, including the turmeric-haired man who had assaulted Marcy Ingleston. The signs they waved had slogans such as "Save Our Kids," "No Simes in Clear Springs," and "Don't Donate."

It appeared that Reverend Sinth and his followers, outraged by the city's rejection of their favored candidate, had turned out in force to show their displeasure. There was an ugly undertone to the way they screamed out one of their favorite hymns, declaring their intent to close down the Sime Center once and for all. They had gotten away with one assault on a donor, their attitude plainly said, and they were ready to commit another.

Den and Rital hurried downstairs and out the front door in the hope that their presence might deter outright violence. Den considered calling the Clear Springs police, but they had barely stepped outside when any such effort became moot. A group of about twenty college students in faded denims or wraparound skirts turned the corner and approached the demonstration, singing a scurrilous drinking ballad at the top of their voices. *Rampant individualists, one and all,* Den thought with a wince. They can't even agree on which verse they're trying to sing, much less in which key.

In the front rank were Marcy Ingleston and her friend, Silva. Den recognized other faces from the debate. Many of them wore white T-shirts with a tattered stocking silkscreened on the front in fluorescent orange. Underneath, in similarly orange letters, was printed **OLD SOKS**. Some wore faded knee socks or stockings as headbands, armbands, or decorations on the rim of a hat. Some carried signs, but these read:

IF WE WANT YOUR ADVICE, WE'LL ASK FOR IT

MIND YOUR OWN BUSINESS

and

YOU'RE LYING!

As Den shook his head in disbelief, they finished their song and began to chant, "Save Our Kids, you're a lie! You don't care if children die!"

The din grew even louder as some members of each group broke ranks to scream at each other.

"How the blazing shen can anyone get through *that* to donate?" Rital asked in horror.

The sidewalk beyond the free-for-all was clear for the moment, but the Collectorium would open soon. Den saw one of their regular donors, Birneece Holderman, turn the corner. She paused, looking in dismay at the near-riot on the sidewalk, but then shook herself and strode toward the Sime Center in a determined fashion.

Two sock-adorned counter-demonstrators approached her. They spoke for a moment, then the students each took one of the woman's arms. They had taken only four steps when several of the anti-Sime Center demonstrators converged, waving their signs and screaming warnings as they tried to block the sidewalk.

However, the counter-demonstrators had also converged. Being equally enthusiastic and, on average, twenty years younger than their foes, they reached the woman first. Linking arms in a flying wedge, they ruthlessly shoved a path through the mob, depositing several of Sinth's followers on the sidewalk and Holderman safely on the Sime Center side of the fray. They cheered as she started down the path to the Collectorium, then began to chant tauntingly, "Bad makeup, bad dress, Save Our Kids, you're a mess!"

Silva sighted Den and Rital and waved. She leaned over to say something to the young man next to her, then took his hand and pulled him across the lawn to greet the Donor.

"Sosu Milnan, it's good to see you again," she said, grinning broadly. The bruises on her face were almost gone. "You remember my boyfriend, Tohm Seegrin?"

Tohm was a short, stocky Gen with a neatly trimmed beard and dark blond hair. He was wearing worn denims with his **OLD SOKS** T-shirt and a button reading, "**This Sime Center stays OPEN!**" Silva's brown hair was cut slightly shorter than Tohm's and she wore a faded calico skirt and brown boots. She also had a button, but hers read, "**OLD SOKS gives a darn**."

"Silva, you're looking well," Den greeted her. "What brings you here today?"

"We're with OLD SOKS," she explained, gesturing to her sweatshirt.

"Well, I can see that there are some old socks with you, anyway," Den agreed, surveying the footwear adorning their outfits.

"It stands for 'Organization for the Legal Disruption of Save Our Kids' Strategies,'" Tohm explained.

"It's kind of a mouthful, but the uniform is cheap!" Silva added.

"And what exactly is this organization of yours?" Rital asked skeptically.

"We're Reverend Sinth's worst nightmare," Tohm boasted.

"After Marcy got hurt and the police refused to investigate, much less prosecute, we decided to make sure those fanatics don't force the rest of us to abide by *their* beliefs," Silva elaborated. "Two of the law school students wanted to circulate a petition and the political science types insisted on an election of some sort. Everybody else wanted to do something that would actually help. More and more students count on money from donating to help cover living costs and Sinth and his group are getting way out of hand."

Tohm winked mischievously and took up the tale. "We decided to make sure everybody who wanted to get into the Sime Center, could."

"We were pretty successful, just now," Silva pointed out. "With us here, I think old Sanctimonious Sinth is going to find it a lot more difficult to block your sidewalk."

Den believed her, although he found her enthusiasm for combat somewhat daunting. In-Territory, such shoving matches between Gens would never happen. The probability of one or the other combatant being injured was too great for any Sime to tolerate. In-Territory Gens learned early that it was easier to stay away from fights than to face hysterical overreactions from every Sime in zlinning distance.

In the absence of further customers, both sets of demonstrators had broken into song again. Save Our Kids chose a favorite hymn about the triumphant day to come when Simes would cease to exist and their church would rule unopposed. OLD SOKS countered with a bawdy ballad that detailed the amenities available at a (Den sincerely hoped) fictional bordello. Several of Sinth's followers took exception to the subject matter of the latter musical offering, or perhaps to the OLD SOKS membership's lack of singing technique. There was a certain amount of shouting back and forth, none of which reflected well on the maturity of the shouters.

Tohm turned toward the noise. "Duty calls," he said, extending a hand to Silva. "Come on, heartless wench."

Silva giggled as he grabbed her and stole a hearty kiss. "Stop that, you animal," she scolded, impotently beating at his chest, then reaching down to pinch him in a suggestive spot. "You see what I have to put up with?" she complained happily to Den.

Den laughed at Tohm's answering leer.

"Tell me," Rital asked. "Why the choice of songs?"

Silva grinned. "It annoys them," she answered succinctly.

O ver the next few days, a battle royale raged over possession of the Sime Center's front sidewalk. The only thing that distracted the two sides from abusing each other was the appearance of a visitor to the Sime Center.

As the week came to an end, Reverend Sinth and his followers had still not found an answer to the sheer youthful energy of the counter-demonstrators. Although no Sime Center visitors suffered worse than minor jostling, the casualties among the feuding participants included two pairs of glasses and a prized pocket watch that were dislodged and trampled during the daily shoving matches. Three regular Save Our Kids mothers who had formerly brought their small children along to the demonstrations found babysitters or stayed home instead.

Hank Fredricks showed up on the third day of the battle and Tohm and Silva gave him an extensive interview. He was interested enough in their efforts to publish a half-page article. Although Rital worried that the shoving matches and screaming would deter Gens from donating, the opposite proved true. The number of donations rose dramatically. Some were Gens who had stopped donating after the assault on Marcy Ingleston, like Carla Lifton's elderly father, Mr. Duncan. Others were students, including many of the OLD SOKS counter-demonstrators but not all of them, to Den's surprise.

He did not, however, get a chance to explore the contradiction. The next evening Sosu Siv Alson arrived from Valzor to give Rital transfer. The day after that, Den was on the train back to Valzor for his monthly transfer. He had never been more eager to leave Clear Springs for this time, as Rital had promised to arrange, he had a full four days of leave afterward in which to attend the East Nivet Model Flyer's Convention.

CHAPTER 12

FLEDGLINGS

After living for so long next to the battlefield of the Clear Springs Sime Center's front sidewalk, Valzor seemed even more of a surreal paradise to Den than on his last rotation back to civilization. It was strange to hear Simelan spoken outside a Sime Center. At the train station, he found himself reflexively tensing when one of the renSime baggage handlers addressed him as "Sosu" in a voice loud enough to be heard by a trio of passing Gens.

I've lived too long out-Territory, he decided, as the Gens hurried past to welcome a young Sime woman with hugs and joyous greetings. Thanks to Reverend Sinth's unrelenting campaign, Den had come to expect every Gen around him who was not Sime Center staff to hate or fear Simes as a matter of course. The Donor was even starting to accept having random strangers verbally abuse him for his choice of profession as normal behavior.

"But it *isn't* normal and the fanatics barricading your Sime Center are not right," Eddina pointed out when he stopped by the warehouse to ask whether she and Jannun had managed to transport the 'Spirit of Valzor' to the test site. "If you accept their false premise as a starting point, they've won the argument before it begins."

"I know," Den allowed. "However, Rital and I can't ever let down our guard, because even the Gens who do support us are dangerously unpredictable. We're not just staying alert for random accidents. We're guarding against actual attacks."

Eddina looked up at him skeptically. "Are you sure you and Rital aren't getting a bit paranoid, imagining attacks and conspiracies that don't exist?"

"I'm not sure of anything," he admitted, "except that I've been assigned out-Territory far too long." Vowing to relearn how to live a normal life, he left to pick up his transfer assignment.

Den's assigned channel for transfer was Hajene Nalod. Nalod had a Proficiency Rating and sensitivity slightly lower than Rital's. His selyn draw and capacity were a little smaller, too, which made giving him transfer less personally satisfying for Den. However, channels had to have a transfer with a Donor who overmatched them every now and then: someone whom they couldn't injure, no matter how demanding their selyn draw. Since Den couldn't give transfer to Rital every month, he was willing enough to serve Hajene Nalod instead.

The channel was eager to take Den's selyn, since he had been making do with not-quite-adequate Donors for several months. The rare freedom to draw to his full speed and capacity exhilarated any channel and Nalod's thanks as they parted were heartfelt.

Low field and truly off-duty, as he never quite could be in Clear Springs, Den changed into civilian clothing and caught the shuttle bus hired for the North Nivet Flyer's Convention. This year, the organizing committee had moved the event just outside the city limits, to a farm owned by the parents of one of the committee members, Kithra Borfin. The farm had a large pasture with a steep hill that would be perfect for flight trials.

Den got off the bus and walked around the house to the barnyard, wrinkling his nose at the smell. Although the area had been meticulously swept in preparation for the conference, no amount of last-minute sanitation could completely disperse the pong from fifty cows.

The conference attendees were crowded into a machine shed behind the milking barn. After the farm equipment had been parked in the adjoining field, there was enough space around the walls for display tables assigned to the various model flyer clubs and the vendors whose supplies supported their obsession. The open space in the middle had rows of hay bales to provide seating, set up to face an antique, horse-drawn wagon too dilapidated to move out with the other equipment. Making a virtue of necessity, the organizers had placed the speakers' podium in its bed.

To the best of his knowledge, Den was the only First Order Donor in East Nivet who was also a model flyer enthusiast. Even just after transfer, his nager stood out to every renSime in the area. He found himself swarmed by friends and acquaintances, all eager to catch up with the events of the past year. The wing contest was the primary topic of interest, of course, but Darvon ambrov Frihill's controversial new book was also creating quite a stir.

"Not that I believe her thesis for one moment," confided Pellit Adjans, a sandy-haired Gen man from Iburan.

"I haven't seen a copy yet," Den admitted. "I've been posted out-Territory where the bookstores don't carry Simelan titles. However, I do have to agree that the idea of using airplanes as a military weapon is just silly. How could you capture enemy soldiers or territory when you're flying half a mile above them? And even the Ancient flyers had to have specialized roads and facilities to make a safe landing."

There was a snicker from Cincee Fragg, a renSime who had traveled all the way from Capital for the conference. Bowing with a flourish of tentacles, she declaimed grandly, "General Milnan, I wish to invade your Territory. Please ignore the swarm of trains supplying the construction crews who are building a landing road conveniently close to your strategically placed secret military base."

The men chuckled. "Even if you wanted to use flyers to spy on enemy troop movements, they'd have to return to a secure place to land," Den observed.

"Which would kind of limit the useful range to just along the border," Pellit agreed. "However, Darvon's illustrations recreating some of the high-performance Ancient aircraft are amazing, although I expect her calculations regarding the speeds at which they were designed to fly are... overly optimistic."

"I look forward to her presentation this afternoon." The Donor caught sight of Eddina and Jannun beckoning from the other side of the room and excused himself. "How did our contest entry turn out?" he asked when initial greetings had been exchanged. "Were you able to get it here undamaged?"

"*It's* undamaged, apart from a few minor scratches," Jannun reassured him. "The warehouse's north window, my left shoulder, and Polma Bagget's clothesline are somewhat the worse for wear."

"We ended up making it in three pieces: the two wings and a reinforced plank that ties them together and carries the crate on its underside," Eddina said. "It's surprisingly heavy, despite being hollow. Jannun thought about making the wooden parts of your design thinner, but he was worried about structural integrity."

"Can I see it?" Even low field, Den had to control his excitement, lest he overwhelm the defenseless renSimes in the area.

Jannun laughed. "Of course. Darvon is selling books hand-and-tentacle. Going by the line at her table, the program won't continue for at least half an hour."

The launch site was down a farm road that wound through a pasture and up a steep hill. The side of the hill that faced them was topped with a cliff-like precipice as tall as a three-story building. The road snaked around to the rear, where the slope was more reasonable. The roof of a hay barn was barely visible, peeking over the cliff. The road was pocked with hoof prints and less savory offerings. Den didn't have a spare pair of shoes with him and watched his step carefully.

The barn at the top of the hill had been cleared of hay bales, but the six-inch deep scattering of loose hay across the floor had been left intact to offer padding for the contest entries. There were ten in a variety of shapes and sizes, ranging from a beautifully finished all-wooden design to one with double wings constructed from bamboo and a tarp, held together with duct tape and wire.

Each entry was bolted, strapped, or tied to a standard packing crate. Several extra crates sat over to one side. Den looked the scene over, grinning so widely it threatened to split his face in two. "They're beautiful!" he announced. "It's like a copy of *A History of Ancient Aviation* come to life. Only it's better, because we're moving forward, not just looking back to the Ancients. Where is the 'Spirit of Valzor?'"

Jannun led him to where their masterpiece had been carefully assembled and bolted to its packing crate. The Donor walked around it, stunned by the reality of his design brought to life. It was larger than he'd visualized, and sturdier. The slightly upswept wings arched smoothly and Eddina's aunt's trick with shrinking the fabric onto the wooden frame had produced a solid covering. The tea stain that had prompted her to donate the bolt of cloth occupied a place of pride at the end of one wing.

"You did an amazing job with this," Den said. "Do you think it will fly?"

"I don't know," Eddina admitted. "It's sure going to be fun to launch it, though!"

Jannun nodded. "Even if the 'Spirit of Valzor' doesn't win, everybody here will learn from seeing all these different designs launched."

"That's the point, after all," the Donor reminded them. "By next year, or maybe the year after, we'll know how to build a wing assembly out of modern materials with the strength, durability, and flexibility to handle powered flight."

Den managed to pick up a copy of Darvon's book and get it autographed before her talk started. Flipping through it, he raised an eyebrow at some of the more exotic flyer shapes she had discovered while excavating an Ancient ruin in the arid southwestern corner of Nivet. It didn't seem likely that such oddly shaped structures could fly. With a certain amount of skepticism, he settled down on a hay bale between Jannun and Eddina to listen to her speak.

The slide projector was quite functional. However, the screen was improvised from a sheet and the machine shed was far from light-proof. By squinting, Den was able to see just enough to follow along with Darvon's talk in his copy of her book. He was not the only member of the audience to do so.

Despite his skepticism, when the historian spoke, he had to provisionally accept her analysis. The Ancient site had definitely been used as a parking structure and service area for flyers: it had all the structural features seen at other such facilities and a good scattering of known late-period flyer designs. The oddly shaped craft had been placed in the flyer parking garages, not those reserved for ground vehicles, and they did have wings of a sort. There simply wasn't a more plausible use for them that he could think of.

"...and so, the evidence found at the Moav Desert site shows that just before civilization collapsed, Ancient flyers became much more varied than was previously believed. We have yet to understand why they changed a perfectly functional design to such a strange extent."

She ended her talk to applause from the audience, then stepped back to yield the podium to the master of ceremonies, Kithra Borfin. Borfin was young, barely out of First Year, but she had the organizational skills of a good manager.

"Thank you, Darvin ambrov Frihill, for sharing your findings with our gathering." She turned to the audience. "Are there any questions for Darvin?"

Half the audience surged to its feet, but Kithra deferred to Den's Donor-sized nager and called on him first.

"Tuib Darvin, I have a possible explanation to suggest for why you might find such a cluster of very atypical flyer designs."

"I am very eager to hear it," Darvin said politely.

"Just before your talk, I was looking over the entries for our own flyer contest. They, too, have a wide array of materials and designs. Is it possible that the Moav Desert site was used for research into new flyer designs? If so, isn't it likely that many of the designs you found were prototypes, built to answer particular design questions, and were never intended as practical flyers? At least, not in the form that you found them?"

Darvin looked surprised, then thoughtful. "That's certainly a possibility," she agreed.

Having contributed what he could to the discussion, the Donor settled down to enjoy a very technical discussion among the engineers in the audience regarding how the controversial wing designs might have performed.

Den hadn't been able to immerse himself so whole-heartedly in his hobby since going to Clear Springs. Even his trips to the university library had been colored by guilt, since they left his cousin at the mercy of inadequate Donor support.

When the afternoon's presentations were over, the convention adjourned to the top of the hill, where the catapult was rolled out for inspection. It was a simple machine: a short track ending at the cliff face along which the packing crates (which had been fitted with wheels) would be pulled by a rope-and-pulley. When the crate reached the end of the track, a quick-release latch would release the pulley, launching the crate and its attached wings off the cliff.

A selyn-powered winch normally used to lower stored hay bales over the cliff to the cows had been modified to power the catapult. Now, the rope from the winch was attached to a sling wrapped around a boulder. The boulder rested on a platform that extended out over the cliff, right over a trap door. Once a wing assembly had been attached to its packing crate, the trap door would be released. The boulder would fall, pulling the crate along the track and launching it at the end of the tracks. Between launches, the winch would slowly pull the boulder back up to the platform.

I t rained overnight, but cleared by mid-morning, when everyone assembled again on top of the hill. A steady breeze blew in their faces as they looked over the cliff which, if the author of the Rick Toeffin book was correct, should actually provide a bit of extra lift.

Kithra, as mistress of ceremonies, reviewed the rules of the contest. "And I have a very special announcement to make," she concluded, beckoning forward a distinguished, middle-aged renSime woman. "This is Fridda Polburn from the Economic Development Board. Let's hope we can convince her that we are well on the way to solving one of the technological barriers to redeveloping powered flight!"

Loud applause greeted this suggestion, then attention turned to the long-awaited contest.

The first design was the double-winged, bamboo-and-tarp entry. This proved to be the work of young Mandle, the would-be test pilot, who had apparently taken Den's lecture to heart.

When Kithra asked Mandle to explain her design before the launch, Mandle said, "This is my 'Right Flyer.' I wanted to build a real wing like a bird, because birds fly well, but my brother Nervin," she nodded at her assistant, "said he didn't know how to build a wing, but he could build a box kite and box kites fly well, too. We used bamboo from the back yard and the old tarp from the woodpile."

Den was not the only conference-goer suppressing an amused smile at Mandle's youthful enthusiasm and low-budget approach. The launch, however, was disappointing. The packing crate hurtled down the short track with impressive acceleration, but the quick-release latch didn't. The entire assembly came to a sudden halt at the cliff's edge, sending the wings whiplashing forward, then back. A strip of duct tape let go under the strain, leaving a flap of tarp to flutter in the breeze.

Mandle's face crumpled in woeful disappointment, but her brother assured her that the damage could be fixed and went off to borrow some duct tape and twine.

The 'Right Flyer' was removed from the tracks, packing crate and all, and set aside for repairs. After the quick-release catch was readjusted and tested to ensure that it would work properly, the next entry was secured in place. The 'Junker' was a design with thick, solid wooden wings. It was the heaviest entry, but its four renSime makers got the crate into place first and then secured the wings with heavy ceramic bolts. At launch, one bolt failed under the strain, causing the affected wing to sag. The wind caught the other, sending it back into the cliff. Crate and wings shattered against the unyielding granite.

"But the wings did catch the air," Eddina observed. "It just didn't fly straight, with the one wing sagging so badly."

There was a pause while Kithra ran down the hill and scavenged thicker, stronger steel bolts from the mowing machine. Using these, her entry, the 'Normal Seagull,' was attached to a new crate. This entry had wider, rounder wings made of canvas stretched over a batwing skeleton frame. Everybody held their breath, but this time the catapult functioned properly, launching the crate over the cliff. The wings caught the air for a moment, but the weight of the crate was too far forward. The entire assembly stalled, tilted forward and then went into a dive, crashing not far from the base of the cliff.

It had flown, even if briefly, and it wasn't a small model, either. The audience erupted into a cheer and willing hands helped move the next entry to the catapult.

The 'Birdwing' had also been designed to resemble birds rather than Ancient machines. It had actual joints, held together by wires, and a fanned tail. When launched, it dove off the cliff, caught the air and rose a little, then executed two swoops to rousing applause before landing nose-first on the hill, fifty yards beyond the 'Normal Seagull.'

The 'Mono-cock' had hollow wings of fiberglass. One of them clipped the winch just after launch, sending it into an unrecoverable dive. The wooden wings of the 'Piper Kitten' had warped in the damp weather in spite of its coat of bright yellow paint. It veered off course but did make some forward progress, as well. The plywood 'Enola Grey' performed the best yet, managing to sustain a glide in more or less the right direction and hitting halfway down the hill.

By this time, the Gens were getting hungry and Kintha reluctantly called for a lunch break. The conversation was spirited as the Gens ate sandwiches and the Simes sipped tea, lemonade, cold well water, or the pomegranate juice that was being served from an absurdly out-of-place, elegant punch bowl. Not all of the discussion was optimistic, however.

"Den, Eddina, I think we may have a problem," Jannun said as he returned from inspecting their contest entry. His worry was evident even to Gen eyes.

"What is it?" Eddina asked, as she and Den followed him over to the 'Spirit of Valzor.'

"Apparently, the hay barn roof leaked last night. The fabric on the right-hand wing is soaked, although the other is dry. It's still stretched tight enough to catch air, as you see, but…"

"With one wing dry and one wet, it won't be balanced," Den finished the thought, running a careful hand over the wet wing to determine the extent of the wet spot. It was definitely too large to ignore. "Can we dry it off?"

Eddina shook her head. "It's muslin. Even if we had heaters, we don't have the time to get it really dry."

"If we can't dry it, we'll have to get it balanced another way," Den said. When the others looked confused, he elaborated, "What matters is that both wings weigh the same, right? So if we can't have them both dry…" He looked pointedly at the refreshments table.

Jannun picked up a pencil and began sketching a mirror image of the wet spot onto the dry wing as Eddina went to scavenge liquids. Alas, aeronautical experimentation was thirsty work. The water pitcher contained enough to dampen only part of the required area and even adding the dregs of the lemonade and tea was not enough.

"We've got to have more," Jannun observed. "It's really soaked, not just damp."

Eddina appropriated the still half-full punch bowl and handed it to Den. "You thought of it," she said. "You can do the honors."

Den poured carefully, wincing as a splash left a brilliant scarlet stain on his shirt. The effect on the wing was equally intense, but more variable. Where the alkaline well water had initially dampened the fabric, the pomegranate juice turned bluish. The acidic, lemonade-soaked parts were scarlet and the areas where they overlapped were purple.

"We win the prize for 'most colorful entry,' anyway," Jannun observed.

But Eddina said, "If it flies straight, who cares how it looks?"

The 'Barriot Chariot,' entered by the Barriot City Flyer's Club, used guy wires to add stability to its wings. While this concept was sensible in theory, when a wind-blown paper caught in one of the wires during launch, the result was the same tight spiral into the cliff face that the 'Junker' had flown.

Den, Jannun, and Eddina moved the 'Spirit of Valzor' into place. Its odd coloration drew some surprised looks. Eddina double-checked that the bolts were secure, the quick-release latch correctly positioned, and the audience at a safe distance, then signaled Kithra to launch.

The 'Spirit of Valzor' accelerated smoothly down the track and launched over the cliff. Den held his breath as it dropped, then caught the air. Den's idea of one continuous wing seemed to be working. The colorful wetting agents had done their job: the wings were more or less even, directing the assembly away from the cliff. They were heavier than he had allowed for in his calculations, however, so it dropped rapidly. The crate hit the ground squarely about fifty feet beyond the wreckage of the 'Enola Grey.'

A collective cheer thundered out as the assembled enthusiasts swarmed the edge of the cliff, sharing estimates of the distance achieved. An alarmed Kithra grabbed her microphone and warned everyone to step back from the edge of the cliff. Nobody listened.

Den took shameless advantage of being the only Donor in the crowd and sent a rude pulse of disruption through the ambient nager. As the ren-Simes, at least, were distracted into looking at him, he shouted, "Come on, people! Stop shoving each other and take turns looking. If somebody gets pushed over the cliff, the press will cover that story and forget what we've done here. There will be plenty of time for everybody to see the distances, now that we're done launching."

The crowd obeyed with good-natured grumbling. It was muted enough that a wail from the corner of the shed was clearly audible. "But we're not done launching!" Mandle protested. "We've fixed the 'Right Flyer' and it's ready to go again."

Mandle's brother, Nervin, nodded his agreement. After its repairs, the box kite design looked even more like something thrown together from yard waste, all held together with duct tape.

However, the crowd was in a good mood. Nobody had the heart to deny the child a chance to fly her creation. Kithra started the winch and willing hands helped the children drag their crate over to the catapult. The hands were so willing, and the wings so light, that one strut came loose at the back. Shaking his head, Mandle's brother took a ball of twine out of his pocket and tied it back into place.

When he was done, he absent-mindedly set the twine down on the nearest flat surface, which happened to be the crate, and performed a brief inspection to make sure that the rest of his repairs had held. Nodding his head, he told his sister, "We're ready."

Grinning broadly, Mandle gave the order, "Launch it!"

The rock dropped and the 'Right Flyer' was catapulted off the cliff. The wind, which had picked up a little, caught the tarp-covered wings. After an initial swoop, the lightweight assembly actually lifted until it was almost level with the cliff.

"Nervin, you're an idiot!" an outraged Mandle berated her brother. "Your ball of string is stuck onto the back end!"

Den blinked. Mandle was right. The ball of twine that her brother had set down on the crate had started to roll off during launch. However, as it fell, the end had stuck to an incompletely secured piece of duct tape on the lower of the two wings, right up against the packing crate. Under the combined acceleration of gravity and the catapult, the twine unwound until there was a twenty-foot tail hanging off the back, ending in a wooden dowel that had acted as a spool.

Now, however, the dowel and attached twine were acting as a stabilizer, much the way a kite tail would. The 'Right Flyer' dipped and recovered as a sideways gust of air hit it, then steadied into a shallow glide path that quickly outdistanced both the 'Enola Grey' and the 'Spirit of Valzor.' The crowd held its collective breath until the dangling dowel finally caught in a bush, jerking it sideways. One lower wing grazed the ground and the entire assembly disintegrated. The wreckage slid to a halt not far from the pasture gate.

Thunderous cheers threatened to bring down the hay barn's elderly roof. When relative quiet had been restored, Kithra invited Fridda Polburn, the representative from the Economic Development Board, to comment. "I'm very impressed with what I saw here today," she admitted. "Yes, there are issues that have to be solved before developing powered flight can be considered practical, but you have made great progress today. I look forward to seeing your progress next year!"

Den made a point of seeking Polburn out as the group started the long walk back through the pasture. He introduced himself and said, "I hope today has demonstrated that powered flight is an achievable goal."

"Flight, perhaps," Polburn agreed dryly. "It appears that landings will take a lot more work."

"We'll get there," Den promised confidently. "The Ancients left us with a multitude of designs. The challenge is to discover which of them work best with our current range of materials. Give us another year or two and we'll have a workable design."

"Sosu Milnan, you know as well as I do that wing design is the least of the hurdles," Polburn chided him. "I've read the proposals submitted by your fellow hobbyists. The Ancients managed powered flight because they had lightweight, powerful engines fueled by hydrocarbons. We can't solve that problem the way they did because they used up most of the world's fossil fuels. It would require substantial research to modify our selyn-based technology to produce an equivalent."

"It will," Den agreed, choosing a more optimistic grammatical tense. "The technology, once developed, will find a lot of other applications besides powering flying machines. Smaller, lighter batteries will provide huge reductions in the amount of industrial selyn to run the sliderail trains, for instance."

"You and your fellow hobbyists make a strong case," Polburn admitted. "After today, I'm willing to consider powered flight as a potentially achievable technology instead of a fantasy. If the selyn supply grows sufficiently to risk developing such an energy-intensive technology, I will cast my vote in favor of powered flight."

Which, Den reflected, put the burden squarely back on him, as the only Tecton Donor who had both a personal interest in the revival of powered flight and an assignment to a struggling out-Territory Sime Center located in the center of the greatest supply of untapped selyn known to the Tecton.

This latter point was emphasized by District Controller Monruss in a private meeting before he was scheduled to catch the train back to Valzor. "I realize that locating any Sime Center so far from the border was bound to be controversial," he pointed out, not *quite* in a scolding tone. "I had hoped that resistance would fade once they had a chance to get to know you. However, Hajene Madz reports that there are still demonstrations against the Sime Center and that these sometimes get violent." He placed a tentacle on the stack of files in front of him, which the Donor recognized as Rital's last four monthly reports.

"Donations are up this past month, in spite of the demonstrations," Den pointed out weakly.

"Perhaps they would go up more, if you started making a real effort to reach out to the people of Clear Springs," Monruss suggested. "Unlike your cousin, you don't have to wear retainers when you leave the Sime Center. Get out and introduce yourself. Offer to teach their children how to survive changeover without Killing. Let people know that they can get quality medical assistance at their Sime Center. Don't just hide and hope they'll forget about you."

Den nodded weakly, trying not to imagine how Reverend Sinth and his followers would react if he walked into their children's school and told the students to ignore everything they had been taught about Simes by their parents and teachers. "I'll do that," he promised. "But it's difficult to leave the Sime Center when I'm the only available First Order Donor."

"Well, that's about to change," Monruss told him. "The donation rate *has* gone up this past month and Controller Madz has requested additional channeling staff. I've found him Hajene Tyvi ambrov Frihill. You'll accompany her back to Clear Springs today and Sosu Alson will stay to take care of her. She's worked at some of the border Sime Centers and her English is fluent. She's waiting to meet you in the conference room down the hall."

Monruss moved the stack of Clear Springs reports firmly to the "out" basket for filing and picked up the next item from the overflowing "in" box. Taking the hint, Den went to meet his new colleague.

CHAPTER 13
CONSPIRACY THEORIES

Hajene Tyvi ambrov Frihill was a relatively tall woman, for a Sime. She was politely aloof when he introduced himself, but seemed competent enough. *A typical Householding channel,* Den thought, dismissing her attitude with a shrug. She'll work with us poor, houseless people for the good of the Tecton, but that doesn't mean she has to socialize with us.

She was, however, a necessary part of the Clear Springs experiment. If the Economic Development Board's willingness to develop a motor that could power a working flyer was contingent upon an increase in industrial selyn, Den was more than willing to work overtime to make that happen. Hajene Tyvi was willing to take on the challenge of winning over more donors in spite of the opposition of Reverend Sinth and his followers, so she was on Den's team and he could and would work with her.

The success of the "Spirit of Valzor" with minimal help from Den had made him rethink his role. There were plenty of engineers among the community of model flyer builders, mechanics like Eddina, woodworkers like Jannun, and even youngsters like Mandle, who knew so little about Ancient flyers that she could approach building a flyer of her own from a completely new perspective. Den would research specific issues for them in the Clear Springs library and cheer on their efforts but in truth, a First Order Tecton Donor simply did not have the training or the time to participate in building a new technology. However, as the only First Order Tecton Donor who had a personal interest in developing that technology, he was in a unique position to help overcome one of the fundamental impediments to redeveloping Ancient technologies.

If the Clear Springs Sime Center failed, the Tecton would assume that no Sime Center could succeed in the interior of a Gen Territory. The border Sime Centers would probably continue to provide enough selyn to run the trains and maintain current levels of industry, but there would be no large surplus of industrial selyn to spur modern technology.

Den very much wanted to live in the sort of world the Ancients had built, a world of unlimited energy that freed its inhabitants to let their creativity run wild. To free himself to fly, he first had to ensure a selyn supply of such abundance that the Tecton would no longer have to make difficult choices between supplying the selyn its renSimes must have to survive and a healthy economy.

Unfortunately for Den's newfound dedication, the citizens of Clear Springs didn't share his desire for progress. The chaos on the sidewalk settled down into a grim battle of attrition as the summer progressed. That didn't prevent the donor rolls from increasing when the tuition increase passed by the university's Board of Regents proved even larger than anticipated. Unfortunately, the new donors were almost all poverty-stricken students. The long-term residents of Clear Springs, even most community leaders who supported the Sime Center, kept any personal support they cared to offer strictly theoretical.

While Den was in Valzor, Carla Lifton had reconsidered her decision to leave the Conservative Congregation church. She might have lost respect for Reverend Sinth personally, but she had invested too many years in her church-based friendships to reject them, as well. She no longer managed the daily roster of Save Our Kids demonstrators, but she dropped by to participate on the days Reverend Sinth was otherwise occupied.

In late summer, Annie Lifton defiantly joined both OLD SOKS and the Sime Center's roster of donors. This finally prompted her mother to stop demonstrating against the Sime Center entirely. "It's just too embarrassing to have her friends in Save Our Kids asking why her own daughter is working against them," Annie explained.

At around the same time, Annie's brother Rob stopped coming in to donate. When Rital inquired as to the reason, Annie shook her head with the scorn of a younger sibling. "Rob is making a fool of himself over Reverend Sinth's niece, Bethany. She and her stepbrother, Zakry, moved here a year ago. Rob's scared she'll find out if he donates and she's even got him going to the Save Our Kids meetings." She grinned wickedly. "Of course, he tells me exactly what they're planning afterward. Then I tell our fearless leaders, Silva and Tohm, who figure out what to do about it."

"After the way Rob argued his mother into letting him donate, I'm surprised he quit," Den remarked to his cousin as the now low field Annie rejoined the OLD SOKS group on the sidewalk.

"I'm not," Rital said, putting her file away. "Rob never was comfortable with the idea of letting a Sime take selyn from him. He couldn't quit just because his mother wanted him to but at that age, how could donating possibly compete with the girl of his dreams?" Rital rolled his eyes at the folly of youth, then added, "In the long run, the information he's passing on to OLD SOKS may be more valuable than the small amount of selyn he could contribute as a donation-shy GN-3."

Controller Monruss was delighted with the progress at the Clear Springs Sime Center, which was finally becoming a reliable exporter of selyn. That took some of the pressure off its beleaguered staff, as long as they could maintain that momentum.

That month, the university's facilities manager, Alvon Desmond, finally talked the university's staff union into allowing him to issue the Sime Center a key to the basement room that housed the selyn batteries. It was only then that Den discovered that the key whose ownership Desmond's union had contested so fiercely also opened the main doors to the building. As such, copies were issued routinely to every employee who might conceivably have to enter the building outside of class hours. This included the clerical staff, janitors, professors, graduate students, undergraduate student lab assistants, and even the outside contractors who filled the vending machines.

The thought of random, untrained individuals having access to the machinery at the heart of a vital utility was utterly alien to Den. Desmond's people weren't completely devoid of common sense. The electrical generators and steam plant were housed in a restricted-access room opened by a different key. The windmills were protected by a fence tall enough to discourage adventurous students from climbing it. Yet the university authorities apparently felt that a simple safety grating was sufficient protection for their prized selyn batteries: a grating that any Sime could open, or any Gen or child with a good pair of wire cutters, for that matter. It was clear to the Donor that nobody among the university's personnel had bothered to learn the first thing about how their new batteries operated or how to handle them safely.

In addition to sending more staff, Monruss also asked Den for a report on how his outreach efforts had improved relations with the city and university. Unfortunately, the Donor had no idea. Quite the contrary: he doubted that there had been any lasting change. His most recent offer to present an informative talk had been met with stony silence from the Chamber of Commerce and the local schools. The battery-room key issue was hardly something he wanted to hold up as an example of his diplomatic prowess. In search of successful outreach efforts, he asked Tohm and Silva to meet with him.

"There's often some trouble when a new border Sime Center opens out-Territory," he explained when they had settled in the Sime Center's small library, "but it's never been this strong or lasted this long. Usually, the problems stop when around 10% of the Gens in the area have donated at least once. Clear Springs passed that point weeks ago, but there's no sign that things are calming down. True, most of our donors are students and we are unusually far from the border, but I wouldn't think it would make that much difference."

Silva shook her head. "The distance from the border isn't the problem. Clear Springs has demonstrators because of Reverend Sinth."

"A man whose dedication is exceeded only by his ego," Tohm added gratuitously.

"Sinth is obnoxious, I agree, but how could one man make that much difference?" Den asked. "I expect his congregation supports his efforts, but there are only three hundred or so of them and that's not enough people to cause this kind of trouble."

"Exactly!" Silva grinned. "So instead of fighting you with just the small minority of Clear Springs residents who are willing to take action against the Sime Center, he pools the efforts of similar groups from all across the Territory. Let me tell you how it works." She plopped down on the couch and Tohm sprawled beside her, one arm possessively around her shoulders.

Den listened with utter astonishment as the two out-Territory Gens described a paranoid's nightmare: a conspiracy to convince the conservative organizations in New Washington Territory to make shutting down the Clear Springs Sime Center a top priority. Sinth had started traveling around the area, giving a lecture to like-minded churches and other groups on the dangers of Simes. His talk contained many references to children of pro-Sime citizens who had gone into changeover and children of God-fearing, righteous individuals who had established. (Somehow, he neglected to mention that the ratio of changeovers to Establishments was identical in both groups.) The presentation was lavishly illustrated with graphic photos of children in changeover and Gens Killed by berserkers. By insisting that Tecton channels were responsible for this human devastation, Sinth had gleaned dedicated volunteers from each audience.

This increase in numbers had allowed him to expand his recruitment efforts to involve mailing lists, phone solicitations, letter-writing campaigns to newspapers and legislators, and even door-to-door visits in selected neighborhoods. Sinth had also asked religious leaders from most of the more traditional denominations to urge their congregants to pledge a day or week as a demonstrator outside the Clear Springs Sime Center, in hopes of fooling the Tecton and the Clear Springs city government into believing that they represented a majority of the town's residents. Out-of-town demonstrators were given free food and housing at the homes of local volunteers.

Such tactics were utterly alien to in-Territory politics. When even the most single-minded of Sime activists could zlin their opponents' sincerity and outright lies were readily detected, there was much more incentive to find a solution that everyone could accept.

"Most Save Our Kids members haven't ever been to Clear Springs and even so, about half of the demonstrators on any given day are from out of town," Silva concluded.

Den shook his head in disbelief. "I find it hard to believe that anyone could get that many people to stand outside all day, waving signs and chanting themselves hoarse, just by mailing some letters and making a few speeches."

"Why not?" Tohm asked matter-of-factly. "How did you think we get people to join OLD SOKS? We put up some fliers, get some letters into the newspapers, ask some of the more liberal churches to write us up in their newsletters…"

"Of course, we have it easier than Sinth, because there are more people in Clear Springs in favor of the Sime Center than opposed," Silva added. "On the other hand, we're strictly local, while Sinth has built a Territory-wide organization. But the principle is the same."

Den clenched his fists in frustration, knowing that the Tecton would find such tactics as unbelievable as he did. *No wonder Rital hasn't tried to explain this to Controller Monruss. Monruss would put it down to paranoia and have Rital on the next train back to Valzor.*

"There's got to be some way to fight them," Den said, trying desperately to think of one.

"Of course there is," Tohm reassured him. "Sinth's demonstrations haven't been nearly as successful in 'convincing' people not to donate since OLD SOKS started escorting people through their lines. The letters they write are only effective if no one writes back to correct their lies. If you folks are finally willing to start standing up for yourselves, they won't have a chance. For instance, my sister works for the *Clarion*. Why don't I get her to ask Fredricks if you can write a regular column to answer peoples' questions?"

"Umm…" Den tried to think of a way to decline politely.

"Good." Tohm clapped him on the shoulder. "Get both sides of the story out before the public and we can't lose. Now, one of the City Councilmen, Dav Senberg, has introduced a resolution drawn up by a committee of our law student members. It calls for the police to vigorously enforce the laws governing demonstrations outside the Sime Center, to prevent injuries. There's going to be a public meeting tomorrow night. You ought to be there. Marcy isn't the only one who's been hurt by those bullies."

That afternoon, Den sent a strongly worded report back to Monruss. "These people are crazy," he wrote in frustration. "There hasn't been a single school teacher who would invite me to speak to her class for fear of complaints from a few parents, yet some of those same teachers push through a mob of angry demonstrators to donate. Some of the Gens who spend hours every week helping donors through the demonstrations openly admit that they, themselves, would never even consider donating. The activists on both sides frequently issue wildly inaccurate statements and no one seems to mind. Please, get a professional diplomat out here before I become as crazy as they are!"

Early the following evening, the Sime Center was called to pick up a child in changeover. By the time Den and Rital arrived it was too late to move the girl, but her parents agreed to let the channel and Donor take care of her in their house.

"It's our fault that she tried to hide it," the girl's mother said, wringing her hands. "She only turned thirteen last week and we just haven't gotten around to talking about it with her."

The girl was untrained, of course, but she was good at following instructions and there were no additional complications. However, by the time Rital had given her First Transfer and her mother had fussed around packing her a suitcase, the City Council meeting was about to start. Rital had the ambulance driver drop Den off at City Hall on the way back to the Sime Center.

The auditorium was packed. Den scanned the sea of faces until he located Tohm and Silva, who were seated with a dozen or so other OLD SOKS members in the second row back. They were carrying their usual signs, but Silva had a new button pinned to her headband with the defiant slogan, "**Pro-Sime and Proud.**"

She saw him and waved. When Den had worked his way through the crush to her side, she indicated the empty aisle seat beside her. "I saved you a place, but I was beginning to think you wouldn't come."

"I had to help Hajene Madz with a changeover," he explained absently, surveying the crowd with disbelief. People were beginning to stand along the back wall. "I had no idea that city government was such a popular attraction."

"Most of the time there's less than a dozen people," Tohm said. "Sinth brought in supporters from all over: they've been shuttling people from the train station to their church all day."

"Ironic, isn't it? They travel in selyn-powered trains to speak against a Sime Center," Den commented with a wry grimace.

Tohm shrugged. "Rob Lifton reports that Sinth is very worried. If they have to leave a clear path into the Sime Center at all times, their ability to intimidate people will go way down. A lot fewer people will be interested in tramping up and down on your sidewalk all day."

Den nodded. "It would certainly make *our* jobs easier," he agreed.

The council members trickled in and Mayor Kroag called the meeting to order a mere ten minutes late. They voted unanimously to skip all new business and all old business except for Senberg's proposal. Because of the large number of people present, Mayor Kroag announced that those officially representing each side would be allowed fifteen minutes to present their arguments for or against the resolution. After that, anyone who wanted to speak could have three minutes and three minutes only. "And we'll be timing you!"

First to speak was Tohm, the primary author of Senberg's resolution. "As a law student," he said, "I fully support the concept of freedom of speech, even when that freedom is used to support causes I despise. The law specifies that any group demonstrating in front of a place of business must leave a clear path at all times and that those who use such paths to enter the business can be engaged, but must not be verbally harassed or physically intimidated.

"During the past few months, I have watched the members of the Save Our Kids campaign break these laws on a daily basis. They routinely fail to leave a passage into the Sime Center—in fact, I can't recall one time when they *have* left such a passage. Anyone who tries to get onto the Sime Center's grounds is the target of verbal harassment and physical intimidation. I have seen anti-Sime demonstrators scream obscenities and threats at a thirteen-year-old girl who wanted information for a school assignment. I have seen the bullies beat men old enough to be my grandparents with their signs—and believe me, a club doesn't hurt any less just because you tack a piece of cardboard onto it. Just ask Marcy Ingleston.

"These actions are not legal and the people who perform them are criminals. The police have proved unwilling to enforce the law, leading to at least one serious injury. My resolution does not restrict the right of Save Our Kids to demonstrate legally at the Sime Center. However, it does ask the officials responsible for law enforcement to curtail the illegal portion of Save Our Kids' activities before we have another Marcy Ingleston heading for the hospital."

The pro-Sime Center people in the room applauded loudly as Tohm sat down. Sinth's followers booed and hissed.

Sinth was the official speaker against the resolution, as the founder and acknowledged leader of Save Our Kids. His face was flushed with passion and he shook his head in hurt innocence as he paced slowly in front of the podium, ignoring the microphone, and said in martyred tones, "I'm deeply hurt by what I just heard. Bullies, vicious criminals who beat children up.... Those are harsh accusations. Particularly from a self-proclaimed radical rabble-rouser who lives with his girlfriend *without benefit of marriage.*" He turned to glare at Tohm, who put his arm around Silva and winked impudently. "Why, his group holds their weekly meetings at the Sudworks Brewery so they have an excuse to drink beer.

"My followers are God-fearing, church-going, sober and respectable people: upright citizens of this Territory. We do not hate the misguided souls who have been enticed to seek out the Simes. We care deeply for them and their families. And in our love, we are driven to share with them what the Scriptures say about Simes: that by donating, by willingly giving themselves into the tentacles of evil, they give the Devil unfettered freedom to turn their siblings, or their children, or their grandchildren, into blood-thirsty, murdering Sime demons!

"We are not breaking any laws. Why, Ezra Tains, our Chief of Police here in Clear Springs, has even joined us on occasion as we try to save these poor souls. Now, I've gotten to know Ezra pretty well since I moved to Clear Springs as pastor for the Conservative Congregation. If there's one thing you can be sure of, it's that he takes his responsibilities very seriously." Sinth's voice rose to a crescendo. "If we were breaking any laws, don't you think that the police chief would be arresting us, not helping us?

"This resolution Mr. Seegrin has talked Councilman Senberg into presenting for him is simply a blatant attempt to harass us as we do God's work. **AND IT WILL NOT WORK!** It will not prevent us from carrying God's message to those who need it most!"

The applause and hallelujahs were much louder this time, thanks to the reinforcements Sinth had bussed in.

Mayor Kroag pounded her gavel for quiet. "At this time, I would like for those who wish to address us on this issue to line up in the center aisle, behind the podium." Over half of the audience made a concerted rush for the microphone. As they jockeyed for position, she raised her voice and continued. "I would like to remind everyone once again that you are limited to three minutes and we *are* timing you. Also, please give your name and city of origin, so that we can keep our records straight."

Since Den's seat was on the aisle, he had managed to grab second place in line. Marcy, who had been seated directly in front of him in the first row, was first. As soon as things were quiet, she began speaking. "My name is Marcy Ingleston and I'm going to college here in Clear Springs. Reverend Sinth is lying about what Save Our Kids is doing. They not only pushed and shoved me, they were so full of loving concern for my welfare," her voice dripped with sarcasm, "that they stood by while their friend broke my collar bone with his sign. Then instead of helping me, they stood around screaming about how I was damned forever! For all they cared, I could have lain on the sidewalk all day. I'm asking the City Council to pass the resolution and put those bullies out of business!"

She yielded the podium to Den, who had just remembered how much he hated public speaking. He swallowed to relieve his suddenly dry mouth. "I'm Sosu Den Milnan, senior Donor at the Clear Springs Sime Center," he began, gaining confidence as he saw that all five council members were paying respectful attention. "I would like to bring up an additional legal question that Tohm Seegrin did not address. Due to the retainer laws, all Sime Centers are legally considered Sime Territory. By blocking access to a Territorial border, Save Our Kids is also in violation of the free travel provisions of the First Contract. The Tecton is very concerned about the situation here. If these demonstrations continue unchecked, you may have an inter-territorial incident on your hands."

"Good point," Tohm leaned over Silva to whisper. "I hadn't thought of that angle."

As the evening wore on the talks started to run together, but there were a few moments that Den was always able to remember clearly:

A highly distraught woman who failed to identify herself before she sobbed, "When are you going to get those slimy snakes out of Clear Springs and save our children?"

Reverend Sinth's nephew, Zakry, a shorter-than-average thirteen-year-old whose slight frame was not quite hidden beneath at least fifty extra pounds of fat, gazing up at the City Council with the ecstatic, otherworldly (and more than a little vacant) stare of a mystic as he explained, with many scriptural quotations, how his faith would make him Gen unless he or his family were exposed to in-Territory contamination. The look of total hatred that he turned on Den as he said this haunted the Donor for days.

A similarly hate-filled expression on the face of a local shopkeeper, as he ranted against the "heresy" of the scriptural interpretations Sinth used to justify his anti-Sime Center stance.

Florence Grieves, whose daughter, Annie Lifton's friend, Rachel, had gone through changeover, Killed her sister, and been murdered in turn by her parents, insisting, "The Sime Center caused both my daughters to die!" When Mayor Kroag asked if she had called the Sime Center for help, the woman indignantly retorted, "Of course not!"

Several donors described in lurid detail how they had been pushed, shoved, and screamed at by anti-Sime demonstrators in their attempts to follow their own consciences by donating. Those same demonstrators flatly denied doing such things.

In all, there were thirty-two speakers in favor of the resolution and sixty-four speakers against, nineteen of whom lived in Clear Springs. When everyone had had their say, the council voted three to one to pass the resolution. One council member thought that the City Council shouldn't get involved in the issue if the police thought the demonstrators' activities were legal and one had gone home early because his babysitter couldn't stay past ten thirty.

It was after eleven when Den finally left City Hall. He was making his way across the parking lot, not paying much attention to his surroundings, when the trouble started. Afterward, he realized that he should have been more cautious, but he had never had to defend himself against a physical attack in his adult life. As a First Order Donor, his nager was zlinnable for quite a distance and Simes jealously guarded the well-being of any Gens in their vicinity. In-Territory, even criminals were well aware that the quality of the transfers and medical services available to them depended on the willingness of channels and Donors to work in their neighborhoods. Thus, Den could stroll through high-crime areas of Valzor in the secure knowledge that his Donor's nager and the Tecton crest ring on his finger would protect him from harm.

He discovered that night the profound difference in reaction his profession invoked on the Gen side of the border. As he passed a group of well-dressed college students who were talking by the bicycle rack, one of them looked up and recognized him.

"Hey, it's the Sime-lover," he called with a predatory sneer.

The others clustered around Den, pushing at the Donor and shouting, "Devil-worshipper!" "Why don't you go kiss a Sime?" and "Sime-lover, you're no better than a whore!"

As the students pushed him from one side of their circle to the other, Den struggled to stay on his feet. In the brief moments between shoves, he tried to locate any of the OLD SOKS members. It seemed incredible that he could be roughed up on the outskirts of a large crowd without attracting their attention. *But it's dark here and there aren't any Simes to zlin that I require help.*

"What's going on here?" a deep, authoritative voice demanded. The mob suddenly disintegrated back into a group of students, who meekly allowed the uniformed police chief to push through them. He hooked his thumbs behind the leather gun belt that strained to hold in his more than ample belly and glared meaningfully at the students. "What do you think you're doing?" he repeated, staring them down one by one until he reached the blond young man who seemed to be their leader.

"We didn't mean any harm, Chief Tains," the blond student drawled insolently. "We just wanted to teach the Sime-lover a little lesson, that's all."

Tains scowled. "We have law and order in Clear Springs, kid, and don't you forget it. Now, I don't want to have to arrest you to protect the likes of him," he nodded towards Den, "but I will if I have to. So you go on home and I'll pretend that none of this happened."

In ten seconds, the students had hopped on their bicycles and pedaled away.

"Thank you," Den said a little stiffly as the last one disappeared down the road.

A fat globule of spit landed half an inch from the toe of Den's right shoe. "Get back where you belong, Sime-lover," Tains said contemptuously. "I don't want any more trouble in my town." He turned and strolled back to the parking lot.

CHAPTER 14

MAKING HASTE SLOWLY

The passage of the demonstration-rule enforcement resolution made little difference in the days that followed, since the Clear Springs police continued to ignore its provisions. In fact, the only real change was the addition of "Anti-Sime, anti-sud, Save Our Kids, you're full of crud!" to OLD SOKS' repertoire of chants in response to Sinth's denigration of their favorite meeting place, the Sudworks Brewery

Den's public relations program was also largely unsuccessful. He got a few telephone calls in response to his fliers, mostly from teachers seeking background information for lectures leading up to Union Day, which celebrated the signing of the First Contract. Politicians and diplomats being what they were, this holiday took place some six months after Faith Day. However, the Donor's offers to visit the teachers' classes himself, or give them and their students a tour of the Sime Center, were always politely declined. Apparently, those few teachers who were courageous (or foolish) enough to tackle such a controversial subject at all felt safer going to Valzor's Old Center. As one teacher explained, "If I 'balance' the Old Center with a tour of the Church of the Purity cathedral and museum across the river and throw in the amusement park and a few art museums to round out the package, the kids and their parents go for it. There'd be less paperwork if I just had you come in and give a lecture, but I'd be fighting for my job within a week."

Hank Fredricks was delighted with Tohm's idea of a Sime Center guest column in the *Clear Springs Clarion* and duly sent over a packet full of guidelines and suggested topics. When Den submitted his first attempt, Fredricks not only printed it, he decided to make it a regular feature.

As Union Day came closer, the number of volunteer general-class donors increased to unprecedented levels despite the best efforts of the anti-Sime demonstrators. To minimize the donors' wait times, Rital requested and received two more channels for the Sime Center's staff.

Zir Asthan and Reyna Tast were both Third Order channels. Zir was a few years younger than Den and a competent amateur musician, while Reyna was the embodiment of everyone's favorite grandmother. The Thirds, with their much slower recovery times, could not take nearly as many donations in a shift as a First like Rital. They also lacked the control and sensitivity to handle difficult or unpredictable cases like untrained children in changeover or particularly frightened new donors. However, they could handle the routine, confident donors and patient monitoring duties, freeing the two First Order channels to focus on the more challenging work.

In response to the increase in donors willing to brave their blockade, the Save Our Kids campaign took out a full-page ad in the *Clarion* calling for all "citizens of good will" to support their efforts to save the town from Simes. The following day, there were nearly twice as many people as usual on the sidewalk outside the Sime Center, but most of them joined the counter-demonstrators. Many of the new Gens also donated in protest against Sinth's tactics. As one irate, middle-aged woman put it, "Any time folks like that are against something, chances are I'm for it."

For the first time, all four channels were working in the Collectorium at the same time. The numbers ebbed the next day, but remained higher than before Sinth's advertisement. Rital changed the schedule so that either he or Tyvi was on call to take care of the "virgins," as Seena still insisted on calling them, while Zir and Reyna handled experienced donors. This was a sensible division of the workload, but the strain of handling transfer-shy Gens all day was taking its toll on both Firsts.

Four days after Rital's turnover, the usually patient channel snapped at Ref for burning his toast and during the resulting nageric disruption, Tyvi broke the handle off of her tea mug. Den and Tyvi's Donor, Siv Alson, informed their respective charges that no more donations were to be taken by either channel unless a Donor was present to block the nageric chaos.

Neither Rital nor Tyvi objected very strenuously.

A week before their transfer date, Den and Rital arrived at the Collectorium ten minutes before it officially opened to find two Gens already waiting for them. Den didn't know the young woman, but he recognized her older companion immediately.

So did Rital. "Mayor Kroag, it's good to see you," he said with genuine pleasure.

"Controller Madz, Sosu Milnan," she greeted them, shaking hands automatically with the practiced firmness of a professional out-Territory politician, but Den knew that Kroag meant it as a gesture of trust and respect.

"I'd like you to meet my daughter, Meg," she continued proudly, drawing the girl forward with an arm around her shoulders. "When I told her I was coming here this morning, she said she wanted to come along and donate also."

"It seemed like the right time of year for it, with Union Day coming up," Meg said a little shyly. "My literature class is reading Tharson's novel about the last campaign against the Raiders this fall and we have to write a paper on it."

"So you decided to do some extracurricular research?" Rital asked, amused.

"It can't hurt," she shrugged, nervously twining the end of her braid around one finger. "Miz Ross's honors class has been using the same reading list forever. I've been trying to think of something original to say about the stupid book for *weeks*."

"I'm glad to see that the spirit of free inquiry is still alive and well." The channel winked, and Meg grinned back, more at ease.

"I have some more good news for you," Mayor Kroag interjected. "Clear Springs is going to be hosting a convention of city government officials from all over this part of the territory next week. Some of the participating towns have been following the situation here with interest and are considering whether they should ask the Tecton for Sime Centers of their own. Electrical power grids are expensive to maintain, after all."

Den nodded in agreement, hiding his elation at this development. Clear Springs was not the only untapped source of selyn in New Washington Territory. Even better, Reverend Sinth did not have enough volunteers to harass, say, a dozen or so Sime Centers.

Mayor Kroag was still talking. "Some of the delegates have expressed interest in visiting your Sime Center while they're here, since it's so much easier to get to than the one in Valzor. If it's all right with you, I'll have my secretary call and make the arrangements."

"That's wonderful," Den responded, glad that he would finally have the chance to give his carefully prepared speech.

Reyna had arrived by now, holding Mayor Kroag's file.

"Meg, why don't you come with Den and me," Rital suggested, "and we'll let Hajene Tast take care of your mother."

Meg swallowed and looked at her mother for reassurance. At Kroag's nod, she followed them down the hall to one of the small collecting rooms. She looked curiously at the transfer lounge as Rital sat behind the desk and Den perched on a stool behind him, but took her place in the visitor's chair without prompting.

Rital pulled out a copy of the medical history form and absent-mindedly fished in his uniform pocket with two handling tentacles for a pen. Meg watched the channel's tentacles in fascination, then blushed when she realized that she'd been caught staring. "I was just wondering what they felt like," she explained lamely.

"See for yourself," Rital offered kindly, holding out a steady hand with one dorsal tentacle extended.

Den leaned forward, ready to shield his cousin if the girl became frightened. *Come on, kid, you can do it,* he urged silently.

Meg hesitated a moment, then cautiously reached out and lightly brushed the proffered tentacle with a finger. "They really aren't slimy, are they?" she said with a note of discovery.

"No, they really aren't," Rital agreed.

After that, it was easy. When the paperwork was finished, Meg lay down on the transfer lounge and offered her hands with a confidence rivaling that of some experienced donors. She hardly blinked when Rital made the transfer contact and when he finished draining her GN-3 level and let her go, she asked in a surprised voice, "Is that all?"

"That's all there is to it," the channel confirmed. "You're low field now."

When Meg had rejoined her mother in the waiting room, full of inspiration for her book report, channel and Donor exchanged indulgent grins.

"You're dangerous, cousin, did you know that?" Den teased. "You've gotten so good at working with out-Territory Gens, I'll bet you could seduce one of those hymn-singing fanatics on our sidewalk into donating, if you put your mind to it."

"They're hardly likely to give me a chance," Rital laughed.

"More's the pity," Den agreed.

There was a continual stream of Gens coming in to donate all day until by early afternoon, Rital had to delegate the pre-donation paperwork to Seena while Gati kept the traffic flowing smoothly. This increased the number of donations he could take, but also gave the newcomers less time to get used to him before donating.

By mid-afternoon, as he and Rital were escorting a white-haired but still active farmer back to the waiting room, Den was looking forward to the end of the shift and dinner. Gati intercepted them before Rital could pick up the next folder.

"We may have a potential problem here, Hajene," she said, lips pressed together in concern as she tapped the file she held in her right hand against her left.

"What is it?" Rital asked.

"An adolescent, not quite old enough to be a university student. She *seems* to be under control, at least as much as any of them are, but Zir agrees her nager is weird and there's something not quite right about her." Gati shook her head. "It's probably nothing."

"Your instincts are usually pretty sound," Rital reassured her. "If the girl's likely to cause trouble, I'd best see to her now."

Gati held out the file folder. "Seena just finished helping her fill out the paperwork. The girl didn't look at her once. And the friend who came with her brought along some of those pamphlets that the nuts outside are so fond of passing out."

"Is the friend donating, too?" Den asked alertly. One possible Simephobe was bad enough.

"No, she's not."

Rital took the folder and flipped it open. Den peered over his cousin's shoulder and scanned the information inside.

The girl had given her name as Bethany Thins and she was fifteen natal years old. That was a little younger than most out-Territory Gens started donating, especially if no other family members donated. Den couldn't recall any other Gens named Thins but he didn't know every new donor in the area, so that might not be significant. There was nothing in the girl's medical history to suggest a problem except, of course, that she had been raised out-Territory. That was more than enough complication, in itself.

Den glanced casually out into the waiting room, where seven Gens sat waiting for the channels. There were only two women young enough to be fifteen. One of them, a small, anxious-looking mouse in a dark brown dress, was holding a pamphlet and showing it to her friend. Because the other girl was facing away from him, all Den could see of her was the dark hair that spilled over the back of her chair.

"Is Bethany the one facing us?" Rital asked Gati as he snapped the file closed.

"No, the other one."

Rital zlinned the girl as well as he could, given the chaotic ambient nager of the waiting room. "Zir was right, she's strange. Not frightened, particularly. It's almost a kind of…voyeuristic curiosity mixed with self-righteous revulsion. I'd expect that from one of the demonstrators out there, not a prospective donor." He zlinned her again, trying to make out details, until Den stepped closer and lightly touched one arm, breaking his concentration.

"You'll have plenty of time to zlin her," he scolded tolerantly. "Right now, you'd better get her away from that friend and her pamphlets before she changes her mind."

Nodding agreement, Rital stepped around the reception desk and called, "Bethany Thins?"

The dark-haired girl looked around with a start, dropping the pamphlet she was holding. "Me?" she asked in a small voice. Now that he could see her face, Den recognized the red-skirted girl from his tour group at the Valzor Old Sime Center. *What the blazing shen is she doing here?*

Rital smiled at her reassuringly. "I'm Hajene Madz," he introduced himself. "Would you come with me, please?"

Bethany gave him a calculating glance, taking in his slight build and carefully retracted tentacles, then nodded agreement and stood up.

"Bethie…" the friend objected in a wavering voice. Bethany whispered something, too quietly for the Donor to hear, then followed Rital to the collecting room, Den bringing up the rear.

Shen, Rital's good, Den thought as he perched on his stool and made himself inconspicuous. His cousin was deliberately moving slower and less gracefully than usual: almost like a Gen.

It was working, too. With the desk between them, Bethany was already less wary. Rital limited himself to neutral topics—general conversation and the information on the medical history form. *Where does he get the patience?* Den wondered. He'd sit there making small talk for half an hour, if that's what it took.

In the end, it took only five minutes before Bethany's distrust eased. When she was ready to listen, Rital began to describe what went on during a general-class donation, as patiently and completely as if he hadn't been giving new donors the same briefing all day. Strangely, the girl virtually ignored the channel's reassurances about what she would (and would *not*) feel during the donation, although every other first-time donor Den had seen in the last week had been vitally interested. *Maybe she's been doing some background reading, so that information isn't new to her?*

But when Rital asked her if she had any questions, she asked several that showed an appalling ignorance. Den's favorite was, "Are there any aftereffects?"

Den struggled to keep a straight face as his cousin reassured Bethany that the only known aftereffects of donating were a lessened susceptibility to some infectious illnesses and a temporary inability to attract berserk Simes if there were other, high field Gens around.

Gati was right, this is a weird one, Den thought as the channel finally coaxed the girl into reclining on the transfer lounge. *From her questions, she could have learned everything she knows about Simes, Gens, and transfer at Reverend Sinth's knee. However, no one with that kind of background should be so calm just before donating for the first time.* Annie Lifton and her brother, Rob, had both been terrified, despite their previous encounters with Rital.

Of course, there was no guarantee that Bethany would remain as calm (relatively speaking) *during* the donation as she was before. Rital seemed to have everything under control as he took her hands but just in case, Den laid his hand on the channel's shoulder and let their fields merge.

As Rital slipped neatly into the full transfer contact, Den watched Bethany's face as closely as he could, ready to intervene if the girl panicked. To his surprise, she looked more startled than frightened. She hesitated a brief moment, then tried to move her head and break lip contact.

That's funny, Den thought. Most out-Territory Gens who struggled tried to move their arms first. Not that it made much difference.

When she couldn't free herself, Bethany began to struggle in earnest. As her eyes widened in fear, Den increased his support of Rital. "Relax, Bethany. Hajene Madz isn't hurting you," he murmured as reassuringly as he could. "It won't take much longer."

She seemed to hear him: at least she stopped struggling. When the channel let her go a few seconds later, she wilted bonelessly back into the lounge, eyes closed with relief. Rital waited until she opened them. "That's it," he said with a friendly smile. "It's all over. You're low field now."

"What?" Bethany asked, looking at him in a bewildered fashion. "You mean you really did…?" She hesitated, then blurted out, "But I didn't feel anything happening at all!" She sounded almost indignant about it.

"Most Gens don't feel anything during a routine donation," Rital explained, getting up from the lounge and returning to his seat behind the desk. He scribbled the proper notations on her file and a voucher form as Bethany stood unsteadily. When she realized that she was unharmed, she walked back to the desk.

"Here you are," Rital said, handing her the voucher. "If you will give this to the receptionist, she will see that your check is sent to you."

Bethany took the voucher from the channel at arm's length and left. Since Rital usually escorted donors back to the waiting room, Den turned to his cousin as soon as the door closed behind her, worried that the girl's fear had done more harm than he supposed.

"I'm all right, Den," the channel said, waving him away. "She didn't hurt me."

"I'll be the judge of that," Den said, taking his cousin's hands and examining the laterals and ronaplin glands for signs of prematurely raised intil.

Rital cooperated, letting his laterals extend to demonstrate their steadiness. "See?" he said. "I sent Bethany back alone because she was nervous about me." The channel frowned, sheathing his laterals. "It's strange. Usually they're *less* frightened after donating, not more. I wish I knew why she came in." He stared at the wall blankly for a moment, then recalled himself with a shrug. "Oh, well, I'm sure she had her reasons."

Den explained about seeing Bethany in one of his tour groups.

"See? I'm not the only one in the family with a talent for convincing unlikely Gens to donate." Rital grinned in delight and gripped his cousin's shoulder, letting a handling tentacle briefly caress the back of the Gen's neck. "Let's get back to work."

When they returned to the reception desk to swap Bethany's file for that of their next client, they found Gati vainly trying to smother a snicker.

"I could use a laugh," Den told her. "What's so funny?"

"Your mystery Gen's mousy friend," she said, grinning broadly. "When you took Bethany back to the collecting room, her friend started reading one of those pamphlets out loud, all about how nasty donating is."

"Shen!" Den swore. Apart from Bethany and her friend, there were no less than three college students in the waiting room whom Den didn't recognize. He didn't want to think about how such propaganda might affect already nervous Gens anticipating their first donations. "What's funny about that?"

"She happened to be sitting next to Mr. Duncan," Gati explained, "who has very little patience with that kind of hysteria. He took the pamphlet away from her, tossed it into the wastebasket, and told her that he knew from personal experience that donating wasn't anything like that. He also told her that she was a fool for believing Sinth, since he's never donated. Then Miz Farral chipped in and told the girl not to worry, her friend was in good hands, or tentacles as the case may be. I don't know if they convinced the girl, but she shut up pretty quickly."

Den grinned at Gati, then went to help Rital with the next Gen. *Maybe the Powers That Be were right to set up the Old Sime Center in Valzor as a tourist trap,* the Donor thought. *If making Bethany watch that donation back at Valzor prompted her to come in and donate herself, my playing tour guide wasn't a total waste of time.* Not that he was about to volunteer for such duty again any time soon. *And if she talks it over with her friend, that's two Gens who are less likely to show up on our sidewalk to harass donors.*

A few days after Mayor Kroag's visit to the Center, Den found his cousin in the latter's office, staring glumly through the window at the mob outside. "What's the matter?" he asked, putting a hand on Rital's shoulder.

The channel relaxed as his Donor's presence dispelled the unconscious, Need-based conviction that he was going to die, but he didn't smile. "I was just wondering how eager those visiting dignitaries will be to have Sime Centers in their own towns, when they have to get through *that* to meet us." He nodded out the window.

Even though the Collectorium would not open for another fifteen minutes, the combatants on the sidewalk were already preparing for battle. Den could hear "There's nothing here for Gens to fear; Save Our Kids, get out of here!" from the OLD SOKS contingent as they performed warm-up stretches. Not to be outdone, Sinth's followers paused in passing out signs and unpacking pamphlets to reply, "Sinners, we won't go away, we will stay right here and pray!" (Or maybe it was "prey.")

"I see what you mean," he said, as OLD SOKS switched their chant to "Anti-Sime, anti-Gen, who the hell do you *like*, then?" He considered the problem for a moment, then brightened. "The Collectorium doesn't open until nine and the demonstrators usually don't arrive much before then. What would happen if we started the tour here at eight, so they don't get hassled when they arrive? We give them a quick tour, feed them tea and some of Ref's good pastries, then pack them back into their bus and run them out to the Center for Technology to show them that selyn power is the wave of the future. If we do it right, all they'll see of the demonstration is a brief glimpse from the bus window if we run late."

"It just might work," Rital agreed, looking happier. "Why didn't I think of that?"

"I think I know why," Den said suggestively, running a careful hand along his channel's arm and delighting in the Need-swollen ronaplin glands. *What better way to celebrate Union Day than a transfer with one of my favorite channels?*

Two days before the touring dignitaries arrived, Den accompanied Reyna Tast to the Center for Technology to refill the selyn batteries. As he fished the Sime Center's own, shiny new key out of his pocket, he was encouraged by even this slender evidence of progress.

His optimism faded as they descended the narrow, concrete stairs and entered the musty-smelling room that housed the building's selyn batteries. The threadbare carpet still covered the front third of the concrete floor and the muddy footprints had never been mopped up. From the battered table to the sagging, olive-green couch with white stuffing showing through the rents in its cushions, the atmosphere was one of total gloom. The only objects in the entire room that looked less than twenty years old were the first aid kit on the table, the shiny new safety grating with its warning signs in Simelan and English, and the selyn batteries it protected.

"Those politicians are going to take one look at this place and decide they can live without us," Den complained as he helped the channel remove her retainers.

"It's not quite that hopeless," Reyna said, surveying the room with the eye of an experienced hostess. "All it will take is a good cleaning and a bit of staging. There are some very attractive carpets in storage and a matching blanket will hide the holes in the couch cushions quite nicely. If you use one from the cedar storage chest, that will help get rid of the musty smell. Put one of our red gingham tablecloths and some of Ref's refreshments on this thing," she poked the table with a tentacle, "and they won't notice how shabby it is." She frowned thoughtfully and pushed the table again with her hand. "Though you'd better prop up that short leg first, or you'll have tea all over the floor."

"You're a genius, Reyna," Den said, following her across the room to the safety grating. "I'll start rounding up some of what we'll require as soon as we get back."

Reyna released the Gen-proof lock on the grating, pulled open the gate, and grimaced at the three batteries inside. However, she dutifully began to unhook the orgonics cable from the first one. As she reluctantly extended her laterals toward the contacts, Den moved unerringly to the exact spot where he could best support her.

She looked over her shoulder at him and smiled in appreciation. "Sometimes, Firsts are very convenient to have around."

The Clear Springs Center had both an arrival and a departure the next day. Due to two unexpected channels' changeovers and an injury, Siv Alson was recalled to Valzor to give an emergency transfer. As a tacit apology, his replacement was Tyvi's son, Obis, who was supposed to arrive the following morning. Tyvi bravely expressed her delight at the prospect of having her son for transfer and immediately retired to the highly insulated deferment suite to wait for him.

The new arrival was Sera Coney, a freelance reporter researching a human-interest story about isolated Tecton outposts for one of Nivet Territory's leading news magazines. She was a stunning redhead with the luscious curves only a Gen could have. She made no secret of her interest in Den, although she knew better than to expect a Donor to have more than a theoretical interest in romance so close to transfer.

The Donor didn't care much for reporters, as a general rule, but he was seriously considering making an exception.

The visit of the out-Territory politicians went more smoothly than even Den had dared hope. Most seemed genuinely impressed with the Sime Center's facilities and comprehensive services. To the Donor's relief, only one man asked about the demonstrators outside. As he listened to them speak among themselves, Den was forced to radically alter his view of out-Territory politics. From their conversation, these men and women had been elected, *not* because of their ability to solve problems in ways acceptable to most people, but because they had been more successful than their opponents in identifying and avoiding reasons for the voters to dislike them.

Suddenly, the tactics Save Our Kids and OLD SOKS had been using began to make more sense. It was no wonder that neither group of demonstrators was interested in objective truth or compromise. They were showing the politicians how many people would vote against a candidate who took the opposing side. It didn't matter to anyone that a majority of Clear Springs residents supported the presence of the Sime Center, so long as that majority didn't feel strongly enough to switch its vote accordingly.

What a backward way to run a Territory!

At the Center for Technology, over refreshments of cookies and imported trin tea that many of the out-Territory Gens discarded after the first sip, several of the visitors made casual inquiries about where they might get more information, should their own local councils decide to ask the Tecton for a Sime Center in their towns. In a purely hypothetical sense, they hastened to assure the Donor.

"And won't *that* look good on our next monthly report!" Den exclaimed happily as he finished bringing Rital up to date.

"It's marvelous," the channel muttered, staring glumly at the file folders on his desk.

Realizing that his cousin was too close to active Need to feel anything else, Den reached for the channel's hands to control it, regretting the thoughtlessness that had led him to inflict his unrestrained ebullience on Rital when his cousin was unable to share it.

Unexpectedly, the channel withdrew. Den paused in confusion. Unlike some channels with whom he had worked, Rital seldom refused his Donor's assistance.

Zlinning his cousin's faint hurt, Rital tried an apologetic smile. It looked more like a grimace of agony. "Please don't, Den," he requested. He rearranged the files in front of him with two tentacles, not meeting the Donor's eyes.

"There's no easy way to tell you this," he said with a sigh. He reached for a pencil, tapped it on the desk a few times, then set it down and pushed a green transfer-assignment card toward Den. "The train from Iburan was delayed. Sosu Obis missed his connection in Valzor and won't get here until tomorrow morning, so I'm reassigning you to Tyvi this month."

"You're WHAT?!" Den sat suddenly in the visitor's chair.

"She can't wait, Den." Rital pushed one of the files across to the Donor. "Here's her file. See for yourself."

Den thumbed rapidly through the materials. "She's been shorted lately, but tomorrow morning is well within her tested endurance ratings…"

"And what would happen if Sosu Obis is delayed again? You know what the trains are like around the holidays. By the time we learned of the problem, you'd be low field. Valzor doesn't have anyone; that's how this whole mess started in the first place. I can survive another few days until Obis gets here, if necessary. Tyvi's been in the deferment suite since yesterday. Losing her assigned Donor a second time just before her transfer is going to be hard enough on her. If there's no replacement within a hundred miles, she might crack."

Den knew Rital was right, but he didn't have to like it. "And where does this leave you?" he demanded. "You've been under stress lately, too. If this Sosu Obis is a good match for Tyvi, he'll be totally inadequate for you."

"He's actually rated a little higher than his mother and he's young enough to have grown some since his last testing. He may surprise me."

"You don't believe that," Den stated.

"There's always next month." Rital finally met Den's eyes and the Donor recoiled at the misery he saw on his cousin's face. "Do you think I *want* to give you up?" the channel demanded brokenly. "Looking forward to a transfer with you is all that's gotten me through the last two months. But I'm Controller here and that means I have a responsibility to look after my people. All of them, not just you and me."

Thoroughly ashamed of himself for making a bad situation worse for his cousin, Den reached for the piece of green cardboard.

D en was still aching with frustrated sympathy for Rital's condition (not to mention aggravation at the channel's stubbornness) when he arrived at the deferment suite. He paused outside the door, disciplining his emotions. There wasn't anything he could do to change Rital's mind and it would be grossly unfair to subject Tyvi to his resentment. *She's hurting just as much as Rital,* he reminded himself, *and she is also worthy of my concern. Even if she is a Householder.*

Besides, there was no point in all of them having an inadequate transfer. Calmer, he thumbed the door signal and when Tyvi opened the door, Den was able to summon a genuine smile.

"Hi, there," he greeted her softly. "Obis didn't make his connection, so I thought I'd steal his date."

Den had hoped to get a laugh, or at least a smile, but Tyvi merely nodded solemnly and stood aside for him to enter. The apartment's sitting room was dim and plush, with blue carpeting on the floor that matched the overstuffed furniture and velvet draperies. It was carefully designed not to allow the slightest outside stimulus to irritate the Need-sensitized nerves of a channel, but Den found the whole effect smothering. He liked to have fun during a transfer—why else would one bother?—and he found the funereal atmosphere inhibiting.

It was Tyvi's inhibitions that were his current worry, however. He could feel her Need, but she wasn't responding properly to his nager. Den looked her over carefully, wishing that he knew her better. Her reserve could simply be part of her personality, or the result of some Householding exercise in self-control. Alternatively, she might have been shorted so much in recent months that she was no longer able to let go and trust her Donor to keep up with her, even when that Donor had speed and selyn to spare. If that was the problem, Den had forty-five minutes to convince her that she couldn't hurt him or she would automatically hold back this time, as well.

He told her as much, adding, "So why don't we have a cup of tea while I get to work?"

She murmured agreement, filling two mugs from the pot of trin tea steeping on the small table in front of the couch. Her handling tentacles shook slightly as she handed one to him. Den relieved her of the mug with one hand and with the other pulled her down beside him on the couch.

"I know you were looking forward to having your son for transfer," he scolded gently, "but holding yourself back with me won't help either of you."

"I know." Tyvi sipped from her mug, then gave Den an embarrassed smile. "I'm just worried about Obis, travelling alone out here. His English isn't very good."

Den shrugged. "It's kind of hard to get lost on a direct train, unless you're a piece of luggage, and the same out-Territory Gens who would run screaming at the sight of you are perfectly willing to help out a fellow Gen. If your son is anything like I was at that age, he's probably enjoying the adventure. Don't worry, he'll make it."

"It's a parent's habit, I suppose, to worry long after a child is grown. I'll try to behave myself."

"Good." Den drained the last of his tea, put the mug back on the table, and reached for her hand. He inspected the tentacles above it, then sighed. "We've got a long way to go before you're ready, so let's get started."

Tyvi tried hard and so did Den but with less than five minutes to go, she was still unable to fix on him properly.

"I'm sorry," she apologized, flushed with an embarrassment that she shouldn't have been able to feel so close to transfer. "It's been so long...."

"And I'm not the Donor you want," Den completed the thought for her. She nodded miserably.

Den shrugged, letting go of her hands and withdrawing nageric support. "Well, if you'd rather wait for Obis to get in tomorrow, I'm sure Rital won't object." He got to his feet, ignoring her astonished stare, and started for the door.

He had taken only three steps when he heard the loud *crash* of the table being overturned, sending the teapot and mugs flying. Before he could take a fourth step, Tyvi had charged around to block him in a flicker of Augmentation. She snarled, pure predator, and reached for Den, eyes vacant as she focused all her attention on his selyn field. A Sime in this hyperconscious state could neither see nor hear.

Tyvi, of course, could recognize Den by zlinning as easily as by sight or sound. Her channel's discipline reasserted itself before she touched him. She forced herself duoconscious, aware of both selyn fields and the five senses she shared with Gens and children, as channel's control reasserted itself to prevent her from attacking an unwilling Gen, even the Donor assigned to her.

"Don't stop now," Den said, grinning in relief as he reestablished the nageric linkage.

Channel's ethics satisfied, Tyvi threw herself at him, intent only on slaking her Need as quickly as possible. As the selyn flowed from him, swiftly but not quite fast enough to really satisfy him, Den concentrated on how good it felt, providing the feedback Tyvi required as much as his selyn. He did not allow himself to remember how much better it would have been with Rital.

When Tyvi stopped—too soon for Den—he held the channel as she cried out all the frustrations of the past weeks, shedding a few tears himself at his missed opportunity.

CHAPTER 15

FESTIVAL

Afterward, low field and off-duty, but not feeling the usual wave of post-transfer euphoria, Den wandered down to the library for something non-technical to read. Tomorrow might be Union Day, but he wasn't in the mood to celebrate. Unity seemed very far away in Clear Springs, with its apathetic non-donors and anti-Sime demonstrators.

Sera was at the reading table, struggling laboriously through the morning's extra-thick, holiday-issue *Clarion*. Den translated a few English words that were giving her trouble, then borrowed the front page and settled down beside her to scan the headlines. Even this far out-Territory, they were full of the upcoming peace conference between Cordona, Amzon, and Zillia. Progress toward Unity had stalled there, too, as the two Gen Territories each insisted that the Tecton pressure the other to give up all claim to disputed Ancient sites as a precondition to discussing an end to hostilities. Chief Tecton diplomat, Sosu Quess ambrov Shaeldor, was still officially optimistic about the chances of building a lasting peace, but the slight note of exasperation that crept into his carefully worded statement made Den feel better.

I'm right, he thought. *Out-Territory political discourse is irrational enough to get on the nerves of anyone, even a Householding diplomat!*

He had turned the page and was scanning a schedule of the Union Day celebrations when Sera gave an exclamation of disgust.

"What's the matter?" he asked.

"Take a look at this," she said, handing him the editorial page and pointing to a letter. "What is it about living out-Territory that turns people into idiots?"

Den skimmed the letter, which was another incoherent version of the standard "my religion says Simes are bad, so my tax money shouldn't go for pro-Sime purposes and the Sime Center should be closed down" argument. A few months before, he would have agreed with her assessment of its author, but after the insights he had gained into out-Territory politics, he had been forced to reassess Silva and Tohm's lecture on the tactics used by OLD SOKS and their rivals.

"How can this…" Sera peered over his shoulder to squint at the name printed below the letter. "…Ephriam Lornstadt get that kind of nonsense published in a respectable newspaper?" she asked again. "The Sime Center is supported by donations and the initial expense was funded by the Tecton. I've been doing my research; I know that information has been printed in this newspaper on several occasions, most recently in your column from last week. Why does this Ephriam Lornstat think his taxes pay for it?"

"Oh, I expect he knows the truth," Den said, a little cynically. "Lornstat is Reverend Sinth's second in command and he's also a member of the school board. Mayor Kroag told me that several Save Our Kids members have been going over the city budget in detail to see if we had any sources of funding that they could cut off. They didn't find any, of course."

"Then why is the man lying?"

"Out-Territory politics," Den answered. "You should get some of the counter-demonstrators to explain it to you—I'm not sure I really understand—but but basically, the important thing for them is to have anti-Sime letters in the paper frequently. It doesn't matter if their content is fact or fantasy, because few people will bother to check. Since they know the Sime Center poses no threat to anyone, they circulate lies to keep the pro-Sime faction busy with damage control and prevent us from recruiting donors."

Sera's mouth twisted in disgust. "The more I learn about out-Territory people, the worse they sound. What kind of unprincipled lorsh would use a strategy based on lies?"

"A desperate one representing a small but determined minority. They haven't been able to convince a working majority of the townspeople that the Sime Center is dangerous. The Tecton is building a reputation for safety here, a legacy of trust that includes even the Gens who never donate. Unless that trust is betrayed, Sinth and his crew can only delay our inevitable acceptance, at best."

Sera gave him a thoughtful glance. "You know, you're pretty eloquent this morning. Though why you would want to defend people who've made a hobby out of attacking you and your cousin is beyond me."

"You can't judge the whole town by the two hundred or so idiots who choose to spend all their time waving signs at each other and making everybody else miserable. The vast majority of Clear Springs residents aren't involved in the demonstrations—on either side."

"I find that kind of hard to believe, after what I've seen in the last few days," Sera admitted.

"Come on, then," Den suggested. "The paper says there's a Union Day fair over at the university campus today. Give me a moment to throw on a civilian shirt and I'll show you what these people are like when they aren't being political."

* * * *

The campus was packed with people in holiday clothing. A mix of students and townsfolk from Clear Springs and the surrounding communities crowded into the walkways between row after row of booths on the central lawn. Packs of shrieking children dodged through the adults, many balanced precariously on the wheeled boards Den had seen before. Even some of the college students were using them since, unlike a bicycle, they were easy to carry when not in use. There were food booths selling pies, drinks, sandwiches, egg rolls, and large chunks of grilled animal flesh that Den was careful not to inspect too closely. Craft booths sold overpriced jewelry, leather goods, handmade shoes, paintings, pottery, cheaply made clothing dyed in fantastic colors, and wooden instruments.

It wasn't totally apolitical, of course. There was a whole row of booths run by groups favoring development and slow growth, economic parity, various politicians, and inevitably, the campus anti-Sime organization, Students for a Sime-free City. While Sera looked through earrings in a neighboring stall, Den glanced through their materials. Their pamphlets were the same ones that Sinth's Save Our Kids demonstrators were passing out, but there was also religious jewelry and buttons and bumper stickers with anti-Sime slogans. Front and center on the table was a clipboard with a sheet of paper. "If you would like more information on this issue," it read, "please leave your name and address." On impulse, Den scribbled down Eddina's name and the number of the out-Territory post office box Jannun had rented to receive English-language model flyer publications. Maybe, if his friends saw some of the anti-Sime literature that was being circulated, they would stop thinking that he and Rital were paranoid.

OLD SOKS also had a booth, but it was much busier. Den preferred to believe that the attraction was in the chance they provided to work toward Unity and not just in the opportunity they offered to wear funky clothes, sing lewd songs in public, and attend weekly beerfests at the Sudworks Brewery.

Den and Sera bought lunch at one of the food booths and wandered for a few hours, stopping here and there when something looked interesting. They learned how to identify the six most common agricultural pests, watched pickle barrels being constructed, and then found themselves lured into an open-air "magic show" sponsored by the Chemistry and Physics Graduate Student Associations to entertain small children while their parents rested.

The magic show was held in a sunken garden that abutted the Center for Technology. A paved path, too steep for bicycles, started at the upper lip of the depression and wound its way down to the bottom. The area did make a decent improvised amphitheater, however, with the basement doors providing secure pre-show storage for chemicals and other props.

Like many charitable efforts, the magic show was well-intentioned but lacked professional showmanship. The audience was full of restless wiggling that even growing ash "worms" and lemon juice "invisible ink" couldn't quell. The vinegar-and-baking soda geyser and fun-with-springs demonstrations were only marginally more successful, largely because Professor Fibes, who was hosting the show, had no stage presence. His pause after each "trick" to explain the scientific principles behind it didn't help. Several mothers frowned as the chemistry of pH indicators was demonstrated by adding acid to a basic extract of anthocyanins to produce realistic fake "blood."

"Why are those women upset?" Sera asked him. "It's a good trick."

"It's a fine trick and uses easily accessible materials," Den agreed. "In short, it's just the sort of thing that children love to do to impress their friends—and make a mess. Good thing the anthocyanins in red cabbage aren't quite as concentrated as in pomegranate juice." He still mourned the shirt that he had sacrificed to pomegranate stains to balance the 'Spirit of Valzor.'

Professor Fibes announced, "To end our show today, I'm going to make some cement that hardens when I say the magic word, then goes soft again on command. Do you think I can make cement like that?"

As those children who were still paying attention expressed skepticism, three of Fibes's graduate student assistants dragged out three large washtubs and set them in a row, touching one another. A fourth student used a hose to fill them part way with water while her fellow minions fetched industrial-sized sacks labeled "Magic Cement." The white powder was poured into the tubs and stirred well with hoes to make a gloppy, viscous mixture like wet concrete.

"What is that stuff?" Sera asked.

"I'm guessing corn starch," Den speculated. "This should be a little more exciting than some of the other tricks."

Professor Fibes took one of the hoes and poked slowly at each tub, demonstrating that the material within was liquid enough to allow the hoe to reach the bottom of the tub with little effort. "The magic cement is soft, like normal wet cement. Now, I'm going to say the magic words and make the cement set so hard that my assistants can run across all three tubs without sinking in. Are you ready?"

As he talked, the graduate students set up ramps on the two end tubs and took off their shoes. With great ceremony, Fibes proclaimed the magic words: "Non-Newtonian fluid with high shear rate!"

The first graduate student jogged up the ramp. Keeping up a brisk pace, he crossed the tubs in three strides, stepping squarely in the middle of each. The "magic cement" dipped a little under his weight, but held. He trotted down the ramp on the far side of the tubs with mostly dry feet as the footprints he'd left behind dissolved away.

"Just to demonstrate that we're not cheating, I'm going to turn the magic cement liquid again," Professor Fibes said. Picking up the hoe, he said, "Non-Newtonian fluid with low shear rate!" and poked the hoe down to the bottom of one washtub as before. "The magic cement is liquid now. Why don't you help me make it solid again?"

After several tries, the audience managed to murmur something vaguely approaching, "Non-Newtonian fluid with high shear rate" and the second graduate student ran across. There was another pause as the "magic cement" was shown to behave as a liquid again.

"How are they doing that?" Sera asked Den quietly. "I can't see them adding anything to change the consistency."

"If I'm right about the corn starch, they don't have to," Den told her. "A corn starch solution of the right concentration liquefies under a gentle pressure, but hardens when hit sharply."

"Like when they run on it?"

Den nodded. "My parents showed Rital and me some tricks to play with corn starch, one rainy morning when we were driving them crazy, but they never let us make up a whole tub of the stuff and walk on it."

"You obviously had a deprived childhood," Sera commiserated as the children in the audience chanted, "Non-Newtonian fluid with high shear rate!" in more-or-less unison.

The third graduate student, a scrawny young man with unkempt, overgrown brown hair that contrasted with his indoor pallor, was trotting toward the washtubs. The audience grew quiet with anticipation.

Thus the high-pitched scream of, "Whoa-oh-oooah! Look out!!!" that reverberated through the amphitheater caught everyone's attention.

Glancing around, Den spotted a carrot-headed boy precariously balanced on one of the ubiquitous rolling boards. He was hurtling down the steep path into the amphitheater at a speed far too fast for safety, arms flailing as he struggled to keep from falling.

About half way down, the boy lost the battle. The board swerved suddenly and he jumped off. As his feet separated from the board, it soared through the air, tumbling through two complete rotations before it smashed into the table on which most of the demonstrations had been staged, bounced back into the air for another rotation, and finally rolled to a stop against the building. Flying glass and chemicals peppered Fibes, his assistants, and the audience. Over the screams as people scattered for safety, Den clearly heard an outraged cry.

"Raymond Ildun, you little monster! I told you never, ever to touch my board!"

It was the third of the graduate student assistants. He had paused to watch the unfolding disaster and without the impact of his moving feet to harden it, the starch solution had liquefied, leaving him knee-deep in a washtub of goo.

Den was already on his feet, propelled by reflex and training. He pushed through the milling crowd into the glass- and chemical-spattered space at the epicenter of the disturbance. Professor Fibes was frozen in shock, dripping blood from a scalp wound. Several damp splashes on his lab coat were smoking as the cloth blackened. Three of the four graduate students had similar injuries, as did some of the closer members of the audience. It was more than one Donor without a channel or medkit could handle.

"Someone contact emergency services," Den called loudly, making eye contact with as many people in the audience as he could.

A bearded man who had been watching from a second-story window shouted back, "I'll call from my office."

"Thank you," the Donor responded.

"It's the least I can do, under the circumstances," the man said, looking unaccountably guilty. He disappeared into the Center for Technology.

Den turned back to address the crowd again. "If you and your children are not injured, please leave the area in a calm and orderly matter," he ordered. "Anyone hit by flying glass or chemical splashes, come this way. Be careful. Don't step on the broken glass or into a puddle. You, there," he continued, pointing to the only uninjured graduate student, who was still mired in the washtub of starch. "What's your name?"

The student looked vaguely alarmed, but stammered, "It's Branlee Arnborg."

Den nodded. "Branlee, put your shoes on, then turn on that hose and start washing the chemical splashes off of people's clothing. Start with the professor's coat, before that acid soaks through and burns him."

The student recognized the voice of authority and moved to obey, wading through the starch quicksand toward the nearest ramp and his shoes.

Den spent the next half hour checking cuts for slivers of glass and improvising pressure bandages. He was vaguely aware of Sera and several other Gens sweeping the broken glass into piles for disposal and setting chemical containers out of harm's way. The university police arrived with paramedics and an ambulance for Professor Fibes and a half-dozen other victims whose injuries were beyond the scope of first aid.

As the crowd of injuries began to ease, the lead paramedic, a stocky woman wearing a uniform with 'Alizon' embroidered on the pocket, began making rounds, checking for any additional injuries or damage that might have gone unnoticed. She dropped by the corner where Den was applying pressure to a little girl's cut arm with the aid of her father's handkerchief. She looked at the Donor's work critically, nodded approval, then opened a small box of bandages, tape, and other basic supplies and held out a neat stack of sterile gauze pads. "I think you'll find these useful."

Den took the pads, substituted them for the bloody and unsterile handkerchief, then expertly secured them in place with the tape she offered. "Thank you," the Donor said absently, looking around for the next patient as the little girl and her father went on their way.

"No, thank *you*," Alizon corrected him. "Your fast response minimized the severity of the injuries, as I'm sure you know, Doctor…?"

"Sosu Den Milnan," he introduced himself. "I'm the senior Donor at the new Sime Center."

This, she had obviously not been expecting. "You work with the channel there, taking care of the changeovers?"

"I do, among other things," Den admitted.

She hesitated a moment, then spoke in a rush. "I know there are plenty of good folks who didn't want the Sime Center around, but I'm just as happy there's somebody else taking some of the changeover calls. They're nasty."

The Donor sighed. "They don't have to be, you know. Changeover takes time. If parents and children learn to identify the early symptoms and get a channel's help, then nobody gets hurt."

Alizon nodded. "That may be, but most folks here don't want anything to do with you people. I don't think that's going to change much before I retire."

Sadly, Den had to agree.

The amphitheater cleared rapidly as the paramedics tended the last injuries. Sera surrendered her broom to a graduate student with training in handling chemical spills. She came over to Den and said, "I think the crisis is over."

Den looked around and nodded. He walked over to one of the washtubs and poked at the surface gently. It gave easily, but stiffened when he tried a slap. "It seems a pity to waste this setup," he observed wistfully.

"Oh, go ahead and give it a try," a voice urged from behind them. "It's fun and you've certainly earned it."

Den turned.

Branlee Arnborg grinned at them from underneath his overgrown mop of hair. "Why not? I'm only going to dump the stuff. Might as well get some use out of it first."

The Donor glanced at Sera, who seemed intrigued. He grinned back at Branlee. "Why not, indeed."

Stripping off their shoes, Den and Sera jogged across the goo, laughing as their feet slapped wetly on the solidified cornstarch solution. While they were rinsing the splashed flecks of starch off their feet with the hose, Den's attention was caught by something lying against the building. It was the object whose meteoric entrance had so disrupted the magic show. Curious, he picked it up and examined it.

The general shape was similar to that of the board-on-wheels toys the local children rode. However, this was obviously no child's toy. The main body was a plank about the length of his arm and a handspan wide. The material it was made of had never been pulled off an old packing crate or pallet. It was very thin and slightly flexible. Despite the abuse it had taken, the board was essentially intact: some scratches marred the surface and a small chip was missing from one corner. The top surface was covered with sandpaper to improve the rider's grip. The wheels were of high quality, turning freely and with very little friction. Technologically, it was as far beyond the toys Den had seen as a modern sliderail trail was beyond toy trains for children.

"What is this thing?" he asked Sera.

She shrugged and admitted, "I've never seen anything like it."

"It's my custom rollerboard," Branlee said, walking over to join them. "I made it out of lab surplus." He took the board from Den, turning it to show off its features. "The wheels are a special, low-friction design that I salvaged from a remotely controlled device that was going to be thrown out. Once I cleaned the cobwebs off, they were in perfect working condition."

"What's the board proper made of?" the Donor asked. "I've never seen a material like it."

"That's because we just invented it," Branlee said, with no little pride. "It's a fiberglass analog composite for chemical storage tanks. It's chemically inert, like fiberglass, except it uses a carbon-based fiber instead of a silicon-based one. That gives the material a lot more strength and makes it less brittle. Combined with the wheels, this board can run circles around the ones the kids use."

"It doesn't steer right," grumbled a childish treble. The carrot-headed child walked toward them, ignoring the detritus from the magic show his misadventure had ended so abruptly. Up close, he seemed strangely familiar. "I couldn't make that board stop swerving back and forth. It shouldn't have done that and you should fix it."

"*You* shouldn't have stolen my rollerboard when I told you to leave it alone, Raymond Ildun!" Branlee retorted. "And whatever got into you, that you thought going down a path that steep was a good idea? And on a type of board you've never ridden before? I'm surprised you made it halfway down before wiping out."

The freckled face grinned broadly. "Wasn't it great, the way the bottles and stuff went flying? And all the ookey blood and stuff?"

"No, it was *not* great!" Branlee's glared down at the juvenile delinquent in outrage.

The boy's attention turned to Den and his eyes widened. "Hey, you're the guy who did the tour of the Sime Center."

That provided the connection Den required to remember where he had seen this child before. "You're the boy who wanted to know what it was like to donate."

Raymond nodded enthusiastically. "Yeah! It's gross, with all the tentacles and things. Changeover is even better. My babysitter, Nozella, went through changeover." He frowned. "You wouldn't let me see her tentacles."

Den was starting to understand Nozella's grudge against her erstwhile charge, even if his ability to spot her changeover early had saved her life. "A lot of people got hurt here," he pointed out. "Don't you think they have a right to be angry at you?"

"I got hurt, too, and I'm not mad at myself," Raymond countered disingenuously. He raised his left hand in demonstration. The littlest finger extended sideways in a decidedly unnatural fashion and was starting to swell. "It's disgusting, isn't it?" the child asked cheerfully.

Den held out his hand, aware of the irony that with four work-starved channels facing entran across town at the Sime Center, he was the one spending his holiday tending injuries. "Let me take a look at that," he ordered.

With obvious pride in his battle wound, Raymond complied.

A quick examination confirmed that the finger was dislocated. The Donor couldn't zlin the details of the damage as a channel would, of course, but there were no obvious broken bones or skin damage. The key to treating dislocations was to get the joint back into place before swelling made movement impossible. On the other hand, reducing a dislocated joint was a painful process and he had neither a channel's ability to block a patient's pain nor access to pain-deadening medications.

It was a holiday and the sun was hovering just above the horizon. It might take hours for the boy's parents to find an out-Territory doctor to tend the injury. Den looked at the unrepentant grin on Raymond's face, thought about the number of others who had been hurt by his escapade, then gripped the injured finger firmly and popped it back into place.

The boy screamed at the intense pain, then glared at the Donor. "Why did you do that?" he demanded indignantly.

"Your finger is back in place now," Den pointed out. "Branlee, would you hand me a piece of that painter's tape?" He nodded toward a roll of brown tape left behind by the cleanup crew, grunted thanks as it slapped into his palm, and taped the injured finger securely to the uninjured finger next to it. "There," he said, releasing the boy's hand. "That will hold you until your parents can get you to a doctor tomorrow. In the meantime, Sera and I would like to enjoy at least a little of our holiday."

"You should go see the dog races over at the sports arena," Branlee suggested. "They started," he glanced up at the four-sided clock that occupied place of pride on the tower that formed the high point of the Center for Technology building, "about half an hour ago, so you should be in time to see the final heats."

"Dog races sound like fun," Sera agreed.

Branlee obligingly provided directions. "Enjoy the show for me," he ended wistfully. "I've got to stay and finish the cleanup. The Chancellor and his evil minions are giving some Very Important Guests a guided tour of their shiny new Center for Technology tonight. With Professor Fibes injured, I'm the one who gets to spend Union Day in the lab, twiddling my thumbs while I wait for the Chancellor's very good friends to arrive."

Following Branlee's instructions, they soon found the sports arena. They rested their tired feet on the bleachers as they watched sausage-shaped, short-legged dogs race after a much-chewed rabbit pelt. The whole stadium cheered when Frankfurter beat Muffin and Fritz for the grand prize. As Frankfurter's owner accepted the rubber pull-toy ceremoniously presented by the president of the Veterinary School Student Association (while unsuccessfully trying to keep the champion from grabbing it instead,) Sera convulsed with giggles.

Den was post enough to notice that she had a very nice giggle.

"You were right," she admitted as the crowd filed out of the bleachers. "Once you get them away from Simes, these are normal people. Or at least as close to normal as you can get with only Gens."

Den agreed, steering her toward a bench where they could sit and talk while they waited for the mob to clear. "Which is to say, as set in their ways as any of the old junct families. People don't change their fundamental world view unless they have a very good reason to do so."

"And yet, you've devoted yourself to getting them to make exactly that sort of fundamental change," she pointed out. "Aren't you just another crusader following an impossible dream?"

"Me, a dreaming idealist?" Den whooped with laughter. "Rital, maybe. He'd really like to convince the people here that they don't have to fear Simes. I, on the other hand, am quite happy to let the Gens here deal with their own existential crises."

"This from the man who is obsessed with flying like a bird?" Sera grinned at him in challenge. "That sure sounds like a dreamer to me."

"I'm not obsessed with flying as a goal in itself," Den corrected her. "I want to re-create the Ancient technology of flight as a practical means of transportation. There's a difference."

When she looked at him in confusion, he elaborated. "If we don't refine selyn technology into something much more efficient during our lifetime, future generations would probably keep our current technology base, but couldn't expand it to recapture other Ancient technologies in the future."

Sera shook her head. "That's not what I was asking. Why develop flight, in particular, as opposed to any other Ancient technology?"

"Technology is never 'in particular,'" Den argued. "If we can develop a smaller, lighter selyn battery that can be used in a flyer, it would also hugely reduce the amount of selyn used by the sliderail train system. If we can learn enough about the weather to use flyers for transportation, the information will also be used to fine-tune agriculture and produce more food with less work. But as to why I, personally, want flyers…"

He looked up at the sky for a long moment, remembering. After a moment, he said quietly, "Rital and I were raised together because his parents died when he was five. They were trying to rescue a group of people stranded by a flood and drowned when a collapsing bridge dropped their train into the raging river. They knew the bridge pilings had been undercut, but the refugees were running out of time, so they gambled their lives that the bridge would hold. And lost." He met Sera's eyes squarely. "An airscrew-flyer like those the Ancients used routinely would have gotten them safely to the other side."

"I think I understand," she said quietly.

It was dusk when they started on the long walk back to the Sime Center, pleasantly tired and too relaxed to talk much. Across the street from the arena, the Conservative Congregation's church was brilliantly lit. Den was debating whether it was the proper moment to invite Sera to spend the night with him, before she returned to Valzor the following morning, when he was distracted by a low moan and the smell of vomit.

Physician's instincts alerted, Den followed the sound toward the Center for Technology and discovered a youngster huddled under the bushes. "Are you all right?" Den called softly, already suspecting what was the matter.

"Go away!" The adolescent voice cracked over two octaves. Ducking under a branch, the Donor knelt by the boy's side. Den could feel his own selyn production rate increasing rapidly. He knew what he would find even before he touched the boy's neck and felt the glands swollen with change-over.

The boy cringed away from his touch with changeover-induced paranoia and Den murmured, "Don't be afraid. I won't hurt you. Do you think you could stand if I help you? You'll feel a lot better once you've had a chance to clean up."

The boy slowly sat up, as if only then becoming aware of the dirt and less pleasant things that were spattered on the front of his lightweight jacket. With a jerky nod, he allowed the Donor to help him to his feet and they stumbled out of the bushes to where Sera waited. Gesturing for her to support the boy's other side, Den steered them toward the door to the battery room. It was at least well-insulated, private, and close. "There are steps," he warned the others as he unlocked the door with the key he had neglected to put away after the morning's tour. "Let me get the light," he advised as he pulled the door open and groped for the switch. He flipped it, blinking in the sudden brightness. He turned to help the others down the stairs, then stifled a groan as he recognized the boy.

"You!" Zakry Sinth snarled, pulling loose from Sera's grasp and stumbling backward a few steps.

CHAPTER 16

BERSERKER

"Well, if it isn't the self-proclaimed holiest boy in the Territory," Den said, with less-than-perfect empathy for his patient.

"Get away from me, Sime-lover! I don't need any help from the likes of you."

Den looked at the boy sourly. "Yes, you do," he corrected. "You can't even stand up straight and it's going to get worse before it gets better. Or didn't you know you're in changeover?"

Zakry, already pale, turned even whiter. "No!" he insisted, swaying dangerously. "I'm not a Sime. I can't be. I've prayed every day and besides, only thin kids turn Sime." He turned to run away, but his unsteady legs collapsed. He yelped in pain as his arms hit the ground, then began crying.

Den gave Sera a long-suffering look and knelt by Zakry's side, already regretting the sense of duty that wouldn't let him walk away. "It's true that Simes tend to be thin and light-boned as children," he explained, "but you can't change your genes by overeating. You'll lose those extra pounds very quickly, now that you're an adult Sime."

"I'm no murdering demon," the boy insisted.

"Of course you're not," Den agreed immediately. "There's no reason at all for you to have to Kill. That's why the Tecton sent me out here to Clear Springs." *Instead of some place civilized, where there aren't any nut cases like you,* he finished the sentence silently. Without wasting time on more arguments, he scooped the boy up, grunting at the weight, and carried him down the stairs.

He deposited his latest patient on the sagging couch, still disguised with a sweet-smelling blue wool blanket from the morning's tour, and began to unfasten the buttons on the boy's vomit-encrusted jacket. After depositing the coat in a nearby wastebasket, he unbuttoned the boy's shirt cuffs and rolled up the sleeves.

The changeover was more advanced than he had expected. The new tentacles were well developed, but the sheaths had not yet begun to swell with fluids in preparation for breakout. Zakry must have been hiding for most of the day.

"There's a medkit under the table," he told Sera in Simelan. "Could you get it for me? And a cup of tea, if there's any left."

"Sure," she said.

Either her moving field, the sight of the growing tentacle sheaths on his newly-bared arms, or both, proved too much for Zakry. He moaned and clutched at Den dizzily. *Stage six transition,* the Donor identified. Ignoring the incipient bruises that the boy's Sime-strong hands left behind, he nodded his thanks as Sera handed him the kit and a mug of cold tea.

"Here," he said, passing the tea on to Zakry and opening the first aid kit.

Zakry sipped cautiously, then spat vigorously into the wastebasket. "What is this stuff?" he complained. "It tastes awful."

"It's just trin tea," Den reassured him as he inspected the vials of medications. "It's perfectly harmless and there isn't any water."

Zakry looked unconvinced.

Den found the mild sedative he was after, double-checked the dosage, and extracted two brown pills from the vial. Offering them, he said, "These will make you feel a little better."

"I don't want any medicine from Simes," the boy protested, pushing Den's hand away.

"The last time I looked, Sera and I didn't have any tentacles," Den pointed out. "You, on the other hand, have a fine set of tentacles growing there. Do you think that medicine for Gens would do you any good?"

Zakry looked down at his swollen arms, gave a muffled sob, and reached for the pills.

While the young Sime-to-be gulped the sedative, Den sent Sera off to call the Sime Center for a channel, but kept his full attention on Zakry. He didn't even hear the door close behind her. It was too late to take Zakry there: the boy had less than an hour before breakout. The basement was adequately insulated, however, and everything seemed to be progressing normally. Zakry even seemed to have an adequate selyn reserve.

This last surprised the Donor. It was very unusual for untrained out-Territory children to get so close to breakout without using up most of their reserves. *The kid is probably so sure his God wouldn't let him go through changeover that he took longer than usual to figure out what was happening to him.*

However, now that Zakry knew, he was not at all enthusiastic about cooperating. It took painful spasms to persuade the boy to try some breathing exercises and he did his best to ignore Den's descriptions of life in-Territory.

The mutual dislike between Donor and patient was not helping matters any. Den could keep his feelings from overrunning his nager but no matter what he did, Zakry would still think of him as the "evil, Sime-loving Devil-worshipper" who was his uncle's opponent in the clergyman's battle against pro-Sime heresy. Of all the channels and Donors in Clear Springs, Den was probably the worst choice to help Zakry through changeover.

Good choice or bad, however, Den was Zakry's only chance of survival and the boy was not the only one in the room with moral standards. The worst insult in Simelan was "lorsh," a person who abandoned a child in changeover, and Den was a better person than that.

As the boy's tentacle sheaths began to swell with fluids, Den tried to calculate exactly how long it would be before help could arrive. He frowned as he realized that it would be close; maybe too close.

Zakry gasped and tried to clench his fists as fluid began to fill his tentacle sheaths, building pressure against the thinning membranes at his wrists. "No, not yet," Den warned, straightening the boy's hands. "Just relax and save your strength. I know it tickles, but you're not ready for breakout yet."

The boy would be ready soon, though, and there was no sign of the channel. For the first time since Rital had spoken to him that morning, Den was glad that he had not given his cousin transfer. If he had done so, by staying with Zakry he would have risked an unpleasant death by being drained of selyn entirely. As it was, although the Donor was technically low field, the inadequate transfer with Tyvi had left him more than enough selyn to satisfy a renSime. Den began to offer Zakry more nageric support, preparing to give the boy First Transfer if necessary.

It wasn't something he would have done in-Territory for a renSime in changeover. Zakry's Need was so shallow that it was difficult for Den to respond properly and despite the sedative, the boy resisted the Donor's attempts to calm him and moderate his fear-induced excess selyn consumption. It was as if Zakry's self-hatred at becoming Sime prevented him from zlinning the Donor's compassion, because to acknowledge that concern was to admit that a Sime might be worthy of it.

Den didn't know enough about Conservative Congregation theology to even guess what arguments might be effective in winning Zakry's cooperation. The Conservative Congregation had broken away from the anti-Sime Church of the Purity shortly after the First Contract was signed because, unlike their parent sect, they considered any end to the Sime~Gen wars other than total extermination of all Simes to be rank heresy. On the other hand, Zakry hadn't tamely reported to his uncle to be murdered, which suggested that the boy's adherence to this goal had some flexibility, at least when it came to himself.

The basement door opened and footsteps clumped rapidly down the stairs. "It took you long enough!" Den scolded in Simelan. "Did you stop to check out the Union Day fair displays on the way over?"

"Silence, Sime-lover!" Reverend Sinth commanded, brandishing a double-barreled shotgun as he paced grandly into the room. "You will not use that heathen tongue around decent people." A scared-looking Bethany Thins trailed in his wake.

"Well, Zakry," the preacher continued, flushing with anger as he glared down at his nephew. "I thought better of you, at least. What did you do to give the Devil a foothold in you?"

Despite his weakness, Zakry struggled to sit up on the couch. "I didn't do anything, Uncle Jermiah," he insisted with a peculiar mixture of sullen fear and self-righteous belligerence. "It was all her fault." He pointed at Bethany, wincing as the movement brought pain from the developing tissues in his arm. "If my two-faced sister there hadn't gone sneaking off to donate selyn last week, this would never have happened."

Bethany is Sinth's niece? Den wondered why he was surprised. Now that he was looking, he could see a family resemblance. *She actually did learn everything she knows about Simes, Gens, and transfer at Reverend Sinth's knee!*

Whatever Sinth had expected to hear, this was obviously not it. He turned on Bethany, who flushed red with shame.

"I didn't mean to!" she insisted, suppressed guilt bursting out of her like pus from a lanced abscess. "I was trying to do what you suggested, but it didn't work out right."

"And when did I suggest that you give the snakes your selyn?" the preacher demanded icily.

"At the last SOK meeting," Bethany quavered, avoiding his glare. "You said that it would really help if someone could get into the Sime Center's waiting room and tell people what they're doing to themselves. You said if even one person could be persuaded to walk out without donating, a lot of others might follow."

"I also said that the idea wasn't practical because the snakes wouldn't allow us time to work," Sinth said in a voice cold enough to cause frostbite. "What prompted you to go against the judgment of your elders?"

"Well, Myra and I…" She looked down at the floor, kicking it with one foot. "We haven't been demonstrating much, so we figured the Sime-lovers wouldn't recognize us, especially if I gave a false name." She shot a guilty glance at Den. "I was going to say I wanted to donate selyn and Myra was supposed to 'talk me out of it' by reading your pamphlet aloud. We were hoping that when we walked out, some of the other people would come with us."

"So you endangered your friend as well." Sinth's voice neared the temperature of liquid nitrogen. "What went wrong?"

"Well, we'd hardly gotten started when their leader—Controller Madz—called me. So I told Myra to try talking to some of the other people while I stalled to give her time to work. I was going to say I had changed my mind at the last minute, but…" She shot Den another glance, then met her uncle's eyes for the first time. "It all happened so fast!"

No, Hajene Tellanser was slow, when she watched him demonstrate donation at the Valzor Old Sime Center, Den recalled, realizing the source of Bethany's miscalculation. *She had no idea that channels usually work much more efficiently.*

"You donated selyn," Sinth finished for her. "You deliberately endangered your soul and that of your friend. Not to mention your vulnerable brother's life, when you knew he was of the dangerous age. And while you and Myra seem to have gotten off lightly, your brother is not so lucky. Watch closely while I do what I must and remember that if you had obeyed my instructions and stayed away from the Sime Center, your brother would not have to die to protect the lives of others!"

Bethany began to cry. Ignoring her, Sinth turned toward Zakry and worked the action on his shotgun, setting shells into the chamber of each barrel. He pointed the business end of the weapon at his helpless nephew's face. He glanced to see if this was making the proper impression on Bethany, but she had her face buried in her hands. With a snarl, Sinth adjusted his aim to Zakry's abdomen.

Den stepped between them. "Nobody has to die," he said firmly. "Not Zakry and certainly not anybody else. Reverend Sinth, Zakry will be reaching breakout soon. Please leave, so that I can take care of him until the Sime Center's ambulance gets here."

Sinth grinned unpleasantly. "Oh, don't hold your breath waiting for reinforcements. That lady you sent isn't getting near a phone until I get back to the church and give the order personally."

Back to the church? Den thought in disbelief. *Sera, don't tell me you were stupid enough to walk into the anti-Sime headquarters of Clear Springs and ask for a phone to call a changeover in to the Sime Center!*

Sinth nodded. "I see you understand your position. Now understand mine. Scripture clearly teaches us that a child who dies in changeover can still hope for mercy, but a child who survives to Kill is damned forever. I can't yet stop you from meddling with the salvation of other children, but you will not meddle with my family! Now, will you step aside while I fulfill my responsibility to my nephew or do I have to shoot you first?"

"Uncle Jermiah," Bethany protested weakly.

"Silence, girl!" Sinth ordered. He leveled the barrel of the shotgun at Den. "Move."

The diameter of the barrel suddenly seemed to triple. It swayed back and forth as the hand holding it wobbled.

Den stared at the unsteady gun barrel and the white-knuckled hands clenching it so tightly, mesmerized. Sinth's right index finger rested uncomfortably close to the trigger. Its nail was thick, almost clawlike, and there was a slightly orange tint to it. Startled, the Donor looked more closely at Sinth's face. The preacher's pupils were dilated and he was sweating freely, although the basement was cool. There was a peculiar odor to the sweat, almost like crushed tomato leaves, and that was enough for Den to make a diagnosis. *He's been chewing melic weed,* the Donor realized.

The leaves and seeds of melic weed produced a powerful high in Gens, during which the user felt invincible. There were also some very interesting toxic side effects that gave addicts a slow and unpleasant death from liver failure as they consumed ever-greater quantities of the drug. From Sinth's relative coherence and the strength of the crushed-leaf smell, he must have been using melic weed long enough to build up a high tolerance.

Handling belligerent drug addicts was not Den's specialty, but he knew enough. It was usually possible to distract them with conversation until they got so confused that they forgot why they were angry. There was nothing to lose by trying.

"Reverend Sinth…" he began, in a soothing voice.

The gun barrel wobbled a fraction of an inch as Sinth's finger squeezed the trigger.

There was a thunderous explosion—far louder than Den would have expected—and a metallic *zing* as the pellets in the shell missed Den's left ear by two inches, ricocheted off the concrete wall, and embedded themselves in the ceiling.

Sinth looked surprised that he had missed, but recovered quickly. "If you don't move aside, the next one will hit you," he warned the Donor.

He means it, Den thought in shock. *He's willing to shoot me if that is the only way he can murder Zakry!*

Den swiftly reconsidered the situation and concluded that, contrary to his previous analysis, handling *armed* and belligerent addicts *was* outside his area of expertise and that he had a great deal to lose by trying. Slowly, the Donor stepped aside, begrudging every inch, but knowing that allowing himself to be murdered wouldn't save his patient.

"I see you've decided to be practical," Sinth approved. "Suppose you stand over there," he gestured with the gun barrel toward the safety grating, "—while I show you how we deal with Simes out here."

Den backed slowly toward the grating, trying desperately to come up with a scheme that might stop Sinth from murdering his own nephew. *If I were a hero in a story, it would be simple,* he thought glumly. *Some unex-*

pected plot device would jump out of the author's fevered imagination, shift reality upside down, and save the day...

But the only thing that shifted was the safety grating, as his shoulder bumped the gate and it swung open. *Reyna must have forgotten to check that it was locked after the tour this morning,* he realized.

"Excellent," Sinth said, motioning the Donor to step through the grating. To Den's dismay, the preacher pulled the gate shut behind him. There was a click as the lock engaged. It was a low-security mechanical device, not one of the new selyn-powered locks that required a channel's precise nageric control to work. Still, the gate took tentacles and Sime strength to open, so the battery enclosure made an excellent Gen-proof cell. "By rights, you should have been locked up a long time ago," Sinth commented, as he tested the gate and nodded in satisfaction. "I suppose that one of your Sime friends will come along to let you out eventually. But *not* until I've done my duty by my nephew!" He took out a handkerchief and wiped the sweat from his forehead.

"Uncle Jermiah!" Bethany warned, just as Zakry gave a choked grunt and convulsed with breakout contractions.

Sinth whirled and fired wildly.

The pellets tore a new hole in the back of the couch.

Sinth paled as he remembered that he had already used his other shot and realized that his gun was now unloaded.

And Zakry gave a triumphant cry as his tentacles broke free.

Den might be helpless when faced with a drugged and armed Gen, but a berserk Sime was well within his capabilities. "Reverend, Bethany," he called softly but urgently. "Both of you, come this way. Slowly! And keep your emotions under control."

Bethany, who was closest to Zakry, paled and began to inch toward the Donor. Sinth, more angry than frightened, did not. Instead, he stared at Zakry's bloody tentacles, face twisted with revulsion.

Den struggled to gain control of the ambient nager. It was difficult when he was so low field, but Sinth was a non-donor and Bethany had donated less than a week before. He was actually carrying more selyn than either of them. If he could coax the two out-Territory Gens close enough, he could turn the berserk Sime's attention to himself. *And the lock won't stop a Sime.*

Zakry lunged to his feet in an Augmented bound, his face reflecting the screaming emptiness inside of him. His eyes unfocused as he zlinned for the life he Needed, then he began to stalk the Gens.

Den calculated that at this distance, he and Sinth were about equally attractive to the young Sime while Bethany, who was closest, was too low field to be worth the trouble. He projected love, compassion, and acceptance as hard as he could, trying to fix Zakry's attention while he verbally urged Sinth to come closer. "*Don't* run for it," he warned as Sinth eyed the distance to the door. "You can't possibly outrun a Sime."

Zakry's attention wavered between the two Gens, then fixed on his uncle. Sinth's rage erupted as he saw the vacant gaze and extended tentacles, proof that by Church doctrine, his nephew's soul was lost. The preacher broke and ran despite Den's warning, *not* for the door, in an attempt to escape, but directly toward the berserk Sime, gun held high in both hands as a club. In a last-ditch attempt to avert disaster, Den slammed his hand against the bars, hoping that the pain carried on his stronger nager would attract Zakry. The boy turned his head toward the Donor for a moment, but his uncle's moving field was closer. He brushed Bethany aside and pounced.

The gun went flying. Sinth tried to use his fists instead, too filled with drug-induced anger to experience fear. He was so obsessed with destroying the object of his hatred that he kept trying to punch Zakry even as the boy's tentacles whipped around his arms with bruising strength and pulled him forward. He was still snarling curses as their lips met.

It wasn't until Zakry actually began drawing selyn that Sinth comprehended his mortal danger. In sudden terror, the Gen struggled briefly as his nephew voraciously stripped him of selyn, too driven by Need to recognize whom he was Killing. Then Zakry dropped him in a boneless heap. The boy chuckled with glee, eyes closed, too caught up in the pleasure of Gen pain to understand what he had done.

"Zakry, you've Killed Uncle Jermiah!" Bethany accused her brother.

Distracted from his inward satisfaction, Zakry's eyes popped open and focused on the corpse at his feet. The joy drained out of him, replaced with horror. Stricken, he fell to his knees and shook his uncle's body, desperately searching for a sign of life. "NO!" he screamed when there was no response.

Before Den could say a word, the young Sime turned and sprinted up the stairs with Augmented speed. The heavy, fire-resistant door slammed shut behind Zakry and the Donor gazed after him in despair, hands clenched into fists at his sides, as he saw all the trust that he and Rital had struggled to build in Clear Springs crumbling before his eyes. Unless he sought refuge at the Sime Center, Zakry would survive only a few short months at best before he was hunted down. However, the Gens he Killed in that time would far outweigh, in the public perception, the lives that the Sime Center had saved.

In the quiet Zakry left behind, the painful rattle of a labored breath was clearly audible.

"Uncle Jermiah!" Bethany cried, running to Sinth's side. "He's still alive!"

"He won't be for long, if he doesn't get help," Den told her. "Can you bring him over here so I can take a look at him?"

"I think so." On the third try, Bethany managed to drag her uncle over to the grating.

Den knelt and poked two fingers through the mesh. He snagged the nearest wrist and searched for a pulse. It was fast and irregular, but there. "Talk about undeserved luck," the Donor muttered. "If he hadn't been high on melic weed, he would have resisted Zakry's draw sooner and it would have Killed him outright."

"You mean his sinful addiction saved his life?" Bethany asked, holding back tears.

"No, if he'd been sober, he wouldn't have been stupid enough to attack a berserk Sime with an unloaded gun and no one would have been hurt."

Sinth's skin was moist and cool with shock, so Den had Bethany fetch the blue blanket from the couch. Seeing how her hands shook as she covered her uncle with it, Den reminded himself that however much he personally disliked Sinth, others saw the man differently.

"He's got a chance, at least," he told Bethany. "If we can keep him breathing. Bring that medkit over, would you? And also about half a cup of tea, if there's any left in the pot."

When Bethany complied, Den pointed out the glass bottle with concentrated fosebine and had her pour a generous dose into the stale tea. He hesitated to imagine what the mixture would taste like, but Sinth would require the medication immediately if he regained consciousness. Not that that was likely, if he didn't get help from a channel.

In aid of which… "Put that cup over here by the safety grating, where you won't knock it over accidentally, but you can find it again in the dark."

"In the dark?" Bethany asked.

"Yes." The Donor got up and went over to the selyn batteries, inspecting the leads closely. "There isn't a telephone in here, but there are plenty upstairs and since the Chancellor is conducting a tour this evening, people will notice that the lights aren't working," he explained. Carefully, he unhooked the organics cable from the first battery, setting the leads to one side. "It shouldn't take them long to trace the power outage to us," he continued, removing the second battery from the circuit. As the last set of cables was unhooked, the steady throb of the selyn-powered electrical generator faltered and died. The lights flickered and went out. "They'll have a channel out here in half an hour or so," Den predicted optimistically.

It seemed like hours to Den, listening for each gasping breath to tell him that his patient still clung to life. He had not felt so helpless since he completed training. He *knew* exactly what must be done to save Sinth's life, but locked away from his patient and without a channel, that knowledge was useless.

Twice, the tortured rhythm of Sinth's breathing stopped. The first time, Sinth began breathing again on his own. The second time, Den had to coach Bethany to breathe into her uncle's lungs. The unsteady pulse under his fingers faltered and the Donor thought for a sickening moment that his patient had lost the fight for survival, but then the heartbeat steadied and the unconscious Gen gasped once out of the rhythm that Bethany had established.

"Stop a moment, Bethany," Den directed. "Let's see if he can breathe on his own."

Bethany obeyed, sighing with Den as her uncle took a second breath. "Do you think he'll make it?" she quavered.

"I don't know," Den answered honestly. "I haven't seen a lot of transfer shock cases. It just isn't that common in-Territory. Being a melic addict won't help. Your uncle's a fighter, though, or he wouldn't have survived this long. My cousin, Controller Madz, is pretty good at repairing damaged nerves. If your uncle survives, he'll be hurting for quite a while, but at least he's got a chance."

Bethany sniffled. "It was all my fault. Why didn't Zakry attack me instead?"

"Because you're still low field from donating last week," Den said, surprised by her ignorance. Realizing that this might sound like an accusation to her, he continued reassuringly, "It wasn't your fault. You aren't trained to handle such situations, but you did exactly what you should have. You followed directions and left Zakry for me to handle. If your uncle had had the sense to do the same, he wouldn't have been hurt."

"But if I hadn't donated, God wouldn't have turned Zakry into a Sime in the first place!"

Den rolled his eyes in exasperation. "Bethany, there were plenty of changeovers in Clear Springs before there was a channel to take anybody's donation. On average, one third of the children of two Gens will be Sime and no amount of praying or sinning has ever changed that."

"But the Scriptures say…"

"If Zakry cheated on his classwork and the teacher punished you instead, I expect you'd lose your respect for that teacher. Is a God who would punish your brother for what you did worth worshipping?"

Bethany made no reply.

When the door at the top of the stairs finally opened, only the necessity of maintaining a professional facade in front of Bethany kept Den from cheering.

Streaks of light from a portable lantern preceded Rital's voice. "Shuven!" the channel swore as he zlinned the three Gens, then the shadows danced wildly as he clattered down the stairs.

He crossed the room in four long strides, dropping the lantern on the table as he passed it. Struggling out of his retainers with more haste than prudence, Rital knelt to examine Sinth. Bethany shrank back at the channel's closeness, but didn't object when he scooped her uncle up, blanket and all, and deposited him on the couch. She looked away and swallowed hard when he used his handling tentacles to rip off his patient's shirt.

Reyna Tast, who had followed Rital into the room, opened the safety gate for Den. The Donor planted a hasty kiss in the vicinity of her right ear, murmuring, "Thanks, dear, I love you forever, would you reconnect the batteries?" and hurried past her to his cousin's side.

For the next half hour, Den held the fields steady as Rital, with infinite patience, coaxed Sinth's damaged nerves to heal. The task was complicated by the effort to avoid placing undue strain on a liver badly damaged by drug abuse. Den was vaguely aware of the lights coming back on and a decrease in the nageric turbulence as Reyna took charge of Bethany.

When Rital finally straightened, looking as exhausted as a Sime ever did, Sinth was breathing normally, if shallowly, and his skin was no longer ash-grey. Satisfied that the Gen was not in immediate danger, Den turned his attention to his cousin, letting his own sympathy well up to control the ache of deferred Need.

"You don't have to nag, Den," Rital said tiredly, sitting down on the edge of the coffee table. "I promise I'll rest when we've gotten Sinth back to the Sime Center."

"This isn't the kind of job you should take on when your transfer has been delayed."

"I'm not actually overdue for a few more hours." The channel gave a lopsided grin. "Besides, if I weren't in Need, Sinth wouldn't have responded so strongly to my field and he'd probably have died."

"Good riddance," Den muttered. "The lorsh is nothing but trouble."

"This from the man who is single-handedly responsible for saving said troublesome lorsh's life?"

"My training overcame my good sense."

Rital's grin vanished. "What happened?"

Den explained briefly, leaving out the reason for Bethany's donation the previous week. Rital wasn't in any condition to cope with that. "It's all my fault," he finished, clenching a fist in remembered frustration. "If I'd been able to reach Zakry, convince him to trust me, he would have been fixed on me before Sinth arrived."

Rital shook his head. "I don't think it would have made much difference, not with a high field Gen actually attacking him." The channel paused as one of Sinth's arms moved. "Speaking of which, is there any fosebine? He's going to wake up pretty soon."

Den turned and located Bethany in earnest conversation with Reyna. Her eyes were reddened with crying and there was a damp patch on the channel's uniform. *Everybody's favorite grandmother, indeed.* Grinning, he asked Bethany to bring over the trin-fosebine mixture. She brought it, eagerly noting her uncle's visible improvement, then stopped short in sudden fright as Rital absentmindedly reached for the medicine with one tentacle.

Shen, that's right, Den remembered as he quickly steadied the fields. *Rital was the channel who took her field down. When she didn't want him to.*

For a long moment, Bethany eyed the channel warily, but then her uncle moaned and she handed Rital the cup.

The channel accepted it with a nod of thanks and expertly forced the contents down the barely conscious Gen's throat. Sinth didn't gag, so Den assumed the preacher was not yet aware enough to truly taste the concoction. A few minutes later, their patient finally opened his eyes, then quickly closed them again with a pained hiss, one hand futilely trying to massage away his headache.

Den, who had suffered through his share of minor transfer burns during training, was very glad that he couldn't zlin. "Just lie still for a few minutes," he suggested softly. "We've given you something for the pain, but it will take a time to work."

Sinth obeyed, biting his lower lip.

"Good," Rital approved. "You've been badly burned. You'll require a lot of care for the next week, so we're going to take you back to the Sime Center."

Sinth's eyes snapped open. With an effort, he focused on Rital, then his face hardened with a peculiar mixture of fear and hate. "Get away from me, Sime!" he ordered with more strength than Den would have credited. "I'm not going anywhere with you."

Rital sighed. "Reverend Sinth, the nerves that control your lungs are badly damaged and your heart is affected, too. I've done what I can for now, but it's going to take a lot more work to get you back to health."

"No," Sinth insisted more quietly, but with utter determination. "I won't go along with your plot to subvert me the way you did my niece and nephew."

"Uncle Jermiah," Bethany said, forgetting her wariness of Rital as she came close enough to take her uncle's hand. "They saved your life. Please let them help you."

"Bethany, I can't help what they did to me when I was unconscious, but that slimy snake isn't going to put a tentacle on me when I'm awake. If God means for me to live, I will live."

Rital picked up the empty cup that had held the fosebine. "If that's how you feel about it, I'll have to abide by your wishes." He crumpled the cup and pitched it into the wastebasket on top of Zakry's coat, which was still filling the room with the sour smell of vomit. "You do understand that without further treatment, your chances of survival aren't very good?"

"Dr. Hardstrom can treat me."

"The out-Territory medical establishment isn't noted for its success in treating transfer burn," Den pointed out.

"If I save my life at the cost of my principles, I'm no better than Mayor Kroag," Sinth retorted.

The Donor shrugged and began repacking the remains of the first aid kit. "If you want to die early, that's your business. Just don't let this doctor of yours give you any opiate derivatives for pain. You're having enough trouble breathing as it is. And stay away from melic weed." Closing the kit, he stretched, stifling a yawn, and went to put it away.

Rital stooped, retrieving his discarded retainers from the floor. Den moved to help his cousin put on the loathsome devices, while doing the least possible damage to the Need-swollen ronaplin glands.

"No, please, he didn't mean it," Bethany pleaded, finally realizing that they intended to leave. "You've got to stay and help him!"

Rital met her eyes with infinite sadness. "I can't. Quite apart from the ethical considerations, there isn't much more I could do for him without his cooperation."

"But..."

"We'll call emergency services and tell them to send an ambulance when we get back to the Sime Center," Den said, leading the two channels toward the door. "If he changes his mind about treatment, let us know and we'll come pick him up."

Bethany stared after them from her uncle's side, silent tears running down her cheeks.

CHAPTER 17
LOCAL STANDARDS

Sera was furious when they rescued her from the church. She spent the entire trip back to the Sime Center describing the habits and morals of out-Territory Gens who, in her opinion, were not only lorshes, but proud of their bigotry. Den concluded, sadly, that his attempt to show her the normal side of out-Territory life had backfired. All he could hope for was that the long train ride back to Valzor would give her time to reconsider her anger and that she would not write anything too inflammatory about her experiences.

When they got back to the Sime Center, Den insisted that Rital spend a few hours resting. To make sure that his order was obeyed the Donor sat by his cousin's bed, letting his nager keep the channel's Need at bay. By the time Rital got up, much refreshed, Sera had long since gone to bed. It was just as well. Den was no longer in the mood for anything but sleep.

The following morning, Tyvi's son, Obis, arrived, even though his luggage didn't. He and Rital retired immediately to a transfer room while the rest of the Center's staff scrambled to find the young Donor toiletries and a change of clothing. His freckled face was shining when he emerged an hour later and went to greet his mother, but one glance at Rital showed Den that even forcing Obis to his limits hadn't been enough for the channel.

There was no time to worry about it, though, because they would have to hurry to make the Union Day parade. Mayor Kroag had invited them to share the official viewing stand as honored guests, so it wouldn't do to be late.

As it turned out, they were late, but the parade was even later. There was time for Kroag to introduce them to the other dignitaries, among whom were several of the more liberal clergy. Den had small use for religions at the best of times and even less for the way they were practiced out-Territory, but the white-haired Thaddus Webber of the Rational Deists seemed refreshingly open-minded, for a non-donor.

Armed search parties scoured Clear Springs for three days, but failed to locate Zakry. Den hoped the boy had had the sense to stow away on a train headed for the border, where he could find help at one of the border-crossing Sime Centers. Reverend Sinth survived the critical first few days after his transfer burn, but was still unable to leave his bed. Both Den and Rital were relieved that their failure to convince the preacher to accept their help hadn't led to his death.

Curiously enough, while the *Clarion* ran several front-page stories on the events surrounding Zakry's changeover and disappearance, it was not the danger posed by a junct Sime that caught the public's imagination. Berserkers were nothing newsworthy out-Territory. The in-Territory press would have demanded to know how the boy had managed to almost Kill a Gen in the presence of a Donor, but no one in Clear Springs seemed to blame Den. Instead, the letters column was full of horrified condemnations of Sinth, but not because he had tried to murder both Den and his own nephew, or even because he had stupidly gotten himself hurt. No, the public was outraged because Den, during an interview, had innocently told the reporter that Sinth had survived his nephew's attack, in part, because he was high on melic weed!

Den could understand, if not condone, Tohm's angry letter to the editor accusing the preacher of hypocrisy. The Donor was quite familiar with Sinth's frequent, scathing public criticism of OLD SOKS' favorite meeting place, the Sudworks Brewery. However, the harshest criticisms came from Sinth's own congregation. In their world of saints and sinners, it seemed, even a small failing was unforgivable in a religious leader. No one seemed to feel that Sinth deserved either sympathy or help.

Den was so shocked by this unforgiving attitude that he rewrote his weekly column. Instead of the material on early changeover symptoms he had originally planned, he gave some background information on drug addiction and its treatment. He ended by sharply suggesting that those who objected to Sinth's drug use should offer him support to overcome his addiction, rather than condemn him for what was, in fact, a rather common weakness.

Fredricks liked the column so much that he ran it in the Sunday commentary section under the headline "A Little More Compassion, Please," instead of in the Wednesday local news section as usual. The flood of angry letters slowed after that, but even the very religious townsfolk seemed more skeptical of Sinth's anti-Sime position. While this new-found skepticism was welcome, Den found the reason for it disturbing. *As if his fondness for mood-altering drugs has anything to do with the truth or falsity of his religious philosophy regarding Simes or the political activism it inspires!*

There was another unexpected result of Sinth's misfortune. Between his injury and his fall from grace, the preacher could no longer coordinate Save Our Kids effectively. The number of anti-Sime protesters outside the Sime Center dropped precipitously and those who did come were poorly organized and comparatively unenthusiastic.

This overnight demoralization of Save Our Kids caused Den to rethink his overall strategy. Following Tecton conventional wisdom, the Donor's efforts had focused on reaching as many individuals as possible and convincing them that the Sime Center was not a threat. This had worked reasonably well with some Gens, but less well with others. Except for Carla Lifton, who had stopped demonstrating when her daughter joined OLD SOKS, his efforts had had no effect on the enthusiasm of Save Our Kids. What *had* discouraged the demonstrators was loss of faith in their leader and public ridicule of his organization.

"People here view donating selyn as an optional political statement instead of a critical public service," Den told Tohm and Silva one evening over a beer at the Sudworks Brewery. "We've got to change that by bringing public attention to something we offer that most people here will view as a public good. Something that Sinth can't afford to ignore, so that we can discredit him for good."

"And what would that be?" Tohm asked with interest.

The Donor smiled. "Changeover training classes for children in the local schools." He paused to enjoy their surprise, then continued, "Since the Sime Center opened, we've lost three children in changeover who would probably have survived if they'd had training. Also, kids who take changeover classes are more likely to realize what's happening to them in time to get help. That means fewer Gens Killed by berserkers."

Silva nodded thoughtfully. "Some of the school board members might approve such classes, but not Ephriam Lornstat. I think you'd have a better chance if you start by talking to the City Council and writing a column or two for the *Clarion* about it. Once the issue is out before the public, Lornstat will find it harder to convince a majority of the school board to quietly table the matter."

Den, who had developed a healthy respect for her political acumen, listened carefully. Afterward, at their request, he taught them and the other OLD SOKS members present several in-Territory children's songs that were simple, repetitive, and easy to memorize.

"It doesn't matter," Tohm said gleefully. "Those Save Our Kids prudes won't know what the Simelan words mean, so they'll be just as annoyed as if we were singing the bawdiest ballads from the most licentious of shiltpron parlors!"

* * * *

Tohm and Silva were waiting in the City Hall's big meeting room a few days later, when Den arrived to make his presentation at the City Council's weekly meeting. They weren't wearing their OLD SOKS sweatshirts, but Silva sported a new button with the slogan '**I READ BANNED BOOKS**.'

"What's that in aid of?" Den asked, pointing at the button as he slipped into an empty seat beside them.

"It's a show of solidarity," Silva answered with a mysterious smile. "There was a little controversy last time that should be cleared up tonight."

Seeing that she was not going to tell him any more, Den looked around. There were only a dozen or so spectators, so it was likely that the meeting would end at a reasonable hour. Sinth wasn't there, of course, but he recognized the preacher's second-in-command, Ephriam Lornstat, and Hank Fredricks.

The first item on the agenda—the addition of a new bus route to the city transit system—passed with little discussion. A plan to install additional playground equipment in Central Park was tabled until the City Clerk, Jess Rebens, could determine what lumber, tools, and other equipment local businesses were willing to donate.

Den was having trouble keeping his eyes open by this point, but Silva jabbed him awake with an elbow as the next item—something about a library book and a citizen's petition—was introduced. "Listen up," she said, grinning with malicious anticipation. "This should be interesting."

Mayor Kroag asked Jess Rebens to refresh the council's memory of the matter. He skimmed through his notes of the previous meeting until he found the proper entry, then read, "Citizens' Petition. Reverend Jermiah Sinth, Mr. Ephriam Lornstat, and Miz Florence Grieves asked that a newly purchased novel, *Sailing the High Seas*, be removed from the children's section of the library."

Den sat up alertly.

"Said novel was deemed offensive because of unsuitable content, explicit illustrations of immoral acts involving tentacles, and a strong pro-Sime bias that undermines religious values instilled by parents," Rebens continued. "Petitioners presented the City Council with approximately fifteen hundred signatures of similarly concerned citizens. The Council voted to refer the matter to the head librarian, Miz Dilson, for advice."

Mayor Kroag nodded. "I see Miz Dilson out there. Are you ready to give your report?" she asked.

A pleasant, slightly rumpled woman carrying a clipboard made her way to the podium. After a false start, she got the microphone working and said, "Mayor Kroag, members of the City Council, our library has a limited budget, so we try to buy books that fill specific gaps in our collection revealed by patron requests. We purchased two copies of *Sailing the High Seas* after newspaper publicity resulted in our receiving over two hundred individual patron requests. This is the most ever received for a single title. Since their arrival, the two books have received many favorable comments from borrowers. They are so popular that we still have a waiting list to check them out. That is why I was a little surprised to get fifteen hundred signatures asking for their removal from the collection. At Mayor Kroag's suggestion, I put one of our library interns to work investigating the signatures."

She looked down at her clipboard. "There were 1,521 legible signatures on the petition. Of these, slightly over a thousand signers do not live in Clear Springs and its associated counties. Only 307 of the remaining names belonged to people with Clear Springs library cards. Two hundred and twelve of these library patrons have no children with library cards, which is of interest because *Sailing the High Seas* is intended for younger readers. The remaining 95 signatures, comprising some 55 families, represent less than 1% of the children using the collection. Strangely enough, none of these names have appeared on the waiting list for the book. Unless they borrowed the Sime Center's copy, it seems unlikely that any of those 95 parents signing the petition whose children actually use our library have even seen, much less read, the book they find so obscene, immoral, and generally unsuitable."

Silva doubled over with silent laughter, but Den was frozen in shock. *Fifteen hundred people signed a petition to censor a book they haven't even read? And I thought Silva was exaggerating Sinth's influence!*

Miz Dilson put her clipboard down on the podium with a decisive *snap*. "Given the popularity of the book Reverend Sinth wishes to censor, I recommend that both copies be retained for the general collection. Those few parents who do not wish their children to read it can prevent that by simply inspecting their child's selections before leaving the library."

Mayor Kroag nodded. "That seems a reasonable compromise, given the small number of children involved. All those in favor of retaining the books?" Four hands shot up. "The motion carries unanimously. The books will remain in general circulation. And, Miz Dilson, would you add my name to the waiting list? I'd kind of like to read it for myself."

Ephriam Lornstat, who was seated in the front row, was on his feet immediately. "How can you just ignore fifteen hundred people who feel that book is a danger to innocent children everywhere?" he demanded.

Mayor Kroag looked down at him with almost feline disdain. "Mr. Lornstat," she enunciated carefully, "I would like to remind you that the City Council represents the people of Clear Springs, not New Washington Territory at large. It is very thoughtful of your co-religionists in other towns to concern themselves with the contents of our library, but we are not bound to follow their recommendations."

Lornstat reluctantly sat down again.

As the City Council moved on the next item on their agenda, Den made a note of the librarian's name. If the Clear Springs library staff would fight to circulate books on in-Territory life, he could make sure that their budget didn't limit their offerings. He could think of several titles that offered facts to counter Sinth's fantasies. There was also a sequel to *Sailing the High Seas,* he recalled. He would have to find out if it had ever been translated. The Sime Center's slush fund would probably cover a decent selection or if not, he could easily afford to buy the books himself.

The last item of old business was a reorganization of the city workers' pension fund. Den didn't bother to follow the discussion. Then Kroag asked if any of the council had any new business to introduce and the newest council member, Faye Wolk, took the floor. It seemed that a seventeen-year-old girl in Cloverdale, twenty miles from Clear Springs, had unexpectedly gone through changeover. The girl had died, not surprising at that age, but the incident raised concern about Clear Spring's liability if one of the many teenagers employed in the city-sponsored summer work programs should survive changeover long enough to Kill.

"Currently, the city hires only those above the age of sixteen precisely *because* of the danger of changeover in younger workers," Wolk concluded. "It seems to me that we ought to raise the age of employment above the age of possible changeover."

"That will eliminate a vital source of income for many young people," Mayor Kroag said. "Those are exactly the individuals that program was supposed to help."

"I know," Wolk said unhappily. She had been elected on a platform of student issues. "I'm open to suggestions."

Mayor Kroag searched the audience, then beckoned to Den. "Sosu Milnan, could you give us some information?" When the surprised Donor reached the microphone, she asked, "What is the latest age where changeover is possible?"

"I believe the oldest changeover on record is nineteen," the Donor said. "But you don't have to restrict hiring to those twenty and older to avoid that sort of accident. All you have to know is that a particular prospective employee is Gen. The Sime Center would be happy to issue letters certifying that individuals have Established. That lets you avoid the liability of late changeovers without depriving young men and women of their jobs."

Wolk brightened at the idea of such an easy solution and a motion was quickly formed to require job applicants under twenty years old to present proof of Establishment. Mayor Kroag was preparing to call for a formal vote when Lornstat interrupted.

"Now just a minute," he complained, putting both hands on his hips in an argumentative stance. "This proposal of yours strongly penalizes those who believe, as I do, that association with Simes is sinful. You want to prevent youngsters of my faith from being eligible for jobs, while giving jobs to kids who have other beliefs. That's not fair, it's not right, and furthermore, the city's charter forbids that kind of discrimination!"

"The city charter does nothing of the kind," Steth Marden, the city attorney, opined. "Miz Wolk's motion is legal because it has a secular purpose—to limit the city's liability—and because it does not force anyone to acquire proof of Establishment. I don't think there's any doubt that it would stand up in court."

After a little more discussion, the motion passed. Den resolved to speak to Rital about selecting a few dates for mass Establishment screenings. Looking at Lornstat's furious scowl, he leaned over to ask Silva, "Is this the proper time to introduce the idea of changeover classes? Lornstat's pretty upset already and his position on the school board gives him a position of strength to oppose them."

Both Tohm and Silva urged him to go ahead. "It's the same tactic they've been using against us," Silva pointed out. "If Save Our Kids has to organize to get the proof of Establishment business repealed, they can't fight changeover classes as effectively, much less barricade your sidewalk. Particularly with Sinth out of the way." She winked. "Better yet, they may try to do all three and overextend themselves."

Mayor Kroag finally opened the floor to new business from the audience. Before Den could get to the microphone, a short and very irate man had captured it and demanded that the City Council restrict public parking on his residential street, which bordered the campus. Apparently, the inadequate size of the university parking lots and high cost of parking permits forced students to seek on-street parking during class hours.

When Mayor Kroag had promised to look into the matter, several times, the man was finally persuaded to surrender the microphone. This time, Den managed to grab it. He briefly explained what changeover training entailed, why it was important, and asked the city to consider offering such classes through the summer recreation program and through the schools when they reopened in the fall. When he was finished, he handed an information packet to each councilmember, as Silva had suggested, and sat back down.

"Good job," Tohm said. Silva nodded in agreement.

It was getting late, so the city council voted unanimously to refer the matter to the school board and adjourned. Seeing the stormy look on Ephriam Lornstat's face, Den took the precaution of giving Hank Fredricks a copy of his information packet as he left.

After discussing it with Rital, Den picked a date ten days away for the first mass Establishment screening and advertised the event in the *Clarion* and its sister papers in nearby towns. Since many private businesses had immediately declared their intention of also asking teenaged job applicants for proof of Establishment, Den was smugly anticipating a large turnout.

Reverend Sinth, now largely recovered from his transfer burn, gave a masterful sermon that Sunday from his pulpit in the Conservative Congregation's Clear Springs church. He tearfully admitted his error in chewing melic weed and blamed the evil influence of the Sime Center for his failing. He did not explain how this influence could have extended back years before the Sime Center opened. As further proof of the Sime Center's pernicious nature, he described in lurid and highly inaccurate terms the proposed changeover classes, which were characterized as being an attempt to win the congregation's children for the Devil.

Faced with this horrifying possibility, the entire congregation rushed to forgive Sinth and by Monday, Save Our Kids was once again filling the Sime Center's sidewalk with angry demonstrators. His credibility among his followers restored, Sinth retaliated for Den's exposure of his drug addiction by publicizing the accidental donation Rital had taken from his niece, Bethany. The first Den learned about it was when Ref, the cook, handed the Donor a copy of the morning's *Clarion* at breakfast, folded to show a full-page advertisement.

"I thought you should see this," he said simply.

The advertisement was carefully designed to look like a legitimate news article, with a headline that screamed, "**SIME CENTER CHANNEL ATTACKS 15-YEAR-OLD GIRL!!!**" The text underneath continued, "Hajene Rital Madz, Controller of the Clear Springs Sime Center, forced 15-year-old Bethany Sinth, niece of Save Our Kids' leader Reverend Jermiah Sinth, to donate selyn last week," the text began. "Miz Sinth had gone into the Sime Center Collectorium to witness to the unfortunate souls who were being deceived by the Simes. Hajene Madz refused to allow her to leave until she had submitted to him and let him take her selyn." The article went downhill from there, blaming Rital for Zakry's changeover and ending with the warning that any Established Gen who attended the screening would be forced to donate before being given the required letter proving Establishment. It also called for a massive increase in anti-Sime Center activities.

"Has Rital seen this?" Den asked.

"I expect so. He likes to read the paper as soon as it comes. He hasn't been in to breakfast, though."

"It probably spoiled his appetite." Den knew that his own had fled at the prospect of losing all the hard-earned progress of the past few weeks. It was already too late to do anything more than try to contain the damage and protesting Rital's innocence would never still the doubts Sinth's innuendos would raise.

Ref nodded in understanding. "There's an interview with the girl in the local news section and an editorial, too," he said. Then he mercifully left the Donor in peace to study the magnitude of the disaster.

Den turned to the interview, which was headlined, "**CHANNEL AC-CUSED OF ATTACKING GIRL.**" It was written by Hank Fredricks himself, which surprised the Donor. In the past, Fredricks had always been a staunch advocate of the Sime Center. When Den saw the subheading, "But Alleged Victim Tells a Different Story," he began to relax and by the time he was finished with the interview and Fredricks' editorial, he was chuckling with relief. The canny newsman had managed to get all the details out of Bethany, from her initial decision to disrupt the Collectorium to her failure to inform Rital that she didn't intend to donate. There were several interesting quotes as well, including what sounded suspiciously like praise of both Den and Rital for saving Reverend Sinth's life after Zakry's changeover. The appearance of the interview in the same edition as Sinth's ad would make the more reasonable members of the community very skeptical about any claims of forced donations, during Establishment screenings or at any other time. The unreasonable members of the community would never have come anyway.

Considerably cheered, Den went to find his cousin. Rital was in his office, the desk in front of him covered with paperwork which he was ignoring in favor of staring at his hands. His tentacles were retracted far up their sheaths, knotted in balls of tension. He glanced up as he zlinned Den, noted the newspaper the Gen was carrying, and said flatly, "You saw it."

Den nodded, slipping into the visitor's chair. "Hank Fredricks got Bethany to admit what really happened. I don't think the out-Territory Gens will blame you for it. Even Bethany admits you made an honest mistake."

However, it wasn't the response of the out-Territory Gens that concerned Rital at the moment. To a Tecton channel, taking selyn from a nonconsenting Gen was as indefensible as rape. "I should have guessed," he confessed, staring at his hands again. "I knew something was wrong. It just didn't *feel* right: her nager, the questions she was asking... I should have taken the time to find out what was going on. But no, all I bothered to zlin was a high field Gen standing in the Collectorium, so I blithely pressed ahead and took her field down." He gave an abrupt, humorless bark of laughter. "You even said it that same morning: that I could seduce one of the demonstrators if I tried. Then I had to go and prove you right!"

Den rudely snapped his nager, causing the channel to look up in surprise. "Will you, for once, try thinking with your brain instead of your laterals?" the Donor snorted derisively. "Bethany Sinth may be a willfully ignorant lorsh, but she isn't stupid. She knew you believed she intended to donate selyn before she went into that collecting room. She had plenty of time to tell you—or me, if she preferred to talk to a Gen—that she had changed her mind, but she didn't. Do her the courtesy of allowing her to accept responsibility for her own mistakes!"

Rital stared at Den, wanting but not quite daring to believe.

"Look, Rital," the Donor continued in a softer tone, "I know you can't take a donation from an untrained Gen without feeling protective. It's part of what makes you so good at what you do. But I don't think Bethany would thank you for assuming that she is too witless to understand that a Collectorium is where Gens go to donate selyn. As it turned out, being low field saved her life. She was actually closer to Zakry than her uncle was, when the boy fixed on him. So there's no harm done."

"No harm?" Rital asked, still unconvinced. "Donating can be traumatic enough at first for some out-Territory Gens who really *do* volunteer. Look at Rob Lifton. A lot of Gens who decide to try donating are only able to do it because they trust that they have at least some control over the situation."

The Donor shook his head. "Rital, that makes no sense. Have you forgotten the basics of channeling? You control during a donation, start to finish. How else can you protect a Gen who doesn't know how not to resist selyn flow from being burned?"

"If you're going to bring up the bedrock principles of Tecton doctrine, they are also clear that a Gen must give explicit consent before a donation is taken," the channel argued.

"She did consent." Den said firmly. "That she assumed there would be a convenient time later on at which she could withdraw that consent doesn't matter. She gave you her hands. From then on, it was your call how or whether to proceed. Not hers."

"According to Tecton law, yes," Rital agreed. "But it's not that simple. Many of our new donors genuinely don't know whether they can let a Sime, even a channel, touch them. They are willing to try the experiment because they trust that I won't force them into anything they can't handle. What are they going to do when they find out that I betrayed that trust?" His tentacles, which had begun to relax, knotted back up again at the thought. "Will any of them be willing to let me touch them after this?" he asked himself in a whisper.

"Did you read Hank Fredricks' interview of Bethany, or just Sinth's fantasy?" Den demanded. "I doubt that many out-Territory Gens will take Sinth's accusations seriously, not even among his followers. He's too well known as an anti-Sime Center activist. Anything he says will be viewed as a political fundraising tactic, not an unbiased accusation. Trust me, they aren't going to believe that you attacked his niece."

"But I did!" The channel clenched his fists, face twisted with guilt. "I assumed without verifying. I never bothered to explicitly ask her whether she intended to donate. If I had, I'd have zlinned the lie when she said yes."

"You had every reason to assume that a Gen who walked into the Collectorium and put her name down on the donor's waiting list was there to donate," the Donor said firmly. "Particularly when she cooperated better than many of the Gens who really *were* volunteering."

"Legally, maybe," Rital admitted. "Morally?" He spread hands and tentacles in a gesture of surrender. "Most important of all, because it affects the Tecton in general instead of me in particular, how are the Gens of Clear Springs going to react? Will our regular donors keep coming? Will new donors decide to trust us, or will they stay away to avoid the channel who attacked a Gen?"

Den shook his head. "I honestly don't think this story will affect Gens who are thinking about donating selyn. The Gens of Clear Springs have lived with berserkers for generations. They know the difference between an honest mistake and a real attack. Even Bethany doesn't seem to hold it against you. Look here." He flipped to Hank Fredricks' interview and scanned the column rapidly, then stabbed at a paragraph with his finger. "See, here she says, 'I didn't start to get scared until I remembered I hadn't told him yet that I didn't want to donate.'" He moved the finger down the column "And here, 'If I'd gone in there to donate, that's exactly the way I would have wanted it to happen.' At the end, she says that the worst thing about the Sime Center is that donating *isn't* unpleasant, so there's no motivation for the less-than-pious to avoid sinful contact with Simes. At the end, where Fredricks asks her about the different story in Sinth's ad, she says, 'I'm not responsible for my uncle's latest fundraising campaign.'"

Den glared fiercely at the channel, trying to break through the miasma of guilt. "You didn't harm the girl and everybody knows it. Only Sinth is claiming you attacked her and he has to stretch the facts to the breaking point to justify that position, even to himself. I may not have a fancy diplomatic rating, but I've come to know these people well enough to trust them to act rationally—at least as they define rational behavior. Or are you just looking for a good excuse to quit and let Sinth win by default?"

Rital flinched away from the scorn in his Donor's nager, then slowly and deliberately relaxed, letting his handling tentacles emerge from their sheaths. "You're right, I guess I did lose my sense of perspective," he admitted. "Thanks for bringing me back to my senses."

Den nodded, unsure whether his cousin's senses *were* restored.

Abruptly, Rital stiffened. "Shen, we were due in the Collectorium ten minutes ago!" He exploded from the desk chair and leaped for the door.

If Rital was willing to go back to work, then he was as close to normal as he was going to get. However, it was obvious that the channel's confidence had been badly shaken. Den was afraid that his cousin would abort if any of the Gens became frightened. Such proof that the channel was *not* in full control of the situation might scare the donors much more than simply having the channel complete their donations, quite apart from the damage that would do to Rital.

Fortunately, Union Day was over and the next round of tuition wasn't due until the start of the winter term, so there were fewer new Gens visiting the Collectorium. Zir was taking care of the most experienced, but Rital's confidence grew as he zlinned that the Gens coming in for second and third donations, nervous as some of them were at the prospect, still trusted him not to harm them.

An hour into their shift Seena announced that the day's first "virgin" had arrived. Rital flinched visibly at the word and Den realized with real concern just how superficial the channel's self-confidence was. He debated calling in Tyvi to take over, but that would be sanctioning his cousin's insecurity. The sooner his cousin confronted the issue, the better.

As the Gen, a middle-aged man who had given his name as Karl Seegrin, followed them back to the collecting room, he admitted, "My son, Tohm, has been after me to donate for months and I just couldn't make myself do it. It was this morning's paper that decided me. I figure that if even Reverend Sinth's niece didn't mind it—well, it can't be so scary after all."

Rital did a double take at this novel interpretation, then truly relaxed for the first time that morning.

Den shook with silent laughter, knowing that the crisis was over.

CHAPTER 18

LEAP OF FAITH

In the days that followed, Clear Springs greeted Sinth's forced donation story with a yawn and even the anti-Sime fanatics were too embarrassed to repeat it. (OLD SOKS, in contrast, was having a marvelous time telling anybody who would listen the differences between Bethany's version of the event and her uncle's.)

As many of the Sime Center's staff expressed their bewilderment with this non-reaction, Den began to realize just how well he had learned to think like an out-Territory Gen and what a valuable skill that could be for a Donor posted to Clear Springs. Being able to correctly anticipate how the city would respond to Sinth's anti-Sime crusade was a large step toward countering it.

Considering how useless the diplomatic textbooks had proved, the Donor wondered if a trained expert in inter-Territorial relations would have been able to do as well. It felt good to know that he was making a real difference in the world. With some surprise, he realized that apart from wanting to design another full-sized flyer for the next summer's flying contest, he was no longer looking forward to leaving Clear Springs. Even then, he was eager to finish exploring the aviation section of the Clear Springs University library before tackling his next design.

Five days before the Establishment screening, Den was working late on his newspaper column. Although the threatened increase in demonstrations had not materialized, there had been several misleading letters and advertisements in the *Clarion*. Den wanted to focus on debunking the most persistent rumors being spread by Save Our Kids.

As he worked, Den cast occasional longing glances at the Simelan typewriter sitting on a rolling table in the corner, wondering if it would be worth the trouble to learn to type in English. He was putting the final touches on the much-edited page and hoping that Gati would be able to decipher his handwriting when the phone rang.

"Den, it's Gati."

"I've finished, I've finished," he assured her. "I'll put it in your box this evening and you can type it up tomorrow."

"Good. You've got an outside call on Line 1. Sounded pretty urgent."

"Put it thorough," he directed. "This is Den," he said in Simelan. "What's the problem?"

There were a few seconds of silence and then an uncertain voice asked in English, "Is that you, Mr. Milnan? This is Rob Lifton."

The last time Rob had contacted the Sime Center late at night had been when he had mistakenly believed that his sister Annie was in changeover. "Rob, what's the matter?"

"Bethany and I went to a Save Our Kids meeting tonight," Rob said, sounding obviously upset. "Reverend Sinth is really mad about this proof-of-Establishment thing and he's determined to stop it. They're calling in activists from all over, enough to block both Sime Center entrances. To keep OLD SOKS from stopping them, they're going to start two hours before the screening starts. No one will be able to get inside."

"Shen," Den swore.

"If we'd known Annie was Gen, Mother would never have believed Reverend Sinth when he told her she was sick with changeover. Bethany may hate me for this, but what they're planning is wrong. Trying to talk people out of donating selyn is one thing; forcing them to stay away from the screening is something else."

"I agree," Den said. "It's also illegal to demonstrate on Sime Center property. Thank you for calling. If it's any consolation, I think you've done the right thing, even if Bethany doesn't."

"Thanks," Rob said glumly and the line went dead.

Den located Rital in the library, immersed in a volume of New Washington Territory history. Rital listened, appalled and outraged, as Den outlined Sinth's latest plan. "I'll get in touch with Tohm and Silva," the Donor ended. "Maybe they can get enough volunteers together to keep a pathway clear."

Rital snapped the oversized book closed. "No," he said with absolute finality.

"What?" Den shook his head in confusion, not certain he had heard correctly.

"We don't call in OLD SOKS for this one," the channel repeated. "What those demonstrators do on the sidewalk is a matter for the out-Territory government, but the Sime Center is under Tecton law. Preventing people from entering a Sime Center has been illegal since the Distect Revolt. If Sinth and his lorshes block access, they will be arrested and prosecuted to the fullest extent of the law."

There was no room for compromise in his cousin's level gaze, but Den had to try. "Rital, have you thought this through? The people here neither know nor care about Tecton law. Arresting Sinth and his crowd will turn them into martyrs. The out-Territory press will go wild and the Tecton will pull us out of Clear Springs if there's too much fuss."

Rital's jaw firmed. "Den, I've spent the last six months watching those bullies harass, intimidate, and sometimes physically assault Gens trying to enter here. Nothing you or I have done has made them listen to reason. Now they want to go after children." His tentacles lashed with anger. "I want Jermiah Sinth to pay for every lie he's told, every scared, bruised Gen who's fought through his followers' abuse to donate selyn, and every child who's been murdered because he told desperate parents it was a sin to call us for help. It may cost me the Clear Springs Controllership, but Sinth has to be stopped."

Den wasn't sure he like this new and vengeful attitude in his usually pacifistic cousin. He sat down on the couch next to Rital, placing one hand on the channel's arm to still the restless tentacles. "Will you at least let me try to talk them out of it before you have them arrested?" he asked gently.

Rital considered a moment, then nodded reluctantly. "Go ahead. But any demonstrator still on Sime Center property by eight will be arrested. I want the entrance clear before the kids arrive."

"All right," Den said, standing up. He chuckled suddenly. "I have an idea that should really dampen their enthusiasm!"

Three days later, Rital suffered a very rough turnover, making it through his usual duties by sheer stubbornness. Den couldn't completely erase the effects of too much stress and a late, inadequate transfer. He consoled himself with the thought that in two more weeks, he would be able to give his cousin a proper transfer.

The newspaper headlines were full of the peace conference on the Southern Continent, but the carefully worded official statements said absolutely nothing of substance. Den wondered what was actually taking place behind the closed doors of the meeting room—not to mention the equally closed doors of all three warring governments, New Washington, and the World Controller's offices.

A thick envelope arrived from Hajene Nalod in Valzor. Tucked inside was an article torn from a magazine. At the top, Nalod had scrawled, "What the blazing shen is going on out there? I hear Monruss is furious." The article was from a popular news magazine and the text, written by Sera Coney, rivaled his worst nightmares.

Clear Springs was pictured as a town full of anti-Sime fanatics and Den and Rital were portrayed as heroes battling singlehandedly to force sanity on a bloodthirsty mob. The anti-Sime demonstrators' activities were described in detail, but there was hardly a mention of OLD SOKS or the other out-Territory Gens who supported the Sime Center. Worst of all, there was a graphically detailed account of how Sera had been held prisoner by Save Our Kids while their leader, Reverend Sinth, went to murder his nephew.

This is just as slanted as the stuff Sinth writes, Den thought in disgust. *Sera, I thought better of you.*

The day before the screening, Den was scheduled to talk to the school board about the proposed changeover classes. To save time and more easily transport his displays and handouts, he took the Sime Center's staff car. When he arrived at the Southside Upper School, classes were just finishing for the day. He threaded his way through the parking lot in search of an empty spot, narrowly missing several youthful pedestrians who were heading for the busses with total disregard for other traffic. *It's a wonder any of them survive long enough to* require *changeover training*, he thought, jamming on the brakes yet again as a pair of giggling young women stepped directly in front of his car. One of them stopped long enough to make an obscene gesture; the other never paused in her chattering.

Out-Territory law considered all of these youngsters children, even though a good proportion of them had already Established as Gens. He had always thought that a ridiculous legal fiction, but these young men and women were acting as irresponsibly as children, at an age at which in-Territory youngsters were earning their own livings, paying taxes, and starting families. *You don't learn responsibility until you are held responsible,* he realized as he maneuvered the car into a visitor parking spot. *And both children and parents out here have a natural reluctance to face that the children are growing up, since that brings the possibility of changeover.*

Well, perhaps he could persuade the school board to let the Sime Center's staff make that dreaded possibility less mysterious and frightening.

He found the small meeting room filled to overflowing with all six members of the school board, the principals of Clear Springs' two upper schools, and an elderly secretary ready to take notes. Ephriam Lornstat was openly hostile, of course, but the other five school board members were polite, if reserved. *Good,* Den thought optimistically, *they haven't already made up their minds to vote against me.*

They wasted half an hour reading the minutes of their last meeting and discussing such uncontroversial matters as funds to purchase two new flutes for the music department. Eventually, they got around to the main item on the day's agenda and asked the Donor to introduce his proposal.

Den had spent a great deal of time revising his speech, with critical help from Tohm and Silva. Also helpful had been a book on curriculum disputes recommended by Miz Dilson, who had been very glad to have the Sime Center donate books to her library. The revised talk was carefully crafted to appeal to the moderate majority of the school board, paying particular attention to the issues that Sinth's followers had been raising in the *Clarion's* letter column. By answering the objections before they were raised, Den could make Lornstat look unreasonable at best or inattentive at worst if he insisted on bringing them up again.

It seems to be working, the Donor thought with satisfaction, noting the attentive faces as he ended his presentation by emphasizing that change-over classes would require parents' written permission. *Even though that will deny help to those children who require it most.*

At least the kids whose parents refused them training would be able to get some information from their friends.

When he finished, the school board members began a spirited debate. It was soon apparent that two of them were moderately in favor of the classes. Lornstat was predictably opposed and the three remaining members were political opportunists unwilling to commit themselves either way until they had a chance to assess public opinion.

For the first time, Den realized the value of Sinth's tactics. If he had tried speaking to the school board first, Lornstat would have tried to per-suade the other members to quietly drop the proposal, simply because none of the more liberal members cared enough to oppose him. Silva's sug-gestion of presenting the idea at the City Council meeting had prevented that, but Sinth's letter-writing campaign seemed to have given three of the school board members second thoughts. What should have been an easy decision in favor of the classes had become an uphill fight.

But it's a fight we can win, Den promised himself and the children of Clear Springs, politely reminding Lornstat for the third time that since the classes would be offered by parental consent only, there was no question of children's religious values being undermined behind their parents' backs. Even the uncommitted members of the board were beginning to look an-noyed at Lornstat.

After an hour and a half, the school board voted to postpone the final decision until their next meeting in two weeks. Den made sure that each board member had one of his information packets. *Got to get some to a place parents can look at them. Maybe the library?* He made a mental note to pay another call on Miz Dilson as the meeting came to a fairly cordial close. Even Lornstat, perhaps recognizing the liability of his earlier be-havior, deigned to offer his hand to the Donor. However, before Den could shake it, the conference room door was flung open by a hysterical junior secretary, followed by an equally frantic Rob Lifton.

"Oh, Mr. Buchan, come quickly!" the secretary cried, wringing her hands. "That Sime they've been hunting is on the roof holding one of our girls hostage. He wants to speak with someone in authority or he'll Kill her!"

"The sharpshooters'll make quick work of that monster," said Lornstat, almost oozing satisfaction.

Principal Buchan calmed the young secretary, told the older secretary who had been taking notes to call the police, and left to supervise the evacuation of the building. The school board followed him out with an excited babble of conversation, leaving behind Den's carefully prepared information packets.

Shen! Den swore silently, trailing after them. Sharpshooters were more likely than not to shoot the hostage, as well. While that might be acceptable to the out-Territory police, who probably believed the hostage was already as good as dead, Den lived by a different standard.

I've got to do something, he thought. Rital would have been a better choice to handle Zakry, but there wasn't time.

"Mr. Milnan," Rob Lifton said, tugging at the Donor's sleeve. "Zakry's hostage is Bethany. We went up on the roof to have some privacy. I was trying to talk her out of joining the Sime Center blockade tomorrow. Zakry jumped out of hiding and grabbed her. Please don't let him Kill her!"

"He won't if I can help it," Den promised, finally catching up to Buchan. "Principal Buchan," he called. The principal was too busy to listen until Den grabbed his arm and forcibly restrained him. "Principal Buchan, I think I can persuade Zakry to surrender. If you start shooting at him, he'll Kill his hostage if the police don't murder her first."

Buchan shook his head. "He might try to Kill you instead and I'd be held responsible."

"I'm a Donor," Den reminded Buchan. "Zakry can't Kill me. Let me try, before anyone else gets hurt."

Buchan pondered for a moment, then nodded. "All right," he agreed. "I'll show you the roof access door and I'll ask the police not to shoot unless the Sime tries to run away."

"Thank you," the Donor said. He turned as Rob began to open his mouth and continued, "No, you may not come along."

"But..."

"No," Den repeated firmly. "The fewer Gens are up there, the better chance I have of controlling Zakry. Promise me you'll stay here."

"Oh, all right," Rob agreed reluctantly. "I promise."

* * * *

Ten minutes later, Buchan showed Den the access door onto the roof, which was a trap door reachable only via a rickety ladder. "Are you sure you want to do this?" the principal asked. "That Sime's been on the run for almost three weeks now. He may be close to Need."

"I'm counting on it," Den said, putting his right foot gingerly on the first rung. "It'll make it easier for me to control him. A Sime in Need might be willing to Kill a Gen, but he probably won't murder one." The rung held. Den made his way carefully up the ladder and opened the trap door. "Make sure the police don't shoot us all," he called over his shoulder as he squirmed through the opening.

The roof of the school was mostly on one level, with air vents and other pipes in irregular clusters and occasional puddles from last night's rain. A solid brick chimney blocked Den's vision and he worked his way around it, hoping that the young Sime hadn't already escaped down the fire ladder with his hostage.

"Who's there?" Zakry called from behind the chimney, his voice quavering with tension.

He should have zlinned me sooner, Den calculated. *Or maybe he just doesn't know how to interpret fields yet. ...*

That could be a real advantage for the Donor.

"Come out slowly, or I swear she'll die."

Den continued around the chimney and located Zakry on a raised section of roof, perilously close to the edge. He was still in the blood-spattered clothing he had worn at his changeover, the tattered remnants hanging loosely on his newly Sime-slender frame. He held Bethany in front of him, her head forced to an uncomfortable angle by the handling tentacles pulling her long hair.

Den eyed the swollen ronaplin glands on the other arm, confirming what his body's response to the Sime had already told him. Zakry had used so much selyn escaping the search parties that he was in hard Need, barely three weeks after his near-Kill of his uncle. It wouldn't take much to provoke the boy into attacking his sister. *And she isn't low field anymore.*

However, Den was also substantially above mid-field and this time, he wasn't separated from Zakry by iron bars.

Bethany stopped struggling when she recognized him, hope displacing some of her fear. Though after Sinth accusing Rital of attacking her and her current plans to help her charming uncle stop our Establishment screening, *I wonder how she dares expect me to rescue her,* the Donor thought resentfully. However, he couldn't help feeling responsible for Zakry's misfortune. *If I didn't dislike him so much, maybe I could have tempted him to turn to me for First Transfer.*

Den took his anger at himself and directed it at Zakry, climbing onto the raised roof section and marching toward the Sime and his hostage. When Zakry took a nervous half-step backward, Den stopped.

"Just what do you think you're doing, young man?" Den demanded, putting his hands on his hips as he glared at Zakry.

"Well?" he demanded. "I hope you have a good reason for causing this circus." He gestured towards the parking lot below, where police cars swarmed like angry wasps, disgorging passengers to the accompaniment of wailing sirens and blowing horns.

"Shut up, Gen." Zakry shifted his grip on his sister, who gasped as a handling tentacle grazed her neck. "Now that I'm a Sime, I don't have to answer to anybody. I can do whatever I want and anyone who tries to stop me will end up like Uncle Jermiah."

"Is that what you want?" Den asked. "To hurt your relatives?"

The boy forced a chuckle, unnaturally loud and completely devoid of humor. "That was poetic justice," he said contemptuously. "Uncle Jermiah thought he'd just waltz in and shoot me, but his prayers didn't protect him from evil Simes any more than mine kept me from becoming one. The only difference is, he's a dead Gen and I'm a live Sime. And you know what?" he blustered. "I'm glad of it!"

Bethany choked at this callousness, but Den knew bravado when he heard it. "Your uncle isn't dead," he said gently. "You burned him badly, yes, but Controller Madz was able to save his life." Den watched Zakry closely to gauge the effect of his words. The boy had to be feeling a tremendous amount of guilt, but he couldn't express it and begin to heal until he regained his sense of self-worth.

Zakry shook his head in denial, both wanting to believe Den and fearing that the Donor was right.

"Your uncle didn't give you a choice about whether or not to attack him, so his injury does not make you evil," Den continued, letting his nager reflect his conviction. "Once you've overcome the need for pain, there's no reason you can't live a moral and upright life in Sime Territory."

For a moment, Zakry's resolution wavered, but then, "Are you kidding me?" he asked incredulously. "Why should I settle for third-rate good when I can be first-rate evil? You and your channel friends have been trying to get a foothold in this town for six months and most of the Gens have ignored you. *I'm* going to show them the kind of damage a real Sime can do, if they don't show me the proper respect."

Why? Den wondered frantically. Zakry was behaving like a Freeband Raider out of the history books, attracted only by negative emotions like fear, hatred, and pain. *Because he fears and hates what he has become?*

Well, if fear and hatred were all the boy could comprehend at the moment, that was the argument to use. "Zakry, you can't force people to respect you by Killing them. All you can make them do is try to murder you first. Make no mistake, the sharpshooters down there will do just that, if you try to run." He directed the boy's attention to the clusters of sharpshooters in the parking lot below.

Zakry's eyes unfocused as he zlinned the policemen, then he moved a few paces closer to Den, preferring the Donor's honest anger to the deadly intent from below. "They're only Gens," he said, trying to convince himself as much as Den. "I'm stronger and faster than they are. They can't hurt me."

Den shook his head at the boy's fantasy. "You can't Augment faster than a bullet. Haven't you learned anything about being Sime in the past few weeks?"

"I've learned how to Kill uppity Gens like you!" Zakry dropped Bethany absently as he began to stalk the Donor. Den thought for a moment that she had fainted, but then she began to slowly crawl away, heading for the cover of an air intake vent.

Good girl, Den cheered her silently. He backed slowly away from the stalking Sime, drawing him away from her. "You haven't learned anything since your changeover, have you?" he taunted cruelly. "You're still the same self-righteous, arrogant bigot who stood up in front of half the town and declared that his total ignorance would make him be Gen."

Zakry's fists clenched, tentacles lashing, too angry and too close to Need to think. He took several more steps toward Den, then stopped and screamed, "I'll show you what a Sime is!" He suddenly turned on Bethany, tentacles outstretched.

"Don't!" Den commanded, but Zakry was hyperconscious and couldn't hear him.

The Donor had a half-second to regret the necessity, then he lashed out viciously with his nager. Zakry gave a muffled cry and dropped to the graveled rooftop in a fetal ball, fighting the agony of being shenned out of his attack. In the absence of a channel, it was the only way Den could keep Zakry away from Bethany. *If he Kills her, they'll never let him leave here alive.*

Den motioned for Bethany to get farther away, then knelt by her brother, hoping that the damage wasn't irreversible. With all the skill at his command, the Donor soothed the young Sime, straightening twisted selyn currents and averting the incipient convulsions.

When Zakry finally uncurled and opened his eyes, Den looked down at him sternly. "Lesson number one about being a Sime," he lectured. "Never argue with a Donor." Zakry shrank back, eyes widening in fear. *Good. If he learns he isn't an invulnerable monster, he might be more amenable to reason.*

He took the boy's hands. "If you want transfer now, I'll give it to you," he offered. Rital would never miss the small amount of selyn a renSime could take. "Or if you prefer Controller Madz, you can wait until we get to the Sime Center. However, I'm not going to allow you to attack your sister or anyone else."

Zakry's laterals were emerging eagerly from their sheaths, dripping with ronaplin, but he glared back defiantly and spat out the worst insult he knew.

"Sime-lover!"

Den froze in astonishment, then guffawed, almost dropping the boy's hands. As his concentration slipped, he lost his tenuous control of Zakry's Need. Immediately, powerful handling tentacles lashed around his arms.

"All right, if that's the way you want it," Den agreed, then bent forward to complete the contact.

Den felt a faint surge of selyn movement as Zakry began his draw, excruciatingly slow compared with even the lowest-rated channel. It took all the discipline he could muster to keep himself from grabbing control. Zakry's draw petered out, long before the Donor's shallowest selyn-storage levels were empty.

Aching with frustration, Den let the transfer end. When Zakry released him, he sat back on his heels. "See?" he said, pushing a stray hank of hair out of his eyes. "You don't have to Kill to survive."

Zakry got to his feet slowly, staring at the Donor. "You're not dead," he said accusingly.

"That's right." Den stood and held out a hand. "Why don't you come back to the Sime Center with me now? You'll feel much better after a shower and some clean clothes."

The young renSime stared at the outstretched hand for a moment, then slapped it away.

"I'll see you in Hell first!" he snarled.

Whirling with Augmented speed, he ran for the edge of the roof and leaped off, right over the sharpshooters. There was an explosion of gunfire and Zakry jerked in an obscene dance as his body was riddled with bullets.

He was dead before he hit the ground.

Den walked to the edge of the roof and looked over at the pitiful, blood-stained bundle of rags. The police were slapping each other's backs and pumping fists in triumph, cheering their victory over a confused, unarmed boy. Fighting tears that he dared not shed out-Territory, Den turned made his way back to the trap door.

Bethany met him part way, highly indignant. "You're sorry he died!" she accused him. "He almost Killed Uncle Jermiah, he threatened to Kill me, and he tried to Kill you. He wasn't worth saving."

All the pent-up grief and guilt came to the surface. "I seem to remember that I'm not the only one who claims the children of Clear Springs are worth saving," he snapped.

Her jaw dropped in silent astonishment. Pushing past her, he stalked to the ladder and started down.

"Why did Zakry do it?" Den asked Rital later, turning haunted eyes on his cousin. "He knew the police would shoot him, even if he managed to survive the fall. He had so much to live for. Why did he deliberately choose to die?"

"Perhaps he truly believed the teachings of his religion." Rital refilled Den's tea mug from the pot on his desk. "There's no place in Conservative Congregation theology for a Sime who doesn't Kill and I suppose even being an evil monster is better than being nothing."

"He was ranting like a Freeband Raider, all about how he was going to Kill any Gen who didn't show him respect, starting with his own sister." Den closed his eyes, but couldn't block out the memory. He got up from his chair and began to pace. "I thought I had him convinced after I proved he couldn't Kill me, but he broke out of my control. I wasn't expecting him to jump."

"How could you?" Rital asked. He came around the desk and placed both hands on Den's shoulders, grasping the Gen's biceps firmly with his handling tentacles. "Den, *it wasn't your fault.*" He shook the Donor once to emphasize his point. "You did everything you could to give that young man a chance to live and he turned you down. Twice. Thanks to you, he was the only one who died."

Den listened politely, unconvinced.

The channel gave an exasperated sigh. "Cousin mine, not quite a week ago, a certain Donor accused me of patronizing young Bethany by failing to hold her accountable for the consequences of her decisions. Well, you are guilty of the same thing if you assume responsibility for Zakry's death!"

Den froze for a moment, then began to laugh almost hysterically at being caught in his own trap. "You win, Rital," he gasped, groping for his chair. The channel steered him to it, then held him as the laughter turned to tears of grief for a boy who was so intent on salvation that he refused to be saved.

CHAPTER 19

JUST RETRIBUTION

The news of Cordona Territory's decision to join the Tecton, combined with the signing of a permanent peace treaty between Cordona, Amzon, and Zillia Territories, created a wave of pro-Tecton sentiment. Donations all across New Washington Territory climbed to near Faith Day season levels for the two days after the treaty was announced and the New Washington government nominated Quess ambrov Shaeldor for an award to honor his central role in stopping a centuries-long war.

Unfortunately, this love fest sparked an equally strong counter-movement among the Conservative Congregation and the more reactionary members of the Church of the Purity, who saw the increased social acceptance of selyn donation as a threat to their traditional, pre-Unity way of life. Pledges of support poured in to Save Our Kids' headquarters and both Rob and Tohm called to warn Den to expect several hundred protesters for Sinth's massive demonstration against the anti-Establishment screening.

The morning of the Establishment screening dawned at last, with a cool, fresh, clear blue sky of the sort that inspires poets to write odes to fall. In the pre-dawn chill, Den directed Alyce and her gardening staff in last-minute preparations, acutely aware of the Tecton police in the parking lot. At Rital's request, Valzor had sent a handpicked squad of six post-transfer renSimes and four high field Gens trained to hold the ambient nager steady as they worked crowd control.

By six thirty, everything was ready. Den watched from the lobby window as Sinth arrived with the first wave of demonstrators. They set to work unrolling a banner that read:

"DON'T LET YOUR CHILD BE DAMNED!"

in blood-red letters a foot high. New arrivals were issued pamphlets, signs, and buttons. Many of the demonstrators carried prayer books, which they read loudly to their neighbors.

By twenty past seven, nearly two hundred people were packed onto the Sime Center's front lawn and the paths leading from the sidewalk to the Collectorium and main entrance could no longer be seen. Rital inspected the blockade and said, "You've got forty-five minutes to talk that mob into leaving, cousin. Better get started on this mysterious plan of yours."

Den grinned. "You're right, it's about time for the fun to begin." He used the house phone to contact the basement maintenance room. "All right, Alyce. Turn 'em on." He turned back to the window, saying, "Come watch, Rital. You won't want to miss this!"

For a moment nothing happened, then with a *whoosh* of spraying water, the Center's lawn irrigation system turned on. Alyce and her crew had re-adjusted the sprinkler nozzles bordering the sidewalk so that the pavement was soaked as thoroughly as the grass. A moment later, portable sprinklers joined them, pumping gouts of cold water into the crowd of Gens.

After two seconds of shock, pandemonium reigned. Half the demonstrators fled immediately with screams of outrage. Others paused long enough to try to rescue boxes of pamphlets.

Sinth and a few of the other men began to search for a way to cut off the water. They did succeed in turning off the portable sprinklers. However, the shutoff valve to the permanent system was in the Center's basement and the pipes that fed it were buried under the grass. In addition, it was next to impossible to turn off or adjust individual nozzles when the water was on. Den snickered as Reverend Sinth half drowned himself in an attempt to beat one nozzle into submission with a wooden signpost.

By quarter to eight, only thirty or so demonstrators were left. Den recognized most of the hardcore Save Our Kids leadership, including Sinth and his niece Bethany, Ephriam Lornstat, Florence Grieves, and Chief of Police Ezra Tains.

Den phoned Alyce again and asked her to turn the water off. "*Now* is the time to talk them into leaving," he told his cousin. "Wish me luck."

"I do," Rital said. "But I'm sending the police out in fifteen minutes to arrest anyone who's left."

Shaking his head at his cousin's vengeful attitude, Den threw on his cape against the morning chill and slipped out the back door.

The demonstrators were cursing and shivering in their soaked clothing, but they quieted as Den approached and drew together to glare at him.

"Folks, I'm afraid I'm going to have to ask you to leave," the Donor began.

"We're not going anywhere," Sinth interrupted, wiping futilely at a runnel of water that wandered across his forehead to drip off his nose. "You're not going to doom any more children to damnation even if we have to sit here in wet clothes all day."

Den ignored Sinth and addressed his followers. "The grounds of this Sime Center are legally part of Nivet Sime Territory. Under Tecton law, it is illegal to block the entrance to a Sime Center. Unlike the Clear Springs police," he threw a pointed glance at Tains, "the Valzor District police are quite willing to arrest and prosecute you."

"We are within our rights to let people know what the Scriptures say on the danger to their children!" Sinth insisted.

Den shook his head. "I don't think an in-Territory court is going to be impressed by your scriptures. Under the anti-Distect Laws, blocking the entrance to a Sime Center, harassing people attempting to enter one, or demonstrating on Sime Center property are crimes. For a first offense, the penalty is a mandatory six months in jail and a substantial fine. The police will arrive in about ten minutes to arrest anybody who remains."

"I'm glad you decided to call in the police," Sinth said complacently. "Police like to take their time and issuing warnings requires so much less paperwork than a criminal prosecution, particularly for such a minor thing as trespassing. It will take them quite a while to get around to actually doing anything. In fact, I calculate they should be making the first arrests about nine thirty, right in front of the parents and children you want to convince of your harmlessness." His eyes gleamed with the pleasure of a hunter seeing his prey walk directly into the trap. "I've also taken the liberty of inviting the press to drop by around then. Innocent demonstrators being dragged off by uniformed Sime police..." He smiled beatifically. "Just think what they'll make of it!"

"Your group is not exactly innocent," Den pointed out. "In-Territory law treats blocking access to a Sime Center as reckless endangerment of the entire community, not as trespassing. That you are blocking access to a Sime Center located in New Washington Territory also violates key provisions of the First Contract between our two governments. Your government doesn't approve of loose cannons who cause diplomatic incidents any more than the Tecton does."

Some of the soaked and shivering demonstrators looked uneasily at each other at the thought that their own government might disapprove of their actions, but Reverend Sinth was not convinced. "You're bluffing," he announced. "I don't believe you have any Tecton police here."

"Normally, we don't," the Donor admitted. "When we learned of your plans to shut down the Sime Center today, we arranged for police to stop your criminal activities. They have already made the trip out from Valzor. They aren't going to be deterred by a little extra paperwork."

Den looked past Sinth and spoke directly to his dripping followers. "I'm giving you the chance to leave without legal consequences, so long as you do it now. If you don't, you'll be removed under arrest. One way or the other, you'll be gone long before the press arrives." The Donor made eye contact with as many of the demonstrators as he could as he issued his final warning. "Unless you want to spend the next six months in a Tecton jail—inside Sime Territory—I suggest you leave."

The demonstrators exchanged uneasy glances, then several broke away from the group and started slowly down the path to the sidewalk.

"Come back here!" a furious Sinth ordered. "Are you so weak in your faith that you refuse to make the sacrifices God demands of you?"

One of the men paused and turned. "Sorry, Reverend," he said regretfully. "If it were just me, I'd stay, but my Tilda can't run the farm alone. If I spent six months in jail, the bank would own my place before I got out." He turned and followed the other deserters.

"Let us pray for our weaker brethren, that they may find strength," Sinth snarled, his piercing gaze threatening instant damnation to any other demonstrator who dared to leave.

As the shivering, dripping group began to recite some litany about defeating Sime devils, Captain Yanif, the renSime who led the Tecton police squad, ambled up at the head of nine police officers. They looked formidable in their forest green uniforms. Each had a dart gun in his or her belt holster and several of the renSimes also carried gas canisters.

"Are these the ones who refuse to leave, Sosu Milnan?" Yanif asked in Simelan. He zlinned the group of Gens carefully, one handling tentacle resting absentmindedly over the manacles looped on his belt.

"Apparently," Den said. "I'd hoped that a few more would give up, but they're a stubborn lot. It doesn't look like they're going to behave sensibly."

Yanif waved away the tacit apology with one tentacle. "It's better than the mob that was out here before you turned the sprinklers on," he pointed out. "That was a great idea."

"Thanks." As Yanif turned and signaled to his squad, Den warned the demonstrators in English, "This is your last chance to leave peacefully."

Sinth and his followers formed a huddle, with the women behind and the stronger men in front. Fists were shaken belligerently and the volume of their prayer increased.

Den shrugged and told Yanif, "They're all yours, then." He stepped back to watch.

"The wind's just about perfect for us," the police chief said, as he raised his right arm.

At the signal, the tenth police officer drove a prison transport bus onto the lawn. Den and the four Gen police officers took a few precautionary steps backward. At Yanif's command, the renSime officers carrying the gas canisters activated and tossed them. A wall of thick blue fog swirled out of the canisters and drifted rapidly toward Sinth and his shocked followers.

As the leading edge enveloped the first rank of the demonstrators, screams rang out and they tried to scatter. Unfortunately for them, they had to breathe in before they could scream. Most dropped where they stood and among the rest, only one managed more than two steps before collapsing.

The exception was Reverend Sinth. Alone among the group, he had the presence of mind to hold his breath as the fog enveloped him. Instead of attempting to escape, he ran forward to attack. He gasped in a breath of air as he emerged from the fog bank, staggering sideways because his clothing was tainted with the sedative gas. However, the stimulant in the melic weed Sinth had chewed that morning allowed him to shake off such an incidental exposure. It also greatly increased his natural aggression. Shaking off the disorientation, he clenched his hands into fists and started purposefully for the police.

Yanif drew his dart pistol, aimed carefully, and squeezed the trigger. Sinth yelped in surprise and stopped, looking down at the small dart lodged in his thigh. A look of outraged understanding crossed his face, then his knees buckled and he collapsed to the lawn.

"Let's get them out of here," Yanif ordered.

The renSime police moved forward, dragging the unconscious Gens clear of the gas cloud in small groups. Their Gen compatriots then took over. Breathing through nose plugs, they placed the unconscious prisoners in padded restraints.

The gas the Tecton police had deployed was a rapid-acting, Gen-specific sedative originally invented pre-Unity by professional junct Gen hunters. The goal was to rapidly and safely capture entire groups of Gens without harming their market value as Kills. The gas didn't affect Simes or children at all and very few Gens suffered complications after breathing it.

As the manacled demonstrators began to regain consciousness, twenty-one were helped onto the bus while still too groggy and confused to resist effectively. The remaining six, including Reverend Sinth, snored on. After Rital had zlinned them and confirmed that they were not suffering from potentially dangerous allergic reactions, the renSimes carried them onto the bus as well.

It took just fifteen minutes for the police to arrest and load all twenty-seven demonstrators. When one of the Gen officers reported to Captain Yanif that the gas canisters had been retrieved and all prisoners were secured and ready for transport to Valzor for booking, he waved acknowledgement.

"That's it, then," he told Den. "We'll get out of your way now and let you get on with your business."

As the bus started for the train station, where it would be parked in a boxcar for the long trip back to Valzor, a dozen members of OLD SOKS arrived, ready to escort parents and children through a massive anti-Sime demonstration. They were astonished to find Sinth and his followers gone, but cheered loudly when Den explained what had happened. Then they set to work helping Alyce's staff clean up the soggy pamphlets, signs, and prayer books that littered the Sime Center's front lawn. By the time the first family arrived for the screening, the only remaining signs of Sinth's massive demonstration were the tire tracks that the transport bus had left in the water-softened lawn.

A steady stream of youngsters seeking Establishment certificates attended the event, enough to keep all four channels busy. In the absence of chanting demonstrators, the mood of the waiting clients was peaceful despite the crowding. A fair number of the parents and young Gens decided that they might as well donate selyn, as long as they were at the Sime Center anyway. Other parents, learning that their child had not yet Established, inquired about changeover training classes. Gati and Seena covered three pages with names and addresses of children whose parents were willing to send them to the Sime Center for lessons if the school board refused to sponsor them.

When the reporters Sinth had alerted arrived, Den and Tohm gave them a guided tour of the Sime Center, complete with interviews of channels, Donors, staff, and Gens who had used the various services the Sime Center offered. Over the next week, most of the local papers published at least one favorable article on the event and the *Clear Springs Clarion* did a whole series on the Sime Center. The newspaper reports mentioned in passing that some demonstrators had been arrested. However, because there were no photographs available and the prisoners were too far away to interview easily, the accounts did not devote much space to it.

The new acting Clear Springs police chief promptly announced that he would enforce the laws governing demonstrations outside the Sime Center. With Save Our Kids' leaders and its most dedicated rank-and-file membership in Valzor awaiting trial, the demonstrations in front of the Sime Center almost disappeared. Most days, there were only one or two people ostentatiously praying on the sidewalk, but these seemed to have lost their taste for harassing the ever-increasing number of people who came to the Sime Center to donate selyn, to get Establishment certificates, or to take one of the changeover classes that Rital had started as a stopgap measure until the school board made up its mind whether to offer them.

Den found the visible daily progress deeply satisfying in a way that his in-Territory work had never been. Watching the pallets of batteries leave for the train station made him feel that he was an essential part of the effort to bring technological innovations to the modern world. He missed working with Jannun and Eddina, but they and the other model flyer enthusiasts were more than capable of carrying forward the effort to recreate Ancient capabilities.

He found himself wondering in odd moments just what would happen in Clear Springs if he were rotated back to Valzor. Would his replacement understand that most of the local Gens were not particularly anti-Tecton? Would the demonstrations begin again when Sinth and his core group of followers were released from jail in the spring? Most important, would the kind of diplomatic specialist Monruss had requested for Clear Springs, trained to negotiate with Gen governments, understand the very different tactics necessary to handle citizen-based groups like Save Our Kids and OLD SOKS?

Den doubted that the Regional Controller's Diplomatic Office had any-one who could deal with Clear Springs' problems as well as he had. In fact, the training given to inter-territorial troubleshooting specialists might well be more hindrance than help. There was a world of difference between politicians, who were accustomed to dealing with facts, and groups of fa-natics who already knew all the "facts" they cared to learn. The only way to combat an out-Territory style political movement was with an even more effective counter-movement.

The more Den thought about it, the more convinced he became that the only real solution was for him to stay in Clear Springs and see the matter through. He would miss the conviviality of in-Territory life—the Sudworks Brewery was no substitute for a certain shiltpron parlor not far from the Valzor Sime Center complex—but the lack of civilization in Clear Springs was easier to bear than knowing that his hard work might be destroyed. Mentally, the Donor began to compose a letter to Monruss, requesting an extension of his temporary assignment to Clear Springs.

Considering how hard it is to find people willing and able to work out-Territory, Den thought ironically, *this is one permanent assignment that I might actually get!*

In fact, things were going so well in Clear Springs that neither Den nor Rital thought to consider how the fall's events would look to those unfamiliar with the out-Territory city's recent political history. It was thus an unpleasant surprise when Gati handed Rital an official communication from Monruss, just as they were preparing to set out for the Center for Technology to recharge the batteries.

"If they're redoing the transfer assignments again, tell them I quit," Den said, not quite facetiously, as he opened up the channel's retainers.

Rital skimmed the message, then gave Dan an appalled look, all eight handling tentacles extended in shock. "We're summoned to Valzor for an official investigation into 'certain recent events,'" he said numbly. "Now that there's a treaty with Cordona, the Regional Controller's Diplomatic

Office has finally found time to deal with problems on this continent. They reviewed the reports that Controller Monruss sent with his application for a diplomatic specialist for Clear Springs and they didn't like what they saw. They're blaming us for everything Sinth's done since the Sime Center opened!"

Den snatched the page from the channel's fingers and scanned it rapidly. "'...ordered to return to the District offices in Valzor by one week from today...answer to certain charges...why you have been unable to win the trust of out-Territory Gens in your area...before a panel of impartial investigators from the Regional Controller's Diplomatic Office...possible disciplinary action...'"

He looked up at his cousin, equally horrified.

"Oh, shen!" they swore in unison.

Two days before the channel and Donor were scheduled to return to Valzor to face the judgement of the professional diplomats, two unexpected visitors were shown into Den's office: Rob Lifton and his mother, Carla.

"We want to travel to Valzor," Carla announced as she seated herself on one of the visitor's chairs.

"Why?" Den asked. Although Carla hadn't demonstrated against the Sime Center for almost nine months, she openly sympathized with Reverend Sinth and his goals. She had studiously avoided having anything to do with the Sime Center and its staff, not an easy task when her daughter was an enthusiastic member of OLD SOKS.

"Our friends and neighbors are in jail," Carla said, a little indignantly. "Is it so strange that we should want to visit them?"

"Actually, yes." Den rearranged some of the papers on his desk. "It's been over a week since they were arrested and you're the first people to inquire about a visit."

"I know," Carla said, "but Rob wants to see Bethany, and I..." She swallowed. "I got a letter from Florence Grieves yesterday. She sounded very depressed. She wrote that hardly any of the other inmates speak English and those who do aren't friendly, not even the Gens. Florence saved my sanity after my husband died. How can I desert her now?"

Den sighed. "Well, if you really want to go, you'll have to make an official request. I'll ask our receptionist, Seena ambrov Carre, to help you fill out the forms. Then you'll have to wait for an Escort."

"A what?" Rob asked.

"An Escort is a channel or Donor who can keep you from provoking nearby Simes and translate for you. All out-Territory Gens traveling in Tecton-governed territories are required to be Escorted. It prevents accidents."

"How long would it take to get one of these Escorts?" Carla asked.

"Rital and I will be travelling to Valzor in two days. If you get the paperwork done by then, you can come with us. Otherwise, it could take a while."

"We'll go in two days, then." She nodded in satisfaction, reaching for her purse. "My boss won't be happy about such short notice, but Florence is more important than the spring inventory."

"Fine. Sometime before you go, you should both come in and donate selyn."

Carla, who had started to stand, blanched and dropped back into her chair. "Is that really necessary?" she asked.

"I'm afraid it is," Den said apologetically. "It's not precisely illegal for non-donors to travel in-Territory, but few hotels, restaurants, or taxi drivers will accept their business and the exceptions are usually limited to organized tour groups. Besides, do you really want to wander around a city full of renSimes when you're high field?"

Carla slumped in defeat. "All right, then. If I have to, I will."

Rob gave her hand a reassuring squeeze. "It's not that bad, Mother. Really."

"If you say so." She shuddered. "But please…"

Her voice trailed off and Den lifted a politely inquisitive eyebrow.

"Could it be Hajene Madz?" she asked in a small voice. "I don't know if I could let a strange Sime do…that…to me, but Hajene Madz is different."

"Unable to win the trust of out-Territory Gens,, indeed! Den thought gleefully. *Wait until the Regional Controller's office hears about this.*

"I think that can be arranged," he assured Carla.

I f the four travelers headed for Valzor on the night train, only Rob was excited about the trip. He kept asking Rital questions about life in-Territory, which the channel answered in monosyllables, too worried about the upcoming inquisition to carry on a conversation. Den was completely occupied with minimizing the inevitable damage that eight hours on a moving train while in Need and wearing retainers was doing to his cousin. Carla, too, was subdued. She had managed to donate to Rital the day before, but neither had enjoyed it.

They arrived in Valzor early in the morning and found a restaurant near the train station, where the Gens ordered breakfast. Afterward, they took a taxi to the hotel where the two out-Territory Gens would be staying. There was a message for Den waiting at the desk, informing him that Terressa Bowlers, the Third Order channel who was supposed to take over as the Liftons' assigned Escort, had been caught up in an emergency and asking the Donor to fill in until she could get free. So, while Carla and

Rob installed their luggage in their room, Rital headed for the Valzor Sime Center complex to get more information about the progress of the Regional Diplomatic Office's investigation. When the two out-Territory Gens were ready, Den Escorted them to the jail where the twenty-seven demonstrators were imprisoned.

The district prison was in the oldest section of the city: a squat, heavily fortified stone building that had once housed captured out-Territory Gens waiting to be auctioned off. Den arranged with the prison warden for Rob and Carla to see Bethany and Florence Grieves. When they were settled in the bare, depressing interview room, Den headed for the infirmary, hoping to find a mug of trin tea and more congenial company than the guards would provide.

Hajene Rassam, the Second Order channel in charge of the prison's small infirmary, was a middle-aged woman with hair grey as iron and a temperament just as yielding. She was obviously unhappy with her less-than-prestigious assignment and inclined to take it out on anyone nearby.

"Those lorshes!" she exclaimed, when Den confessed what had brought him to the jail. "Why anyone would want to visit them is beyond my comprehension. They've been nothing but trouble from the moment they arrived." She busied herself getting the Donor some tea. "I'm supposed to zlin incoming prisoners for contagious diseases. You would have thought I was a Freeband Raider going for a Kill, from the fuss those idiots put up."

Den shrugged, accepting his tea and sipping cautiously at the hot liquid. "Well, where they come from, berserkers are a lot more common than channels and their religion prohibits them from having contact with Simes."

"They're lorshes," she insisted. "Won't donate, haven't the faintest idea how to behave themselves..." She snorted in open contempt. "We had to put six of them into isolation cells. The other Gen prisoners were getting a little tired of being preached at and threatened to shut the idiots up permanently. I can't blame them. I had the leader, Reverend What's-his-name, in here for a few days—melic withdrawal—and my Donor was about ready to strangle him. The things he was saying...and that's when he *wasn't* hallucinating."

"Have there been any injuries?" Den asked worriedly. The out-Territory press might have been willing to accept the arrests without too much comment, but physical abuse of helpless prisoners in a foreign jail was a terrific story to boost newspaper sales.

Rassam shook her head. "Some of them got shoved around a bit, that's all. They refused to let me look at them, so they can't have been hurt too badly."

Remembering how Sinth had refused treatment for a life-threatening transfer burn, Den wasn't convinced of this, but he didn't think it was worth arguing.

When he returned to the interview room, he found Rob and Carla looking content, if not happy.

"Did you have a good visit?" the Donor asked.

Carla nodded. "We prayed together and talked about what the Scriptures truly mean. They don't specifically forbid donating selyn, you know."

"I'm not surprised," Den said. "They were written shortly after the downfall of Ancient civilization, weren't they? That was centuries before there were any functioning channels that a Gen could donate selyn *to*."

"God knew about channels," Carla insisted. "And His written words will tell us His wishes, if we have the wisdom to understand them properly."

Den had a hard time understanding how a book could be considered authoritative on subjects that didn't exist when it was written, but there didn't seem much point to arguing religion with a True Believer. When Carla stopped off at the bathroom, he asked Rob how his talk with Bethany had gone.

"She's mad at me for telling you folks about the demonstration," he confessed, "but when I told her what you and Hajene Madz did for me and Annie last summer, she said she understood."

"Then she forgave you for spying?"

"Well, mostly," Rob said hopefully. "She's not as convinced all Simes are demons as she used to be. In fact, she wouldn't have been at the demonstration at all, if her uncle hadn't made her. This past week, she's been talking to some of the Gens who live here in Sime Territory. It hadn't really dawned on her that there are people whose friends' and relatives' lives depend on the selyn those Gens in Clear Springs donate. She thought it all went for trains, cars, and cheap lights."

"But she understands now?" Den asked tiredly, wishing Bethany's change of mind had happened before she was arrested.

Rob shrugged. "She hasn't quite decided what to do about it. Her uncle still insists that all contact with Simes is sinful, or at least he did before they locked him in an isolation cell."

Somehow, Den wasn't surprised that Sinth was one of the six out-Territory prisoners who had been put in isolation.

On their way back to the hotel, Rob and Carla began to argue over the interpretation of key passages of either their Scriptures or some theologian's commentary on them, the Donor wasn't sure which and didn't really care. He had read excerpts from the Church of the Purity's Scriptures in his class on out-Territory culture during Donor training and found them full of hatred and violence, even downright obscene.

Den listened as the two out-Territory Gens came up with two very different meanings for one sentence, neither of which made the least sense. As far as he could tell, there were only two rules to the game: the phrases had to be contained within the Conservative Congregation's version of Scriptures and despite obvious discrepancies, nothing in the scriptures could be called a mistake. Even if two sections flatly contradicted each other, they both had to be considered correct.

The current discussion hinged on a reference to "slimy" tentacles and the religious obligation for the pious to avoid them. Both Gens, of course, knew from personal experience that Sime tentacles were not slimy.

While Den appreciated the lessons spiritual philosophers could teach as much as anyone, the modern world knew a great deal more about Simes than the Gen religious leaders who had compiled their Scriptures shortly after Ancient civilization collapsed. Looking at the clear meaning of the passage, Den concluded that the church elder who wrote it had made it up as he went along.

Instead, Carla was insisting that Sime tentacles must have "spiritual" slime, whatever that was supposed to mean, while Rob claimed that the passage in question referred only to new Simes, whose tentacles were covered with the blood and other fluids of breakout, and not to adult channels. Deciding that the two Gens could solve this weighty issue without his help, Den introduced them to the substitute Escort who was waiting for them back at the hotel. Then, he went to the Valzor Sime Center in search of his cousin, eager to share the most amusing aspects of the discussion.

Rital pounced as soon as he entered the main administrative building. "Monruss wants to talk to us," he said.

"When?" the Donor asked.

"Now," the channel said, turning to lead the way.

All thoughts of out-Territory theology fled.

CHAPTER 20

A CHANGE OF TACTICS

"What the bloody shen have you two been doing out there in Clear Springs?" Monruss scolded, looking like an indignant pigeon ruffling its feathers. "Den, I told you to find a way to stop the demonstrations against the Sime Center and six months later, you have a blockade instead. Not a great improvement."

Den squirmed uncomfortably, but before he could open his mouth to explain, Monruss had rounded on Rital.

"And you, Rital. Even if your cousin there didn't understand the consequences, you've worked with out-Territory Gens long enough to know better. Don't you two ever speak to each other?"

Rital also tried and failed to get in a word of explanation.

"Now I have the jail warden complaining about being stuck with twenty-seven Gens who won't donate and who spend their time trying to convert the other inmates to their lunatic religion," the Controller's rant continued. "The newspapers are printing lurid tales of a reporter being held at gunpoint to prevent her from getting help for a child in changeover and the Regional Controller's office is on my neck, wanting to know why I haven't pulled you out of Clear Springs for incompetence and offering to do it for me." He glared at them, daring them to speak.

Both prudently remained silent.

"I've done what I can for you," the District Controller continued somewhat more calmly after a moment of silence. "The investigating team is reading your reports today, so they probably won't want to talk to you until tomorrow. That will let you have transfer first, at least. Now get out of here and let me get some work done."

When they reached the privacy of the deferment suite, Rital turned lost eyes on Den. "If they pull us out of Clear Springs, neither of us is likely to get out-Territory again!" he said, stunned by the enormity of the penalty. "Den, what have we done?"

"We did what we had to," the Donor insisted as he guided his cousin over to the transfer lounge and mentally berated whichever lorsh from the Regional Controller's office was responsible for dragging them back to

Valzor for this inquisition just before their transfer. "And it worked! We're finally rid of the demonstrations and the Sime Center is now shipping pallets of filled selyn batteries back to Valzor. Whatever the diplomats decide, they can't take that away from us."

"It's all right for you," Rital said, just a little scornfully. "You'd rather work at an in-Territory Sime Center anyway and no Controller is going to mind one blemish on the otherwise excellent record of a First Order Donor."

Den shook his head thoughtfully. "Six months ago, I would have agreed with you. But I've discovered that I have a talent for out-Territory politics, just like you have a talent for dealing with individual out-Territory Gens. I want to keep using that skill and I don't want to see my work in Clear Springs messed up by someone who doesn't understand the situation."

"And you think you do understand it?" Rital asked skeptically.

"Not as well as I'd like, but I do know one thing." Den let himself feel his cousin's Need and felt that Need begin to grow in response. "Reverend Sinth and his followers aren't out there screaming every day because they're afraid you might hurt someone. They hate you because they know you won't. Your existence makes them question the fundamental assumptions that their religion makes about the universe and their place in it. That's more threatening than any number of berserkers."

"I hadn't thought of it that way," Rital admitted, sitting on the transfer lounge.

Den began massaging away the knots of tension in his cousin's shoulders. "No one in the Tecton thinks of it that way," he observed. "We think all we have to do is prove that channels won't hurt out-Territory Gens and then they'll magically accept us. But until we understand *why* they perceive us as a threat and to what, how can we prove anything to them?"

"But they *do* fear that channels will hurt them, at least at first," Rital insisted. "I zlin it every time I take a first donation."

"Oh, sure they're nervous," Den shrugged it off. "But *that* fear they can face, if the channel takes the time to win their trust—and you're an expert at that. That's not the fear that motivates the demonstrators or the kind of political campaign Sinth has been running."

"That." Rital groaned, covering his face with both hands. "How can we convince the Tecton that that sort of politics even exists, much less that the two of us are able to fight it effectively?

Den nodded. "It's not only the out-Territory Gens who have trouble accepting new ideas, is it? This whole investigation is one big misunderstanding on the part of the Diplomatic Office. They mean well, but if they pull us out of Clear Springs, Sinth will have won and the whole city will know it. On the other hand, given six months to work while he serves his sentence, we could have the city so pro-Sime that Save Our Kids would have to give up."

Rital's laterals extended, searching for the selyn they Needed.

Den smiled ruefully and held out his arms in invitation. "This may not be the best time to mention it, but I was going to ask you and Monruss for a permanent assignment to Clear Springs so I could help it happen. That is, if you want me."

"Want you!" Rital was finding it more difficult to speak as his Need rose to the surface, but the possessive strength with which his handling tentacles gripped the Gen's arms left no doubt of his feelings. "Though I may not have the authority to approve a permanent assignment for the roaches in Alyce's gardening shed, by the time this is over," he warned, letting his laterals slip into contact at last.

"Then we'll win or lose this one—together." Den leaned over to make lip contact, knowing that his cousin was probably unable to hear his words, but also knowing that he would zlin their meaning.

They had always had good transfers. They were closely matched and they knew each other well. However, ever since Rital had first become involved in the Clear Springs Sime Center, their closeness had been lessened by mutual awareness that their goals and commitments were very different. With this barrier removed, there was an extra empathy between them that Den had never felt before, not even on the long-ago day when he had first Qualified as a Donor.

Then, he had been barely more than a boy, facing a nebulous future. Now, he knew exactly what he was committing himself to and the knowledge that his cousin was working for the same thing gave him the confidence that they would succeed.

We did so much when we were working separately. How can we fail now that we are working together?

That evening, Den picked up a bag of ginger cookies to share and visited the Flyers Club to check on the progress his friends had made on their design for the new and improved "Spirit of Valzor II." He found Jannun hard at work gluing leftover fabric across a six-pane window frame.

"I think the window would work better if you used glass," the Donor observed.

"Very funny." Jannun stretched the fabric tight and secured it with staples. "It's an experiment. If we're going to develop a flyer that can actually be used for transportation, it's got to be able to withstand a little moisture without getting so soaked it affects the weight. So, I thought I'd try out some glues and other coatings to see how they work. It'll make the fabric more airtight, too."

"Good thinking," the Donor agreed, then did a double take as he spotted a heap of bamboo and old tarp in the far corner. "What's that doing there?" he asked, pointing at the remains of the "Right Flyer."

"The Valzor Model Flyer's Club has a new member," Jannun informed him as he placed the window frame carefully on a bench and set out five assorted pots of glue. He handed one pot and a brush to Den, indicating which section he should treat, then started applying a different glue to another section.

"Really?" Den asked, obediently applying the glue in a nice, even coat. "Who is it?"

"Young Mandle," Jannun chortled. "Her parents finally decided they weren't going to talk her out of flying, so she might as well indulge her interest in the presence of informed and sensible adults."

"Have they actually met you and Eddina?" Den inquired with feigned surprise, then made a show of cringing away when Jannun shook the brush at him.

"She's a smart kid and a hard worker," Jannun explained, going back to his painting. "Best of all, by bringing her in, we've got great shot at building next year's winning wing assembly."

"Combining the teams behind the two best designs from this year is a great idea," the Donor agreed. "The timing is right, too: Clear Springs is finally on the way to yielding the quantity of industrial selyn required to allow research on power-hungry new technologies. I'd like to go further, though." He inspected the glue-permeated fabric thoughtfully.

"Further, how?" Jannun asked.

"Some of this year's wing assemblies flew before they crashed and the others just crashed," Den mused aloud. "None of them were very stable in flight and all were pretty much destroyed when they hit the ground."

The other Gen shrugged. "Landing wasn't part of the challenge."

"True," the Donor conceded. "However, unless we can build a wing that can survive a less-than-optimal landing, we'll never be able to risk sending a human pilot up, even if we develop a lightweight selyn-powered engine."

Jannun frowned. "The Ancients used a lot of metal in their flyers, just like they did for their other technologies. We simply don't have access to that. If we redevelop powered flight, we'll have to do it using the materials at hand."

"Using the materials at hand," Den repeated, staring hard at a stain on the far wall but not seeing it. Instead, he was caught up in a vivid memory of a rollerboard, made by a graduate student out of a material that happened to be at hand. A rollerboard that had survived a spectacular crash into the chemistry magic show with only minor damage. "Of course!"

"What is it, Den?" Jannun asked. "I know that look. You've come up with another mad idea."

"This one is sane," the Donor assured him. "I met a Gen in Clear Springs, a graduate student at the university. He was experimenting with a new composite material that is stronger, lighter, and more flexible than wood. Using that material, or something like it, has to be our next step. We also have to start thinking about how to stabilize the assembly in flight and during landing." He grinned at Jannun. "You see, I don't want to just win contests. I want to fly!"

They were discussing how best to procure and test suitable samples as they finished applying the glue to the windowpane experiment when Eddina arrived. She fixed Den with a baleful glare.

"All right," she demanded, hands on hips as she scowled up at him like a miniature thunderstorm. "Are you the one who told every anti-Tecton organization in New Washington Territory that I was interested in becoming a member? Because it isn't funny."

Den wasn't about to let her spoil the hard-won optimism he had managed to find while talking to Jannun. "Why, Eddina," he said, smiling. "I'm so glad to see you again. Would you care for a cookie? I brought a bag of those ginger ones you like."

"Cookies!" She glared at him, then suddenly began to chuckle. "All right, I'm sorry. I didn't mean to snap at you."

Den accepted the apology with a graceful gesture, then asked, "What was that about anti-Sime organizations?"

She frowned. "For the last month, I've been getting two or three letters a day from various groups asking me to join them in their fight against Simes, or at least send money. Most of the letters are full of vicious lies about Killer channels and Tecton conspiracies. I've gotten over twenty individual requests to come and demonstrate against the Clear Springs Sime Center. You are the only one who both has a connection with Clear Springs and knows that I can be reached at Jannun's box number, so I assumed you were having a little joke." She looked up at him uncertainly.

"I did give your name and that address to the student-run anti-Sime group in Clear Springs," Den said slowly. "They were offering free information on their organization and activities to anyone who signed up. I thought it might give you a better idea of what we were facing out there. But I swear, I didn't sign you up for any other groups."

"Then how did I end up with a sack full of hate mail?" Eddina asked.

Den thought it over for a long moment, then remembered Thom and Silva's lecture on Sinth's recruiting tactics. "Mailing lists, of course!" he exclaimed. "Eddina, I've got to see those letters. If I'm right, they'll show those diplomatic types from the Regional Controller's office exactly how the tiny anti-Sime minority in Clear Springs has managed to cause such a fuss!"

Neither Jannun nor Eddina understood why Den was so excited, but the renSime obediently handed over a large canvas tote bag full to overflowing with letters. Most had been mailed in the cheapest available envelopes, with URGENT, *Dated Material,* and Immediate Response Requested splashed on the outside in equally cheap red ink.

"They started coming the week after Union Day," Eddina explained. "With one thing and another, I didn't look at them until yesterday. They were so awful that I almost tossed them all in the garbage. However, one of my nephews collects stamps, so I was going to let him have them."

"It's a good thing for me and Rital that you didn't get rid of them," Den said, bringing the two of them up to date on the happenings in Clear Springs as he sorted the envelopes by the date on the postmark. When he had finished, the pattern sketched out by the stacks of envelopes was clear.

"See, Students for a Sime-free City—that's the university's anti-Sime group—not only sent you the information they'd promised, but also gave your name and address to Reverend Sinth's Save Our Kids," he explained, pointing at the relevant envelopes. "That's why those are the earliest letters. According to our friends, Tohm and Silva, Sinth recruits his new members by buying or trading membership lists with other organizations with similar interests. That must be how these conservative church groups in other nearby cities and towns got your name. Those groups sold their lists of members and prospective members to commercial purveyors of religious literature and artifacts. And, of course, political organizations also buy such lists and they can afford to send sample copies of their magazines or newsletters to prospective members. If a certain percentage join up, it's worth their investment." Den picked one such publication up and thumbed through it rapidly. "And what do you know, here's a three-page article written by Sinth himself, urging people to come and help him stop our Establishment screening!"

With growing excitement, they began to read through the material more closely, tracing the strategy Sinth had used to recruit and organize his demonstrations. By the time the Gens had finished off the last of the cookies, Den was reasonably confident that he had the hard evidence to convince the investigating team of diplomats that the anti-Sime activism that had plagued the Clear Springs Sime Center did not represent the majority opinion of the city's actual residents.

If they believed it.

* * * *

Early the following morning, Den placed a strategic telephone call to Tohm and Silva before joining Rital in the conference room for the investigation. The Regional Controller's Diplomatic Office had sent three representatives. Hajene Alim Fassmij was a young and idealistic First Order channel who was being groomed for a Controllership of his own. Sosu Kirlin Mayori was a career administrator who had gone through her Donor's training at Rialite a few years ahead of Den's class. The committee's chair was the renowned Sosu Quess ambrov Shaeldor, fresh from his triumph in Cordona Territory. Quess was a balding Donor of indeterminate years, dressed in a spotless uniform and fully awake in spite of the early hour. He was not participating in the subdued conversation between his fellow committee members, preferring to look Den and Rital over with a measured intensity that made the younger Donor want to squirm like a small boy.

Householders, Den thought resentfully. *Why do they always look down on non-Householders?* The Householdings might have founded the modern Tecton, but it wouldn't have survived long without us "houseless" channels and Donors.

Of the three committee members, only Quess had spent a significant amount of time outside of the Tecton-governed Sime Territories. Den thought the senior Donor's experience of alien cultures made him the most likely of the three to accept Den's account of what had been happening in Clear Springs, but that was cold comfort. Even the more open-minded Householders tended to judge people by their results, not the difficulty of the task. If Quess decided that they had failed where success was possible, he would probably rule against them.

Fassmij was too inexperienced to appreciate the differences between out-Territory Gens who lived near the border and interacted frequently with Simes and the Gens of Clear Springs who had never seen channels before the past year. Kirlin Mayori probably didn't care about the out-Territory Gens' opinion of the Clear Springs Sime Center as such, but from her expression she was annoyed at them for causing a situation and hauling her away from her comfortable office at the regional capital. Both Fassmij and Mayori would most likely follow the recommendation of Quess.

So it's Quess the inter-territorial diplomatic hero that I've got to convince, Den thought as he and his cousin took their seats. *Shen.*

Monruss was present in an advisory capacity only and did not have a vote. He was inclined in their favor, Den knew, if only to justify his actions in sending them to Clear Springs in the first place, but he had already displayed his basic lack of understanding of the situation. Any help he tried to give might do more harm than good.

When everybody had filled their tea mugs and the Gens had helped themselves to muffins and donuts, Quess cleared his throat. "Hajene Madz, Sosu Milnan, we have gone over your official reports from Clear Springs and discovered several areas of concern," he began in a carefully neutral tone. "First, the continuous, violent demonstrations since the Clear Springs Sime Center opened. We expected some trouble when we approved a Sime Center so far from the border, but this has gone far beyond our predictions. Second, there have been a number of events involving one or both of you that seem to have been grossly mishandled. In the past two months alone, these include public accusations that Hajene Madz forced an unwilling out-Territory Gen to donate—" Quess nodded toward Rital, "—and a child in changeover who attacked and almost Killed an out-Territory Gen in your presence, Sosu Milnan."

Even though there was nothing he could have done to prevent Zakry from attacking Sinth, Den had an overwhelming urge to squirm under the older Donor's implied accusation.

"Last but not least, while the arrest of twenty-seven out-Territory Gens for attempting to block access to your Sime Center was legal, the Clear Springs Sime Center is the only one that has required police action to stay since the Distect Revolt a century ago. Taken together, these incidents show a consistent lack of trust on the part of Clear Springs' population. We realize that the reports don't tell everything, so we would like to hear your version of these events and any explanations for your actions that you might wish to offer." He settled back in his chair and prepared to listen.

Den took a deep breath and began talking. He explained the tactics that Reverend Sinth had used to forge Save Our Kids into an effective weapon against the Sime Center, using the library censorship attempt and the letters and magazines that Eddina had received as documentation that many of the protesters came from outside Clear Springs. He described how Ezra Tains' refusal to keep the protests within legal limits had led to OLD SOKS and the passage of Tohm's resolution.

Rital explained Bethany's accidental donation and Den confirmed that there had been no way for Rital to have known her real purpose in coming to the Sime Center. Den told the committee how Zakry had managed to nearly Kill Sinth.

Most importantly, Den described the fundamentalist worldview of Sinth and his supporters and how it would never allow them to accept the presence of channels, precisely because they did *not* present a danger. He used Sinth's refusal of Rital's help and Zakry's suicide to illustrate their willingness to die before giving up their convictions. Finally, to emphasize that only a small number of Clear Springs Gens shared those convictions, he told them of the virtual disappearance of the demonstrations after the arrests. "If there were hundreds of Gens in Clear Springs who wanted us gone, getting rid of only twenty-seven of them wouldn't even have slowed the protests," he finished hoarsely. He took a sip of stone-cold tea from his mug, only then realizing that he had been talking for nearly three hours.

Quess shifted in his seat, discretely stretching his cramped muscles. "This has been very interesting, Sosu Milnan, but I've never heard of the kind of tactics you describe in all the time I've spent out-Territory and I'm not sure I believe they really exist. May I borrow those letters of yours? I'd like to read them more thoroughly."

"Certainly." Den repacked the stacks of letters into Eddina's sack and pushed it across the table to the older Donor.

Quess gathered it up. "I suggest a two-hour break to examine this new evidence."

Everyone began to stand, stretch, and gather belongings.

"Did I convince Quess?" Den asked his cousin, privately, as they headed for the cafeteria.

"I don't know," Rital admitted. "His nageric control is incredible. I couldn't zlin anything except bland neutrality."

Den sighed. "At least he didn't fall asleep."

When they reconvened after lunch, Kirlin Mayori pushed the sack of letters back across the table to Den. "These are all very interesting, Sosu Milnan," she said a little petulantly, "but I really don't see how they prove your claim that you and Hajene Madz were acting appropriately. It was your job to prevent trouble, not to combat it once it started. If anything, your evidence this morning demonstrates a complete inability to anticipate events that anyone familiar with out-Territory culture could have predicted."

Den glared at her. "May I respectfully remind you that neither my cousin nor myself has any training as a diplomatic troubleshooter?" he asked icily. "Rital was assigned to open the Clear Springs Sime Center because he's good at handling people, not politics. If he hadn't succeeded, Reverend Sinth would never have seen him as a threat and Save Our Kids would never have been founded. I was assigned to Clear Springs because your office was too busy with other problems to send the expert Controller Monruss requested. I improvised as best I could and along the way, I learned a few things about how out-Territory politics works on a local level. I'm not sure anyone from your office could have done better."

"Oh, come now," Mayori objected.

"I'm serious," Den said. "I had no diplomatic training, but I consulted the relevant textbooks.

The suggested strategies centered on convincing community leaders that a Sime Center was in the community's best interests. That was never

Clear Springs' problem. The mayor, the university, and the newspaper were on our side from the first and most of the rest of the town is at least willing to go along with them. In fact, during the Union Day rush, almost a third of the population were willing to force their way through an angry mob of anti-Sime demonstrators to use our services."

Fassmij dropped his pen onto his notepad, grimacing with disgust. "If you had the whole town so convinced, why was that mob of demonstrators there in the first place?" he demanded.

"Because they value the integrity of their religion over worldly self-interest," Den answered wearily, trying to find a way to make the committee members understand his insight. "The core members of Save Our Kids are willing to spend huge amounts of time and money to fight our presence, even if that means the disapproval of the rest of the town. They firmly believe that they are helping to save the souls of the donors they shove and scream at. You can't negotiate with fanatics. To them, compromise is surrender to the forces of evil. All you can do with people like Sinth and his followers is limit their efficacy. My methods may have been a little un-orthodox, but they worked—and if I can finish what I started, when Sinth returns from exile, Clear Springs will not greet him as a martyr and hero."

Monruss cleared his throat. "There have been some recent developments I believe you ought to know about before you make your final decision," he told the investigating committee. "First, this inquiry has somehow become public knowledge in Clear Springs and a number of the out-Territory Gens don't seem happy about it." He emptied a box of phone message slips onto the table. "My inter-territorial phone line has been tied up all morning with Gens expressing confidence in Hajene Madz and Sosu Milnan. Mayor Kroag reports that several nearby towns are thinking about asking for Sime Centers of their own and says," the channel cleared his throat and read in accented English, "'Don't scramble your eggs before they hatch by getting rid of your best representatives.' While it's an odd idiom, the meaning is pretty clear, I think. The editor of the *Clear Springs Clarion* wants an interview and he doesn't sound happy."

"This puts a different perspective on the situation," Quess admitted, leafing through the stack of message slips. "I find it incredible that so many out-Territory Gens would call to support a specific channel."

Even Den found the number of messages hard to believe, if not their existence and subject matter. He would have been pleased with a dozen calls, but there seemed to be roughly ten times that. *I should be feeling guilty*, the Donor reflected. However, if the investigating panel accepted the phone calls as representing a cross section of Clear Springs citizens, Den wasn't about to enlighten them. After all, he told himself virtuously, he had explained in detail exactly how such tactics worked and they hadn't believed him.

"But the constant demonstrations," Fassmij protested. "What about those twenty-seven prisoners sitting in the district jail?"

"That's even more interesting," Monruss answered. "Guss Narlin, the prison warden, phoned me during the break. Apparently, the twenty-one out-Territory prisoners who are not in solitary confinement prayed together last night and decided that their religious doctrine doesn't forbid association with all Simes, after all. Eighteen of them have told the warden that they are now willing to donate selyn—but only to Hajene Madz. I gather they don't trust anyone else. Narlin thinks they're *all* insane, but he wants Hajene Madz over at the jail instantly if not sooner, before they have a chance to change their minds."

For a moment, Den thought that the committee was ready to rule in their favor on the spot, but then Quess fished a sheet of paper out of the stack at his elbow, and passed it over. "Tell me, Sosu Milnan," he said sternly, "if you are such an *expert* on out-Territory politics, how do you explain this?"

With dismay, Den scanned the letter that he had sent to Monruss with his first interim report.

The Householder continued implacably, "I don't mind telling you that it raises serious questions about whether you should be allowed an out-Territory license at all."

Den quickly controlled the icy dread that gripped him at Quess's statement, but not before the channels were able to zlin it. "Look," he said desperately, as his hopes for the future began to crumble, "I'm not going to pretend that I don't feel that many, maybe even most, out-Territory Gens are less than rational on the subject of Simes. Of course, by their standards, every Gen in this room is certifiably insane for wanting to be a Donor and our system of government is just as incomprehensible to them as theirs is to us."

"Their Congress isn't so different from our Tecton Council," Quess corrected impatiently. "I've dealt with it often enough."

"But it is!" The Donor stopped trying to control his nager, letting the channels zlin how deeply he believed what he was saying. "The superficial structure may be similar, but the whole philosophy behind it is distorted beyond recognition *because no one out there can zlin.*"

"I think we know that, Sosu Milnan," Fassmij said, in a patronizing tone.

"But do you understand what it *means*?" Den insisted. "No one can tell how people really feel about an issue unless they say it publicly. It's shaped their whole political system. Except for the few issues they personally care about, out-Territory politicians cast their vote for the loudest and most energetic activists. Everybody in Clear Springs knows and expects this and so it works pretty well for them. Then we came along, opened our Sime Center, and instead of running the aggressive publicity campaign they expected, we just sat there behind our fence and let the anti-Sime faction tell lies about us. Some of the local Gens are still wondering what we're trying to hide.

"Every time I've made progress, it was because I discarded the techniques developed to win over junct Sime towns and adopted the same tactics that were being used against us. If the Tecton wants to keep a Sime Center open in Clear Springs, it will have to run its public relations by Clear Springs' rules. I've spent the better part of a year learning those rules, largely through trial and error. I may think out-Territory Gens are crazy, but my publicity campaign worked. This last week, the Sime Center's sidewalk was clear for the first time in a year. How will it help the Tecton to win over out-Territory society, if you take away my license just because I achieved the right results by an alternative method?"

The three committee members broke into a babble of comment. Most of it, to Den's dismay, seemed to center on whether it was ever permissible for a Tecton Donor with Den's lack of diplomatic credentials to improvise while blithely ignoring the accumulated wisdom of experienced diplomats.

I've lost, he thought numbly. *It's all over except for setting our punishment. He slumped in his seat, too dejected to try defending himself any more.*

At last, Quess called for the vote.

"The out-Territory Gens *I've* met haven't been insane or unreasonable," Fassmij said, with the unconscious arrogance of youth. "If they can't convince the town to trust them, I say let someone else try."

Mayori shrugged and indicated the stack of phone message slips. "They've obviously won the trust of *some* Gens out there. It's hard to find channels and Donors willing to work so far out-Territory. If those two actually *want* to stay in Clear Springs among the Simephobes, I'm inclined to let them."

Quess sighed and looked at his laced fingers. "It's my decision, then," he said tiredly. "I'm not convinced that the two of you have handled these incidents as well as you should have, and I don't like your attitude at all, Sosu Milnan." He met Den's glare calmly, then indicated the stack of reports. "However, neither can I ignore the support you've gained. If the mayor and the local newspaper both want you in Clear Springs, pulling you out of there might do the Tecton more harm than good. So, after due consideration I'm casting my vote with Kirlin, with the recommendation that Controller Monruss keep a closer eye on the situation to prevent further incidents."

We've won! Den thought in disbelief, exchanging relieved and triumphant grins with Rital. *They're going to let us see it through!*

EPILOGUE

Den and Rital spent the rest of the afternoon at the jail, where Rital took donations from twenty nervous Gens. Two of the three holdouts changed their minds when they saw that their fellows were unharmed. Afterward, Den and Rital treated Rob and Carla to a celebratory dinner at Den's favorite restaurant and then all four boarded the night train back to Clear Springs.

It was only an hour after dawn when the train pulled into the station. After seeing the two out-Territory Gens on their way, channel and Donor wearily headed for the Sime Center.

Tohm and Silva were waiting for them in the main lobby, looking disgustingly wide-awake to Den. "What did they decide?" Silva asked eagerly. "Will you be staying?"

Rital nodded. "It looked pretty bad there for a while, until over a hundred people spontaneously decided to call Valzor to express their support for us. Isn't that strange?"

"I'll say," Tohm agreed. "We had over three hundred people who promised to call."

"Most likely, they couldn't get through," Den suggested. "The Valzor Sime Center only has one inter-territorial phone line. Controller Monruss was a little upset about having it tied up all day."

Silva shrugged. "Oh, well, at least it worked! But could you give us a little more warning next time? These things are easier to coordinate if we have time to get organized."

"Speaking of organization," Tohm broke in smoothly, "the school board is meeting tomorrow night to consider your changeover classes. Since Save Our Kids doesn't have the bodies to keep folks out of the Sime Center the way they used to, they've focused on keeping you out of the schools."

Tohm lifted a worn leather briefcase onto the reception desk. He and Silva bent over it, sorting through the papers inside.

"This is a copy of the petition they've been circulating door to door," Silva said, passing a clipboard to Den.

"Here are the misinformation pamphlets they've been leaving in mailboxes," Tohm added, waving them at the Donor before plopping them down on the petition.

"They've been sending letters to the papers, of course," Silva continued as a dozen copies of editorial pages from the *Clarion* and other local papers landed on top of the petitions and pamphlets, "but Hank Fredricks had a copy of your information packet—smart move, that—and did this feature on the classes." A copy of the local news section was balanced precariously on the top of the stack.

"We've both got morning classes today, so we've got to run," Tohm said. "But we'll be by this afternoon to talk over plans."

The two young Gens waved goodbye and trotted briskly away. Den tried to free a hand to wave back, then swore as the newspapers were dislodged from their precarious resting place and cascaded to the floor.

Rital knelt to gather them, prudently trying not to laugh. He collected the sheets of folded newsprint into a neat pile and presented them to the Donor with a flourish.

"Welcome home, cousin," he said with a grin.

ACKNOWLEDGEMENTS

Mary Lou Mendum

I first encountered Jacqueline Lichtenberg's Simes and Gens when I was in high school. I was immediately fascinated by the concept of an intelligent predator that must come to a civilized accommodation with its equally intelligent prey if either is to survive. Over the next decade, as more books in the series were released, I started to play with writing "missing scenes" that I felt should have been included, expanding them into stories and then novel-length pieces that were published in the Sime~Gen fanzines as my writing skills improved.

The era that I found most interesting was the century after the wars between Sime and Gen Territories had ended, when the former enemies had to set aside their very rational fear of each other and cooperate. The broad sweep of that history was outlined in the then-available books, but while treaties negotiated between warring governments usually manage to keep the peace, they often fail to convince the common citizens to forget the past and move on to the future.

It's relatively easy to convince people to help sandbag a flooding river so it doesn't wash away their town. It's quite another matter to convince them to relocate their homes out of the floodplain or to permanently increase their taxes to build and maintain the dams, levees, and other flood control structures that prevent the river from flooding in the first place. The first option provides a brief opportunity to be a hero; the other choices are more effective, but require a fundamental change in how people think about riverfront property.

I created the character of Den Milnan almost 30 years ago to examine how the process of peacemaking would play out in the day-to-day lives of ordinary Simes and Gens. Den isn't a diplomat, he doesn't belong to an elite Householding, and he neither knows nor cares about Gen Territory culture and values. Nevertheless, he is assigned the job of convincing the Gens of Clear Springs to set aside their well-justified fear and hatred of Simes and create a new, blended culture.

Unfortunately for Den, the people of Clear Springs already have a culture that suits them just fine. Some are open-minded and willing to embrace change, while others view change as a threat to public decency. Most simply see no reason to rearrange their comfortable lives for Den's convenience.

Den's first adventure was published in 1990 in the paper fanzine AM-BROV ZEOR and others followed. Eventually, they were posted in Rimon's Library on simegen.com. When Jacqueline asked me if I would consider reworking the first two of Den's stories into the next professionally published Sime~Gen novel, we added several subplots to the existing storyline. The result, I hope, will contain enough new material to satisfy even readers who are already familiar with the original version of Den's story.

Jacqueline Lichtenberg and Jean Lorrah:

One of the principles of writing science fiction is that the writer does not tell or even show the reader all of the world that is envisioned, at least not all at once. But everything in the story must be consistent with the un-revealed background.

So there are many "truths" the characters live with which few readers ever see or care to know. That is how Sime~Gen novels have been written. With each novel, the reader finds out new bits of background, and the sweeping dynamic of the thousand-year future-history of humankind that has been envisioned.

These novels are not post-apocalyptic, but rather post-post-post-apocalyptic. The story begins at the first thrust to rebuild civilization, when one person (Rimon Farris of the novel *First Channel*) discovers (with the help of his beloved) that he is capable of doing something nobody else can do. And the story ends many centuries later at the point where his self-discovery has changed several whole galactic civilizations.

The fans of these novels who have re-read the books in various orders have compiled the bits of the universe into a wiki. The finalization of that work has been done by Zoe Farris and Karen MacLeod with the help of Eliza Leahy whose illustrations are magnificent. Eventually that work will be converted into a publishable concordance. It will reveal much that has not made it into the novels.

Each of the novels discusses in thematic depth one or another premise behind the Sime~Gen Universe concept. Jacqueline Lichtenberg acknowledges Mary Lou Mendum and all the writers who contributed to the anthology, Sime~Gen #13, *Fear and Courage*, which highlighted various views of how humanity has changed as a result of the Sime~Gen Mutation. Lack of Compassion is now a capital offense against Nature.

Mary Lou Mendum has provided us with the Clear Springs Chronicles, the fleshed out and enriched version of her fanzine stories about her original characters, Den and Rital.

The Clear Springs Chronicles, the story of Den and Rital in Clear Springs, make clear one of the fundamental distinctions of the Sime~Gen Series Universe: Humanity is Creative.

Fantasy Genre novels very often depict humans as lacking in originality and creativity. If some magical formula or artifact, device, grimoire or Book of Shadows ever existed and revealed something "powerful" that humans can do—then the only way to do that in the current world is to hunt down that object or bit of knowledge, that one special person who has conquered the technique, and get it from that source. Never once does anyone in the Fantasy genre novels think something like, "Well, it's rumored that so-and-so did such-and-such. I bet I could do that." Or, "I bet I could do it better, cheaper, faster, more elegantly."

Sime~Gen is not Fantasy Genre. It is Science Fiction. It shares a lot of ostensible elements with Fantasy Genre (such as ESP, and Mysticism), but approaches those elements from the view of science, not caring how they did that, but rather imagining how I can do that, and do it better.

There is a Householding in Sime Territory called Householding Frihill. They are the archeologists who are insatiably curious about the Ancients (us), and are always digging up clues we have left behind and writing academic papers and even novels built from those clues.

Mary Lou Mendum picked up on that decades ago and ran with it. She grasped immediately that neither Simes nor Gens would lack the creativity and initiative to do these miraculous things themselves, once the right people got wind of the basic idea, or thought it up themselves from scratch.

Thus, in these novels of Clear Springs, Mary Lou has presented a step by step chronicle of the events in Clear Springs, a small university town way out in Gen Territory, when a Sime Center comes to town.

The basic premise of Sime~Gen, the one thing that makes it take a thousand years or so after the collapse of our civilization due to the Sime~Gen mutation, is that Creativity happens when Simes and Gens live together.

They don't come together to rebuild our Ancient civilization. The nature of humanity has changed. They have no use for the way we do things today. Where Sime and Gen come together, they create something new, something that has never existed before, an entire galaxy spanning civilization rooted in Compassion.

The Clear Springs Chronicles tell the story of how that new human civilization begins to industrialize and innovate a whole new technology.

ABOUT THE AUTHORS

Mary Lou Mendum

Mary Lou Mendum moved to Davis, California, for graduate school and never got around to leaving. After several postdocs resulting in academic publications in subjects as diverse as grape genealogy, walnut tissue culture, and food poisoning bacteria, she found a niche editing plant science journal articles. She has been writing Sime~Gen science fiction for fun since the 1980s.

Jean Lorrah

Jean Lorrah is the creator of the Savage Empire series and co-author of the Sime~Gen series. She is also an aspiring screenwriter, with an optioned screenplay, *Coal for Christmas*, written with Lois Wickstrom. Be sure to look for her Nessie's Grotto books with Lois, folk tale favorite Rooster Under the Table, and Jean's one-off vampire novel, *Blood Will Tell*. Jean lives in Kentucky with two dogs and two cats, and does pet therapy with Bianca, a Maltese, and Splotch, a big ol' sweet-natured tomcat.

Jacqueline Lichtenberg

An active science fiction fan since 7th Grade, I created the Sime~Gen Universe when I was 10-15 years old. When I was 25 and a new mother, I sold the first story to be published written in this universe. It is *Operation High Time*, and was bought by Fred Pohl, who later also bought my first non-fiction book, *Star Trek Lives!* I was a *Star Trek* fan before there was a *Star Trek* fandom because *Star Trek* flung my own visions onto the TV Screen.

As I was learning to write, practicing the craft by writing *Star Trek* stories set in my Kraith Universe (now posted online for free reading at simegen.com/fandom/startrek/) I was also writing Sime~Gen novels for the traditional publishing market. *Star Trek* fans began writing stories in my Kraith Universe, and for a few years there was not an issue of a *Star Trek* fanzine that did not have a Kraith story or discussion in it. By managing the 50 or so creative contributors to Kraith, I learned how to integrate different visions into a master-plan. I used that practice to incorporate Jean Lorrah's vision of one of my characters, Rimon Farris, into the Sime~Gen Universe vision.

This was easy because Jean, too, is a *Star Trek* fan and fanzine writer whose *Night of the Twin Moons* is as famous as Kraith. Jean went on to sell a number of *Star Trek* novels for the paperback market, and as the Sime~Gen universe grew, we became partners and Incorporated to manage the Sime~Gen franchise.

We have always planned to add more writers to the professionally published series, and were delighted with the publisher's request for an anthology (Sime~Gen #13). We have many plans for the future, so keep in touch via Facebook.